THE KILLING PLAN
THE MACKENZIE PARISH TRILOGY

BY

TERENCE F. MOSS

1

Contents

Other works by the author

Angels and Kings (Musical)
Soul Traders (Musical)
The Inglish Civil War (TV Comedy)
Closing Time (TV Comedy)
Dave (TV Comedy)

Novels
The Prospect of Redemption
The Tusitala
Be Happy with my Life
Death of a Sparrow

Terence F. Moss can be contacted at
butchmoss@OUTLOOK.COM
Terence F. Moss on Facebook

Dedicated to Wendy
For her kind forbearance, love, and patience

Many thanks to Caroline, Nick, and everybody who has been put through the ordeal of reading this book in the initial stages and to all the other people, too many to mention, who have given me their help, guidance, and advice along the way. And finally, to Chris Schuler for the initial editing and proofreading.

THE KILLING PLAN

BY

TERENCE F. MOSS

Glossary of Terms and Acronyms

Amarium: New mineral energy resource first discovered in disused Welsh coal mines

AMGS: Atlas Matrix Guidance System. Used to control the speed and distance between all vehicles travelling on province roads.

Artemis: Police database.

Balingo: Security service database.

BART: Collective name for Artemis and Balingo

Deliverance: The walled residential and farming province along the south coast.

Ghettazone: The de-controlled areas of the Republic of Britain beyond the walled provinces.

Glundes: Generic Low intelligence, Unemployable, Unregistered, Non-Christian, Drug-addicted, or Ethnic. Residents of the Ghettazone.
ISA: Implant Standards Authority for VRS implant receptors.

Plutomarium: Combination of amarium and plutonium, producing a non-radioactive energy source.

Progression: The amarium mining area of North Wales, surrounded by a wall.

Protton motor car: The only available form of personal transport.

Providence: The gated province of London, surrounded by the M25 wall.
Redemption: The gated industrial production province of the Midlands, surrounded by a wall.

SCOMTEL: The shopping conglomerate now controls all hypermarkets.
VRS chip: Virtual Reality Simulation Chip. Creates a virtual reality experience.

VRS interface: The interface docking receptor is implanted just behind the right ear.

Chapter 1

2023. For reasons never clearly explained at the inquest, the car in which they were travelling untethered itself from the left-hand carriageway matrix, crossed the electronic central reservation and re-tethered itself to the right-hand carriageway oncoming vehicle matrix. Strangely, no alarms sounded. The sixty-ton SCOMTEL freightliner practically obliterated the vehicle. Rendering it utterly unrecognisable after nine sets of giant wheels had passed over it. Eventually, the freightliner pulled to a halt approximately two hundred yards past the point of collision.

At first, the police did not believe the wreckage was a car but something that had fallen from the back of a lorry. However, closer inspection of the debris – coupled with the frantic emergency telephone call from the driver of the freightliner – indicated that something far worse had occurred.

The ferocity of the impact had left no part of the flattened vehicular collage thicker than the width of a finger. This meant there was insufficient body mass to immediately confirm the involvement of people. The tech team could only find scraps of body tissue, blood residue and some tiny fragments of bone. Most of the blood had soaked into the road by the time the emergency services arrived. This could easily have been attributed to a hedgehog or a badger, but it was enough for the forensic team to later confirm from DNA analysis that two people had been involved and who they were.

The only item from the car that appeared undamaged by the impact was the tiny plutomarium isotope from the

1

vehicle's power system. Somewhat conspicuously, this was lying in a small pool of quietly bubbling mahogany brown liquid. It glowed with a shimmering shade of pink, a chemical reaction usually triggered by the presence of saltwater.

The road was closed for two days while the forensic investigation team tried to discover how a vehicle could break free of the AMGS (Atlas Matrix Guidance System) and then reattach itself on the wrong side of the road. The many failsafe procedures built into the road and the computerised guidance system integrated into every Protton vehicle's electronic brain made it technically impossible. Nevertheless, it had happened. It was eventually determined at the inquest that it was probably due to an anti-transient system malfunction of an unspecified nature, whatever that was supposed to mean.

Part II
Catherine

It was a late summer's day in 2009. Still warm but soft, delinquent breezes had begun to blow, heralding nature's autumnal transition. It was a time when unforgiving temperaments had mellowed and were starting to prepare for the equinox that would eventually sweep them, imperceptibly, into the cold depths of winter. However, before those darker days arrived, there would be a period of graceful light and long shadows. Hopefully, these would soften the sharp edges of the harsh reality that was to follow.

The first golden leaves were beginning to fall. Each caught up in a spiralling vortex as if waltzing to Strauss at a Venetian ball in the Doges' Palace before breaking free and wistfully pirouetting to Mother Earth. Occasionally, one or two would find a final breath of wind. And for a few moments, in silent desperation, they would swirl upwards one last time to dance around the gates of Downing Street. Amid the hustle and bustle of daily life, each leaf seemed to believe it was an integral and indispensable part of the proceedings. That was before surrendering to the inevitable and eventually settling onto the cold grey pavement. Finally, it was preparing to shrivel away and turn to dust or be swept away by the council street cleaners.

Sergeant Mackenzie Parish, as he was then, first noticed Catherine on one of these days – their lives would always be marked by such moments. She was part of a delegation of trainee doctors visiting Number Ten to present a petition. They objected to the excessive hours they were forced to work in hospitals during their final years at medical school. They believed this practice jeopardised the fundamental integrity of the job for which they were being trained. Catherine had only been at medical school for just over a year but still felt passionately enough about their grievance to join the committee that had prepared the petition. The fact that she was stunningly beautiful had not been wholly lost on the other committee members. To some degree, they were guilty of co-opting her into assisting them with an established marketing tenet. The media were always slightly more responsive to and supportive of a cause with a visually attractive and articulate spokesperson – and a justifiable complaint. A patronisingly sexist ploy to present an argument, possibly. But doctors live in a world of pragmatism - not a make-believe Disneyland where dreams come true and there is always a happy ending. They needed all the media attention they could muster, and Catherine was the means to that end.

Parish was there on routine security duty when he first noticed her in the crowd of interns chanting and waving placards. She was hard not to see. She was also holding the petition, patiently waiting her turn to present it to the Prime Minister's aide. He eventually came out from Number Ten and up to the railings that now barricaded both ends of Downing Street. The days of handing over a petition, with all the attendant kudos of a photograph in front of the famous black door, were long gone. Catherine had read somewhere that the colour you painted your front door indicated something about you. Black, oddly, was considered to convey the message, 'Stay away! We don't appreciate visitors – Private.'

On the other hand, Red meant you were probably a liberal-minded extrovert, an exhibitionist, al-fresco sex sort of person. Green suggested a traditionalist, staid, conformist; white, organised, religious, neat, and clean, and so on. It was all vacuous rubbish, of course, but it filled a couple of pages in a Sunday colour supplement once a year.

Although she was some ten yards away, her zeal and animated desire to make her point were plain to see. It was this burning desire that first captured Parish's attention. Charming itself into his imagination, where it ran wild. When their eyes met, it was just one fleeting glance, but in that split second, he could see the fiery passion in her soul.

Something that had been missing from his life for a very long time.

Catherine turned back to speak to the aide from Number Ten, and the moment was gone. She handed over the petition, thanked him with a smile, and press photos were taken. Garrulously walking away with her friends, momentarily exhilarated at having succeeded in her mission. She turned back – the frenzy of the previous moment's elation now abated – and gazed at Parish for the second time. The apocryphal tales of love, at first sight, were never further from either of their minds. But in that one fantastic moment, any preconceived cynicism was shattered like an enormous explosion in the brain. She turned around and made her way slowly back through the jostling crowd toward where he stood. It felt like one of those stupid slow-motion moments in a film when the camera was over-cranked and re-run at normal speed. He continued to gaze at her as a stunned gazelle mesmerised in the glare of headlights. The traffic's commotion and noise became muffled and grey and began to fade from his consciousness. He felt his heart pound in his chest as if it were about to burst. This wasn't really happening, he thought. I've been watching too many romcoms. Maybe I should get out more and socialise with ordinary people. All these thoughts raced through his mind when she suddenly stood before him, gazing up interrogatively, without a splinter of shyness.

'I'm Catherine,' she spoke quietly and smiled disarmingly. 'Would you like to come for a drink? We're celebrating.' The lilting quality of her voice seemed to hang listlessly in the air.

I didn't answer immediately. I needed to make sure I hadn't imagined it. My throat had chosen this particular moment to dry up for some inexplicable reason, so I couldn't respond, even if I had wanted to. After a few moments, sufficient moisture returned to my throat, and I was able to reply to what was now a somewhat perplexed Catherine.

'Eh, yes,' I eventually spluttered out, 'but I'm on duty right now. Could it be tonight? I'm off at six.' I suddenly felt like a little boy back at school, explaining to a potential date that I had to stay behind in detention and couldn't walk her home. It all sounded so embarrassingly feeble, and we both knew it.

'Oh! You're a police officer!' she replied coyly. 'I didn't realise.'

'Eh, yes,' I replied a little cautiously. I think my eyes instinctively opened a little wider despite the sunlight. They tended to do that under certain circumstances, this being one of them. Probably has something to do with the brain suddenly demanding more visual information to fully assess how that admission affected someone's demeanour. Body language, expression, eyes...

'Is that a problem?' I asked, suddenly aware of a hint of intractability in her voice. I was unaccustomed to being asked out by an attractive woman, especially one I had never met before. Her precocious suggestion had caught me completely off guard. Catherine had also detected the thin, martyred air of remorseful anguish in the tenor of my voice. She later told me she found it quite endearing. It was as if this liaison might suddenly end because of who I was, and all would be lost. Like most women, she was hard-wired with the mysterious ability to extrapolate a meaningful inference from the tiniest gesture or inflection - as far as men were concerned.

'No, not at all, I just didn't realise,' replied Catherine reassuringly. The words were enough to staunch any further loss of confidence I might have felt, and I think she knew that. I had half expected some dry political comment, conditioned as we were to be taunted with all manner of cleverly constructed, politically biased epigrams at these assemblies - but none was forthcoming. 'Aren't you going to arrest me then,' she asked playfully? Her face lit up with contained pleasure as she swivelled playfully on her high heels, her eyes never losing contact with mine.

'Why should I arrest you? I asked. I was surprised at the question and unsure how I should reply. 'Have you done something wrong?'

'No,' she replied, 'but I'm sure you could think of something... if you really wanted to.' I smiled; unbelievably, I knew I was already falling in love. We stood there silently for a moment - just looking at each other as if unsure what should happen next.

'Pen!' she suddenly spluttered, holding out her hand and waving it around jauntily.

I rummaged desperately through my pockets and eventually found a pencil, which I held up, maybe a little over-jubilantly. Catherine smiled kindly, trying not to laugh. She took it and scribbled down her telephone number on a scrap of paper she had produced from her jeans pocket and handed them back to me. 'Call me when you are...' Catherine paused for what seemed like an interminable amount of time, carefully considering which word to use to close the instruction before eventually settling on 'available.' She uttered the word slowly, letting it drift out of her mouth on a small breath of air - with all the hidden agenda she could marshal into four tiny syllables without sounding slightly demented. Then she smiled again.

I was initially slightly surprised at her manner, but then again, I was not. This was who she was. Catherine reached up on her toes and kissed me gently on the cheek, 'there you go.' Then she turned on her heels and sashayed her way back to her friends, waving goodbye with her hand above her head as she disappeared into the crowd. I didn't move; I couldn't. Somehow, I knew I must remember this moment. Commit every detail to memory, every word, every gesture, and every inflection, for it would never happen again. I called her at six-thirty that night, and we arranged to meet up at a pub near Trafalgar Square, and our life began.

Part III
Jade

2023. Jade had been staying at a friend's house on the other side of Providence near Harlow for a couple of days. Catherine had agreed to pick her up that night as Parish was working late, and she had a few things to do on the way. It was nearly nine o'clock, and darkness had descended when Catherine arrived at Tasha's home.

She was going to toot the horn to alert Jade she had arrived. It was cold outside, and she was warm and cosy inside the car and didn't relish the thought of getting out into the freezing wind, even if only for a few minutes. But noticing how quiet it looked – it was an attractive neighbourhood, with pretty, tall, narrow townhouses and ornate lampposts. The residents would probably not appreciate their peace and tranquillity being rudely interrupted by some inconsiderate stranger sounding a car horn in the street. Not while they were all quietly dozing in front of their holavisions. She reconsidered her decision, slid out of the car, gathered her coat tightly around her to fend off the biting wind, and quickly made the short journey to the front door and rang the bell.

Jade answered the door with a smile - already wearing her coat, scarf, and pink woolly hat. 'Hi, Mum.' She kissed Catherine on the cheek. 'I'm packed and ready to go.' She pointed to her small rucksack by the door. She knew she was not the best timekeeper in the world - but she had obviously made an effort to be ready on time today. It would be a long drive home in the dark.

'Bye, Tash. See yer later,' Jade shouted up the staircase. 'Thanks for everything.'

'Bye, Jade. See you Monday,' came the disembodied reply. Jade smiled, picked up her rucksack and slammed the front door behind her. The wintry night air seemed to have no effect on her.

'Tash is having a bubble bath,' muttered Jade as they walked down the path. 'She'll be hours. She likes to put all those little pink candles around the room, burn incense and play whale music while soaking. I had one earlier… it's very soothing, music, candles and everything….'

'Sounds lovely,' said Catherine, but she did wonder about the whale music. 'I think maybe I'll have a bath when we get back.'

Jade threw her rucksack into the back of the car and flopped down next to Catherine.

'The bath has made me a bit tired, Mum. Is it okay if I go to sleep?'

'Of course, it is. I'll join you in a few minutes anyway,' replied Catherine. Jade pressed a button to lower the back

9

of her seat into the sleeping position and closed her eyes, and Catherine drove away.

Catherine didn't enjoy driving long hours at night, so she, too, would sleep once the car was locked onto the AMGS network. There was nothing further for her to do until they arrived home. She looked across at Jade, now snuggled up into a ball. Already blissfully asleep, her face a serenely calm marble sculpture peeking out from her hood, flawless and untainted by the ravages of time, obligation, or responsibility, with no concept of what fate might await her. The triumphs that she might reach out to touch - the disappointment when they recede just beyond her grasp. You never know what might lie ahead in the years to come. Oh, to be young again. Oh, to be you, thought Catherine. Not a care in the world – a free spirit without… without what, she pondered? I have Parish, I have you, and I have a career. What more could there be? She admonished herself for one fleeting moment of selfish ingratitude - then wondered from where she had conjured those thoughts. Instead, she pushed the corrosive line of harmful indulgence from her mind and deliberated over the unmistakable similarity between father and daughter. It was still a remarkable aspect of human design to assiduously carry forward small, unique traits from parent to child. The same features would always endear and cement families. Nearly everything would change throughout their lives, but certain things would forever remain the same.

Maybe it was time to have another baby. Maybe her hormones were playing games with her mind; she was not getting any younger. Jade would be off to university soon, and then she and Parish would be alone again. Was it wrong to have another baby to alleviate the pain they would feel when Jade had gone? I will mention it to Parish tomorrow; yes, I will do that. She made another mental note to broach the subject over dinner the following evening and tried to settle down to sleep. But sleep wouldn't come.

Her mind flashed back to the day they first met. She smiled, thinking of the first few weeks of their relationship. Chaotic rotas to juggle just so they could be together. Intense candlelit meals in a quiet bistro or restaurant when neither was hungry. The food was played with but seldom eaten. Sometimes, the waiters would ask if something was wrong with it - but there never was. They were just too immersed in each other to eat. Too involved with each other, talking about anything and everything. And then there were the long nights of lovemaking at Parish's flat. Catherine lived in a shared house with three other girls, which was not ideal for what they had in mind. Sometimes, in the mornings, they would have exotic feasts, figs, guava fruit and eggs benedict or smoked salmon, wild strawberries, and pink champagne. A little decadent, maybe, but an essential respite to allow them to regenerate and replenish their exhausted bodies and prepare them for the labours of the days ahead.

Those deliriously irrational days and nights stretched into weeks and months, then years - but the passion of their frenzied existence had now slowed a little since Jade was born. The three of them had eased into a gently quixotic intermezzo - a pause before the raging storm.

Chapter 2

It must have been towards the end of October 2023. Janice was making one of her regular monthly visits to stay overnight at Rose's house. The air was bitterly cold and damp, and the piercing wind swirling around the empty streets chilled her to the bone as she walked the last few yards to sanctuary. It felt as if she were naked before God on Judgement Day for all the protection her coat and jumper afforded her. But hostile elements would never deter her from making the arduous journey to see her beloved daughter. Like sirens of the sea chanting demands for atonement, the winds seemed to be beckoning her to join them. But it was an allusion, for there were no sins unspoken for which she must repent, so she ignored their wailing. Her hour of redemption had not arrived just yet, and she had memories of far worse nights than this.

They sat huddled together on the sofa in the comfort of Rose's lounge, watching the roaring flames of the open-hearth fire. The medullary rays and shakes on the oak-panelled walls came alive with the reflection of the firelight and the flickering imitation candle bulbs in the traditional wall lights. Winter had come again; it always seemed to be winter these days, and they were so much longer and colder than Rose could ever recall.

But Janice could remember the story of a cold winter night. A story she had been told many times as a child. The memory of which she did not care to revisit too often. She was haunted by the similar circumstances surrounding the conception of her child, Rose. An event of which she had little recollection, only the living evidence. Her family had indeed suffered much at the hands of men. One day, there would be a settlement, an atonement that would deliver her salvation and finally bring the nightmare to an end.

'I think... I may be getting close to finding him at last...' said Janice. She spoke quietly, almost whispering. It was as if she thought their conversation might be overheard by a concealed listener. While staring into the fire all the time, watching the flames conjure up fearful illusions from her darkest imaginings. All life had begun with fire and would probably end the same way. For a few moments, she was miles away, back to 2001 and a night that changed her life forever. She cradled her glass of German Riesling in both hands. Crushing it so tightly, her knuckles began to pale as the colour of life was squeezed away from every capillary.

Although no longer fashionable, it was still her favourite wine. Far too sweet for Rose, who preferred the dryer, flowery fragrance of her Pinot Grigio. Rose touched her arm to comfort her and whispered a few kind words of reassurance. The tension slowly eased. Her fears and uncertainties were alleviated... for now.

Like a thief in the night, summer had surreptitiously crept in unnoticed under the cover of darkness. And it had swiftly left again, taking with it the last few fleeting moments of pleasure from another year. Rose could only remember it being warm enough for them to sit outside for dinner on two occasions during the summer. It had started to rain on one of those. During the previous year, on a whim, she had made a valiant attempt to re-stain the wooden patio table a dark mahogany colour. But it had already defaulted to the dull, sullen shades of winter grey.

Janice glanced at Rose, expecting her to say something, but Rose did not reply. She just carried on gazing at the flames, looking into the past. The glow highlighted her

Eastern European heritage. Her alabaster skin almost too delicate for the purpose it was intended. Her blonde hair cascaded around her shoulders. The Aryan influence that had jumped a few generations brought an erotic pang of agony to Janice. There was another malevolent influence somewhere inside a tiny chamber in her mind, but Rose had never noticed that and never would.

'I'm meeting someone in a few days...' whispered Janice, sounding cautiously optimistic, 'someone who may be able to help me at last.' Rose knew what she was referring to without seeking any further clarification; sadly, it was never far from Janice's mind.

'That's good,' replied Rose positively, in the supportive way a daughter would. Even though she wasn't sure, her mother's obsession with finding the man who had raped her and was, in fact, her biological father was such a smart idea. Whoever he was, he would never be her real father, and Rose had no desire to meet him, but Janice felt differently. 'It's been a long time in the coming,' continued Rose with a hint of reservation, fortunately almost undetectable to Janice.

'It has,' replied Janice, deep in thought. 'It has.'

'Are you sure it's the right thing to do,' asked Rose meditatively? She was cautious about displaying negativity, but deep down, she felt uneasy about this obsession and apprehensive about how she would deal with the consequences if Janice succeeded in her quest. She was happier with things as they were, letting sleeping dogs lie, but Janice could not let it be.

'Right thing?' asked Janice, unsure exactly what Rose was alluding to. 'What? Meeting the man who....'

'Are you going to meet him?' interrupted Rose, slightly concerned.

'I don't know,' replied Janice. 'I suppose it depends on what I think… once I've seen him… from a distance, that is.'

'But what can that tell you?' asked Rose, sounding confused.

'I don't know,' replied Janice, 'but if I can just see his face, then maybe I'll understand why he….'

'I still think it's dangerous,' interrupted Rose, 'digging up the past, especially with something like this. He may not even remember. He was probably blind drunk, for all you know. You said you had all been drinking that night.'

'Yes, I know, but it wasn't just the… I was in hospital for nearly three weeks after and… well… I wanted to know why he …'

'Three weeks?' interrupted Rose. 'You never mentioned that before. Why three weeks if it was just…' She stopped, suddenly realising she was about to take the hackneyed path so often adopted by the authorities and trivialise her mother's brutal sexual assault by downgrading it to the less significant charge of non-consensual sex, which it was not. She cursed under her breath for even considering the thought. Belittled by a momentary lapse into the cynicism customarily reserved for her clients, never for the only person she had ever loved. For Rose, the act of intercourse had always been – would always be – one of consensual sex for a fee negotiated and paid in advance. This was all she understood, all she wanted to understand. Anything else was inconsequential and had no relevance or meaning. Occasionally, it became a little rough, but she could handle that. She was always in control – total control.

She had no comprehension of a personal and sexual relationship becoming entwined into one. Of course, she knew about this kind of arrangement. She had read many romantic novels, watched countless films, and spoken at length to friends in an attempt to understand the concept. But she had never personally experienced it and could never see herself doing so. She could not allow herself to become involved. As far as she was concerned, these two transitory states must, at all costs and to preserve her sanity, be kept far apart.

For her, love and sex were something entirely different; each had its own mindset and parameters. Rose's feelings about sex had been rationalised and simplified by the very manner in which she lived. Reduced to a basic level of perfunctory gratification exponentially related to financial reimbursement. This, she clearly understood. There was no ambiguity for her - no confusion or misunderstanding in the nudity of simple words and no blurred demarcation lines that couldn't be crossed. Sex was sex - that was it, plain and simple. Rose remembered the first time she realised she could trade her body; she had sold it for a swig of vodka in exchange for a head fuck while she was still at school. Now, she sold it for much more, but that was it. Sex for goodies, nice things, nothing else.

She had different relationships with her mother (whom she loved). Her cleaner, doctor, bank manager and hairdresser (whom she liked). And her clients, who she fucked, despised and held in utter contempt. It was as profoundly simple as that. Love played no part, nor was it a factor worthy of consideration.

'I know what you mean,' replied Janice. 'It was just a quick …' She couldn't say the word. 'So why did I…' she paused momentarily, gazing into the fire. 'But he did things to me that night. I don't know what he did - I only know it took the surgeons a long time to repair the damage... I could never have another child after....' She paused again. 'That's why I had you.' She looked at Rose without expression, unsure how she would react to what she was about to tell her. Janice's eyes fell to the floor as she continued. 'The hospital offered me an abortion... and I seriously considered it... but when they told me I would never be able to conceive again, I declined.' She looked up at Rose and smiled, looking for some response.

'And I'm extremely delighted you did,' said Rose, returning her smile but not sounding too trite.

Janice paused momentarily, opened her handbag and took out an envelope. She handed it to Rose. 'I want you... I want you to keep this somewhere safe. Please don't open it unless something happens. It's... it's just something you should know, in case....'

'In case? That sounds a bit ominous,' enquired Rose, reluctantly taking the envelope, unsure how to react.

'No, it's not really,' replied Janice. 'My grandmother told me something once, something I have never forgotten; I'm just following her advice.'

'What,' asked Rose, now intrigued?

Janice looked at her beautiful daughter and smiled but did not answer. 'Why do you do it, Rose,' she asked instead? Rose was taken aback, almost embarrassed, by the bluntness of the question. They had never discussed what she was - what she did or why she did it. It was something that up until this moment, had been tacitly accepted but never spoken of.

'I am beautiful, Mum, and that is because of you,' said Rose. Janice smiled. 'I have you to thank for that, you and grandma and her mother,' continued Rose.

'Yes, I know you are beautiful,' replied Janice, 'but....'

'Men pay for that,' interrupted Rose, with pragmatism and stillness that left no room for sentiment. 'More than I could ever earn doing anything else. Why should I work my fingers to the bone like you do when I have this?' Rose made a brief gesture to her face and body with her immaculately manicured hands, elongated by pink sparkly painted fingernails. 'You had this, you probably all had this, but you chose to work hard all your life to get what you wanted, but I am weak, Mum. I want it all, and I want it now.'

'But...' said Janice, but Rose interrupted her again.

'No buts, Mum. I do it, and I like it – well, most of the time.' She glanced self-effacingly at her mother and pursed her lips. 'And if not, I think of....' She paused, looking whimsically at her fingers, and rolled them a few times. 'Diamonds.' She smiled again, a smile that lit up the room. 'That's what I think of when they're fucking me: diamonds. And that makes me laugh.' She looked up at her mother with a stoical expression. 'And when I laugh, they give me more diamonds, so what the hell, bang away. Rent-a-body, that's me, but the rates are high, extremely high, but only for so long... We've all got a fuck-by date.' She paused for a moment. 'Sex is my currency, my agency, my investment and my stock, and I'm a day trader....'

Janice was a little shocked by Rose's blasé detachment. She knew she wasn't morally corrupt - she wasn't amoral either. But she was beginning to understand the strict personal boundaries that Rose had set - within which she chose to operate. Janice laughed. She could see the uncomplicated commercial logic in Rose's explanation, and it amused her. She wondered why she had never thought about it like that. Maybe her life would have been a little easier… a lot easier, if…

'Do you think…?' she carelessly murmured, almost unaware she had spoken her thoughts aloud.

'No, Mum,' Rose interrupted. 'You're my mother, and I don't need competition, thank you. You carry on working where you are. I'll look after you.'

They looked at each other, laughed and drank more wine. Janice was still an attractive woman. But that salacious dynamic that could so easily entrap men - that indefinable quality they could not resist and would induce them into parting with expensive gifts for favours rendered, was no longer there. Maybe, in her case, it had never been there. Or perhaps it had been crushed into obscurity by indifference, neglect, and the passing years. She pondered over the wise council her daughter had managed to summarise so succinctly, achingly erudite in its simplicity. It comforted her to know that no one, absolutely no one, would ever be able to take advantage of Rose.

'What did grandmamma say, Mum?' asked Rose. Janice looked at her, the firelight sparkling in her eyes, the shadows flickering on her cheeks like harlequins dancing at the Burning Men's masquerade ball at the carnival of Venice.

'The war picks you, so you must pick your battles,' she whispered quietly.

'Pick your battles? What does that mean?' asked Rose, as mystified as she was intrigued.

'If ever you desire retribution for something done to you, plan it well and plan it carefully. Not rashly, in a moment of anger or rage when you may not be thinking too clearly. True absolution will then be yours. Vengeance is the dessert; it is eaten last when everything else is finished, as the Italians say.' She winced with mild embarrassment for employing the trite cliché, but it summed up perfectly how she felt. 'There will always be the perfect moment. It may only come once, but it will come. You must be patient and wait for that moment to arrive. But remember,' she looked into Rose's eyes, engendering a promise, 'do not open the letter unless....'

Rose had nothing to avenge, so the advice didn't register immediately. Not until a few years later would she think back to this day and consider Janice's words again, this time more carefully, while she prepared her *killing plan.*

'I won't,' said Rose. 'I promise.'

The old-style open-hearth fire, which they both preferred to the central heating, sizzled and hissed as the moisture buried deep within the heart of each new log was driven out by the intense heat. Piles of logs were stacked in baskets on both sides of the hearth, enough to see them through the evening. Janice dropped another couple on the fire. White sparks flew up and out - tiny comets escaping gravity incinerated in microseconds. Flames leapt up, casting mysterious, ever-changing shadows over the back of the hearth. Shape-shifting demons rose up from Hades, accompanied by the primal screams of tortured souls in an endless display of pyrotechnics that had continued to fascinate people throughout the ages despite the advances in science and technology.

Janice gazed into the fire and recalled a story she had often started on evenings like this but never finished. A tale her great-great-grandmother Lara had told her about a dark period in her life, in everybody's life, during the Second World War.

'I was only seven years old when Lara told me this story, and I didn't fully understand everything my great-great-grandmother told me. But I still clearly remember her eulogising about the kitchen hearth and it being the middle of winter in their farmhouse in the village of Lubesk, near Silute in Lithuania. Their very existence depended on keeping the fire going day and night through the long, dark, bitter winter months and...'

Chapter 3

'**He** who would valiant be, let him come hither...' Aiden had sung those words many times before as a child. But never with any real emotion or a passing thought for John Bunyan, toiling in his prison cell, scribbling down his opus to the immeasurable cost of salvation. Back then, they had always remained just meaningless, oddly rhyming phrases in a hymnbook.

Today, they rang in his ears with a rousing, unexplained poignancy, something he had not encountered before and would probably never experience again. Apart from one warm April day many years later, in 2013, when they would broadcast Lady Margaret Thatcher's state funeral on television. On that day, he would hear the words sung out once more. But this time, with aching intensity and jingoistic triumphalism as the party faithful trumpeted their Boadicea's delivery into the lap of God.

A sanguine farewell to the glory days of yesteryear, but they would return one day; he would make sure of that. Like so many others, Aiden was strangely moved by what he had heard that day and the realisation of what she had achieved. The things she had changed against all the odds, accomplishments that would be hard to match and unlikely ever to be bettered. The cost would be immense but worth it in the end.

Today, too, those words sounded different; a sentient resonance touched his heart, raised his spirit, and burnt a pathway deep into his soul. He wondered if Margaret had been similarly inspired by the haunting melody when she sat alone in her cabinet office. Making decisions that would affect many people and change the country forever.

These thoughts he would always keep to himself, for he was a dedicated socialist. But then Thatcher was the natural antithesis of capitalism, so evidently, she must have been a socialist and a true democrat.

The first tentative steps of all great journeys are filled with trepidation and foreboding. But with mounting confidence comes hope, followed by joyful anticipation. Then, only after these distractions have been put aside, the exulted passage into the unknown - the journey of a lifetime truly begins...

Aiden Hawsley's journey started with a dream. A vision of revived English superiority in Great Britain. Inspired by an impassioned speech he had witnessed at a political rally he accidentally attended on a cold winter's day in Trafalgar Square in late 1996. On that day, his life, like the lives of all who change man's destiny, was suddenly redirected by the fates down the road least trodden. He was entranced by the sense of urgency - and the passion imbued in the words. Some of which were admittedly soaked in fascist rhetoric, some of which he would not fully understand until many years later.

Nevertheless, he still passionately embraced the democratising accessibility and the intense commitment of the speaker's eloquent delivery. He spoke well, knowing the value of inspiring words and gestures when they were meticulously assembled. And how magniloquence could so easily influence vacuous souls. Just as gravity, unseen, never given a second thought, surreptitiously pulls us to earth, so too was he drawn inexorably closer, not to the words themselves, but to the message so cleverly concealed deep within the genetic code of every sentence.

The thread of commonality, purpose and accountability instilled in the speaker's rage and the ranting frustration he conveyed ran parallel with his own fears and uncertainties about people and society. This desperate desire for change, the pleading quest to follow the rising phoenix into the jaws of hell if necessary. The intensity of his yearning to make Britain great again drew him into this ethereal web of mindful certainty. This, alone, would be enough to hold his attention then and for the rest of his life. For who would claim to be that which he was not.

Aiden joined the struggling British National Party on that day. Although hugely unpopular, despised, criticised and harangued by all the other political organisations, there was no denying its logical argument and the indisputable facts being so articulately expressed. Aiden was wholly engrossed by the elation of the crowd. They were being so adroitly manipulated by the proselytising speaker. In equal measures, they were mesmerised by the way this man would, with consummate proficiency and pitch control, suddenly lower the tenor of his voice down through the sombre, toneless, deathly cold greys of anguish and torment to surreptitiously draw in the crowd; the crowd over which he had cast this spell, this magical illusion. Then, slowly, like the sound of faraway thunder growing ever closer, he would subtly increase the resonance and volume to please the hushed crowd now straining in absolute silence to hear his every rumbling word. Almost imperceptibly, his voice floated up through the euphoric pinks of passionate endeavour to the exulted oranges and reds of oratory gymnastic ecstasy. It was as if he were some ancient Arabian storyteller, weaving his mysterious spell while imparting a dark and fantastic tale to a group of children captivated by his mastery of the art. Or possibly a snake-oil salesman imbuing the magical properties of his unique elixir of life. It was a cunning stratagem used sparingly but with magnificent effect by all great orators.

Cold shivers of excitement began to run down Aiden's backbone as the speaker delivered his eloquent arguments. He could sense the growing exhilaration slowly overwhelming and absorbing him. Although blatantly patriotic in a dangerously xenophobic way, the speaker managed to engender and instil a sense of guilty pleasure and vulgar arrogance in every listener. Aiden was in awe of this unique ability, this gift of mass communication. He had never experienced it before, but he would learn this art form and learn it well, and one day, he would use it to control a nation. He imagined himself standing on a larger platform addressing a crowd of thousands, all enraptured and enthralled by his every word and mannerism.

'...for this world has changed – and our lives have changed – and we must change. A plague has infiltrated us – and will contaminate us all unless we make a stand. We must act and act soon – if we wait, it will be too late. The party I lead will stand up against the foe – and it will cherish and defend your right to live your life any way you choose – and not allow the invaders to take from us that which is ours. We will build the barricades – and they will stand for a thousand years. And as those years pass – we will rejoice in the knowledge that on the day that we were called to account, we were not found wanting, and we made the right decision.'

Aiden could hear the tumultuous crowds cheer loudly, but he was a dreamer and a dangerous one. But the people had been charmed, mesmerised, and tricked by eloquent dreamers before, and they would be again.

He agreed with the speaker's assertion that natural order and control dissemination had seriously, but not mortally, wounded society. The country needed a new Boadicea to lead from the front, not some chinless Etonian, snivelling and kowtowing under the heel of faceless, imbecilic European bureaucrats. Too much had changed, and not all of it for the better.

Something had to be done to reverse the moral erosion inflicted on their country by previous generations. Now caught up in this intoxicating haze of patriotic euphoria, Aiden began visualising the speaker as a humble disciple. Someone desperately searching for a saviour, and he was subliminally directing his attention specifically at him. This heartfelt call to arms, this impassioned appeal, was a plea to take up the flaming torch of liberty and egalitarianism and to march forward into the darkness to seek out the light.

The manifesto was persuasive, lucid, unambiguous, and succinctly confirmed his long-held belief that society's polarisation had already begun. What it lacked were the essential specific refinements and direction. No longer was the country split between North and South or rich and poor. It was now a clear division between those who contributed to society and those who only bleed something away from it.

Karl Marx said, 'From each according to his ability to each according to his need.' But this maxim had been subtly tweaked by Lenin, Stalin, and Trotsky to '*He who does not work neither shall he eat.*' This was still the message today, but Hawsley's modernistic interpretation would be, 'He who does not donate, neither shall he benefit.' True socialism had returned, albeit irrevocably, but indiscernibly flawed. Communism seeks to share the wealth - socialism seeks to share the poverty.

Aiden began to see himself as the single guiding light, a messiah held aloft. He would lead his country out of the dark shadows created by a cloud of dissent, disharmony and disarray that had hung over the land for so many years since the end of Thatcherism. It was now slowly descending, enveloping, and inveigling its way into every tiny crevice in every corner of every home, choking the very lifeblood out of the country. He would destroy the darkness, and the day would return. 'To be a pilgrim,' he sang heartily at the end of the rally. It was no longer just an old hymn; it would be his battle cry, his anthem to lift the spirits of those who would eventually follow him. The crusader moving forward against the foe, towards a New Jerusalem, waving his flag with glorious indefatigability and evangelistic zeal. He was that pilgrim, and this was his time.

Unknown to him at that very moment, the fates had conspired to send him on a new pathway. Nothing raises the ugly face of nationalism faster than a song, and now he had the song. For Aiden, this was the uplifting experience he had waited for his whole life.

He remembered his father once took him to a pub for a pint. It was just after his eighteenth birthday before he went to university; he wanted a 'quiet chat about things'. After they were seated, his father said nothing for five minutes and just sat sipping his pint. It was an extraordinarily long time to say nothing. He explained that life should be full of wonderfully uplifting experiences, or each day should at least be leading up to one. *'When this no longer happens, it is time to finish it. Because it all becomes a little too tiresome after that.'* Those were his final words that day, but Aiden remembered them for the rest of his life.

Aiden didn't fully understand what he meant until a few years later when his father, who no longer had uplifting experiences, committed suicide at forty-three. He had fastened himself with brown gaffer tape to an old armchair in the garden shed (where they had spent many happy summer days together). He injected himself with a prodigious quantity of the juice he had methodically extracted from the deadly nightshade bush that grew in a wild patch at the bottom of their garden. He had not taped his left arm as he needed one arm free to inject the poison into the other. As he was right-handed, this would have made it more difficult for him to extricate himself from his bindings should he have had a sudden change of heart and begin to panic in his final moments. This was undeniably his penultimate uplifting moment – the final one was the fiery cremation that would soon follow. Aiden's mother, Rosemary, had been surprisingly sanguine about the whole affair. Never mentioning it again except when trimming back the wild patch to put in a rockery a few years later.

After the meeting, Aiden rang Drummond Cleaver and Benny Maranno, two friends from university, and asked them to meet him in the Mortlake Arms public house just off Trafalgar Square at eight o'clock that evening to celebrate.

'Celebrate what exactly?' asked Drummond cautiously, a man not easily extricated from his warm lodgings on the vague whim of a good friend. 'I would rather stay in. We're having a Chinese takeaway and a few beers.' After all, it was cold outside, and it was Friday, a good night on the telly, thought Drummond, but of course, he didn't mention that to Aiden for fear of instant admonishment. He had already been chastised several times for becoming a couch potato and not fully embracing university culture, but he had a good reason.

A few months earlier, in a local pub usually only frequented by students, he had been the subject of a terrifyingly unprovoked attack by a drunk, possibly of Romanian or Ukrainian extraction. The man had suddenly produced a chair leg from nowhere and, for no discernible reason, commenced beating Drummond around the head with it.

Drummond was not a fighting man and had immediately rolled himself into a foetal ball on the floor to protect himself as best he could. As luck would have it – a few moments after the attack began – Aiden arrived and, seeing the commotion, immediately made for the epicentre while the rest of the students were hastily withdrawing. He did not immediately realise it was Drummond who was the target of the assault. Although the raging man was at least four stones heavier than he and obviously much stronger – Aiden, with no thought for his own safety and without hesitation, grabbed hold of one of the bar stools and lifting it aloft, moved towards the attacker.

Sensing Aiden approaching, the man suddenly produced a large knife and turned to face him, armed with a chair leg in one hand and the knife in the other. Aiden continued moving slowly towards the man while holding the chair menacingly aloft. Despite his distinct weight and height advantage, and probable drug-induced bravado, the raging man's eyes met Aiden's eyes, and his resolve weakened for a split second. He was momentarily mesmerised by something he could see but didn't quite understand. In that moment of indecision, Aiden's chair came crashing down on his head, reducing him to a crumpled heap on the floor. He did not get back up. Now standing, Drummond rushed across to thank Aiden. They left the pub together and made for home unaffected by the evening's experience apart from a few minor bruises. Drummond was forever in Aiden's debt. The thought that Aiden had put his own life at risk for him without hesitation would never be far from his mind in moments of indecision or uncertainty in the future.

'A new life!' declared Hawsley, sounding unnervingly optimistic, which was always a serious cause for concern in Drummond's experience. 'I must do something good. This could be it – this is what I have been looking for,' he spluttered enthusiastically. Hawsley sounded almost messianic, gripped by a frenzy of chemical intensity. He had always been prone to severe emotional highs and lows. His mercurial character could be intimidating to a stranger, but Drummond had become accustomed to it. Curiously, it was this trait that had attracted Drummond and Benny to Aiden in the first place. It was as if he were continually atoning for a mortal sin not yet committed while simultaneously searching for the principal objective - the Mecca - the redeeming conclusion that would justify the journey - the means to the end - and his very existence.

'Is it better than this one?' Continued Drummond hesitantly at first. Carefully delving deeper into this week's epiphany while nibbling a prawn cracker and smiling quirkily at Benny. Benny was listening intently to the conversation on the speakerphone but saying nothing. Benny's facial expression indicated he was not interested in going out and was perfectly happy to stay where he was. But deep down, he knew that they would both eventually accede to Aiden's invitation; such was his persuasive manner.

Drummond was biologically programmed to be cautious about any significant change that came about too effortlessly. His life had never been comfortable; he had struggled hard to get through university. And this had taught him one thing – nothing worth having would ever be easy or be presented as a gift. You either earned it by working hard or stole it - if you had a mind. But he had never stolen anything in his life, except for a couple of tins of tomato soup when he was hungry and skint in his early days at university. That wasn't technically theft, as he had no intention of permanently depriving the owner of their contents. And as he understood it, that was the primary defence argument in any legal proceedings.

He replaced them a few weeks later when he received money from his father. With the genuine version, needless to say, not the family budget variety he had *borrowed*. Such was his egalitarian nature.

He had met Aiden Hawsley and Benny Maranno on their first day at university, and they had formed a friendship that would last a lifetime. They had also switched rooms in the student accommodation block on campus and were now all on the same landing during their first year while freshers. This arrangement was mutually beneficial - most of the time.

'It will be,' answered an ecstatic Aiden, who had embraced without reservation the promises and political dogma he had heard that day. 'There's a new world coming,' he added enthusiastically.

Drummond and Benny reluctantly finished their takeaway dinner. Carefully and somewhat precariously, they placed the dishes in the sink on top of the ever-increasing mountain of crockery and utensils – all scheduled for the weekly clean on Saturday. They put on their coats. Drummond always wore an old duffel coat he had acquired from a charity shop for five pounds. It gave him the quirky appearance of an eccentric, philosophising academic. He wasn't. They made their way out of the flat, walking briskly towards the pub, garrulously contemplating, with wide-ranging speculation, the nature of the revelation on which they were about to be enlightened.

After they arrived, Aiden spent the first part of the evening galvanising them with the emotional impact of the epiphanic road to Damascus moment he had experienced that day. He spoke of the profound philosophy of the unnamed speaker from the BNP who had mesmerised him with an impassioned speech. The rest of the night was spent defining and extrapolating its aims and objectives, all with the assistance of copious pints of local ale. Such was his confidence and enthusiasm that he promised them, on his mother's life, unfortunately, senior positions in his government when he was elected leader. Somewhat unforgivably, he forgot that his mother had died five years previously.

'Benny!' exclaimed Aiden, impassioned by the moment but now beginning to mumble and slur his words a little. 'I appoint you as my Minister of Central Logistics and Transport, and you... My trusted ally, Drummond, will be my Minister of Internal Security.' He took another sip of his beer and continued... 'It is crucial to have the right people by your side on the eve of a magnificent battle.' He was now beginning to sound like Winston Churchill reciting an imperfect speech. They weren't ever sure whether he was being serious or playing a game. 'You may think I am pissed...' he took another sip, 'and this may be the alcohol talking, but I can assure you it is not.'

His voice suddenly became clear, articulate, and distinct; he had stopped slurring and appeared perfectly sober. It was a strange transformation which took Drummond and Benny by surprise.

Aiden had always believed that a significant element of intoxication was psychological. A pseudo state induced to befit the occasion. Alcohol, of sufficient quantity to incapacitate most people, apparently seemed to have a negligible effect on him, and drunkenness appeared to be another illusion. It was almost as if he hadn't drunk alcohol at all that night. He focused his attention on the two of them and repeated his pledge with a cold, calculating intensity. He meant what he said, of that much they were sure. They were both incredibly pleased with this sudden, unexpected promotion to the elevated echelons of power, albeit slightly hypothetical in their minds, but they didn't mention this. However, they did celebrate the moment by having another pint of left-wing socialist beer and going for a communal piss.

They spent the last part of the evening laughing and drinking to further excess, for they were friends and happy for him - on what was clearly a joyous and seminal moment in his life. However, they were a little concerned that he kept quietly repeating a few bars of 'To be a Pilgrim' after each salient point. Aiden spent the rest of the evening drifting from blind drunkenness to puritanical sobriety with remarkable agility. Benny found it oddly entertaining, but it disturbed Drummond. He was beginning to see a different side of Aiden, a side he was unsure he liked.

After the pub closed, they struggled back to their campus rooms at two in the morning. Drummond and Benny soon forgot the pledges and undertakings of the night before. However, Aiden did not. True to his word, they would be appointed many years later to the exalted positions of power he had promised them that night.

The three of them had started at university together. And although they struggled during those early years, they would always remain good friends, which would continue to be the case almost until the end. By 2001, Aiden had been working for nearly six years for the party. Two and a half years part-time while he finished his university degree in English and Political Sciences. Followed by three and a half years as their media advisor before being promoted to deputy leader of the BNP. He had initially anticipated becoming a barrister but had been unable to secure the necessary tutelage. He undoubtedly had the essential abilities of shrewdness and absolute dispassion, which would hold him in good stead in the coming years.

But he lacked the unique dimension of the cunning trickster. Someone who could adroitly lead an unsuspecting victim safely across an alligator-infested swamp on an invisible pathway hidden below the water. Only to suddenly disappear along with the path - leaving the victim stranded on a tiny island with no escape, at the mercy of ravenous creatures.

Drummond graduated as a research chemist and worked for the government at the Porton Down Chemical Research Centre on various top-secret military chemical projects. Aiden would later be told that one was a modern variant of a 1960s experimental incapacitant chemical called Pyrexal (lipopolysaccharide). It was euphemistically described as a harmless riot-control nerve agent). Pyrexal was, in fact, a derivative of the salmonella bacterium *Abortus equi*. The original formula had failed at the early testing stage and produced unreliable and inconsistent results. Some unexplained suicides indirectly attributed to its use had finally put an end to the development program.

However, subsequent research and further development in the early years of the twenty-first century solved the original problems. The establishment eventually delivered an active chemical agent for the 'restrained control of assemblies and rallies which had become unruly or overly boisterous' (a polite euphemism for a riot). Of course, it was not merely a riot-control drug but a highly effective battlefield incapacitant called Benacane. At full strength, it could render an enemy incapable of carrying out the simplest tasks - compliant to any verbal instruction, physically incapable of any form of resistance, and yet wholly conscious and compos mentis.

Benny didn't see the point in finishing his degree and left just before graduation as he had received a highly lucrative offer to start working immediately as a computer software designer. In the evenings and weekends, he worked tirelessly for the BNP.

On the night of Hawsley's election as deputy party leader in 2001, he celebrated at the BNP headquarters with Benny and the support workers for most of the evening. Aiden eventually left with a few female acolytes to meet with Drummond at a nightclub. They stayed there drinking and dancing until the early hours before finally deciding to leave. As they could not find a taxi and it had started to rain, they decided to stay at Drummond's flat on the Fulham High Road as it was within walking distance. By this time, however, most of the other girls that had come to the club with them had already gone home. Except that is for Janice Watson, an attractive new girl, tall with long blonde hair and a short dress, and two other staff girls from the office.

Overwhelmed by alcohol and the euphoria of Aiden's election victory, they continued listening to music and talking politics while Janice and her two friends giggled, drank, and kept dancing. After another hour or so and a few joints, Aiden became bored and tired of talking, and his thoughts turned to sex, which he clearly demonstrated to the others. Aiden looked across the room at Janice, who was dancing alone (her two friends had now gone home). Being the only remaining female, she became the obvious subject of his lascivious attention. Acutely aware of what was possibly about to occur, Drummond went to his bedroom and returned a few minutes later with a small tablet in his hand, which he offered Aiden. Aiden looked at the pill in Drummond's palm, unsure what it was or what he was supposed to do with it.

'Whatever your intentions are, for Christ's sake, give this to her first.' Directed Drummond with the prosaic pragmatism that one way or another would influence his life over the next twenty-five years.

'What?' enquired Aiden with a desultory insouciance. His drunken state had rendered him incapable of rationalising helpful thoughts or actions. 'I don't need that. We're only going to fuck her.'

'Not we, mate,' replied Drummond firmly with a slightly uncharacteristic northern twang. 'Don't shag anything without written consent.'

'Lightweight,' harped Hawsley condescendingly. 'What is it anyway?

'Protection,' said Drummond quietly. 'Please give it to her,' he pleaded as he offered the pill again to Hawsley. His tone indicated this was for his benefit, but Aiden was too drunk to appreciate the inflection.

'Against what?' slurred Benny. Benny was slumped in a chair on the other side of the room, dribbling a little and far too drunk to stand. 'The pox?'

'Prosecution, a listing on the sex offenders' register, unrestrained condemnation by your political opponents, probably a short prison sentence and the end of a promising career as a politician,' warned Drummond wryly. 'She's only fourteen. It's statutory rape, and that's illegal.'

Aiden thought about Drummond's words for a few seconds and looked back at Janice dancing in the centre of the room. 'With tits like that, she can't possibly be,' he exclaimed disbelievingly. 'She looks so much older! They're bloody illegal.' The alcohol and skunk had muddled his customarily balanced perception.

Benny laughed, but in his reverie were the tiny seeds of destruction.

'She's fourteen,' confirmed Drummond flatly. 'She told me that tonight at the club.' Drummond appeared to have sobered up relatively quickly, never being one to completely lose control of his faculties. Or maybe he hadn't drunk or smoked as much as the other two.

'Where's the bathroom,' asked Janice with remarkably lousy timing? Until now, she had been too busy dancing to understand the proposed carnal plans.

'Straight through there, second on the right, love,' replied Drummond, pointing toward the bathroom. Janice smiled wanly and wandered off, swaying a little as she went, oblivious to Hawsley's intentions.

'What will it do?' asked Hawsley curiously.

'It won't do her any harm. She just won't remember anything that happens tonight, or for the next twenty-four hours for that matter,' muttered Drummond. 'That's it... more or less.'

'What, not any of it?' slurred Benny, attempting to light a cigarette. 'That is a shame... for her, that is.' Drummond looked at Benny with utter contempt but said nothing. For a moment, he wondered how he had arrived at this appalling low point in his life.

'Nothing,' confirmed Drummond. 'It's something we've been working on for the military. It does, however, have one interesting side effect.'

'Which is?' asked Aiden, who was not too drunk to realise they were considering administering a classified military drug for purely recreational purposes.

'Temporary loss of inhibition and permanent short-term memory loss,' replied Drummond authoritatively.

'And that's it, nothing else?' asked Aiden.

'Not as far as we are aware,' replied Drummond.

'Temporary loss of inhibition?' said Aiden. 'What does that mean?'

'Just that. She'll do anything you tell her... until the drug wears off,' Drummond added as a cautionary qualification.

'Give it to her,' ordered Aiden peremptorily after giving the matter a few moments' further consideration. He was already beginning to sound like a general commanding his troops in battle.

The alcohol had obviously not completely dulled his profound sense of self-preservation. Drummond reluctantly dropped the pill into Janice's glass of wine and swirled it around to dissolve it before replacing it on the table. When she returned from the bathroom, Aiden picked up the glass and gave it to her.

'To labour in vain,' toasted Aiden. He held his glass up high, and they clinked together. She did not understand the listless epigram but swallowed the contents without hesitation, and they continued dancing briefly before Aiden sat back down. The three of them talked and watched as Janice continued to dance on her own. Drummond, however, was becoming increasingly uneasy about what he had been a party to. Like it or not, he had potentially become an accomplice to a serious crime.

Aiden kept a watchful eye on Janice, expecting to see some discernible change in her behaviour as the drug took effect, but there wasn't any noticeable change. This began to annoy him. After another twenty minutes and becoming impatient, he suddenly barked an order.

'Take your clothes off, Janice.' She smiled at him demurely. He had been watching her all night, although appearing to ignore her. She was aware of this. She was also aware that he was now paying her some attention, so now it was her turn to play games. Looking him squarely in the eyes and with charming promiscuity, she took hold of the hem at the bottom of her dress, lifting it off her body and over her head in one slow theatrical motion.

Like a butterfly gently extricating itself from its previous existence, she discarded the dress, throwing it with blithe abandonment over her shoulder. Now freed from any natural inhibitions by the chemicals coursing through her brain, Janice continued to dance, tantalisingly naked except for a black silk G-string. Her large breasts slowly swaying rhythmically with the music were more than Aiden could resist.

'I'm going to bed. I'm tired,' said Drummond. He was perfectly aware of Hawsley's intentions but didn't want any part of what was about to follow.

'Stay!' snapped Aiden. 'It's for free,' but Drummond smiled reproachfully and walked to his bedroom. He had been an accomplice to the proposal but had no desire to witness its execution.

'Take her with you when you go, and please leave her somewhere safe,' implored Drummond. Those were his final words that night.

'Don't nag, Cleaver,' mumbled Aiden contemptuously. 'You are beginning to sound like my mother.' He turned to Benny. 'What about you, Maranno? Don't you want to…?' He made a gesture with his arm and a clenched fist.

'No thanks, mate. I'm pissed and knackered. Go on, Aid, you give it to her. I'll just watch.' The words reverberated in Janice's head.

'Go on, Aid, you give it to her. I'll just watch… Go on, Aid, you give it to….' Suddenly, every syllable seemed to be bouncing off the inside of her skull, muddling itself up into a cacophonous symphonic babble. Now entirely overwhelmed by the alcohol, Benny fell asleep in a drunken stupor on the sofa, curled up into a foetal ball and began to suck his thumb.

Aiden turned his attention back to Janice, who was still dancing and beckoning him to join her. The drug had taken full effect, and Janice could no longer control her mind or body. Aiden glanced carefully around the room; he was looking for something.

The physical injuries inflicted on Janice's body that night constantly reminded her of an event she would never clearly remember. But paradoxically, for the rest of her life, she would never entirely forget. The doctors at the hospital had never encountered such brutal vaginal and anal damage - but despite this, nine months later, she gave birth to a beautiful, healthy girl. She would never be able to conceive again. The hospital offered her a termination a few weeks later after being told she was pregnant. But when the position regarding the unlikely possibility of any further pregnancy had been clearly explained, she decided to carry the child to full term. She would call her daughter Rose. The police investigation into the rape and sodomy came to nothing. The DNA retrieved from her vaginal vault did not match any of the suspects they had block tested, and the case remained on record as unsolved...

Chapter 4

Benny ambled slowly, anxiously around his conservatory. The pervasive, musty aroma of damp earth, greenery, and the warmth of the sun filled his senses. It was pleasurable suffocation, and he adored it for the tranquillity it brought to his tortured soul.

Although the ambient temperature had crept a few degrees higher recently, he was still moving slower than usual. His right leg gave him a great deal of discomfort, which was unusual as the warmth usually helped ease the pain - but he wasn't really thinking about that today. Benny's thoughts were elsewhere; he was more troubled by past events and what the future might hold. A small glistening, silvery bead of sweat slowly ran down his temple, but he didn't notice it immediately. He swiftly brushed it away with his shirt sleeve when he felt it touch his cheek. For a moment, he wondered why life's other problems and imperfections could not be so easily brushed away. But that was naïvely childish; he knew that. The days of innocent resonation were gone and would never return.

Although still only in his early forties, he was no longer a particularly attractive specimen of manhood. He was now grossly overweight due to the lack of exercise brought about by the long-term problems with his leg.

For some reason, known only to him, he always immodestly referred to himself as 'slightly crippled' when in the company of friends. An offensive phrase much frowned upon when discussing other people of similar impairment but not quite so harshly condemned when used self-deprecatingly. There were rumours he did it to engender sympathy, but that would have been cynically specious even for Benny.

He wasn't crippled, merely troubled with a limp. It would have gone almost unnoticed if he didn't insist on using a walking cane, which he'd had deliberately shortened to accentuate the affliction. He had picked up that idea from a story he once read about Marilyn Monroe and her high heels. He had lost most of his hair (this was a hereditary condition) and a large number of teeth due to a gingivitis infection in his early twenties, and despite surgical implants, there was no getting away from the fact that the handsome, energetic figure of his early youth was gone forever. He had aged much faster than expected, looking old well before his time. The lottery of life had not been kind to him. It had promised so much at the beginning, but little had turned out as he had expected. Over the years, he had come to deeply resent the hand he had been dealt.

At school, Benny played rugby and cricket; at one stage, he was simultaneously captain of both teams. His was a much-envied position, as his physical attraction, natural charms, and sporting achievements made him almost irresistible to the most attractive girls in and out of school (as well as the not-so-appealing). These same girls were only too happy to travel with him on their tempestuous voyage through puberty to discover the as-yet-unexplored pleasures of sex. At one stage, he even managed a short dalliance with Miss Marion Perkins. The well-endowed school music teacher, the fantasy fuck for most of the boys, who had taken it upon herself to teach him so many things about the art of making love. This expertise endeared him no end to the other febrile women who made up his remarkable tally of conquests. Each trophy was methodically recorded, possibly apocryphally, as a notch on his cricket bat.

It was a little ironic that there seemed to be a corresponding decline in his sporting prowess with each additional notch. Then, one day, everything changed forever. It was as if he had partaken of a Faustian pact, and his part of the bargain had been called in much sooner than expected. After his school days, his sexual activities diminished considerably. He now had more success with his flowers than he would ever again have with women.

Wandering around the conservatory, he occasionally stopped to gaze intently at the inflorescence of the *Brachycorythis macrantha*. A beautiful purple orchid and a creation of nature he cherished and adored. Despite the odds, it had flourished under Benny's care for some reason, even though its usual habitat was a relatively high altitude in the African rainforest. His eyes were drawn to the column, the fused sexual organ found just above the lip of the orchid. He had read somewhere that it contained both the female and male parts. Inside the column is the anther, which carries the pollen and the pistil, which receives the incoming pollen and bears the seeds. The sex life of a flower was now far more fascinating to him than the human variant. This so often came laden with sentiment, emotion, and an abundance of physical activity, which, for Benny, corrupted the simple purity of the act. He had become bitter, incapable, and cynical with age.

The miracle of self-procreation, which had fascinated him since childhood, was something he had hoped to recreate for himself one day. Although Benny was not averse to sexual contact with women – he regularly used them on a contractual basis to allay his natural physical urges. But due to their transient inadequacies compared to the perfect symmetry of an orchid, he found them less physically and socially desirable.

He did, however, make one exception, and that was Dhalia. Dhalia Vingali, the strange girl with the unusual name and even stranger bedroom appetites. He would visit her once, occasionally twice a month if she were available. Benny knew she was in high demand, which made him sad; therefore, he treasured every moment in her company. More tragic than this was that he could not physically endure her insatiable demands more than once a month. Unless he experienced a youthful surge of athleticism, but that simply didn't happen anymore.

He bitterly regretted his inability to perform better than he did. The real irony was he could still clearly remember how sexually proficient he once was - in his youth— another bitter twist of nature's knife. At times of introspective reflection and critical self-appraisal – something he engaged in more frequently these days – he had started to believe that maybe that person was someone else altogether, not him at all. Somehow, he had subconsciously transposed himself into the character of one of his friends at school. This seemed to assuage the harsh reality of his current inadequacies. It was easier to accept his present circumstances if he could readjust the past to match.

Such were Dhalia's sexual desires that he felt completely drained of life afterwards. It was as if a predatory creature sucked the essence of existence from his body. After she had finished with him, he was spent and needed days - sometimes a week to rejuvenate. He would hide away, wandering amongst his orchids while regaining his inner strength. However, no sooner was he fully recovered than he would once again prepare for another encounter. She had become the opiate to which he was hopelessly addicted. This was so perilously close to nature's path to oblivion, and it deeply disturbed the altered state of his sensibilities. He knew so well that satiated irresistible desires were always accompanied by unforeseen dangers, but he couldn't resist. This unquenchable raging fire kept drawing him back. He knew it would probably kill him in the end, but he no longer cared.

When he was with Dhalia, the pain was gone, and he was young again - if only for a few short hours - and he could feel his tormented soul slowly bleeding away. Dhalia was the ultimate ataxia, the conduit through which all hurt and sorrow left his body, but paradoxically, the one through which all enjoyment entered.

Today, however, his mind was not on life's simple pleasures but clearly distracted by the more daunting task ahead. The slow tap-tapping of his walking cane heralded much. A constant reminder of a catastrophic skiing accident in his mid-twenties. The operation to repair his shattered leg had not gone as well as expected. It sounded slightly muffled on the well-worn, mossy brick pathways stretching out like a spider's endless web from the central atrium to the conservatory's far corners. All roads lead to Rome. In this case, with slightly less opulence, it was a prosaic Victorian partner's writing desk in the epicentre of his glass kingdom. Occasionally, he would stop for a moment and revel in the exquisitely fecund perfection of each delicate blossom. Benny was in awe of its ability to remain unblemished, unfettered and unaffected by the pernicious nature of the environment in which it flourished. On the other hand, people were so easily tainted and corrupted by simple association with evil and malicious temptation.

If ever he was called upon to defend the existence of God, then surely this would be his opening gambit. For they served no other purpose than to enrich the aesthetic senses of man and pleasure those who enjoyed them for what they were. How, he would argue, could something so intrinsically beautiful be created by the whimsical intervention of chance, evolution, and serendipity. There had to be a God. He returned to his desk and sipped cold coffee before wandering off again.

This place was so peaceful, he thought. He could happily live here forever. With just the susurration of Mahler symphonies drifting on a gentle breeze, rustling the flowers, immersing his soul, and caressing his senses. This was all the company he ever wanted or would ever really need.

But these things were the antithesis of who he was - the reality of what he had become and the inevitable realisation of what he must now prepare for. He continued to meander around the conservatory, leaning heavily on his cane as he went. Now carrying a small water spray in his other hand, he squirted a fine mist onto a bloom whenever he thought it appropriate. Occasionally, if he trod awkwardly, a shaft of pain would sear up his leg, and he would wince in agony, but he never made a sound.

After a while, he heard the noise of someone arriving and slowly wandered back to his desk. As he reached it, so did Drummond Cleaver.

'I am so sorry for being late,' apologised Drummond. He had obviously been running or walking fast and was slightly out of breath. 'Everybody's off today, so I've been left alone to do everything as usual. I could come back at another time if it were more convenient?'

'No, that won't be necessary,' replied Benny, smiling benignly. So much concealed within a smile. The Judas kiss reveals nothing unless you are expecting something. 'I think we can sort this matter out today.' He gestured to a chair on the opposite side of the desk, and Drummond sat down, relieved. Benny rustled around the piles of papers and files on the desktop, looking for something. He eventually found whatever he was searching for. Gave another genteel smile, sat in his chair, stretched his legs out, and took another sip of the cold coffee. The pain in his leg seemed to fade for a moment or two - a fleeting expression of pleasure crossed his face, but it didn't stay long.

'I'm sorry, would you like coffee or a drink or something?' asked Benny, almost apologetically, suddenly realising he had forgotten his manners.

'No. No, I'm okay, thank you,' Drummond replied.

'Good, good,' said Benny, sounding slightly distant. He paused for a second or two to get his thoughts clear. 'Look...' said Benny, now adopting a more sombre, almost business-like tone to his voice. 'I'll be blunt; I don't want to waste too much of your valuable time.' There was a conspicuous lack of sincerity in his voice. This could have sounded distinctly patronising to a third party, but Drummond didn't seem to notice, or maybe he just chose to ignore it. Benny leaned back in his captain's chair, crossed his arms, and looked at his friend with the apologetic air of a surgeon about to impart grave news.

'As you know...' he paused again, and his mind drifted off for a few seconds as he gazed up at the sunlight that had started to pour through the conservatory roof. Some low-lying clouds that had been hanging around all day had suddenly cleared, probably moved on by an impatient westerly wind. *Artemis may have felt more accommodating today as no one had yet slain her precious deer.* 'As you know, there have been a couple of unexpected developments recently.' He pointed to nowhere in particular but was obviously alluding to Aiden Hawsley. 'And the LP has asked me to tidy up some loose ends, which is why I've asked you here today.' Benny smiled in a restrained, almost restricted manner as if the expression was on ration.

'I understand,' replied Drummond. He didn't really but thought it best to agree, as it would speed things along, and he was a little pressed for time. He could always raise an objection later were it something disagreeable. All would undoubtedly become perfectly clear in the next few minutes anyway.

'You must appreciate that this is not personal,' said Benny. 'We've known each other for what must be…' he looked skywards again and slightly to the left, with an expression of abstraction as he calculated the years… He thought back to 1998 when they had all gone on holiday to a tiny village in Italy. Drummond and Aiden had just finished university and wanted to celebrate. He had resigned a year before, having been offered a lucrative position as a computer programmer. A fourth friend, Harry, had come with them, but they had lost touch over the years. They were only reunited in a manner of speaking when they all attended his funeral in 2013 after he had committed suicide for reasons never clearly explained. That was another story.

'Nearly thirty years,' interjected Drummond, trying to be helpful. 'And I've worked for the party for over twenty-five of those,' he added. Aiden Hawsley had made him the party spokesman on Defence and State Security just after the Janice Watson incident. It was a token gesture, but Aiden thought it prudent to keep him on a short leash and 'in-house', so to speak. Drummond could sometimes be unpredictable, even strangely ambivalent, on the simplest of decisions. The Watson incident was a case in point.

Drummond had acted in this capacity for twelve years while continuing his work as a research chemist. The CSP (the Christian Socialist Party) – was the new name that Aiden had conceived one year before the general election. The name was adopted to help distance his party from the unsavoury elements and issues that had tainted the old BNP for many years. The CSP was elected in 2014. Drummond continued in the same position, but this time as a Minister in the government for another eight years. Hawsley had kept a promise he made one drunken night many years before. He was if nothing else, a man of his word. Drummond had given up his research job when appointed as a Minister but kept in regular contact with the research establishment.

This arrangement had worked out well, in fact, much better than Hawsley had expected. Drummond had been working on various military drugs for the previous government. When he discussed these projects with Hawsley just after his election, he confirmed that he had been instrumental in producing a new opioid product called Panzanoid. The drug could be used as a non-addictive rehabilitation treatment for Class A addicts. It was made freely available and distributed to all drug addicts to counteract the severe addiction problems that had developed over the past ten years. Its general accessibility would, in effect, kill two birds with one stone.

Wreck the illegally imported drugs trade and solve the country's major narcotic addiction problem.

Drummond had also completed work on the Benacane drug. The prototype of which he had passed to Aiden back at the election party in 2001. However, both drugs had secondary, but more importantly, strategically darker uses, which were not widely broadcast. These were the issues that had caused Drummond some concern. For this reason, he had given up the position of Minister the previous year and returned to working in the laboratory. It was less stressful.

Benny smiled at him again, this time a little more disturbingly than before. 'Twenty-eight years is it?' repeated Benny thoughtfully. 'Well, we have all come quite a long way since we first met, haven't we?'

Drummond did not answer, just nodding nonchalantly.

'That's nearly a working lifetime, isn't it?' continued Benny, sounding energetic and enthused.

'Well, a short one, maybe,' replied Drummond cautiously, sounding slightly puzzled.

'But a very productive life?' added Benny with almost jubilant admiration. 'You invented the drugs that saved thousands of lives in the riots and helped change how we deal with the nation's illegal drugs problem. And there's all the work you did on the plutomarium project. All remarkable achievements.' He was still smiling benevolently, which disturbed Drummond a little.

'Yes, but still short for a lifetime?' queried Drummond.

'Well, it's a lifetime for you,' suggested Benny, still smiling disarmingly.

'Is it?' he replied curiously, not fully appreciating what Benny was alluding to.

'I'm sorry,' said Benny, changing his tone, 'but we will have to let you go… into a less demanding position.' His expression changed, and he pursed his lips, looking genuinely wretched at having to say this to one of his oldest friends. His eyes closed to a squint as his bushy eyebrows lowered and arched slightly.

'Oh, I see,' Drummond replied, sounding surprised. 'I wasn't expecting that.' He went quiet for a few seconds while he absorbed what Benny had said, what it meant, and how it would affect him. It's funny how a few unexpected words can suddenly set the windmills of your mind spinning off chaotically in so many different directions, churning up the settled dust of memories.

'It means you will have more time to spend with your family,' suggested Benny half-heartedly, with a distant hint of a smile.

'I'm not married,' replied Drummond scornfully, staggered that Benny appeared to have forgotten a basic detail about a friendship that had lasted nearly thirty years… 'Surely you knew that?'

'Sorry, of course, you're not. I don't know what made me think you were,' replied Benny, apologising profusely. 'Had you never thought about it?' he queried somewhat vacuously – trying pitifully to deflect some of the contempt he had brought upon himself through his blasé indifference, but he wasn't really interested in Drummond's feelings.

'Never got around to it,' replied Drummond reflectively. His voice momentarily tinged with regret and sadness at missed opportunities. 'Working all day at the laboratory and then working most nights for the party, the time seemed to slip away.' He looked much older than his years; he was still only forty-six. Benny had also noticed he had now developed a slightly hunched back. Which, for obvious but somewhat bizarre reasons at once, put him in mind of Richard the Third, a stereotypical attribution, unfortunately, visited on anybody with a similar affliction.

He was a little overweight but nowhere near as heavy as Benny, something else he hadn't noticed before. It was probably brought on by too many years spent leaning over a desk, looking into a microscope and eating white bread sandwiches. He had developed a pasty, sallow complexion, which made him appear like someone who had spent an extended period incarcerated in a dungeon, permanently deprived of sunshine. He thought he was getting a little extra sunlight today - glancing up again through the dome, but that would not make much difference now.

The personal goals - the markers in time which, as a younger man, he had aspired to with so much energy – were no longer achievable. The children he wanted were now a distinctly remote possibility. But that was principally because he didn't have a woman who would commit to that extent. Drummond had been involved with several women over the years, but each relationship never quite developed into anything more significant for one primary reason. He could never make that final commitment to monogamy; he was already married to his work. But now he was alone with his career, and even that seemed to be slipping away.

'But I'm only working part-time now in the laboratory. Surely things aren't that bad,' suggested Drummond?

'Look,' said Benny, 'when you were working as the minister, you were invaluable, but since you left, we felt you were no longer part of our little triumvirate. Do you understand?'

'It was getting too heavy for me,' Drummond replied defensively. 'I told Aiden that. Those drugs I helped create had a disturbing effect on thousands of people every day and still are, as far as I am aware. I couldn't handle that pressure any longer.' He appeared emotionally exhausted. The drugs were, in fact, being used to control millions of people, but Drummond didn't know that.

'But,' replied Benny animatedly with almost religious fervour. 'Those treatments' – he consciously avoided using the 'drug' word, thinking his euphemism sounded more altruistic – 'are keeping the Glundes (Generic Low intelligence, Unemployable, Unregistered, Non-Christian, Drug-addicted, or Ethnic) under control. Those people are the most serious threat to our new society. 'Your "treatments,"' Drummond registered a curious expression on Benny's use of the word again, 'help to maintain the security of our country and protect the true patriots.' There was an almost jingoistic dimension in his tone. From what he could remember from school social history lessons, the Samuel Johnson quote - *The last refuge of all scoundrels and despots is patriotism* – sprang to mind.

Benny slowly ground the sole of his shoe into the ground as if squashing a spider, but his expression remained calm. 'Aiden understood your concerns, and that's why he transferred you when you asked him to, but that's what you were good at, really good at. Any old chemist can work as a lab assistant. You're much better than that.'

'Oh,' Drummond replied, a little stunned at Benny's unexpected praise and now beginning to feel slightly better about what he had just been told. 'So, what have you got planned for me now?' There was a sense of joyous anticipation in his voice.

'Well, we thought of early retirement. How does that sound?'

'But I'm only forty-six. A bit early for early retirement, isn't it?' replied Drummond, sounding bewildered and not really appreciating the dry witticism of his tautology.

'I would be perfectly happy to continue working in the lab,' he smiled, almost in disbelief at what Benny had suggested.

'I don't know,' said Benny. 'Many people would love to retire early and have fun before they die.'

'I'm not one of them,' Drummond replied firmly. He had no intention of dying soon if he could help it. 'I love my job.'

'Well, actually, you are,' corrected Benny.

'Am I?' Drummond replied, still bemused but now perplexed by Benny's oddly presumptive assertion.

However, 'there is something you have, something we need and something that is particularly important and extremely valuable to us,' said Benny. 'In fact, it is priceless.'

'What?' he replied curiously, still feeling a little concerned but slightly relieved to think he still had something of value which they needed. Maybe there was some light at the end of this dark tunnel he had just entered, after all. Had he been reprieved at the last minute? Was there just one single strand of hope he could hang on to? Possibly. 'Whatever it is, you're welcome to it. What's mine is yours. That's what friends are for,' stated Drummond altruistically. Precisely, thought Benny, quietly amused by the irony of the declaration.

'A generous sentiment and beautifully expressed, if I may say, and I applaud you for that.' said Benny.

Drummond smiled at the compliment and wondered whether this was all a subtle renegotiation strategy for his job. But that didn't make any sense. He knew far too much about too many things. But more than that, he knew where all the skeletons were - all the secrets. Well, one of them, anyway. Maybe this was just a big joke. Any moment, Benny would start laughing uncontrollably and produce a bottle of champagne from under his desk. Dancing girls would appear, and Aiden would pop his head around the corner with a funny hat on, letting off party poppers, and they would all laugh, joke, and get drunk as they used to in the old days...

The flash of light and the first muted pop caught him entirely by surprise. It sounded like a hand slapping a large book. No champagne bottles were popping open, and no corks were flying skywards, as far as he could see. And there were no streams of string confetti - and definitely no dancing girls.

He did, however, experience a sudden unfamiliar pain in his chest, a crushing sensation he had never felt before. The abnormal pressure propelled him back into his seat, and for a moment, he thought he'd had a heart attack, but the pressure eased almost at once, and he bounced forward slightly. Looking down, he could see a damp stain on his shirt, but he wasn't sure what it was.

Everything now seemed to move as if it were a slow-motion movie, and as his head slowly came back up to look at Benny, he saw another flash and heard a second leaden clap. This, too, propelled him back into his chair. Once again, he instinctively looked down to see that a second blot had appeared on his shirt. He glanced up at Benny through the top of his eyes as if seeking an explanation. But none was forthcoming. Then he saw

Benny's gun for the first time; it was aimed directly at him. He thought it must have been hidden under some papers on the desk; otherwise, he would have seen it when he first sat down.

Drummond tried to say something but could not get the words out of his mouth. He realised this was because his throat kept gurgling when he attempted to speak. Even breathing was now becoming a problem. It felt like he was drowning, but there was no water. He looked down again and saw the damp blots were now a darker crimson and spreading as the blood pumped faster from his wounds. His body was desperately trying to coagulate the blood and stem the breach in the wall - but it was failing miserably, unable to perform the miracle that could save his life. When he looked up again, his brain, now dazed with confusion, tried to make sense of what was happening. He could see the eyes of his old friend were tinged with sorrow. He could also see a single teardrop that had fallen from the corner of Benny's left eye - now slowly edging a path down his cheek.

This did not make any sense. Why was his old friend Benny crying, he thought? Never before had he seen him weep. He spat out the liquid that had gathered in his mouth and tried to speak again, but his mouth just filled up with more blood. He was very muddled. They were talking about retirement, and now, suddenly, he appeared to be dying. He had no idea what this moment would feel like. Obviously, he had thought about death many times. Most people do, and he had also considered the many ways it might happen. The older you get, the more time you spend morbidly dwelling on how the end will come. Will it be quick, or will it be slow and painful? Would it be a surprise? Could you take control? All these thoughts visit you more frequently the closer you are. He had never considered what this moment would feel like, but he knew instinctively this was it. He looked down, but his eyes were beginning to close.

The second bullet had entered neatly between two front ribs. It had torn away a large section of his descending aorta, severing it almost entirely before exiting neatly between two ribs. Just nicking one before passing straight through the back of the chair and ending its journey in a water butt just behind him. The butt started to spurt a small jet of water, but Drummond did not know this, and he never would, for he was fast losing consciousness.

He would be dead very soon - he knew there was no coming back. In his last few seconds on earth, he managed to summon enough strength to lift his head for one final glance at his old and trusted friend and flashed him a smile of stunned incomprehension. Then he slumped back in the chair and died, his eyes gazing awkwardly towards an indeterminate point in the heavens. His body would never be found, and the orchids would be even more colourful the following year due to the addition of a highly enriched fertiliser with an organic nutrient.

Chapter 5

It was Christmas Eve 2026, and all was well, or so Lord Protector Aiden Hawsley would have you believe. The VRS Christmas holiday chip had always been a popular product this time of year. It was still sold extensively throughout the provinces. Not surprisingly, there was also a bustling black market for interface implant surgery in the Ghettazone. Some well-known surgeons, not wishing to miss a very lucrative market, had opened clandestine operating theatres with the full blessing of the government.

Although the VRS Mk 1 unit had been available for over eleven years, the Cyberon Corporation (CyCo) had never fully rectified the odd DNA incompatibility problem. CyCo had always maintained it was 99.9% safe. The Implant Standards Authority's marketing campaign always insisted that they could not claim a 100 per cent safety record as nothing was perfect, except their integrity…

The most worrying aspect of the Mk 1 version was the "unstructured customisation issue." A delightful euphemism for a random software design fault. Occasionally, resulting in a matter-mass congestion issue. The unfortunate user would suffer a sudden, unforeseen transmogrification from organic status to that of a small blob of non-organic pinky-grey marshmallow-type gunge the size of a golf ball. This would evaporate in around thirty seconds and leave virtually no evidence of its earlier existence, apart from a small stain that could be quickly removed with household bleach.

Without anything tangible for the police authorities to analyse, there was never any real possibility of contesting a Transmog glitch issue. Product negligence actions brought to court by overly ambitious compensation lawyers were invariably dismissed through lack of evidence. The corporation's legal department simply requested physical proof of the plaintiff's former existence. And as there wasn't any, that would end the matter.

From a strict marketing point of view, it was the perfect product. The VRS2 prototypes were now available for beta testing, and with the unique Family and Friends interface, you could interact virtually with any number of registered members by choice. This would effectively render the tedious obligations of conventional socialisation etiquette redundant.

CyCo received around 150 complaints yearly but never any irrefutable verification. Oddly, there was never any trace of a citizen's registration record after a malfunction. It was almost as if, in the unlikely event of a 'chip malfunction', the Cyberon database, with disturbing synchronicity, simultaneously destroyed all traces of the user's previous computer data existence.

It was no coincidence that CyCo also designed the Artemis and Balingo national database computers that held the records for every registered citizen in the gated provinces. This included information on your medical history, province movement, global travel, product purchases, entertainment preferences, communication data, employment, religious inclination, food and drink choices, ancestry information and probably a lot more,

These computers could not only tell you how much you urinated last Thursday but also what you were probably thinking at the time. There had been many rumours and conspiracy theories about authorised malfunctions of VRS chips by the Lord Protector's office but, not surprisingly, little, if any, compelling evidence.

Conspiracies were, by their very definition and woeful lack of credible evidence, nothing more than vague innuendo, hypotheses, and supposition. Simply unsubstantiated ramblings of hostile province residents. Coincidentally, some of these same "residents" were invariably diagnosed with some rare form of paranoid psychotic behavioural disorder and treated accordingly. Which, in most cases, meant immediate expulsion from the province. If you wanted to stay as a resident in any province, the best advice was to keep your head down and your mouth shut.

If you thought you were on the Hawsley administration blacklist and the SDSD (Social Disorder State Directorate) had their eye on you. You would have to be profoundly stupid to stick a genuine VRS chip in your head. Being stupid was another perfect reason for the SDSD to expel you from a Province.

Hawsley knew the VRS chips reduced seasonal unrest in the Ghettazone at Christmas. This meant the civil guard had fewer Glunde incidents (a political euphemism for civil disturbance) to deal with. But as genuine chips had a direct data feed to CyCo headquarters, the opposite was also possible. For this reason, illegal chips, which had the data feed facility blocked, were also freely available on the black market at considerably less than the official SCOMTEL retail price.

The random nature of the initial data selection made it almost impossible for any two Virtual Reality Trips to be identical. The basic concept was similar to interactive computer games from the early years of the twenty-first century but without the TV screens, consoles, control panels and headsets. You were actually there, part of this virtual life experience. If you were shot, you felt pain, real pain. If you went skydiving, skiing, hang gliding, had sex, or drove a Ferrari, your body felt exhilarated. If you went exploring in the Amazonian forest, you would be able to smell the flowers, and you could be bitten by the mosquitoes (though, of course, you would not contract malaria). If you walked on the moon, you would experience weightlessness. If you played an instrument, or even if you didn't, you could be in any group in the world, past or present, and experience the sensation of fame, adulation, and many other benefits despite having no discernible talent.

But then, talent was never an essential prerequisite to be in a group - not in the 1960s. Blind enthusiasm was all you needed. The options were endless. But as a precautionary measure, a provision had been programmed into every chip to prevent the same person from activating the same version of a chip beyond the five-run limit. This was to avoid addiction. However, as with everything related to software, there were rumours that software geeks could reprogram the VRS Mk 1 chip to facilitate unlimited reruns. Addiction and permanent suspension in your own computer-generated illusion had now become a surreal possibility.

Chapter 6

In the still of the night, a soft velvet blanket of pure white snow had been silently draped over Madison County. Undercover of darkness, it had obliterated all distinguishing landmarks and, a little inconveniently for me, it had also blurred the critical delineation between highway and sidewalk. Signs that would have significantly assisted passing strangers, presumably including me, were completely obscured. As I had no conscious recollection of visiting this place before, I couldn't rely on my memory for guidance. I drove on for another hour until I reached a large road sign with snow precariously balanced on top of it. The sign said I was on the outskirts of a small municipality called Buckridge, with 1,766 residents. The last digit had been an eight crudely amended to a six.

I wondered who might be responsible for keeping a tally of residents and what had happened to the two who were no longer included. Maybe they had left town or died. But then surely there must have been a birth or two unless all the women were past childbearing age. Statistically, that would be a little unusual. Whatever the circumstances, it seemed odd that there had been any change to the number at all…

Underneath the main sign, hanging from two chains, was a smaller sign pointing right at the next junction towards the village of Ellington, where I was headed.

The road narrowed slightly, but I knew my destination could not be too far. I could see the outline of a triangular sign some 100 metres off to the right-hand side of the road. As I eased my foot off the accelerator, the car slowed, and I could just make out the name 'Whit's End' on the sign as it came into focus. I had just turned into the sweeping driveway when, up ahead, a large white owl suddenly appeared from nowhere, flying exceptionally low with ponderous indifference. It almost defied gravity as it slowly drifted from right to left across the driveway, throwing off a diaphanous cloud of snow dust in its wake. As it passed in front of the windscreen, its head slowly turned, and two large brown eyes blinked once very slowly before focusing directly on mine. It continued gazing at me with a mocking expression of indifferent concern as if it had recognised me. Its head continued to swivel, endeavouring to maintain visual contact while it moved inexorably onwards. It was as if it knew something, some dark secret it wanted to impart but could not. Something I didn't know but should.

Startled and fearful of a collision with the owl, I instinctively stamped on the footbrake, but to no avail. The car continued on its journey, unable to gain purchase on the snow-covered gravel. Eventually, the motor car slid gracelessly to a halt. With an air of detached indifference, the owl turned away, disappearing into the early morning mist. I am sure it was smirking as it left the scene.

In that split second, my brain involuntarily reconsidered the wisdom of my decision and began to deliberate on whether this could be an omen that I should take notice of. Nevertheless, after a few more moments spent carefully re-evaluating all the available information, I dismissed that thought as an overreaction to a perfectly reasonable situation. Cautiously, I resumed my journey, pushing any lingering concerns to the back of my mind.

I slowly edged the car past two tall brick pillars on either side of the drive. On top of each pillar was a large, illuminated dome light, but they served no purpose now as dawn broke and the sunlight splattered through the trees from the east. I continued towards the house - I could just make out the external lights in the distance.

The dazzling reflections of the rising sun bouncing off the snow blinded me for a few seconds, so I eased my foot off the accelerator. , I had read, somewhere in the pre-run notes, that as I had selected the 'Christmas Special reality upgrade' option, there was a possibility that the lake in front of the house might be frozen. Under the thick snow covering, it would be almost indistinguishable from the drive. Although the ice might be very thick, it would probably not be thick enough to support the weight of a car.

There were no tyre tracks to guide me, so I pressed the button to lower the driver's window a few inches to listen out for any change to the tyres' noise on the crunchy frozen gravel. The chill of the early morning air surprised me a little. I was unaccustomed to this characteristic's stark reality. It was probably an upgrade they had forgotten to mention when I purchased the VRS trip.

The house seemed to rise out of the early morning haze as the winter sun began to warm the east elevations of the roof, creating a swirling, mystical scene like some ghostly apparition. It reminded me of an old musical called *Brigadoon,* which, coincidently, I had recently watched on Holavision. It lent itself perfectly to my miniaturised, three-dimensional amphitheatre entertainment facility at home. However, I did wonder whether the user's memory was being used as a source of fresh data from which VRS chip designers could extract information for inclusion in newer VRS trips. It would give every experience a unique twist of originality but with a dimension of reassuring familiarity.

The house – a mansion really – was one of those stunning colonial clapperboard properties painted duck-egg blue with the windows and doors picked out in white. It sat in the middle of hundreds of acres of countryside that probably exploded into a million shades of orange, magenta, rust, and ochre every autumn. An enchanted palace waiting to cast its spell.

As I pulled up in front of the stone steps and exited the car, one of the two tall front doors slowly opened. Out stepped two people who, according to the notes, were Jack and Marilyn, my hosts for the duration.

'Hi Macki, how yer doing? Did you have a good drive down,' asked Jack jovially?

'Yes, I did, thank you. No problems.' I replied politely. However, I was a little unnerved and slightly surprised at being addressed by my nickname, which had only ever been used by a few close friends and Catherine. This overly convivial informality gave me slight cause for concern. Somehow, it had clandestinely invaded my natural conservative reserve. I wondered how much more they might know about me.

'Don't you just *luvvvv* Christmas?' said Jack. He had grossly distorted the word love for some inexplicable reason – possibly just for emphasis, but it didn't work. It sounded childish, immature, and typically gauche Americanese. 'I just *luvvvv* being all snuggled up with my Marilyn at this time of year,' continued Jack, with a cringingly personal over-familiarity. He then gave me a huge smile that was even more disturbing. Marilyn jabbed Jack playfully in the ribs. She was obviously also slightly embarrassed by Jack's overtly congenial ramblings. It was reassuring and comforting to know that she empathised with my embarrassment.

'Yes, I do, thank you,' I replied sheepishly.

Jack walked down the steps to the car, grabbed my right hand with both his hands and shook it vigorously. His hands were huge and strangely warm, with many tiny scars, probably from cutting down trees and working the land or whatever it was that people like Jack did to pass the time.

Somehow, he didn't seem the golfing type; that would be too sedentary for him. Blasting away with a big hunting rifle, killing bears and other large animals, was far more likely. Jack wore the stereotypical gingham lumberjack shirt with the obligatory braces and light blue, well-worn jeans. This was a sad reflection on VRS software designers, who apparently did not get out much. Or, possibly even more sadly, they wore similar hillbilly-type clothing, which they had decided to enshrine for eternity in a software reality program.

'It's really great to meet you, Macki,' said Jack. 'We're so glad you've come to stay. Let me get your bag.' He made a grab for the case that I had just taken out of the car.

'You don't have to do that. I can...' But my protestations were ignored as Jack swept the bag away from me and started back up the steps to the veranda. I followed behind.

'You are just gonna *luvvv* it down here, Macki,' said Jack enthusiastically. Am I? I thought to myself.

Marilyn was even more attractive up close. She was well-preserved in her mid-fifties with dark olive skin, probably Native American or Mexican extraction. Oddly, she was wearing a low-cut green silk evening dress, not unlike the ball gown a girl might wear on graduation day or as an extra in a remake of *Gone with the Wind.* It worked well with her skin colour but seemed a little out of place at breakfast. Maybe the software writer was having a sartorially bad taste day as he finished the coding. Perhaps he was having a laugh to prove he had a sense of humour after his hillbilly phase.

If Loretta had inherited her mother's genes, she would be stunningly beautiful, but that was clearly academic in the circumstances. I already knew what she would look like.

'Would you like something to eat, Macki?' asked Jack. 'Loretta is just doing her hair. She'll be down in two waggles of a....' He didn't finish the sentence, leaving me to wonder what exactly he would waggle.

Why did he insist on calling me Macki? It sounded a bit mid-twentieth century and was already beginning to irritate me with the over-accentuated Southern twang.

Catherine used to call me Mack. That was okay, but I took exception to anybody else, apart from a couple of close friends, using the edited version. It was the last remnant of something very personal, something I desperately wanted to hang on to. I resented it being sequestrated by people who didn't exist.

The CyCo agency had all my details, and there had never been a problem with my name being truncated this way before, so I presumed it was just some minor technical glitch. But what the hell? They had me as a guest for the Christmas holiday, and I would be having the pleasure of their company. It was an all-inclusive package, and I was guaranteed an *absolutely wonderful experience.'* That's what the brochure said, so I could afford to be charitable on the irritating matter of my name for a few days. I could have adjusted the situation if I wanted to, but that would have meant suspending the VRS run, which I didn't want to do. I was beginning to enjoy it.

Anyway, if everything went too perfectly, it could all become rather dull and predictable, which was not what this was all about.

'I have just made some hot spicy wine,' declared Marilyn, 'and we are having breakfast out back, so when you're ready, just come on down.'

'Thank you,' I said, following Jack up the stairs to the first floor. Mulled wine for breakfast must be an Arkansas thing, I suppose. Maybe they were breakfast boozers, even full-time drunks, for all I knew. All it took was one bibulous software designer, perhaps the same one who had sartorial issues (maybe that's why he drank), having an off day. Then he dreamt up a new algorithm, and... No, perhaps that's going too far. They were probably just being hospitable, and I was being disingenuous. Anyway, I hadn't tried the mulled wine yet. Maybe it would be enjoyable for breakfast. Try anything once; wasn't that the corny mantra?

'There you are, son, make yourself at home.' said Jack, directing me to one of the five bedrooms off the landing. It was a huge room with a magnificent view looking out across the multi-coloured countryside of Madison County.

'The bathroom is to the right. You come down when you're ready.' Jack wandered off down the stairs, taking the time to realign one of the pictures on the wall as he went. After unpacking and taking a quick shower, I went back downstairs. The breakfast room was enormous, the same size as my parents' terraced house in Bournemouth – nearly twice the size, in fact. No, maybe not that big, but it was big.

Sometimes, it was hard to differentiate between reality and virtuality. Nothing was ever quite what it seemed, but I suppose you can say that about most things in life, especially people. Beyond what you could see, there was always more, much more. The secrets and lies, the thoughts unspoken, the truths that would never be heard. And the question that still haunted me – what was real and what was an illusion, and did any of us really know the difference? Did any of us really know where exactly we were? More importantly, I suppose, did anyone really care?

The glass patio doors ran the entire length of the room's east side, creating a stunning panorama across the valley. It was completely different from the view from my bedroom. The early morning sun bounced off the dancing waters of a fast-flowing river as it snaked down a distant mountain and across the landscape like flaming quicksilver pouring from the sky. The snow-covered hills rose majestically to kiss the azure sky on the other side of the valley. The brilliance burnt my eyes; it was truly breathtaking. A beautiful Navajo rug in the middle of the room depicted a herd of buffalo chased by hundreds of what appeared to be starving indigenous inhabitants. Maybe it was their breakfast time as well.

'So, Macki, has it been a good year for you?' enquired Jack ineffectually.

This was the part I found irritating. All the cheery bonhomie and overt Middle America Baptist charm seemed technically superfluous. I preferred the blunt, dysfunctional, arrogant, and stoical insouciance of the trailer trash you can find in any run-down backwater shit hole in darkest America. At least they were genuine with their sentiment, even if they'd cut your throat for a few dollars. Worn-out whores - cheaper by the dozen. Horseless cowboys looking for a prairie. Good drunks with lousy booze – bad gamblers with good money. Mortgage defaulters with families gone – the ingenuity of tax evaders. Friendly chemical sales executives – men selling cut-price escapism in a box. Gay guys on Harley's looking for fresh   cock. Cold-blooded Capote killers chewing tobacco driving old Ford trucks. The dream makers of yesterday and the cheap liberal politics of tomorrow. This, all of this, was the United States of America.

Was I becoming too cynical? No, I don't think so. This was an allegorical anachronism. That was the real U.S. of A, but were they really united any longer, I wondered? They too, must have been affected by the political change sweeping Europe and Asia.

'Brilliant, sir,' I eventually answered, thinking it best to adopt a slightly obsequious manner - this was the American way. 'The book is really coming on well. I hope to finish it by February, and I've recently been promoted and moved to the *Boston Gazette*. I was hoping that Loretta might help me finish the book.'

Previously, I was asked to complete a small life summary on the VRS database application. To be used exclusively for this trip. It was a work of fiction. But it added substance and background colour to the experience. So I ticked the box on the form saying that I was a novelist as I thought, maybe a little sadly, that this might make me sound more interesting. I tended to opt for a more conventional format these days as the more elaborate stories I had prepared in the past had created some bizarre results. Lies beget confusion, and confusion begets distrust.

'You don't have to call me sir, here, son. Jack is just fine, and I'm glad my daughter is going to help you finish your book.' Jack paused to ensure he had my attention, and his voice dropped a few semitones. 'We always hoped she would find something worthwhile to do with her life. We thought it would never be real and she would never truly have a life unless she created something worthwhile and tangible with it. We all have to take control of our destiny, don't we?' added Jack in a paternalistic tone.

Christ, I thought, that was a frighteningly philosophical statement to take on board just before breakfast - but in a way, he was right. This whole thing was just an illusion, anyway. I wondered why Jack had referred to Loretta as 'my daughter' and not by her name. The odd terminology seemed to add unnatural distance and detachment.

'Oh, I'm sure she will,' I replied.

'Macki, would you like pancakes and maple syrup? We love pancakes in the morning. They are so American, don't you think? So, what we really are, aren't they?' Marilyn sounded tritely loquacious and a little bemused. She was also probably a little confused by the existentialistic drift of the conversation.

Jack looked at her as if to say, *'Not so much talking, dear. You are going on a bit.'* In the secret language that long-married couples use where, nothing is spoken, and polite requests are tersely summarised into a tiny hand gesture or an oblique nose twitch. She did not take offence and graciously smiled back at Jack before turning back to the range cooker and continuing with the breakfast.

'Call me Mack, please.' *Oh shit, why did I say that? I meant to say Parish, but it was done. There was no going back; I would have to roll with it for the duration.* 'I'll have two, thank you, Marilyn.'

'Mack, it is,' said Marilyn, without hinting at trespass on her sensibilities. 'Two all-American pancakes coming right up with lots of....' She stopped and looked at Jack, who blew her a kiss. It was all very touching but a little odd.

'I like Mack,' said Jack, pouring another coffee, 'it sounds a little nineteen fifties, you know Bogart, Edward G Robinson, real men. Gangsters with style, not like those pretty boy actors you see today. I'm sure half of them are fags or paedos.' He spat the words out like some poisonous venom he had just sucked out of a snakebite victim who had been bitten on the arse. Presumably, it was someone Jack was already well acquainted with.

'You're not a gangster, are you, Mack,' asked Marilyn with mocking concern? Jack pretended to have a machine gun - scrunched up his face, and proceeded to shoot silently at the ceiling for some reason. Marilyn looked at Jack with dazed astonishment but said nothing. He was happy in his little world, and she was pleased that he was happy.

'No, no, I'm a writer,' I replied. 'I thought I mentioned that earlier?' I could just as easily have been a gangster for all it mattered. I could have been a heart surgeon, even a movie star, but I had chosen a writer for my sins, so I would have to stick to it. Making character trait changes during a virtuality experience could have unusual, even undesirable, effects on the eventual outcome.

'So, you did, Mack, so you did,' mumbled Marilyn, her voice seeming to fade away towards the end. She appeared a little confused, possibly absent-minded. Maybe she had started on the mulled wine a lot earlier. Perhaps they both had.

'Is that a gun, or are you just pleased to see Loretta?' asked Jack somewhat incongruously, in the worst Mae West accent I had ever heard. Jack laughed at his witticism. I didn't. I felt embarrassed and uncomfortable, but Jack didn't notice; Marilyn did. I wondered whether Jack had early-onset Alzheimer's or maybe Asperger's syndrome. He appeared to lack any ability to gauge embarrassment or awkwardness.

'Jack! Stop being naughty,' cracked Marilyn, wrinkling her nose and looking disapprovingly at him, visually admonishing him for his inappropriate quip. 'You hardly know Mack. He could easily be offended by your Southern crudities.'

I wasn't, but I was confused for a moment as I thought they were something you nibbled with a glass of wine at parties, but maybe I had that wrong. After deliberating for a nanosecond over whether I should make a witty reply that might diffuse the slightly strained atmosphere, I decided to say nothing.   The room fell silent for a few moments. I took another sip of my coffee.

'He was born in Alabama, would you believe,' muttered Marilyn wistfully with a hint of disparagement. She placed a condescending kiss on Jack's head while flashing me a pained expression - as if to say, *I apologise for my husband. It's not his fault. His parents didn't give him enough meat to eat as a child. Things were tough down South.* I found that endearing, and it helped confirm my earlier thoughts on the existence of a secret language only they understood.

'Beam me up, Scotty,' I mumbled under my breath. That is my favourite misquoted line from a nineteen-sixties television sci-fi series. The line was apocryphal; it was never delivered by any Star Trek character. Of such things, legends are made. I would mutter the line to myself, a sort of internal interjection to fill any embarrassing pregnant pause that unexpectedly occurred during a conversation.

'I'm sure Mack knows I'm just having a bit of fun,' parried Jack timidly. The corners of his mouth now turned down like the sad expression of a circus clown who had suffered a severe verbal battering at the hands of his dominant partner.

'No, it's okay, Marilyn,' I replied. 'It's terribly funny, really,' (but I didn't laugh). 'It is a gun, actually.' I removed the snub-nose Smith and Wesson 45 from my shoulder holster and dropped it clumsily on the table. 'Sorry, I always carry it when I'm driving. I should have left it in my bedroom. You can't be too careful; it can be dangerous outside a province's boundary walls these days.'

Marilyn initially looked at me with surprise and general agreement, but then she was programmed to do that. She knew nothing of what the world outside virtuality was really like.

'Absolutely, son, absolutely,' said Jack, who didn't know what I was talking about either. Loretta came down the staircase, stopped a few steps from the bottom and looked directly at me. Pouting her lips in Marilyn Monroe style while placing her left hand on her hip, she dropped her right hip a fraction for the quintessential vamp pose. I was stunned by the visualisation that stood before me. I could not believe how much she looked like Catherine. The linear entrapment characteristic of the software was beyond my wildest expectations. This was Catherine, not just a hologram, someone organic, someone I could touch, feel, and hold again. This whole thing suddenly became too surreal, and my head began to spin.

'Hello, Mack,' she said quietly. 'I've been dying to meet you.' I thought it was all a bit neo-Hollywood, and then everything stopped…

PROGRAM ALERT....... PROGRAM ALERT...... IMPLANT MALFUNCTION... .... TEMPORARY SYSTEM FAILURE...... RESET IN PROGRESS................................

PROGRAM ALERT...... PROGRAM ALERT...... IMPLANT MALFUNCTION... TEMPORARY SYSTEM FAILURE......... RESET IN PROGRESS.................

SYSTEM RECONFIGURED...... RECOMMENCING PROGRAM...

Rewrite....................................

The VRS trip had reconfigured itself. This happened occasionally. It was very peculiar to see your life appear to stop for a few seconds. Then enter a recalibration phase and restart a little earlier - while you are watching it replay. The VRS chip run had restarted, but at moments like this, you question where the actuality stopped and the virtuality began. It also cast doubt on whether reality was reality at all or part of a much larger deception.

At times like this, the question that went through my mind was, could I be experiencing a trip malfunction within a localised trip, within a much larger universal trip? Or, to put it another way, was the whole of our existence on planet earth just one miniscule experimental illusion. Something being played out by some omnipresent heavenly deity getting pissed and having a lark in his laboratory somewhere in the astral cosmos?

'No, it's okay, Marilyn. It's very funny,' I replied. Still no laughter. 'It is a gun, actually.' I removed a PPK automatic from a shoulder holster James Bond style, pulled the ammunition clip, put it into my pocket, and then handed it to Jack. I smiled at Jack as if to say, *'We don't want any accidents, do we?'* Jack understood the unspoken gesture as though it were nothing to worry about. It was technically impossible for him to harm anybody anyway. 'I always carry it when I'm driving. You can't be too careful these days. It can be perilous in the Ghettazone.'

'You're not wrong there, son. It is a nice gun. I bet you could take out a few of those lowlife Glunde varmints with that. Same problem as we used to have with them, there nigger boys.'

'Oh, I have, sir, plenty of 'em.' I hadn't, but it was only a game, so it didn't matter much if I exaggerated a little. However, I was a little taken aback at his comment about the Glundes; as far as I knew, they only existed in reality and not in this virtuality program. Maybe the software writer had included the reference as another private joke. It was a little confusing.

'Good for you, son, good for you,' replied Jack approvingly. 'And it's Jack, remember?' He glanced at me paternally. *'Only those nigger boys call me sir'* ran through my mind for some reason.

'Sorry… eh, Jack,' I replied apologetically, wondering what part Jack would have played if the Klan had still been operational. It's funny how your mind goes off at odd tangents.

'That's better,' replied Jack, smiling. 'Hey, that must be 'Retta coming now,' said Jack, turning to look at the staircase. Loretta appeared at the bottom, and I stood up as she smiled at me. It was Catherine, as I will always remember her. This was worth all the pain and anguish I would suffer later, all the heartache, remorse, and regret I would experience when it was over, and all for one brief moment in time.

She was as stunningly beautiful as the first time I saw her outside Downing Street. Today, she wore tight black jeans, high heels and a white gipsy blouse tied at the waist. I remember we went to a party once when she was dressed exactly the same way. That detail must have been mined from deep down inside my memory bank. Flowing black hair cascaded down her back; her eyes were still the colour of bourbon by candlelight, burning deep into my soul. This was going to be a wonderful Christmas.

'Please sit down, Mack,' she whispered huskily. She sat down opposite. 'Finish your breakfast, then we can walk and talk awhile.' Her voice reminded me a little of Lauren Bacall's in *The Big Sleep*, another old film I had seen recently. She smiled all the time and never took her eyes off me.

'Loretta, honey, do you want some pancakes,' asked Marilyn? Loretta looked away for a second.

'I sure do, mama.' She turned back to look at me and picked up the enormous steaming coffee pot.

'Would you like some more?' she asked, leaning across the table, smiling evocatively, and offering to refill my cup.

'Thank you,' I replied, politely looking more closely into her eyes. 'Be careful you don't spill it,' I mumbled inexplicably. Sometimes, people say the banalest things, and this was one of those times, but I don't think she noticed. Loretta's eyes emitted a flash of bewilderment - she appeared confused by my concern for her safety. She smiled disarmingly, acknowledging my benevolent interest in her welfare, but still seemed slightly confused. It wasn't possible to harm anybody on a virtuality trip - it was just an enormous illusion - but I wondered whether she didn't realise that....

I could not take my eyes off her; it was as if some strange magnetic force was drawing me deeper into her eyes. I had always been fascinated by the vertiginous depth of digital clarity and emotional quality encapsulated within the VRS Mk I chip. I still found it hard to believe that Loretta, Jack, and Marylyn didn't exist except in my brain. This virtuality illusion was all due to the wizardry of a tiny piece of plastic, impregnated with thousands of layers of intricate circuitry - which I stuck in my head.

Sometimes, it felt like I was an integral part of a holographic experience instead of standing outside looking in like an Edward Hopper voyeur. The linear entrapment scanner had trawled the depths of my brain to conjure up this fusion of all my memories. The result was unnervingly precise and achingly beseeching.

'We have some friends coming over tonight for a small party...' interjected Marilyn. She had her back to me, and the conversation was a little unclear, muffled by the splattering crackle of hot oil as she cooked the eggs, bacon, and hash browns. This, fortuitously, broke my concentration and the slight lull in the conversation. Jack was now reading the newspaper while slurping the dregs from his gigantic cup of coffee.

'The governor and his wife will be coming, and a few of Jack's hunting buddies,' Marilyn added as an afterthought, 'will you be able to stay and meet them?' She turned to gauge my reaction. 'They're all dying to meet you,' she added. A *curious phrase* in the circumstances.

'Of course I can, Marilyn. It will be my pleasure,' I replied, slipping inexplicably into a Texas drawl, which even surprised me.

It probably wouldn't, but it would be discourteous to decline, and they were probably Loretta's friends, after all.

There, I'd done it again, thought this was real and that I might offend somebody, but that was just not possible. Still, I might as well go along with it now; I had nothing to lose.

'They can sometimes be boring and dreary, just talking about hunting, shooting, fishing, politics, religion and the clan. But if you could just say hello, that would be wonderful,' said Marilyn. It didn't sound like it would be boring, and I could see that she really wanted me to meet them. So I agreed to her request and ate the half dozen pancakes she had generously covered with maple syrup and fresh cream.

'Then you two can go off into town or for a walk if you want to and enjoy yourselves,' added Marilyn. Then she placed the most enormous fried breakfast I had ever seen in front of Jack. There must have been four, possibly five eggs all sunny side up, six slices of bacon, four tomatoes, a stack of hash browns and two whole tins of baked beans.

'That looks like an excellent start,' remarked Jack wryly, eagerly smiling in anticipation of what he was about to devour. Desperate Dan, the legendary comic book character, sprang to mind. He had the same expression just before he ate one of his infamous cow pies. Jack covered the whole ensemble with lashings of brown sauce and started consuming the feast.

'That's no problem at all,' I replied, looking at Loretta, who had just given me a pleading glance.

'Are you sure that's okay, Mack?' she whispered, sounding slightly concerned but smiling in the way that Catherine smiled, which she knew I couldn't resist.

'That's fine,' I said. 'I'm happy to do whatever you want. I have two weeks before I have to return, so it's no problem.'

My cell phone rang, and the VRS trip automatically suspended itself.

'Parish?' inquired Commander Morgan. I at once recognised his voice.

'I'm on holiday for a few days, sir.' I replied a little abruptly. 'It is Christmas, you know.' They were my first words before any meaningful conversation had started. I instinctively adopted a defensive position whenever receiving unsolicited phone calls. Especially from the station while on holiday. 'Whatever it is, can't you give it to somebody else? I'm in the middle of something vitally important.... at my house,' I added as an afterthought. Of course, I was lying, but Morgan never rang for social reasons – I knew that much – and I didn't want him to know I was on a trip. I could, of course, have just turned the mobile off, but I hadn't. It was a force of habit.

It always felt a little strange walking around a suspended reality run with everybody else frozen in time. So I poked Jack in the eye for fun, but it had no effect. He was just a hologram held in suspension while I communicated with the station in real-time. He wouldn't return to a nonorganic status until I restarted the VRS run.

With VRS technology, Christmas had become a wonderfully stress-free occasion. Friends and families were always happy, and everybody remained amiable for ten long days. If someone malfunctioned and became a problem, you simply removed them using the character elimination button on the screen control panel. But this was rare. This, indeed, was the American dream of utopia, but alive and well in England.

Have a Cyberon Chip for Christmas,
'Cause real life can be a drain,
Have a Cyberon Chip for Christmas,

Cy-ber-ron will take the strain.

The slightly phonetically disjointed final line never did scan correctly. Only serving to highlight the embarrassing lack of musicality in the jingle.

The commerciality of the earworm drove you crazy. The melody was tuneless and monotonous, the lyric uninspiring, the benign sentiment hypocritical. The family quartet of media monkeys performing the hologram were unbelievably believable, which was truly worrying. The really annoying thing was the ubiquitous musical arrangement. It stuck in your brain like some cancerous holiday song, slowly eating away at what little remained of your cultural integrity.

This was subliminal saturation marketing at a level never considered possible or legal before the creation of CyCo. Its unique trading charter gave it the power to repel attacks on its business model. With twenty-four million chips sold every Christmas, approximately fifty-four per cent of the registered and unregistered population, this was good business by anybody's standards.

Lord Protector Hawsley had decided it would be prudent to allow the black-market proliferation of illegal chips to continue, as most of them were sold outside the defined province areas in Ghettazones. This area was sparsely policed, so the legislation would have been impossible to enforce anyway. Unbeknown to the purchasers of illegal chips (which had had the data feed facility blocked) live, personal data was still being transmitted to CyCo for constant evaluation. This was facilitated by another microscopic nanochip data feed device buried much deeper inside the VRS chip.

Virtual Reality has changed the culture of Christmas forever from a traditional family gathering to an event in which you can take part on your own terms. CyCo had the benefit of being able to monitor the thought patterns of all Ghettazone users of unauthorised VRS chips.

The Friends and Family option proved immensely popular, and this alone was a profoundly distressing statistic. It clearly demonstrated how a generation's social/ecological mindset had changed beyond recognition. When this boundary marker was objectively analysed in conjunction with all the other changes that had occurred at some later point in history, it would become painfully clear that the demise of man as a social creature had begun around this period.

'We need you back now, Parish. I'm sorry, but this one (he emphasised the 'one') 'is a little unusual.' There was an unfamiliar note of concern in his tone that disturbed me a little.

'I think it will be a high-profile case from what I've been told so far.' Commander Morgan sounded uncharacteristically agitated for someone who religiously practised tai chi. This, I had been informed, he performed in his back garden to achieve a state of transcendental Karma before starting work each day. I knew him well enough to know he was not someone to over-dramatise an event. Nevertheless, his voice had a sense of measured desperation, a subtle blend of obsequious flattery, natural charm and pleading anguish.

'*This one is a little unusual,*' I thought to myself. They were all fucking unusual, as far as I was aware. A straightforward *bludgeoned to death in the library with a candlestick by the vicar* may have been a bit clichéd, but I missed the format a lot. I had recently started reading Agatha Christie novels for excitement. Occasionally, even watch reruns of old cop shows for inspiration.

'I was really hoping to take the whole weekend off. I haven't had a break for months,' I pleaded, 'can't you get Munford to do it?' I was beginning to sound whingy, so I shut up and listened. Morgan stated his case far more articulately than I had managed, quoting the usual problems of staff illness, pressure from above, other inspectors having families... At that point, he stopped and apologised. Having momentarily forgotten that I, too, once had a family. Then, as a last resort, he defaulted to the old *'You're the best inspector I have for what appears to be a very unusual incident. We need someone with your intuitive insight and blue-sky thinking'* chestnut. (I never fully understood what he meant by 'blue-sky thinking. My interpretation was "a good idea but without any discernible practical use." So, as a compliment, it was sadly devoid of integrity, honesty, and humility. Hence, it wasn't really a compliment at all,

'Alright, I'll be there in half an hour,' I replied reluctantly. I ended the call, and the run restarted.

'Look, I'm really sorry, but they need me back at the station. It's an emergency.'

'I heard...' said Loretta, looking a little tearful.

Christ, this was going to be hard, I thought.

'I thought Mack was a writer,' mumbled Jack, casually glancing up as he devoured his fourth egg.

'He is, but only for now,' replied Marilyn, hushing him. 'You know how it works?'

'Yeah, sure I do, honey,' replied Jack nonchalantly. He had started to work his way through the mountain of baked beans, which, strangely, he had now covered in mayonnaise on top of the brown sauce – but he didn't, not really.

'You heard?' I repeated curiously. I thought about what Loretta had just said. During a trip suspension, I understood that characters only existed in a quasi-two-dimensional format without human characteristics or senses. That piece of information was obviously, worryingly inaccurate.

'Yes,' said Loretta. 'I'm sorry you have to go. I was really looking forward to....' Her last words faded away to become almost inaudible.

'Me too. Look, I could be back in no time at all,' I said a little too hurriedly, making me sound just a little bit desperate, which is never an endearing quality. 'I might wrap it up and put it to bed in a few hours with some luck.'

'That's what I was hoping,' replied Loretta coquettishly. Memories of Catherine's flirtatious mannerisms came flooding back, further confusing me.

'Are you really that good?' She enquired vampishly, smiling provocatively while fluttering her eyelids. This whole exit was turning into a dreadfully bad B-movie.

'I do my best,' I replied, looking directly at Loretta, endeavouring to hold on to a pained expression of dedication to duty before pleasure. I might just as well play up to it as long as possible. The next few hours, possibly days, held little prospect of physical pleasure - that was a given. I felt a little like Humphrey Bogart must have felt in one of his Philip Marlowe roles just as he leaves the '*broad*' and starts his pursuit to find the killer. Or solve the riddle revealed in the first few minutes of the film.

Jack and Marilyn were extraordinarily disappointed but nonetheless understanding. Loretta gave the impression of being genuinely saddened, but that could have been the program – or was I being a little disingenuous? All this self-analysis was beginning to make me a bit paranoid.

'Life's a bitch,' interjected Jack, back in philosophical mode. He looked strangely upset at my leaving – or maybe it was indigestion. He stabbed the last baked bean with his fork, popped it into his mouth, finished his coffee and got up from the table. 'That was delicious, honey.' He gave Marilyn a long kiss, maybe a little too long, then glanced at me nonchalantly and smiled.

'I'll get your case, Mack,' then he wandered off up the stairs.

I turned to Loretta. 'I will get back, I promise. I'll ring when I know what it's all about and how long I'll be. Can you hold things up for me?' I don't know why I said I would ring her because I couldn't; she didn't exist. But it felt so real that I had resorted to conventional terminology and protocol by default.

'Only for seventy-two hours. You know the rules, Mack,' replied Loretta with a reluctant cautionary tone. 'Then we have to move on.' Although she spoke almost in a whisper, her voice had a palpable sense of regret, making me feel decidedly wretched for giving in to Morgan too quickly. It was easy to forget that I was being sequestrated by reality in these situations. That had a prior claim on my time. I had no idea why they had time limits on VRS trips. It didn't serve any purpose as far as I could see and could cause immense frustration, which it definitely did on this occasion.

'I'll be as quick as possible,' I replied resentfully.

'It's your trip, baby,' replied Loretta, holding her arms out to hug me. She wrapped them around my shoulders, pressed her firm breasts into my chest, and kissed me passionately. Now I was really pissed off. I was looking at

Loretta, but all I could see was Catherine - all I could sense and smell was Catherine. She was gone, but she wasn't...

There was no sudden realisation that this was an illusion. I was always aware of that. But that still didn't detract from the knowledge that I could have been experiencing the sensation of exploring and enjoying her warm, sensuous body all night. Instead of which, I would probably be poking around somebody else's cold, rancid, mutilated carcass. Not quite what I had planned for the Christmas holiday.

Jack brought my case down from the bedroom, and I took it and thanked him for his hospitality. 'Anytime, Mack, anytime.' I think he meant it. 'We would all love to see you come back.' I grudgingly waved goodbye as I walked down the steps to the car and threw my case, a little tempestuously, into the trunk. I turned to take one last look at them and the beautiful illusion before settling into the car. Loretta blew me a kiss, and I blew one back. I smiled at all three of them standing on the porch and wished I didn't have to leave. These were nice people. I had the final image of the snowflakes that had just started to fall again and the sun that, rather oddly, was still shining brightly. Loretta looked incredible in a red squirrel fur coat picked out perfectly against the blinding white snow.

I scratched around behind my right ear, took out the virtual reality pin chip and put it into a small leather pouch, which I slipped into my inside pocket. As I removed the chip, the scenery began slowly morphing back to the more familiar surroundings of my house in Providence. I was back again, sitting in the lounge in the dark, where I had always been, back to reality.

Fuck it, I thought, already regretting taking the phone call. I got up, grabbed my coat, hat, and scarf, and left the house. It was as cold outside here as it was where I had just sort of been.

Chapter 7

The Artemis network control unit had already programmed the onboard computer in Parish's car with the incident's details. However, it still requested a security pin number the moment he sat down. Parish mumbled '2929ZB', and the voice recognition system confirmed his identity.

'Good afternoon, Inspector Parish… and what would you like to do today?' the computer asked. It seemed an odd question, almost dilatory.

'Go to incident code…' he stopped for a second and glanced at the computer screen for the code, '17994DD26.' The computer confirmed the address of the incident. The car began to move off, lock into the AMGS and merge into the traffic. Nobody liked the system or the vehicles, but they worked, and nearly everybody arrived where they wanted to be, on time, unharmed and unstressed. Of that, there was no argument except from Parish.

'Is there anything you require?' Asked the computer in the monosyllabic tone of a fast-food operative with partial brain damage. The AMG system was initially designed to mimic the intonation, inflection and tonal variations of the last person to speak to it. The theory was most people liked the sound of their own voices and, therefore, would listen more intently and take notice of instructions. However, early trials had shown the exact opposite to be the case. The programmers subsequently reverted to using the standard monotonic option.

'No, thank you,' replied Parish. He was occasionally tempted to make an obscene suggestion at this point, but this would have been automatically reported to the Network Control Hub. In a few days, he would receive a scathing reprimand for misuse of government equipment, no doubt accompanied by a punitive fine. He derided and despised computers not for the worthy goals they could have achieved but hadn't, but for all the good things they had destroyed. And for all the banal, vapid, and trite garbage they had made possible.

Social networking websites interacting through the plethora of electronic devices available had literally taken control of the lives of so many people, watching their every move. Parish considered this a malicious intrusion into his and everybody else's lives. Contrary to widely held belief, he thought they had considerably reduced the quality of life, not enhanced it. One of his happiest schadenfreudelistic moments had been another cold winter's day, the 21st of October 2016, when the Opendoor X3 operating system collapsed. The innocuous-sounding Viral B virus (classified as being above human intelligence standards) had been covertly programmed into the design format of the X3 system. This was to enable additional personal surveillance by the government. But it migrated to the internet through the DNS root zone. This was the American-controlled protocol prohibiting any two websites from having identical addresses.

Within days, the virus renamed all the world's websites with the same name and address. This created instantaneous global internet chaos and made the universal system completely inoperable. The infinite structure and integrity of the World Wide Web had been comprehensively destroyed. The sub–Viral B virus's exponential growth was so devastating that the internet was condemned as profoundly unsafe. It was officially shut down at the end of December 2016 and never reopened.

One year later, that event heralded the most unusual Christmas Day for nearly forty-five years. When children opened their presents on Christmas morning in 2017, they did not receive computer-based games that replicated the thrill of the kill. They were no longer being produced as they would not run on government-controlled computer terminals. An alternative had to be found. Socks, jumpers, board games and books had made a welcome return, something tangible that children could enjoy without the fear of sudden and unexpected annihilation. It had been proved beyond doubt that mindless war games had immunised two generations against the actuality of death. They could no longer differentiate between playtime and reality. Due to the constant exposure, their brains had become rewired and had evolved to accept gratuitous murder as nothing more than a game option.

Parish sat back and watched the news. The car drove for approximately forty-five minutes before arriving at the flashing blue lights outside the incident scene. It neatly docked itself alongside the pavement. It was only mid-afternoon, but the daylight was already fading fast. Streetlights began to flicker into life, casting their peculiar silvery-white metallic glow onto the drama playing out below.

This was a part of Chelsea that he had never visited before. The snow that had been gently falling for many hours started settling on a scene of gentle serenity. It was strangely reminiscent of the Dickensian-styled Christmas cards his parents used to receive when he was a boy. He could still remember eagerly awaiting each new postal delivery. He looked forward to reading the verse and gazing at the pictures - each imbued with the promise of a renewed opportunity to reacquaint him with charmingly depicted bucolic places and charismatic characters who appeared to live in much happier times. Men doffed their large stovepipe hats and smiled at ladies in crinoline dresses and bonnets. Plump Robins sat on the bare branches of trees that never changed. These thoughts took him back to long-forgotten memories of crackers and chestnuts, turkey and Christmas decorations and a tree with flashing coloured lights covered in silver balls and tinsel. All the rituals people did not bother with anymore. We were all so much younger then, and it was all so different now.

Sadly, the tradition of sending Christmas cards had ceased back in two thousand and sixteen with the collapse of the old postal service. It had become prohibitively expensive due to its antiquated delivery system. Greetings cards had been replaced with the soulless and predictable automated Mailex system. The introduction and installation of a General Access Computer terminal, with Mailex in all public buildings in the UK, was completed nearly five years ago. All that was necessary to access mail was to log on at any GAC terminal or registered home computer with a retinal scan. Any letters, documents and messages waiting would be displayed on the screen. They could be previewed, printed, or trashed immediately, much like the old email system. Mailex made it much cheaper to send a *letter*.

Ornate wrought-iron railings segregated the small garden area in front of each house and the pavement boundary. One single gate led into the front garden. The ironwork had probably been there since the nineteenth century when the homes were built. *You don't see quality like that anymore, Parish thought to himself,* but then he had been saying that for the last twenty years. The house was in a row of terraced Victorian villas in a four-storey crescent where people with serious money lived. A domestic incident was his first thought as he stepped out of the car into a deep, slushy puddle. He felt the ice-cold water slowly run down into his shoe. The drains were obviously not working. The driver seat sensor shut off the engine, and the computer asked, 'Where-are-you-going…? Detective… Inspector… Parish?'

'Fuck off,' he muttered quietly, too quietly for the computer to detect. The water had splashed up his leg and soaked his sock and trouser bottom.

'Bugger,' he muttered as he made his second step towards the house, this one on the pavement, which was a little dryer. He went to shut the car door…

'Bugger is not recognised; please repeat the command.' Asked the computer in the polite but demonstrably demeaning tone it had adopted when conversing with humans. Or was it just him who it had taken offence to? He turned around to let rip with a cavalcade of colourful eighteenth-century naval expletives when, in a flash of mental clarity, he suddenly became aware of the absolute absurdity of not only harbouring grievous physical thoughts about an inanimate object but also actually arriving at that moment in time when he was seriously considering verbally abusing it. It was just a chunk of plastic and metal and didn't have a life. Confrontation was undoubtedly the road to madness. He opted instead to bite his lip and clench the cheeks of his arse tightly together instead. Slowly, the moment passed.

He knew that shouting at, directly assaulting, or insulting his vehicle, or its computer terminal or any other government device for that matter, was deeply frowned upon by the Hawsley administration. They had initiated a policy wherein all government equipment should always be accorded absolute respect. The government had issued a proclamation covering this particular social offence, but Parish had never read it. Conversely, he assumed that inflicting pain and misery on his own computer in the privacy of his home was perfectly acceptable. But then, his home computer was neither patronising nor antagonistic and would never have the audacity to provoke such emotions. He slammed the car door shut and left the computer, confused.

Experience had taught him that most domestic incidents were usually related to one disgruntled spouse attempting to or successfully bringing about the other's premature demise. Don't know why they bothered to call me, he thought. He would have said it aloud, but no one noticed him as he arrived.

There were three police vehicles, a techie unit, and an ambulance in attendance. So, it was reasonable to assume that it was a relatively normal murder – as far as murder could be considered normal. Everything was relevant to your relationship with people. Parish always thought of himself as a sort of independent assessor of souls. It was essential to understand how people worked, what motivated them, what drove them forward each day, and what could cause them to suddenly change direction.

There was always a reason for everything; it might not be immediately apparent, but it is still there if you look hard enough. Nothing ever happened by chance. Every event was governed by the logic of synchronicity. And therefore, to no small degree, it was predetermined but not necessarily premeditated. This, of course, was his personal theory and probably not something to which anybody else on the force would openly subscribe.

Glancing casually around the street, he was struck by the pervasive sense of self-righteous moral rectitude oozing out from under every front door. He thought about the people he could not see. Those secretly peeking out through tiny chinks in their heavy, fully lined velvet drapes and discreet Roman blinds - at the solemn proceedings unfolding before them. Did they ever expect something like this to happen right on their doorstep? In what was the 'nicer part of town'? Would there be repercussions? Would it affect house prices?

Before he started to walk up the path, Parish noticed the only thing missing from this archetypal Christmas scene was the obligatory robin redbreast. At this point, one suspiciously appeared and perched on the iron gate that opened onto the pathway leading to number sixteen's front door. Parish turned his head slightly but not so much as to alert the bird and squinted dubiously at the robin. The robin looked back at him with engaging curiosity. Was this a spontaneous natural event he was experiencing or something darker and far more sinister? Maybe CyCo control was reading his thoughts through his docking interface. And maybe regenerating archived three-dimensional facsimilised images to alleviate his fears about the loss of reality. Possibly to satisfy his deepest desire to recreate the nostalgic memories buried in the archives of his long-term memory bank.

The docking chip interface implant behind his ear was for purely recreational purposes. The CyCo installation centre staff had assured him that its only use was as an interface for the Cyberon Recreational product range. He had no reason to doubt their integrity. They were, after all, the largest recreational implant manufacturer in the world. So, would they jeopardise this unique position by having their professional integrity and autonomous status impugned by rumours of a dark agenda? Or an alliance with a demonic oligarchical third party. But then other organisations had travelled on this road before, and they were gone.

Was he becoming paranoid, he thought to himself once again, or was he growing paranoid about becoming paranoid. He became increasingly more unsure with each passing day. Maybe it was just a robin, after all, nothing more than that, a common garden *Erithacus rubecula.*

Parish had noted the incongruous cinematic imagery of the blue-suited techies masquerading as overweight visitors from another astral plane or planet, possibly Mars. With their new-fangled horseless carriages, idiosyncratically set against the clichéd Dickensian landscape. When Parish reached the front door, he quickly glanced back to see if the robin was still watching him. He was, but now with utter indifference. The robin wiped his beak on his wings in an unmistakable gesture of defiance and flapped them a few times. Parish squinted at the bird in a wholly unnatural, prolonged battle of nerves before eventually conceding defeat and turning back to enter the house.

Parish had served in the Providence Division for just over nineteen years. He had experienced many changes since that bitterly freezing day in February 2006 when he was transferred to the City of London Metropolitan Force. He had worked through the major upheaval created by the Hawsley administration after it was elected in 2014. In the years that followed, Britain was split into five separate areas. Four-walled Provinces with everything else designated as a 'Decontrolled Liberties' area known as the Ghettazone. This area now encompassed nearly eighty per cent of the country. It was partly policed by local vigilante groups, partly by a token presence from the police operating from high-security compounds based in the most significant urbanisations. But it was, to all intent and purpose, a lawless zone or, more accurately, one where different laws applied.

The Ghettazone was home to approximately eighteen million people, including about nine million unemployed with abnormally low intellect. There were another three million immigrants, mainly from central Europe. Transporting them back to their country of origin proved impossible as most were unknown to the authorities. Nearly one million convicted criminals were no longer incarcerated in prisons. Being condemned to live in the Ghettazone was a far harsher sentence than any institution had to offer.

There were also approximately three million unregistered citizens. They had worked all their lives and claimed various forms of social security but never paid any income tax under previous governments. They were automatically expelled from the gated provinces. Finally, there were the remains of an unknown number of minority religious groups who had managed to avoid detection. All these were collectively known as the Glunde.

Parish managed to survive and remained busy during the turbulent and dangerous period of civil riots when the security walls were being built around the new provinces. Since the introduction, three years before, of the Scan-Tech crime investigation department, he had experienced the most notable change of all as far as policing was concerned. Scan-Tech technology was a highly sophisticated DNA air analysis system. It was now possible to detect whether somebody had been present at a crime scene up to twenty-four hours before the air scan sample was taken.

They seldom called him out for a straightforward incident. Most of them were usually resolved without further reference to his office. In a way, it was a pleasure to be asked to attend a murder incident, even if it was his weekend off. It had the beneficial effect of restoring some of the loss of confidence in his professional abilities. Something which had been brought on by a smouldering belief that he had become fundamentally redundant. Worse still was the threat of becoming an anachronism.

'Afternoon, Inspector. Over here,' Heart interrupted Parish's thoughts. Although they had worked together for seven years, Heart still conscientiously maintained the customary rank formalities in front of other officers. He was already wearing his isolation suit, so Parish didn't recognise him immediately. 'The techies have a minor problem which has them a little perplexed.' He wasn't exactly gloating as he spoke - but there was a clearly defined smirk. A tiny hint of professional arrogance that he could not or maybe did not wish to conceal. He, too, had been harbouring the same employment uncertainties as Parish. They enjoyed working together; the whole was stronger than the constituent parts of their relationship, but with each passing year, it was becoming more infrequent.

'You surprise me,' replied Parish a little disingenuously. Fully appreciating the deprecatory dimension of Heart's comment. 'I thought nothing confused the Bofs.' He pronounced the last word with palpable disdain and screwed up his nose and mouth to make a funny face like a mouse. This was Parish's sobriquet for the technical squads. In the main, they consisted of timid, unassuming creatures who erroneously believed the nickname to be a derivation of "Boffin," a not unwelcome epithet as far as they were concerned. In fact, it was Parish's acronym for a Boring Old Farts, though they didn't realise that. At least he didn't think they did.

They were all university graduates and operated and socialised in a remarkably close academic clique. This excluded plainclothes detectives, who, in the main, still came up through the ranks and were considered to be only one evolutionary step above pond life. Their leisure activities tended towards bridge nights, cocktail evenings, summer soirées and the opera. In contrast, Parish was more prosaic in his interests.

He was still fretting about being pulled back from his weekend trip. He held the bof's solely responsible for that. Heart led Parish through the melee of techies loitering in the doorway and the hall smoking cigarettes. This was despite a total ban on conventional smoking in public places.

The Minister for Law Enforcement and Defence had granted officers partial dispensation when working on traumatic incidents. This resulted from the Army threatening to resign en bloc if a similar exemption was not given to soldiers on active service in foreign battle zones. The government had attempted to impose the ban on armed forces personnel on active duty because it was unequivocally detrimental to their health. Especially where fitness was paramount. But the ban had been comprehensively and soundly rebuffed by a spokesman for the armed services. His primary defence argument was faulty, antiquated equipment and surprise bullets essentially had the same ultimate effect. Soldiers enjoyed the sardonic irony – all bullets hitting them were usually by surprise.

The technical supervisor handed Parish an isolation suit in the front hall with an aspirator, headset, and a small air tank clipped onto his belt. Parish took it with some reluctance, smiling a little ungraciously as he did so. After climbing into the plastic suit and fitting his breathing apparatus, he followed Heart further into the house. The sound of breathing through the aspirators affected the clarity of their conversation, which became slower, breathy, and more deliberate as they became accustomed to the apparatus.

'Supposed to be off this weekend,' mumbled Parish. 'Munford was suddenly unavailable, so I understand.'

'Probably playing golf with the Chief Constable,' muttered Heart acerbically. Parish glanced at Heart but said nothing.

'So, what do we know so far?'

'The housekeeper, Maddie Cornwell, found the body.'

'How?' asked Parish, still adjusting his plastic suit, which appeared to be too large.

'Well, she let herself in this morning at about nine. It was her night off,' said Heart. 'Found the deceased at...' he fumbled through his tablet 'about nine-thirty this morning. The call was logged at 9.34 am. She lives in but went to a party last night and didn't return until this morning.'

'Why the delay?' asked Parish. 'That's over half an hour before she reported the incident?'

'She made tea downstairs and had a slice of toast before taking a cup upstairs... to the victim.'

'I presume that's where the body is?'

'Yes,' replied Heart.

'Tell me, Heart...' asked Parish. He paused momentarily, knowing there must be a plausible reason, though he couldn't think of it. There was always an inescapable inevitability about this kind of question being misread. But it was too late. The words had slipped past his tongue and were dangling listlessly in the air, never to be withdrawn. 'Why so many bodies?'

'There's only one,' replied Heart, sounding a little bemused. He led Parish up the staircase past a few blue-coated techies holding various pieces of electronic equipment.

'I meant, why so many techies? I've counted at least eight already. That's got to be a record for a domestic, isn't it?'

'Yes, it is. Six extra techies arrived just after the initial air scans had been carried out - but their vans were immediately driven away - which is a little unusual. Something about not wishing to attract additional attention by having too many vehicles outside.'

'Why have they done that?' asked Parish.

'Don't know for sure, but there's a problem with the DNA air scan results. I know that much.'

Parish knew he knew more. They had arrived at the first landing, and Parish stopped and leant against the bannister to gaze back down to the entrance hall below.

'Don't tell me, Jack the Ripper done it,' replied Parish, adopting an exaggerated cockney twang. He sounded more like Dick Van Dyke in *Mary Poppins* than a real cockney. He did not immediately appreciate how puzzlingly close to the truth that statement would prove to be.

'Not Jack the Ripper, guv,' replied Heart thoughtfully, 'but somebody of a similar emotive cache.'

'Emotive cache!' exclaimed Parish disparagingly. 'You've been working with the bofs too long or wasting too much time on crosswords again - please don't go all poncy on me.' He had always considered them complete nonsense and an utter waste of time. Sometimes, to annoy Heart, he would fill one of his crosswords with all the wrong words just so long as they fitted. Parish found that remarkably satisfying. It would drive Heart to distraction.

Parish was chirpily sarcastic at most of these incidents. Heart usually chose to ignore him, adopting a more formal approach that enabled him to preserve his psychological objectivity. But with his lighter touch, Parish had developed the ability to get behind the invisible barriers and inside the victim's and the suspects' minds to glean his paradoxical perspective on the events. This produced a unique viewpoint on murder and gave the two of them an investigatory edge still not attainable with computer gadgetry.

'Lord Lucan, then,' suggested Parish with a whimsical flourish of acerbity? He knew he had little chance of guessing the suspect's name from the scant information made available so far.

'Close, but not quite. Try Aiden Hawsley.'

'Hawsley – fuck,' mumbled Parish. Sensing an immediate change in the atmosphere, Heart turned to face him. 'That's why they called you.' Heart prepared himself for a rant, but it never came.

'Didn't they try Munford first? He's senior to me,' asked Parish pensively.

'Yes, they tried him,' replied Heart, but his phone was switched off, and anyway, ACC Daniels especially asked the commander to call you.'

'Did he?' replied Parish, sounding slightly flattered, but he didn't show it.

'Yes,' confirmed Heart supportively.

'Well, I suppose that's some consolation.'

'That's what I thought,' said Heart as they ascended the second flight of stairs, but neither of them really thought it was.

'This is wrong on so many levels,' mumbled Parish.

'Is it,' asked Heart? Unsure what he was referring to. Parish stopped on the staircase and turned to Heart.

'He turns his phone off, so I get all the shit. I bet he already knew about the DNA air scan.' Parish was obviously slightly irritated that Munford had effectively dumped on him again. However, his fractious eruption was delicately balanced against the personal satisfaction of knowing he had been specifically targeted to head up the investigation. Could it be one more brownie point towards promotion, he wondered? A high-profile case quickly solved might just do it, but on the other hand...

'It gets more interesting,' added Heart, resuming their ascension.

'Not for me, it doesn't,' replied Parish thoughtfully. The mechanics of promotion would be suitably lubricated if he managed to quickly solve a murder case such as this. But that thought was tinged with an element of concern, as Munford would have also known that. He was further troubled at being landed with an incident that Munford had deliberately avoided for reasons he was keeping to himself. Parish gazed down at the activity in the hallway below.

'I can see my career disappearing down the toilet if Munford has sidestepped this,' Parish mumbled. Heart heard him but said nothing. He knew Parish would cut a limb off to take on a case like this from Mumford, but on this occasion, it had been handed to him on a plate. That unnerved him. The words 'poison' and 'chalice' kept popping into his head.

'He knows something that he's not telling us,' Parish suddenly exclaimed. That was the only rational conclusion he could reach - having carefully considered and discarded all other possibilities. Any other explanation did not fit in with Mumford's underhand nature, which, above all else, was consistent... They arrived on the top landing and stopped.

'Odd you should say that,' replied Heart, 'the same thought crossed my mind.'

'He always knows more than we do. He licks too many arses not to,' replied Parish in a tutorial tone. 'He could smell a dead rat in a sewer.' There was little love lost between Parish and Munford.

'Paints a lovely picture, guv, but I was referring to the toilet.'

'Why,' asked Parish? Years on the job had taught him that most cases were unusual and some were inexplicable. Unfortunately, this case was stacking up to look like one of the latter.

'You'll see in a minute. It'll be a pleasant surprise,' replied Heart, smiling quietly.

'Right, I see,' replied Parish phlegmatically. 'Are we going to have to tread carefully on this?'

'Oh, yes, I think so,' replied Heart gloomily. 'Very carefully.'

'What have they got so far?' asked Parish, alluding to a passing techie.

'Well, there are twelve air scans in total, covering the last twelve hours. Five of them are our people, and one is the victim. Hawsley's was the only name I recognised, but the techies have more information upstairs. They've been remarkably busy.'

'Well, that's encouraging,' replied Parish tartly. 'I only hope the other six aren't the rest of his government. I can't see us being flavour of the month if we have to arrest the entire Hawsley administration.'

'Us?' replied Heart squeakily, showing signs of grave concern. 'That won't look good on my record – "Man who helped to arrest the government". I was hoping to retire in three years with nothing more to do for the rest of my life. Apart from some therapeutic gardening, a couple of pints in the pub every night and the occasional game of flat green bowling. I've always fancied that.' He looked almost sublimely content with his utopian dream until Parish gave him a disparaging glance.

'If this all goes tits up, we could both be gardening, permanently, next week if not earlier,' mumbled Parish, with a sarcastic smirk. Heart remained silent, having long since resigned himself to the uncertain fate which lay squarely in the hands of another at that particular moment. Heart directed Parish along the landing, but Parish paused when he was drawn to one particular hanging portrait. He gazed at the painting for a few moments.

'Do we know anything about our victim yet?' he asked Heart while still reviewing the portrait.

'I'd say she was in her twenties, but it's tricky to tell. Her name is Dhalia Vingali, and she's on the DNA register. But there's a discrepancy there, which the techies are looking into. Heart was reading from his tablet again.

'Dhalia Vingali? Sounds a bit like an extremely hot curry,' replied Parish drolly. Heart half-smiled.

'Well, she appears to be English, although she does have that Asian name. Oh, and she may also be a prostitute.'

'I thought that was an automatic expulsion to the Ghettazone,' queried Parish, still looking at the portrait.

'It is, but she's obviously not actually listed as a prostitute. That's what one of the neighbours told me just before you arrived.'

'Nice neighbour,' replied Parish. 'Probably didn't like Miss Vingali's occupation, but she was too nervous to say anything while she was still alive. So, she patiently waits until Miss Vingali is serendipitously murdered before putting the boot in. This neighbour – is she a woman, by any chance?'

'Yes, a Mrs Daphne Charminster,' replied Heart, rechecking his tablet.

'Thought so. Competition!' said Parish acerbically, looking a little smug. 'Better check her out while we are at it. She has a potential motive.'

'If you say so, guv,' replied Heart, slightly perplexed at Parish's conclusion. 'Mrs Charminster said Dhalia used to have a lot of visitors at odd times.'

'I didn't think that was a crime yet,' replied Parish cynically. 'If she owns a house here, there's probably enough business for them both. So why is she grumbling?'

'I don't think she is, guv, and she has to be eighty if she's a day,' said Heart.

'I thought you said she was about twenty-five?'

'The victim is somewhere between twenty and thirty. Mrs Charminster is….'

'Oh, right. Well, maybe she caters for the more mature clientele,' mused Parish, chuckling to himself. 'The more discerning punter,' he added as an afterthought. 'What do you think?'

'They would have to be bloody fit to climb stairs like those and perform at the top,' replied Heart dryly, ignoring the subtext of Parish's last question. 'Anyway, I don't think she's a prostitute,' he added defensively. 'She seems to be a genuinely nice lady.'

'A nice lady?' asked Parish suspiciously.

'Yes, a bit like my mum was,' added Heart, a little out of context. His expression changed momentarily.

A techie walking past stopped, turned around and, looking a little unsure of himself, tentatively held out a folder.

'D.I. Parish?' he queried, looking at Heart as he was the older of the two.

'No,' said Heart, nodding at Parish. 'He is.'

'Final air scan identification results. I think you'll need these,' said the techie holding out the file for Parish.

Parish smiled and pointed nonchalantly to Heart, signifying that he should give the folder to him. Heart thanked the techie, opened it, and began reading the report. Parish gazed upwards, admiring the ornate leaded dome roof light, glazed with small stained glass panels. Dappled sunlight showered down the atrium, a delicate mix of pale pink segueing into orange and blues and then back to pink.

'It says here that…'

'Lovely dome,' interrupted Parish almost rapturously while scratching the back of his neck. 'Must be cast in wrought iron. It's remarkably similar to a dome I saw in a beautiful house I had to visit in Little Venice a few years ago.' For some reason, Heart thought he was probably reminiscing about happier times with his late wife but was about to be swiftly corrected on that misapprehension.

'The woman there had stabbed her husband in the eye with a solid silver antique marshmallow toasting fork. Apparently, they were a very devoted couple.' Parish turned around to get a different view of the dome and tilted his head slightly as if he had found a minor blemish in the construction. 'Very sad. You don't see many of those anymore.' He spoke with such prosaic inflection that it was hard to tell whether he was jesting or merely recalling some interesting architectural fact.

'What? Wives killing husbands!' exclaimed Heart with jaded surprise.

'No,' replied Parish wistfully, turning to Heart. 'Georgian toasting forks. And that one was ruined, I can tell you. Completely bent out of shape.' Parish continued gazing up at the dome. Heart winced at the thought of the bent fork; he was still squeamish about some aspects of murder, especially when it involved the eyes.

'Oh,' replied Heart. 'Anyway, as I was saying, the report confirms they have isolated eleven positives and one negative air scan. If we discount the five I mentioned earlier and the victim, we are left with six possible suspects.'

'Busy girl!' interjected Parish, whose mind was still elsewhere. 'Are you sure she didn't die from exhaustion?'

Heart continued reading out the file summary. 'Of those six, one is the housekeeper who found the body, one is a waiter who brought food round last night at about 10 pm. Apparently, the victim had an arrangement with a local restaurant. Another is a doctor who lives at number eighteen. The housekeeper called him when she found the body. He was here when the techies arrived, but....' Heart referred to some notes he had made on his tablet, 'he didn't touch anything, so he tells us. Never got closer than six feet to the body. He concluded that life was obviously extinct, so he deemed it unnecessary to examine the body more closely. So he came back downstairs and waited for the ambulance to arrive.'

'Deemed it unnecessary to examine the body?' queried Parish with a Holmes-esque mannerism, looking skywards while musing on the phrase. 'Must be a very clever doctor who can pronounce life extinct from six feet away – or maybe he knew her intimately.' He hated that phrase 'life was extinct'. Whatever happened to 'he or she was dead', he wondered. It was as if professional people were afraid of using ordinary, unpretentious words to explain something in relatively simple terms. Preferring to hide behind a cloak of magniloquence.

Heart looked up from his tablet. 'He did know her quite well, apparently. Popped in quite often to see her, and he confirmed that he arrived here at 9.41 a.m. after Miss Cornwell summoned him from next door.'

'That's very precise,' queried Parish.

'He makes notes on everything he does,' replied Heart.

'Does he?' said Parish. 'That could be handy.'

Heart continued. 'So, if we eliminate those three, that leaves just three suspects. And no, she didn't die from exhaustion, guv. The techies are fairly sure the sword slash that decapitated her probably killed her.'

'Sword slash!' exclaimed Parish, snapping back into reality, his eyes opening a little wider as his brain began to conjugate various gruesome scenarios. This was starting to morph into some sort of VRS horror trip. He suddenly had to take a deep breath to re-orientate himself as to where he was. Sometimes, differentiating between a vivid dream, a VRS trip, a drink-induced stupor, a narcotic haze, and reality was difficult. Occasionally, they even segued into each other, which could be very confusing.

At that precise moment, Loretta – or was it Catherine – blew him a kiss. His mind was playing a few tricks today. If that robin suddenly reappeared and started giving him criminological advice, he would have to go home and lie down in a darkened room for a while.

'We have the weapon,' said Heart exuberantly. 'It's a ceremonial Japanese Samurai sword.' At that precise moment, a passing techie smiled at them and offered Parish an exhibit bag he was holding. On closer inspection, he could see it contained the offending implement. He noticed the smiling techie had two front teeth missing, which diverted his attention momentarily before looking back at the sword.

'It's a nineteenth-century Shinken samurai sword,' confirmed the techie.

That wasn't easy to say with two missing teeth, thought Parish.

'Is it,' asked Parish, sounding a little surprised.

'Yeth,' said the techie, 'very valuable.'

'Right.'… 'Big, isn't it?' remarked Parish casually. 'Looks extremely dangerous.' Another passing techie looked at Parish and started to say something. But changed his mind on recognising him and stayed silent. Everybody seemed to be exercising extreme caution today. Parish wondered why.

'And very sharp,' said the first techie slowly, still holding up the sword. He obviously had no reservations about passing a comment. Unfortunately, the last word came out as Swarp due to his orthodontic issue.

'Swarp?' repeated Parish, a little puzzled.

'Yeth, very,' confirmed the techie.

In itself, this was of no significance, but in the overall picture, it appeared almost surreal. Parish glanced at Heart to double-check he hadn't drifted off on some VRS flashback, but he hadn't; at least, he did not think he had. Parish noticed the sword had an ornate inlaid jade handle and a very bright steel blade with blue damask engraving, stained halfway down with what he presumed to be dried blood.

'I'm beginning to see why they called me,' continued Parish. Heart smirked and beckoned Parish to follow him into the primary crime scene. The pathway to the bedroom suddenly opened like the biblical Red Sea did for Moses as techies stood back to allow him to pass.

Walking into the room, he first noticed it was almost entirely white - the walls were papered with silk lightly embossed with tiny flowers. The furniture was all white leather, and the curtains were white velvet, as was the bedspread. The sheets were made of white silk, possibly satin. He never could tell the difference.

Then he noticed the smell emanating from the room, the sour, rank odour of stale urine. But there was something else as well, something he could not clearly identify. Did the body excrete some kind of enzyme connected to fear, he wondered, a sudden involuntary discharge when the victim faced imminent death? He had never noticed it before, not at any other murder scene he had ever attended, except for one many years ago when he was about eight years old.

His parents had started taking him on holiday to a converted farmhouse in Provence. They used to rent it for the whole of July each year. George, the old farmer who lived in the farmhouse next door, kept various animals – a few chickens, a pig, some milking cows, a donkey and one calf for veal. George would have the calf slaughtered as a special treat for the Christmas festivities each year. Parish later learned that George did not actually eat the whole calf for Christmas but had it frozen so he could eat the rest during the following year.

He also kept a fat pig, which, oddly, he also called George (he was French, after all). George fed George with every bit of edible kitchen waste available, including our kitchen waste contributions during July. The same fate befell the pig every few years, as did the calf. But Parish never realised this until he was nearly fifteen when he mentioned to George (the farmer) that he had noticed that George (the pig) appeared to have changed colour from the previous year and had also lost some weight.

George looked at Parish somewhat wistfully and asked whether he liked the paté his wife had brought around at the beginning of July each year and the bacon he brought them for breakfast each day. When he said he did, he told Parish it was George and laughed. After Parish had recovered from the initial shock, George carefully explained that they kept George to eat all the waste food. When the pig was fat enough, he would have it slaughtered and eat the meat. That way, there was practically no wastage.

At first, Parish was terribly upset, feeling a little stupid and naïve. But after some further deliberation, he realised what an amazingly efficient concept this was, despite the crude casuistry George, the *farmer*, had demonstrated. After that, he began to understand one crucial element of life more clearly, something that would stay with him for the rest of his life.

George always took great delight in showing Parish around the barn where this year's calf was being reared for veal. The calf apparently never saw sunlight. George kept it permanently in the dark, believing it would keep the meat white. Parish, could remember the cloying stench of the calves' sour urine and excrement. Although not always visible, it was clearly evident in the warm, airless room. It had permeated every wooden beam and soaked into the earthen floor. But there was always something else as well, something he couldn't put his finger on.

Although intrigued by George's ancient practice, Parish never really understood why George enforced the incarceration - until much later in life. Then, he began to wonder whether the calf ever had an inkling of what was in store. It always appeared happy and content, even resigned to its destiny, but did it know there was more to life? The other strange smell he had detected in the barn stayed with him forever, locked deep in his memory. Until now...

On to this colour-washed panorama of virginal tranquillity were splattered spots of blood. Each became darker and more intense as they gradually converged. The culmination - a modernistic explosion of deep, dark crimson.

Apart from the technical invaders' blue coats, the only other colour in the room was the numerous ornaments of green jade, which sat on small white marble tables. One was a large bowl-shaped fish; another, which stood nearly a metre high, was the figure of an old fisherman. As Parish's eyes slowly became accustomed to the techies' arc lights' glare, he began to see the other artefacts in the room. Highly decorative carved statues slowly came into view, each one the distinctive hue of milky green that he associated with the better-quality jade.

A woman's almost flawless, naked, headless body lay on the most enormous circular bed he had ever seen. Parish ambled slowly over to the bed and gazed intently at what appeared to be a carefully staged tableau. The centrepiece an alabaster statue of a serenely peaceful headless body in repose. He could not remember ever seeing a young woman's body that did not have some tiny scar, birthmark, blemish, or evidence of suntan or artificial tanning somewhere. *It was as if she had been kept out of the sunlight all her life.*

Dhalia's arms had been carefully arranged with a deliberation that clearly betrayed the emotional state of the person who had placed her on the bed. Her left hand had been carefully placed on her right breast. Her right - had been set over her pudendum. Replicating the manner in which some of the Pre-Raphaelite Brotherhood of painters chose to depict the coyness and purity of young women. Paintings of older women were never so virtuously portrayed. They were merely an allegory of the loss of innocence and youth. In Parish's mind, they were all idealistic betrayals of reality, and here was the graphic contradiction to prove the point.

The final vacuous attempt to provide a measure of decency after her macabre ritual decapitation intrigued Parish. Perhaps it was merely the act of an innocent visitor, an impulsive act to preserve what little was left of Dhalia's dignity, having accidentally stumbled on the body after death. If that were the case, why didn't they contact the police, he wondered? In his mind, however, he had virtually discounted the possibility that any woman could commit such a heinous act.

Maybe this person's social position precluded him from reporting the incident. Perhaps his wife might have

114

objected to the revelation that he was visiting a prostitute. Maybe he was so much in love with her that he couldn't desert her, not abandon her on this, her last day of life and the first day of death. These were their final moments together before the ritualistic journey back to Mother Earth began.

All these thoughts passed through Parish's mind as he considered the possibility that at least one person could have contaminated the scene but not necessarily have anything to do with the killing.

The pattern of blood splattering centred on an area of the ceiling midway between the bed and the window. There was also a large stain of dried blood on the floor directly below, where she would have bled out. Parish surmised that the sudden slash had instantly severed the carotid artery and jugular vein. With her head wholly detached, her heart pumped furiously for a few seconds, desperately trying to recover normal pressure before giving out to the inevitable.

This created a fountain of blood that hit the ceiling, leaving an interesting splatter design. A vision not dissimilar to a classic modern art painting from the nineteen seventies he had seen in an art gallery about six months previously. He did not mention his recollection to Heart. He knew he could be a little squeamish about such indelicate observations.

A space on the carpet where the sword was found had been carefully marked with tape, alongside where the body must have fallen before it was moved to the bed. The killer appeared to have dropped the sword after he (or she) had severed the victim's head. But they still had the presence of mind and the time to allow the body to fully bleed out before moving it to the bed. This would account for the complete absence of blood on the bed cover. Parish wondered what the killer must have been thinking while he patiently waited for the last drops of blood to drain from Dhalia's body.

A red rose had been placed in her navel, once again, typical of the Pre-Raphaelite style of painting. Parish found this detail particularly interesting, as there were no other flowers in the room. Possibly, the rose had been brought to the scene and deliberately positioned by the killer. So, maybe not such an innocent, casual visitor after all. He was leaning more towards the possibility that the killer had meticulously staged the theatrical tableau. Unless, of course, the last visitor had brought roses with him and decided, impulsively, having found the body, to place it on the bed. And then place the head of one of the roses in her navel as a token gesture. This was an unlikely scenario, but then he had seen some unusual murder tableaux in his career. Each precisely set to convey some specific final subliminal image.

'It's ruined the carpet,' mumbled Heart, interrupting Parish's line of thought. Any possible squeamishness that Heart may have suffered previously – was no longer evident.

'What?' asked Parish inquisitively, having missed Heart's offhand comment, his mind still preoccupied with diaphanous visions.

'It's ruined the carpet,' repeated Heart, wishing he hadn't bothered. The moment had now obviously passed, and he'd had time to reconsider the tactless flippancy of the remark. Spontaneity was paramount in these situations; there was no place for mistimed humorous asides.

'And her career,' replied Parish acerbically.

'I've always fancied a really nice white carpet in my bedroom,' remarked Heart, admiring the quality of the flooring.

'It stains easily,' said Parish, glancing at Heart and then looking back at the stain, effectively closing off that avenue of extemporaneous absurdity.

Heart started to say something but changed his mind.

'Any semen match on the air scans?' asked Parish. The question wasn't specifically directed to any particular person in the room.

'We're still working on that.' Came a reply from Dr Geraldine Fitzgerald, who had her back to him. She finished checking the equipment she had been working on and turned to face Parish. She smiled. He smiled back, courteously at first, then he realised he knew her, had known her... almost intimately.

'Gerry! Sorry, I didn't recognise you in the suit and the...' he pointed to the aspirator. 'Long time no see.'

'Very long time,' said Gerry guardedly.

'So how have you been,' asked Parish? Not really the right question, he thought. In fact, it was excruciatingly banal and predictable. But what do you talk about when you meet somebody you once nearly had an affair with. It had initially developed through the intimacy of their close working environment. It might have progressed beyond the formative stages had it not been for his wife and daughter's sudden death. The relationship took on an entirely different dimension after that. The seed of desire that suddenly flowers into rampant sexual chemistry and overwhelms everything for the first few heady months of a new relationship never took root and quickly withered and died. After that, Gerry transferred to another district in the province, and Parish didn't bother to contact her again.

He never understood why he had been attracted to her in the first place, as he was perfectly happy with his home life. Sometimes, things you don't understand happen in life - things you don't have any control over, as with Gerry.

He no longer harboured the feelings of guilt and betrayal he had experienced immediately after the accident. But for whatever reason, relationships with women were now restricted to the relatively safe confines of a VRS experience. He still couldn't deal with anything real that would require commitment.

'Still employed, so can't complain,' replied Gerry.

'So, what are you doing here?' asked Parish, although it was blindingly obvious.

'Is it a problem?' Gerry asked tentatively. Her voice's faint suggestion of concern reminded him of how selflessly she had acted when she suddenly left the district after the accident.

'No, not at all, just a little... surprised.' All sorts of memories flashed through his mind, and he wasn't sure how to react to this turn of events. If he had known that he would meet Gerry today, he might have been able to think it through and work out a mental strategy to deal with the situation. But suddenly, being confronted with the situation's stark reality wasn't quite so easy.

'They asked me to come back, and as it's been over three years, I thought maybe it would be okay now.' She paused for a second to gauge Parish's reaction, but it was hard to tell what he was thinking behind the mask. 'We've all moved on, *haven't we,*' Gerry declared rhetorically. But it could also have been a question - interpretation depending on how Parish wanted to hear the words.

'It's not a problem,' he replied after a few moments, but he didn't completely answer her question. Then he realised just how crass that sounded - almost condescending. What had happened wasn't her fault, but she was the one who had faced the upheaval of moving to another region of Providence. They could easily have carried on working in the same district, but she knew there would always be an awkward tension whenever they met.

'Not... a problem?' repeated Gerry cautiously? She was a little unsure as to precisely what Parish was saying. Was there something she was missing tucked away behind the words? Further enlightenment from his expression was almost impossible while wearing aspirators.

'Not at all. It's great to have you back,' replied Parish, smiling at her reassuringly while trying to get his head around the situation. He hadn't been any help to her before, and she had done nothing wrong. Maybe now he could do something to make amends and put that right. 'Maybe we should get together for dinner or something, chat about the old times,' said Parish.

'Maybe,' replied Gerry, making direct eye contact with Parish and smiling discreetly but looking for some reaction that might help her out. She was not entirely sure what that meant either. Parish was still finding his way.

'So, what do we have,' asked Parish, reverting to a more formal tone? Gerry lifted the aspirator from her face. The whole conversation up to that point had been slightly stilted - it was not easy to read facial expressions through a mask.

'You can take those off now,' instructed Gerry. 'We've analysed and recycled all the air from the top two floors and just finishing the ground floor. The basement will be finished later, but I don't think we will find much down there that will be useful to you.' They gave their aspirators to one of the passing techies, who looked decidedly disgruntled for being treated like a servant.

Parish felt vulnerable for a few moments; it was as if their feelings had been protected by the masks, hidden, as so much is, behind a forensic hijab. But now, with them removed, their faces were naked and could be easily read.

'Well, as always, this is purely a preliminary theory, but I think she was possibly kneeling about here.' Geraldine positioned herself facing the bed with her back to the window behind the main bloodstain.

'She was facing her assailant....' She pointed at Heart with her index finger and smiled at him; they, too, were old friends. Then, she beckoned him to come over and stand before her. Geraldine was nearly ten centimetres taller than Heart but almost sixty centimetres shorter when she knelt down.

'And again, assuming the sword is the murder weapon.' She pointed at the rough shape of a sword on the floor. 'And, I have no reason at this time to think otherwise, then she was struck from the front with one single blow.' She gestured to Heart to recreate a sword-swinging action from his right to left, which he did in slow motion.

'The blow would have neatly severed the head, which landed around there.' Gerry pointed to a spot on the carpet about two metres away, just in front of the door to the en-suite bathroom, where there was a large stain. 'There was a final expulsion of blood from the severed artery, which hit the ceiling before the heart shut down. She would have needed to be looking upwards at her assailant to achieve the correct incision angle on the neck. That leads me to surmise that she was actively participating in the

120

decapitation and aware of what was happening. But, for some reason, she was unable or disinclined to do anything about it. There is no evidence she was restrained in any way.'

'So,' she actually looked the killer in the face as he…?' suggested Heart.

'Yes, I think so,' replied Gerry.

'Pleading for her life?' suggested Heart.

'No. I don't think so,' said Gerry. 'If she was, why weren't there any defence wounds to her hands? There is no evidence of a struggle, so she probably knew her assailant. When someone comes at you with a sword, the natural reaction is to put your arms up to protect your head.' Gerry threw her arms upwards, and Heart acknowledged the point.

'Could she have been struck from behind?' asked Parish for no reason, but no sooner had the words left his lips than he knew it was a stupid question. His mind was still trawling over the past and not concentrating on the matter at hand.

Gerry thought about it for a few seconds, deciding to humour him for a moment.

'She could have been standing up,' Gerry continued tentatively, 'and struck from behind.' But then her assailant would have to be left-handed or ambidextrous to have made such a tidy job of it, and the blood spatter pattern doesn't work quite so well. Oh, and she would still have to have been looking up at the ceiling for some reason. The assailant would also have to have been considerably shorter than her, possibly by about sixty centimetres or more.'

'A midget, maybe,' suggested Heart, looking at Parish quizzically, but Parish did not respond.

'Maybe not from behind, then? Just thought I should explore every avenue,' replied Parish apologetically.

'The angle of entry incision and exit skin tears virtually confirm a right-handed person, but I haven't examined the head in detail yet. So, I won't be able to confirm that until later.'

'Executed professionally then?' inquired Parish.

'Possibly,' said Gerry. 'It was all very neat, very precise, almost clinical. Whoever carried this out must have done this before... and had lots of practice. She flashed a quizzical expression at Parish. I don't think anybody could be this competent on their first attempt.' That thought sent a chill down Heart's spine.

'Do you know that when they executed Mary Queen of Scots, the executioner had to have three goes? The first one missed her neck completely, nearly cut her arm off, and split her back open. The second attempt split her head almost into two. Only by chance did he succeed with the third attempt. The neck's precise position was no longer visible, with exposed tissue and blood spurting everywhere. It was an absolute cock-up of an execution. The media guys were so pissed off with all the bad press they got that they executed the executioner the next day, and a bloody good job too.'

'So, he literally got the chop?' Chirped in Heart, much to the amusement of the other two techies in the room. Gerry and Parish half smiled, but their minds were on other things.

Gerry flipped through a few pages on her tablet. 'There was a dress in the washing machine when we arrived. We've retrieved it, but I don't expect we'll find much to help you. Unfortunately, it appears to have completed a full cycle.'

'Why did he or she put the dress in the washing machine if the victim was naked when she was killed?' asked Parish.

'No idea,' said Gerry. 'Possibly, it was contaminated with something from the assailant, hair, body fluids, fibres, or fingerprints, but it's probably gone now. Maybe he helped her take it off,' she ventured. 'Anyway, she was moved onto the bed and arranged about twenty minutes after death, after being fully exsanguinated.'

'Exsanguinated?' repeated Parish almost in a whisper; the word had always fascinated him.

'It means...' Heart started to say, remembering the word from a crossword he had completed a few weeks ago, but Parish interrupted him.

'I know what it means, thank you,' replied Parish condescendingly, throwing a dismissive glare at Heart that nearly burnt his ears off.

Gerry glanced at Parish, a little startled by his abrupt tone. His expression said nothing, so she continued without comment.

'She is.... was about thirty to thirty-five years of age, possibly of Lithuanian extraction. Our computer records indicate a discrepancy in that detail. As you can see, she is a natural blonde. She died between one and three o'clock this morning. I'm afraid I can't be more precise about the time of death until after the postmortem examination. The central heating was flat out when we got here. So, the body temperature was higher than it would have been under normal circumstances. Couldn't use the head temperature because it had been sitting in cold water. Oh, one other thing...'

'Yes,' said Parish.

'She was pregnant - about three months, I would guess. I'll be able to be more precise about the gestational age after the post-mortem.'

'Pregnant,' repeated Parish as if it were something rare. Gerry nodded.

'That is interesting,' he said but didn't elaborate. 'Where is the victim's head, by the way?' He looked tentatively around the room for signs of its whereabouts.

'Oh, that's still in the toilet,' said Gerry in the casual, matter-of-fact manner you might use at a dinner party to ask someone to pass the salt.

'The toilet!' exclaimed Parish with surprise. 'Why haven't you moved it?'

'Thought you might like to see it as we found it, *in situ* as it were, before we bag it up. It's through here.'

Parish felt a rather unpleasant tickle in his stomach when she said, 'bag it up.' Gerry walked into the en-suite bathroom, followed reluctantly by Parish and Heart. All three peered simultaneously down into the toilet bowl to inspect the head facing up at them.

'That's very odd,' said Parish, not elaborating further.

'I thought it was a bit ironic, really,' remarked Gerry. 'It's almost as if the killer is sending out some sort of pagan allegorical challenge.'

'Allegorical,' repeated Heart?

'Symbolism,' explained Parish. 'It's like a message.' Heart half-smiled

'What, a head in the toilet?' said Heart, not grasping the gesture's significance. From the other side of the bathroom, a techie who was clearing up listened in quiet amusement at this peculiar conversation played out by three people staring into a toilet bowl.

'Well, get this one wrong, and that is where your careers will be,' remarked Gerry sardonically.

'Oddly enough, Heart has already done that one,' said Parish humorously.

'Years ago, they used to stick the heads of traitors on poles outside the Tower of London as a warning to others,' said Gerry.

'Did they?' said Parish. They all raised their heads simultaneously; it was beginning to look like synchronised apple bobbing.

'Attractive,' said Heart, still admiring the head from an upright position.

'Bit late for a date unless you....' Gerry went no further.   'Not my type anyway,' said Heart. Gerry and Parish looked at each other but didn't say anything.

'Pretty green eyes, no earrings,' remarked Parish.

'No earrings. Didn't find any jewellery at all, and her hair was damp.

'Did he flush the toilet?' asked Heart.

'Possibly,' replied Gerry. 'But I don't think that made her hair damp. Most of her head was above the water level. However, we did find traces of urine on her, which could match the unregistered visitor who had sex with her.'

'He pissed on her,' exclaimed Parish?

'So, it would appear,' said Gerry. 'We are checking the DNA, which should tell us one way or the other.'

'But why do that,' said Heart, 'if he'd already killed her?'

'She must have seriously pissed him off,' said Parish thinking out aloud. The pun was unintentional; he didn't immediately realise what he had said. Heart and Gerry looked at him oddly, and the penny dropped.

'Sorry, I didn't mean it quite like that. I meant that...'
They both nodded. There was nothing more to be said.

'So, it is a he already,' said Gerry? Heart looked at Parish, having realised they had both spontaneously opted for the male option again.

'Well, it starts to look that way, and anyway, a woman would have to sit on the pan,' said Parish. He started to adopt the position of a woman having a pee, but Heart pulled him back.

'Somehow, I don't think a woman would do that, and anyway, the head was sticking up too far. Also, it would have made it uncomfortable with her nose sticking up.' Heart couldn't help but snigger like a naughty schoolboy.

'Not necessary,' said Gerry, who was not amused. She could have done it this way.' She faced the loo and positioned herself over the pan, standing up. 'You see – like this.' Heart and Parish both looked on in astonishment.

'You just have to buy a P-mate tube. I'm told it's very liberating.' She gestured as if she were holding a tiny penis. She glanced at Parish with a smirk.

'I have never seen a woman pee like that,' said Parish, a little astonished.

'You should get out more,' replied Gerry with a wink and a shake of her pretend penis.

Heart smiled, and Parish looked at both of them, slightly dismayed by this revelation. Gerry thought it was time to stop jesting and get back to the more salient aspects of the murder.

'Anyway, the three suspect air scans are male, so statistically, it's a reasonable bet that the killer was one of them,' said Gerry.

'But just now you said it could be....' queried Parish,

Gerry smiled. 'We can, but it doesn't mean we do. Anyway, a woman would have to be extremely strong and skilful. The victim was approximately five feet ten inches high with good muscle definition – almost athletic,' said Gerry.

'She did get plenty of exercise,' suggested Heart. Gerry glanced at him but said nothing.

'Obviously, I can't be more precise until I have…' her voice trailed off.

Parish nodded his head, acknowledging what Gerry was referring to.

'So, unless you have an eighteen-stone female Amazonian weightlifter in the frame, then I think it's a man,' continued Gerry.

'How long before we get the semen cross-match with the air scans?'

'Not long. I'll check in a minute,' replied Gerry.

'What do you think?' Parish asked Heart.

'Some kind of ritual thing, but I don't understand the Japanese connection if she is Romanian, Hungarian or Asian. It could be drug-related, I suppose… Russian mafia?'

'DNA scan confirms Lithuanian,' said Gerry. 'Probably second generation, though.'

'Which means?' asked Parish.

'Depleted European gene pool, so probably just one parent or grandparent – or possibly even further back – was originally from Lithuania, and the other parent was English.'

'Right,' said Parish.

'I don't understand the head down the pan bit; all very strange. Still, if we get a semen-air match, we could tidy this up before teatime,' said Heart.

'In my experience, there's a good chance that the last man to have sex with her probably killed her,' said Parish.

'So, you definitely ruled out necrophilia,' asked Gerry, tongue in cheek.

'Well, she'd probably still be livelier than some of the women Heart has known,' replied Parish glibly, which was strangely a little out of character for him. Heart, however, acknowledged the caustic comment with a nod and smile. It was beginning to turn into a Laurel and Hardy sketch.

Parish's throwaway quips occasionally provided an unintentional Freudian insight into a pre-emancipation mindset. Reminiscent of an age before sexual egalitarianism.

'Too much information for me,' said Gerry, glancing at Parish admonishingly before walking back into the hall to talk to one of the techies.

'Sorry, sorry,' replied Parish sheepishly as she walked away, *but not with any genuine conviction.*

'So, it could still be Aiden Hawsley,' asked Heart.

'Can't see it,' replied Parish. 'He might have been having sex with her, but why kill her? He could have had her deregistered and dumped in the Ghettazone in a flash.

'And never heard of her again,' added Heart.

'Quite,' said Parish, 'and he wouldn't have had to bother with all this crap.'

Aiden Hawsley had formulated much of his political dogma and social policies around a fundamental Nietzsche premise. The framework for a perfect society should be based on a totalitarian control system without the encumbrances of God or religion. He considered both vacuous, pointless, and problematical once the discipline of existential logic was applied. In reality, faith and religion in most civilised countries had already been supplanted by holavision, which was now the definitive moral compass of the proletarian masses. God was now all-seeing, all-powerful in glorious 3D and available in every room.

'What if he was the last to have sex with her?' asked Heart.

'Let's wait and see,' replied Parish. Gerry walked back into the bathroom.

'We've completed the DNA air scan and semen cross-matching,' Gerry read from her tablet.

'Benny Maranno had sex with her, and we have his DNA everywhere. The air scan puts Aiden Hawsley here, but he did not have sex with her or touch the body, and there is no DNA evidence to link him to the body or the crime scene. A third unknown suspect had sex with her, and we have his DNA all over the place and on her body, but he did not leave any air scan evidence.'

'So,' said Parish, 'we have two definite maybes, one of which has DNA not recorded on the database and one possible maybe with Aiden Hawsley, but he didn't have sex with her?'

'Not as far as we can ascertain now,' replied Gerry. 'There's no forensic evidence to connect Hawsley to the victim or the murder. Just the fact that he was in the room at some point in the last twelve hours.'

Gerry sounded almost disappointed that she could only report the evidence as she found it - cautiously reluctant about offering any further opinion in the current surroundings. Parish was well aware of her personal views on Mr Hawsley.

'So,' said Parish, recapping. 'She died between 1am and 3am, and the scans confirmed she had sex with Maranno and one other suspect between 9.20 pm and when she died. And there is indisputable evidence that Hawsley was here during that period.'

'Yes,' replied Gerry. 'That about sums it up.'

'Do we know in what order she had sex?'

'Yes, the semen decay puts Maranno first, then the unknown suspect. There was evidence of earlier sex with two other people, but that was before 9.20 pm – probably a couple of hours before.'

'So, let me get this clear,' asked Parish. 'Hypothetically, she had sex at, say, 7pm and then at 8pm and then with Maranno at, let's say, 10pm. And then with the unknown suspect, let's call him Mr X, at 12am, and then she was killed around... let's say 2am. Is that all reasonable?'

'That's a lot of sex?' said Heart, 'four times in one night.'

'It's doable,' replied Gerry, 'and that's about it for now, except for one other oddity. Dhalia Vingali is not her real name – it's Rose Watson. That came up on the DNA scan.'

'Rose Watson. Well, that sort of rules out the Asian theory,' mumbled Heart.

'I wonder why she changed her name,' said Parish.

'Maybe she thought she could charge more with an exotic-sounding name,' replied Heart.

'Maybe,' said Parish thoughtfully. 'Anything else?'

'Nothing worth worrying about. I'll be able to give you more information and a toxicology report tomorrow after I've done the post-mortem. I'm sure that will help.' Gerry smiled at Parish reassuringly.

'Hope so,' replied Parish, deep in thought. 'Can we get a DNA sample from the foetus?'

'Yes,' replied Gerry, 'but that won't help in establishing who killed her. Just possibly who the father is... was,' she corrected herself, 'well, still is, I suppose.'

'So, we have Hawsley, Maranno and this unknown person. Do we know anything about him yet?' asked Parish.

'Nothing yet. Oh, but there is something else you should see,' added Gerry. Parish looked a little anxious, but Gerry smiled, alleviating his concerns.

'It's back here.' She led Parish and Heart back into the bedroom. Set into the wall about one metre from the floor was a fine mesh grill - there was another in the ceiling. On the wall grill, there were some controls.

'That,' said Gerry, pointing at the grill. 'What do you think?'

'I don't know,' said Parish. 'Looks like air conditioning to me.'

'Well, that's what we thought to start with,' replied Gerry with a hint of intrigue in her voice. 'Something to do with an air conditioning system anyway, but then one of the techies looked a little closer, and guess what? It's a DNA air scrub unit.' She glanced at Parish to see whether he knew what that was.

'A what?' said Parish. She was right. He didn't.

'An air scrub-wash system for cleaning the contaminated air,' explained Gerry.

'But who would want one of those?' asked Heart.

'Well, quite a lot of people, actually,' replied Gerry. 'But they tend to use a more sophisticated version. For example, there's one in your police station, and we use one in our pathology lab and the mortuary.'

'But where would you get one of those?' asked Parish curiously.

'Now that is a good question,' replied Gerry, 'and I don't know the answer, not for a domestic model anyways.'

'Ideal for a crime scene where there might be incriminating DNA evidence?' suggested Heart.

'Absolutely,' replied Gerry. 'But as to where you might buy one, you can't. Not without a licence.'

'So how did she get one?' asked Heart.

'No idea,' replied Gerry.

'What exactly does it do?' asked Parish, still very curious.'

'Well, it filters, scrubs and washes the air, removing all impurities in a fixed environment,' explained Gerry. 'It simply removes all airborne matter and leaves clean, fresh air devoid of contamination and, more importantly, DNA.'

'So, it's a posh air-con unit?' asked Heart.

'In a manner of speaking, I suppose you could call it that,' replied Gerry, smiling. She paused for a second. 'You don't hear that much anymore, do you?'

'What? Aircon unit?' replied Heart, a little puzzled,

'No, posh,' said Gerry. 'It's one of those words that has fallen out of popular use over the last few years. It's funny how some words stop being used one day but still bring back memories. My gran used to have a posh frock for special occasions; she always talked about it. She would wear it every Christmas and on her birthday. My mum used to have some *posh* china that she would suddenly produce from God knows where whenever relatives came for tea. After they had gone, it would disappear again.'

'Bit like my bike, then,' said Heart.

'You use a bike?' enquired Gerry, a little bemused by the thought of Heart riding a bicycle.

'No. Not anymore, I don't. It disappeared years ago. Somebody nicked it.' Heart looked genuinely saddened by his loss.

'Oh,' said Parish, trying to appear empathetic but only managing confusion. It went noticeably quiet for a second or two. Parish and Gerry tried to contain their laughter. They weren't sure why they both found Heart's comment amusing, but they did. They still laughed at the same things... that was something.

Gerry continued with her explanation. 'Air-con units re-circulate the air after cooling or heating it. They clean it through an elementary carbon mesh filter; it's all very rudimentary. This unit, however, does something quite different. It cleans the air through a complex water and chemical filtration system. It removes every impurity and pumps it back into the same area without changing the temperature. Air-con units destroy some of the airborne evidence and affect our DNA air scan results' integrity - but not all. But more importantly,' continued Gerry, 'this device removes all trace of airborne DNA and any other pollution, nuclear, chemical, or biological,' explained Gerry.

'So why didn't it bugger up your DNA air scans?' asked Parish, sounding confused.

'Another good question, and the simple answer is - this one isn't working. Somebody had disconnected it,' replied Gerry. 'It's imported, which is unusual, and it can't be more than two or three years old. We've only had the DNA air-scan technology for the last three years, so this is a very sophisticated toy for a prostitute.

'So why are they used in police stations?' asked Heart.

'Absolutely essential to avoid cross-contamination between suspects, investigating officers, techies, and me, etcetera. For instance, if you were to go back to the station now and pull Hawsley in, he could say that as you had been to the crime scene and inhaled some of the air at the scene. Then you returned to the station and entered the interrogation room where he was being held; you could have exhaled some air. Some of which could contain airborne particles of DNA from the victim and the perpetrator at the crime scene. Therefore, you could have contaminated the air that he is breathing and the clothes he is wearing. *Ipso facto,* you have contaminated an innocent party.'

'Sounds extremely implausible to me,' remarked Parish.

'It is,' replied Gerry, 'in fact, it's virtually impossible. But the seed of doubt has now been planted. Any barrister worth his salt would make the jury aware of the forensic evidence's fallibility, which placed the suspect at the crime scene. So any conviction could be deemed unsafe.' Parish sighed at the explanation.

'And' continued Gerry, 'on top of that, if you returned to the crime scene, you could re-contaminate it again simply by expelling air from your lungs.'

'Sounds a bit like we're as buggered as a pretty camel in Kabul,' mumbled Heart. Gerry and Parish looked at each other with amused disbelief at this odd analogy. They both went to say something but could not find the right words, so nothing left their lips.

'So how exactly does the air scan equipment work?' asked Parish, still pondering the camel's fate.

'By analysing microscopic particles of exhaled vaporised carbon dioxide at floor level,' replied Gerry.

'There are millions of miniscule air bubbles exhaled every time you breathe out, and each one contains the DNA of the exhaler. Each bubble is slightly heavier than air, so initially, it drops nearer to the ground. However, through a process known as diffusion, the bubbles eventually decay, and the CO_2 remixes vertically with the atmosphere over approximately twelve hours. Any movement of air accelerates the remixing process. That is why the first few hours are so important. The integrity of the air scan depended largely on relatively tiny amounts of movement in a room. Once mixed, it is almost impossible to un-mix it. That's why the techies have been so successful at doing your job over the last few years as long as they get to the crime scene in the requisite time frame.'

'Sounds to me like we've got too clever for our own good,' added Heart.

'Well, I suppose we have a bit,' replied Gerry. 'We managed to develop the DNA scan technology, but of course, that also meant there was a higher possibility of detecting cross-contamination of airborne evidence. Something that we would never have encountered before because we weren't looking for it – we didn't know how to. So now we can find it, we have more evidence to prove a case, but so have the defence lawyers to disprove it.'

'So, it's back to square one?' asked Heart.

'Not quite,' replied Gerry reassuringly. 'We had a case kicked out a year ago based on that precise argument, which is why we had the air scrub units fitted in all police stations to stop the problem recurring.'

'So, we don't have a problem?' said Parish, sounding a little concerned and desperately seeking reassurance that there wasn't a technical problem with the evidence.

'No problem at all,' confirmed Gerry. 'I just mentioned it because a highly sophisticated filtration system is fitted here. Which is a little unusual, apart from being illegal. I thought you should know about it. Of course, had it been working, we would not have extracted anything from the air scans – just fresh, clean, unpolluted air.' Gerry flashed Parish a pixie grin.

'What about the semen in her body? That's incontrovertible evidence, isn't it?' asked Heart.

'A good brief could still say it was planted maliciously by someone trying to discredit the suspect. Without a supporting positive air scan, you would still be hard-pressed to prove he had ever been here,' replied Gerry. 'Anyway, the suspect could have had sex with her somewhere else, which meant she could still have managed to get home presumably intact.'

'But we are okay, aren't we?' asked Parish, looking a little unsure of exactly where that left them.

'Yes, I think so,' confirmed Gerry. 'So far, that is. The DNA air scan places three people at the scene in the right time frame. You just have to work out which one did it.'

'That's a definite?' asked Parish.

'It's a definite maybe,' qualified Gerry. 'For now, it is, anyway; I'll speak to you after I've completed the autopsy tomorrow.'

'Right,' said Parish. Gerry and Heart left the room, talking about air scan units. Parish turned to Zac, one of the senior techies busy packing up one of the last pieces of SOC equipment.

'Zac, have you anything else that might help?'

'We'll be checking her computer for the usual stuff. We didn't find any other records, so hopefully, her client list will be on the computer. I have requested phone records and all the bank information and should be able to give you a full report by close of play tomorrow. By the way, we didn't find a mobile phone.' Parish went to turn away, then turned back.

'Zac?'

'Yes,' replied Zac, smiling.

I don't suppose there are any CCTV cameras?'

'No. I haven't seen any, but I will have a look in the street before I leave.'

'Good, good,' said Parish, repeating himself. He paused briefly to mull over everything that had happened so far.

'Heart!' shouted Parish, bursting back into life. Heart was in the other bedroom with Gerry.

'Yes, guv,' replied Heart, returning to the main bedroom.

'Right, who do we have here to interview?' Heart looked at his tablet.

'The housekeeper who found the body is downstairs. The waiter who brings her food works in a restaurant just around the corner. I've rung him, and he said to come at any time, and the doctor said he would be in all day.'

'Right, I'll talk to the housekeeper; you can pop next door and talk to the quack. I will meet you back here later, and we can walk to the restaurant and talk to the waiter.'

'Whatever you say, guv,' replied Heart. They walked back down the staircase, and Parish stopped again to admire one of the paintings. Something dark about it had caught his attention, but he couldn't quite grasp what it was. When they arrived back on the ground floor, they could see the housekeeper was still talking to one of the techies in the kitchen. So Parish gestured to Heart that he would step outside for five minutes to get some air. He needed to clear his head.

Chapter 8
Catherine and Janice, 2023

The telephone rang in the kitchen, but the caller's identity did not appear on the screen. Catherine seldom answered the phone unless she knew the caller or they were already on the call register. This was something that had been religiously instilled into her by Parish. He had a phobia about telephone calls from unknown sources, always believing they heralded unwelcome news. For this reason, he refused to answer one without caller ID. He could be right next to the phone when it rang, but if a name didn't appear in the display window, he would ignore it and let Catherine or Jade answer it. This, they found exasperating.

He rigidly maintained that no one would phone him from work on the landline, so it was never for him anyway, and he was annoyingly right most of the time. However, there were occasional moments of great glee and amusement when someone did phone for him, and they handed him the telephone with bubbling self-righteous indignation. Catherine was reluctantly beginning to adopt the same approach. The anonymous calls were increasingly inconsequential, time-wasting sales dribblers or friends of Jade enquiring about her whereabouts because her mobile was not charged. This was either because it had a flat battery (which happened quite often), or she had left it at a friend's house, and they were calling to tell her where it was, which also occurred quite a lot. However, for some inexplicable reason, Catherine answered it on this occasion.

'Catherine… it's Janice Watson - how are you?'

'Oh, my god!' exclaimed Catherine, bursting out with surprise, 'Janni Watson! Christ, we haven't spoken since....' In a puzzling paradox, Catherine had instantly abbreviated Janice's Christian name despite always making it perfectly clear that she hated other people shortening hers.

'..Since I left university nearly sixteen years ago,' answered Janice with a hint of regret. She sounded pleased to be talking to Catherine.

'Where have you been,' asked Catherine? It was a woman's question, one that was cleverly asking so much more but without appearing to pry. 'I tried to get hold of you after you left, but you just disappeared.'

'Things happened,' replied Janice in a quieter tone. 'Life, you know...' she hesitated. 'What about you?'

'I stayed on to the bitter end,' replied Catherine. 'I managed to qualify... just.'

'Bet you passed with flying colours. I'm glad you got what you wanted. You deserved it,' replied Janice, sounding genuinely pleased. 'I knew you would.'

'But so, did you,' replied Catherine, still trying to piece together the past. 'What happened? I don't remember you telling me. You just weren't there one day, and....'

'My mum died,' Janice interrupted. 'That's why I left. She looked after Rose, so I had to leave and look after and protect her and....'

Catherine interrupted as the details slowly trickled back into her mind. 'Your daughter, of course, from....' She paused for a few seconds as the mist of hazy memories began to clear, and the landscape of their university life slowly came back into focus. Then something else she'd entirely forgotten about sprang back to mind.

'The rape.' Janice finished Catherine's sentence, still sounding as cold, blunt, and clinical about the attack now as she did back then. She always spoke of the ordeal objectively, trying to put distance between it and her. It was as if someone else's cancer had been cut away. It was, in a way, but with cancer, it either kills you or you get over it? You stop thinking about it every waking moment. But it's still there, always there as a distant memory, something you encountered, but something you overcame and conquered. Eventually, it does become part of the past, and you move on. The devil that you had smitten down before you rode on to Camelot.

But with rape, it's different. It's there all the time, slowly eating away at you. Only retribution and vengeance can kill this cancer. The loss of control and the annexation of your body, which you cannot resist, creates immense anguish and torment. Sometimes, a memory can be hidden in a box, discreetly tucked away in the back of your mind. But it's never really forgotten, never completely gone.

If only she could put a name and a face to the person who had done this to her. He had not only left her pregnant, feeling wretched and worthless, but so physically damaged she was unable to bear any more children. He had effectively stolen her life, and she carried this emotional baggage, humiliation, and shame into any new relationship. Maybe she could come to terms with it one day, but not knowing who he was meant it could still be any man she met. A man she encountered casually in the street passing a kind word. The man in the SCOMTEL shop – smiling and selling her a lottery ticket. The jovial computer licencing inspector who came every year, always with a funny story to tell. They were all the same to her... Suspects! And that is what all men would ever be. She could never maintain a permanent relationship, for that would have invariably led to the intimacy she so feared. She would never be able to trust anyone except for her daughter Rose and now Catherine again, but never another man, not until she knew...

That was what Catherine remembered most, talking into the small hours of so many mornings. Trying to find a way for Janice to come to terms with what had happened, but they never could. That night had left immeasurable and irreparable damage. Too much to ever be wholly obliterated. The scars of the brutal assault were burnt too profoundly onto the battlefield of Janice's body and mind. The same scars her great-grandmother carried from when she was raped by an invading German officer in 1942. Her grandmother was the progeny of that rape. Now, the result of another violation, Janice's daughter carried the victim's curse forward again. But why had they been singled out... that's what she didn't understand.

'It's okay, you can say the word. I'm used to it now. Anyway, enough of that,' said Janice, now sounding uncharacteristically cheerful. 'In fact, having Rose and watching her grow daily has made it bearable. All these years, the one redeeming feature and the only consolation was a paradox. The living evidence of the worst thing that ever happened to me and the best thing that ever happened. Each completely and utterly dependent on the other, and I can't have one without the other, so I live with them both and get on with life... and that's why I'm calling you.'

'Oh,' said Catherine, a little taken aback by Janice's unexpectedly self-assured and seemingly contented disposition.

'I was wondering if we could meet sometime and catch up on all you've done. I could tell you everything that's happened to me. I need to talk to someone I can trust, and you're the only one I've ever told about what happened that night apart from the police.' Janice paused to gauge Catherine's reaction, wary of proceeding too far. She waited anxiously for the inevitable polite excuse or hint of hesitancy. Some indication that would mean they had moved on too far to return to how they were. She had prepared herself for that and was half expecting it, but nothing came.

'Of course, that would be great. Look, where are you,' asked Catherine, sounding so genuinely pleased that it immediately lifted Janice's spirits and made her smile. But then Catherine had always managed to do that. Even in Janice's darkest hours, she had always been there, loyal, reliable and supportive. Now, she felt embarrassed, having cut herself off from her friend for so long without good reason. But now that was over, they would meet up and renew an old friendship. A friendship that had been neglected for far too long.

'Over on the Southern Quarter Quay,' replied Janice. Catherine flitted through her phone diary and found an available day.

'What about Thursday?' asked Catherine. 'I work in the morning but could be away by 12.30, so say 1pm in Costa coffee on the front near the tower. Would that be okay? We could have lunch.'

'Sounds great,' replied Janice. 'It will be lovely to see you again.' She knew she shouldn't have left it for so long, but there was no point in fretting now.

'You too,' said Catherine. 'See you Thursday. Love you, love you.' Catherine had gotten into the habit of using those closing words as a throwaway line at the end of every phone conversation. Although, in one way, the cliché devalues the currency in which we all trade, in this case, it enhanced its value - for Catherine sincerely meant it. Theirs was a friendship that would last a lifetime, no matter what happened...

'Love you too, and thank you, thank you so much. Bye,' said Janice, touching her phone. Catherine replaced her receiver and thought about those last words. Later that evening, the words came back to her once again. Something about the phrasing puzzled her. *Thank you;* why did she say thank you? It just didn't sound quite right, almost inappropriate. Maybe she was reading something into a few innocuous words uttered slightly out of context. She thought no more about it that day.

On Thursday, Catherine arrived at the café a little earlier than arranged and sat outside after ordering a decaf Americano. She looked out over the harbour, watching the sailing yachts struggling to make headway, becalmed by an indolent wind. *Artemis, the goddess of the hunt, wasn't feeling particularly friendly today - disinclined to send the wind the warriors of the sea so desperately desired. Maybe a sailor had killed a wild hare somewhere, and somebody would have to be sacrificed before the ships could set sail... somebody always had to be sacrificed.*

Catherine had been daydreaming for maybe ten minutes when she heard her name being called. 'Cathy,' said Janice quietly. Catherine turned sideways and saw a woman smiling in her direction. She immediately recognised her, with her shoulder-length, blonde curly hair still as vivacious as ever. The years suddenly seemed to fade away, and they were back having a coffee between lectures on campus. Catherine stood up to greet her, and they kissed and held each other tightly. The bond from all those years ago was still intact. They sat down, smiling at each other, unsure what to say for the first few moments until the waiter interrupted them and asked them what they would like. They ordered more coffee and paninis and began.

'So how have you been, and what are you doing?' asked Catherine. 'Tell me all about your life?'

'Let's talk about you first,' asked Janice. 'All the nice things, anyway. You're married, aren't you?'

'Yes, how did you know?' asked Catherine, a little intrigued.

'The internet still worked when you got married. Don't you remember Goggle and Twaddle?' said Janice, smiling. 'That's what you renamed Facebook and Twitter. You used to love using them when we were at uni.'

'Yes, I did, didn't I? I've completely forgotten about all those social networking websites. They were so morally reprehensible, corrupt and iniquitous. I didn't realise it at the time. I'm glad they've gone,' replied Catherine. Contemptuous in her condemnation of the invasive banality of a technological phase that had come and gone not soon enough as far as she was concerned. 'Hawsley was right on that one.'

'My God, you've become one of his apparatchiks,' replied Janice, astonished at Catherine's apparent change of political allegiance. 'You were always a left-wing socialist.'

'Well, I wouldn't go quite that far, but he's okay.' She nodded from side to side as a gesture of mild indifference. Things are much safer now he's in control,' remarked Catherine with surprising conviction. 'Would you want to share everything you have with Glundes?' Janice didn't answer immediately.

Catherine's reverential support for Aiden Hawsley was something she had not expected. She was perfectly aware that without constructing the walled provinces in 2015, anarchy and civil war would have enveloped everybody, and nothing would have been left. Separatism, paired with elitism, was a socially unattractive philosophy but essential for future survival.

'But he's a bloody right-wing extremist! A social engineer, for Christ's sake... He's practically a fascist dictator!' exclaimed Janice jokingly.

'Only a little bit, though,' replied Catherine, pursing her lips. 'Better than being a namby-pamby, cabbage-sucking, left-wing, flag-waving, pig-eyed, sheep-shagging commie sympathiser,' whispered Catherine with faux venom. Janice nearly peed herself.

'I read that somewhere. Good, isn't it?' said Catherine. She smiled, and they both fell about laughing at her political conversion. At university, they would spend endless nights arguing the jurisprudence of politics, the incalculable geometry of chance, and how it would affect all their lives. How little did they know then how much their lives would eventually be changed by chance? Evenings were never more enjoyable than when they had university boyfriends who could so easily be baited with convoluted, obtuse, and controversial opinions on almost everything.

'I remember seeing some pictures a few years back, on Goggle, I think, of a daughter?' Janice ventured cautiously. The general public's internet service had been closed since 2016; many things were no longer universally broadcast. Personal information was now conveniently vague, sometimes simply unavailable and often outdated. Fortunately, this meant that, to a small degree, elements of personal privacy had been recaptured. Returned to Pandora's box - but the state security service still had full access to all information.

'Yes, I have a daughter,' confirmed Catherine. 'Her name is Jade, and she's nearly thirteen, going on seventeen, and she is gorgeous, like her mother, of course.' They both smiled at Catherine's self-appraisal, but there was no hint of arrogance or conceit, just a mother's maternal pride in her offspring. Catherine was beautiful. There was no denying that, and inevitably, Jade would be just as beautiful. The mention of her daughter brought happy thoughts to mind, and she smiled to herself.

'We are a bit like how you and I used to be,' said Catherine. She smiled again, held out her hands to take hold of Janice's and clasped them tightly for a few seconds.

'I bet she doesn't nick your bras,' said Janice, trying to avoid becoming too emotional. They both laughed, and Catherine took a sip of coffee, and the moment passed.

'I miss you so much,' said Catherine. Her expression changed for a few seconds, replaced by something more profound. A tenacious unity of two friends had reformed, something that would never be broken again except by death. At last, Janice felt a sense of belonging, something she had not experienced for a long time; Catherine was a friend she could trust and depend on.

'I miss you too,' replied Janice. 'So, tell me, what do you do? I presume you work in a hospital or doctor's surgery now?' She knew she didn't, and the slight deceit unnerved her little. She felt a cold shiver tingle down her back. They had only just renewed a bond, and already she had betrayed the trust.

'Well, no, actually. I qualified, but then Jade was born, not quite to plan, and I wanted to be at home with her, so I never practised full time. I work part-time in path lab now, just mornings.'

'Dead people,' said Janice, surprised?

'They don't complain quite so much,' replied Catherine glibly. 'I look after my husband, who works for the Police Department – he's very much alive, but he does complain a bit.'

Janice smiled.

'And then there's Jade, our daughter. Yes, I've become very domesticated - almost a Stepford Wife.' She smiled, tongue-in-cheek at her self-deprecating quip, and they both laughed aloud.

'He's a detective inspector, isn't he?' enquired Janice curiously.

'Yes... how did you know that?' asked Catherine, 'you're remarkably well informed.'

'Oh, I just kept up with the news. I think somebody told me, or I read something. You were always the one that was going somewhere. I just liked to see that you were doing well.'

'Enough about me. What about you? What have you been doing?' asked Catherine.

'Well, I'm not married, and Rose, she's nearly twenty-two now, can you believe that? She has her own business, something to do with the media. I don't understand it, but she makes lots of money. She lives in a lovely house in Chelsea. She even has a lady who works for her to keep the house clean and tidy.'

Janice was incredibly proud of that detail. She had distant memories of her mother, Tatiana, working as a cleaner. Her mother was twenty-four when she left the small village in Lithuania, where she was born, to come to England for a better life. Tatiana had become pregnant with Janice in nineteen eighty-six after a one-night affair. She was still naively innocent about the more liberated European attitudes to sex and had suffered the consequences. Janice was born in 1987. They lived in a council flat in Hounslow, surviving on housing benefits and social security until Janice started school. That was when her mother started domestic cleaning work for an agency.

Janice had gone to work with her mother on most Saturdays from the age of seven. The drudgery of cleaning other people's houses at such an early age left an indelible scar. This spawned a compulsion to work hard at school with the hope of finding better-paid employment than her mother had ever managed. She would find other part-time jobs when she wasn't working with Tatiana on a Saturday. It was at one of these Saturday jobs in 2001 while helping to distribute political leaflets for the British National Party that Janice's life changed so dramatically. She was invited to a party where one of the men was celebrating a minor political promotion. She was drugged, raped, and became pregnant, and her dreams of a better life would have started to slip away had it not been for her mother. Despite having the child, a girl she called Rose, Janice carried on at school and then to university. Tatiana managed to look after Rose during the day and worked nights after Janice came home. But the strain of working nights and looking after Rose during the day eventually took its toll on Tatiana, and she died soon after.

'So, what are you doing now?' asked Catherine.

'Well, that's part of why I wanted to see you.' Janice sounded a little reticent at first. She knew that promises made in happy times could often be forgotten with the passing of years. 'I'm sorry if that sounds a bit insincere, not being in touch for yonks and then suddenly turning up unexpectedly, but I need some help, and I thought of you. We were so close at uni, and you're the only person I could turn to.'

'Friends for life, that's what we promised,' pronounced Catherine with a flourish of cheerful optimism.

'I haven't kept up my side of the promise,' said Janice apologetically.

'Ours was a bond forged in adversity,' replied Catherine, 'and it will always be there even if we don't see each other as often as we used to.' They smiled at each other. 'I remember you shared your last tin of baked beans with me when we were potless, and you lent me some knickers.'

'I don't remember you ever wearing any,' replied Janice casually. They laughed again as only real friends could laugh. They had become good friends at university and had shared lodgings for the first two years. During that time, they built a relationship they believed would last a lifetime.

'Yes, we did promise, didn't we,' replied Janice, sounding reassured and confident but also a little sombre as she moved closer towards the real business of the day. She took a deep breath and prepared herself for what might happen next...

'I managed to get a copy of the DNA report from my rape,' said Janice. The good-humoured atmosphere faded as Catherine absorbed what Janice had said.

'How did you get that?' asked Catherine, sounding surprised? She knew only too well from Parish's discussions about data protection and security that obtaining copies of case files and passing them on to third parties always resulted in instant dismissal.

'I ran into that nice detective some time ago, the one who looked after me during the investigation. We had a coffee and talked about the case. As far as he knew, the file had been closed for years and would never be reopened unless new evidence came to light. So, I asked him why they couldn't trace the man from the DNA, and he said they never found anybody on the DNA register to match it, even though they carried out a block screening.'

'Is that when they...' asked Catherine.

Janice quickly interrupted, '...took the DNA samples of everybody I could have come into contact with. Unfortunately, I couldn't remember anything because of the Rohypnol.'

'And what happened?' asked Catherine.

'He said unless the man reoffended and was arrested, then it was doubtful they would ever find him. So that's why they closed the file.'

'And?' said Catherine. She knew there was something Janice wasn't telling her.

'Well, I asked him if he could get me a copy of the file.'

'And he did!' exclaimed Catherine in amazement.

'Somewhat reluctantly,' replied Janice. 'I had to wiggle my nose a bit, but it worked.'

'As long as that's all you wiggled,' smirked Catherine playfully. 'It's against the law to bribe a police officer, you know.' They both laughed, and the slight tension that had become evident quickly disappeared again.

'Don't you ever bribe a police officer?' said Janice, with a naughty glint in her eye.

'That's different. That's for personal gratification. That's allowed, and it doesn't count anyway,' replied Catherine, laughing.

'So, you have the file, but where can you go with that? It must be the same now as then,' asked Catherine, a little unsure where this was going.

'Well, I was going to try at work first, but I can't tell them I have the file, or they might fire me. So I was wondering whether you could...' Janice hesitated momentarily. She knew this could stretch their renewed friendship to the limit. '..ask Parish to look into it for me? The security database has everybody on it that lives in a province, and it's far more up-to-date now.' She waited for an abrupt refusal, but none came. Twice, she had expected rejection from Catherine or at least a gentle rebuff - but she had received tacit, unwavering support on both occasions.

'But he might live in the Ghettazone,' replied Catherine, 'and I don't think they have any records of the people living there, and anyway, how would you find someone out there? Without any records, that is almost impossible.'

'I know,' replied Janice, gazing despondently into her cup of coffee. 'But it's all I have.'

She paused for a moment, then looked back up at Catherine. The passion in her eyes and the compelling desire for truth were so intense that Catherine could almost reach out and touch it - such was the intensity in Janice's voice. How could she refuse?

'I have to know Cathy - if it's the last thing I ever do, I have to find out who he is and confront him with what he has done to my life.' The irony of her words slipped by, lost in the momentum of the conversation. Only the lucky few have the luxury of knowing all the answers.

'But for what reason?' asked Catherine with a palpable sense of caution. 'What can possibly be gained from dredging up the past? Probably only more heartache. Wouldn't it be best to just let it be?' She spoke as someone who had also experienced deep hurt and anguish.

'I need closure before I can move on,' replied Janice. She hated how the dream doctors had hijacked the word, but it summed up exactly how she felt. 'Is that too much to ask after all this time? I am sorry.' She looked directly at Catherine with a soulful gaze. For the first time, Catherine noticed that the years had not been particularly kind, and the load Janice had carried for so long had taken its toll. The perfection of youth had gone forever, ravaged by the passing years.

'For what? You did nothing,' replied Catherine defensively, still a little confused.

'I just don't know what happened; that's the point. He, whoever he is, is the only person who knows what happened that night.' Neither of them spoke for a while, contemplating what had been said. Janice waited for an answer.

'I'll ask him - that's the least I can do. That won't hurt.' She half-smiled at Janice and thought how lucky she had been with her life and how easily they could have been sitting in opposite chairs today.

'Right, enough of the maudlin stuff,' said Janice. 'Let's have some wine.' She called over the waiter and ordered a bottle of Pinot Grigio and two large glasses. The waiter smiled at Janice, and Catherine smiled conspiratorially at Janice. They both laughed, but the waiter didn't understand why.

'So, tell me all about you and where you work.'

'Well, for the last eleven years, I've worked at the Christian Socialist Party headquarters as a researcher. You know the sort of thing, collating information about this and that and sticking it on the computer database.'

'Christ! You actually work for Hawsley,' exclaimed Catherine. 'The right-wing fascist dictator,' she said, quoting Janice's earlier description verbatim.

'Well, maybe I was a bit hard on him,' she smiled. 'Anyway, I don't work specifically for him. There are a lot of other people working there.'

'Have you actually spoken to him?' Catherine was apparently in awe of knowing somebody who knew Aiden Hawsley, somebody she apparently admired.

'Yes, two or three times,' replied Janice matter-of-factly.

'What's he like?' asked Catherine.

'What's he like? Spooky, that's what he's like, I suppose,' replied Janice without any reservation.

'But how did you get on with him, man to woman?'

'Oh, nothing like that. He frightens me a bit. Anyway, I couldn't have a relationship with any man, let alone one like that, not until I've....'

'You haven't been out with a man?' interrupted Catherine in disbelief.

'Yes, of course I have, but they don't last long. A week, maybe, and then I don't bother for another year. I can't commit to letting myself go completely and falling in love. I suppose I don't want to lose the control I have over my life. Not again if it means having to trust somebody without reservation. I don't know if I can do that. But that's why I want to do this. I hope to move on once this thing is out of my head. Can you see that?'

'Yes, yes, I can,' said Catherine.

'But why don't you ask Hawsley to check it out first? Nobody's going to challenge a request from him.'

'But I would be asking him to break his own laws,' replied Janice cautiously.

'Just explain what happened. You did nothing wrong. Remember that. Hawsley may feel - he should feel morally obliged to do something, as the original investigation didn't get anywhere. It would look good for him if his intervention succeeded when the previous lot failed. Don't you think?'

'Well put like that, I don't suppose there's any harm in asking,' replied Janice, carefully mulling it over in her mind.

'Play to his vanity,' instructed Catherine, forcefully interrupting Janice's train of thought. 'That's always their weakest point. They never realise until it's too late that they've been nobbled.'

Janice was surprised at how forthright and demonstrative Catherine could be. She had always been strong-willed and resolute, but now she had the aggression to follow it through. She felt a sudden lift in confidence with the support of a friend.

'Not their trousers, then,' added Janice derisively.

'That's a close second, but *vanity, vanity, all is vanity.* Remember, their egos are always more prominent than their dicks. They both laughed aloud, almost a witch's cackle. The crowd around them looked over, slightly envious of two beautiful women enjoying themselves without a man in attendance.

'He can only say no,' replied Catherine, smiling. 'He's hardly going to fire you for asking a favour, is he?' Her voice conveyed a hint of doubt, but Janice ignored it.

'If that doesn't work, I'll come round and blow some smoke up your husband's arse,' replied Janice demurely.

'Now, that could be extremely dangerous,' replied Catherine, feeling light-headed. Then, she suddenly fell victim to a severe attack of the giggles. They clinked their glasses together, and some wine spilt on the table. Catherine toasted: 'To Vanity.' Janice smiled. They clinked their glasses again - like two musketeers and toasted, 'To Vanity, vanity, all is vanity,' and downed the contents.

They laughed aloud, thinking about the past and the future, a little drunk on the joy of living. People passing by could be forgiven for thinking they were just two ladies of leisure without a care in the world. Idly passing the time of day, never appreciating how soon the world would change because of something they had casually discussed. But Janice and Catherine were blind to the capricious destiny that awaited them. Unable to hold back the devastating fate into which they and their children were being irrevocably drawn.

Chapter 9

'What's the cleaner's name again?' asked Parish, leaning idly against the front door, hands in his pockets - half-heartedly watching the techies as they gathered up various pieces of electronic equipment, packing them away in battered aluminium flight cases. Cases that travelled with implacable resilience from one death scene to the next. What mayhem and depravity had they witnessed over the years, he wondered? Sometimes, he, too, felt like another flight case. Carefully unpacked at an incident to do a job of work and then neatly packed away again when it was all over. But he wasn't quite so emotionally detached from all he had seen.

Parish turned his attention to the cleaner in the kitchen, talking with one of the techies. She appeared oddly animated. It felt Edward Hopperish in mannerism, voyeuristic and prurient in concept. Furtively invading someone's privacy occasionally served a practical purpose and sometimes even produced unexpected results.

Over the years, Parish had concluded that as much information could be learnt from what a person didn't say as from what they did. Likewise, valuable knowledge could be gleaned from the simple body language of a potential suspect when observed from afar. Occasionally, insignificant, involuntary idiosyncrasies revealed hidden agendas - but little out of the ordinary immediately concerned him about the cleaner. Nevertheless, he would still treat her as any other potential suspect.

'Maddie Cornwell,' replied Heart. Also stood outside the front door, taking advantage of the smoking dispensation. Carelessly blowing smoke into the wintry night air, watching it slowly disappear.

'Do we know anything about her?' asked Parish.

'Nothing on record, guv,' Heart replied smartly. He had obviously already checked Artemis. It was an odd conversation as they leaned idly against the same door frame, looking in opposite directions. To a passer-by with an over-active imagination, they could easily have been mistaken for two poorly disguised secret service agents. Covertly passing highly confidential information, or maybe even a couple of actors preparing for the opening dance routine to a West End musical.

'Right,' said Parish with refocused conviction. 'I'll chat with Miss Cornwell - you can tackle the quack.' Heart stubbed out his cigarette and, checking there were no witnesses, surreptitiously kicked the butt under a small, snow-covered bush before casually wandering off down the pathway.

Parish could see Maddie was now alone in the kitchen. She was taking small sips from a large mug of tea, which she held tightly while gazing listlessly into space. She was possibly preoccupied with thoughts of where she might find other work now that her current employment had been unexpectedly cut short. Cut short! He thought, suddenly realising the unfortunate turn of phrase in the circumstances. Maybe she was wondering how a new employer might react when told of the unusual demise of her previous employer. Or how she would explain her inability to produce a reference if she hadn't mentioned the murder, which was obviously something she wouldn't want to refer to unless absolutely necessary. Or, possibly, she wasn't thinking of anything at all. Parish was prone to flights of cerebral fancy from time to time.

'Miss Maddie Cornwell?' asked Parish.

'Yes,' replied Maddie quietly, returning from her cerebral meanderings to look at Parish. She smiled disarmingly. Maddie was an attractive girl, about nineteen or twenty, he guessed. She reminded him a little of how Catherine used to look when they first met.

'My name is Parish, Detective Inspector Parish. I would like to have a few words with you if that's convenient. Can we go somewhere private and...?'

'The study is over there,' pre-empted Maddie with some trepidation. 'We can use that if you want?' She pointed across the hallway to a closed door with a notice attached to it declaring 'AIR SCAN COMPLETED'. Maddie led Parish across the hallway into Dhalia's study. Parish closed the door behind him to cut out the noise of the techies still working in the hall. The room suddenly fell silent. Maddie looked awkwardly at Parish for direction; she appeared unsure whether to sit down or wait for him to suggest it. It seemed a bit incongruous that she should feel the necessity to wait to be told what to do when he was the visitor in the house where she lived and worked. But then it also felt equally inappropriate for her to sit in her employer's part of the house before being invited.

Parish made a mental note about this momentary indecision. It would seem unlikely that someone who couldn't decide whether to sit down - because she apparently felt intimidated by authority - would be capable of the gruesome act that had recently been committed just two floors above them. He gestured towards a chair on one side of Dhalia's desk, and Maddie sat down. He took the seat opposite, but before starting the conversation, he took a few moments to cast his eyes around the room at the large number of books stacked on shelves. Parish needed to collect his thoughts. He noticed more Chinese and Japanese ornaments. Presumably, Dhalia had collected them over the years from appreciative clients.

'So, Miss Cornwell, how long have you worked for...?' Maddie interrupted Parish again before he could finish. It was almost as if she didn't want to hear Dhalia's name mentioned.

'Nearly four months.'

'Not long, then?' replied Parish.

'No, I suppose not.' That may have accounted for her reluctance to just plop herself down, thought Parish.

'And what exactly did you do?'

'Everything, really. I do...' Maddie paused for a second and corrected herself. '*Did* all the cleaning, washing, and ironing, running about picking up food, household things....'

'And did you get on well with her?'

'Yes, she was really nice to me, and she pays... paid me well, and it's a nice flat, not like some employers who have you live in, treat you like a Glunde and pay you a pittance.'

'So, how did you hear about the job?'

'Through the agency. They told me about it. So I came for an interview, we got on really well, and Miss Vingali hired me immediately.' Parish glanced around the room.

'Do you know what she does?' asked Parish, surreptitiously studying her carefully for a reaction.

'You mean did, don't you,' she said politely but firmly? Parish smiled. Any impression he may have formed about her timidity was quickly dispelled.

'Yes, did,' said Parish grudgingly. 'Did.'

'Not to begin with, but I soon realised that...' She didn't finish.

'And that didn't make a difference to you?'

'Why should it?' replied Maddie with what almost appeared to be belligerent naivety.

'Why indeed,' replied Parish.... 'but prostitution is still illegal, you know?' Maddie looked at him incredulously as he realised how ridiculously pompous that sounded. They lived in an age where CyCo now supplied a range of VRS fantasy chips. Each one a twenty-four-hour Bacchanalian orgy, and all for the price of a double cheeseburger and coke.

The question now was, does the law on morality, common decency, and behaviour regarding previously illegal sexual acts such as paedophilia still have any relevance. Especially when these practices were now being conducted within the confines of a Virtual Reality experience. Something that only happened in the brain of the user. Illegal VRS chips were now manufactured in China to explore the most debased forms of depravity known to civilisation and some as yet unknown. Could you be prosecuted for unlawful acts you committed in your brain?

'I didn't say I thought she was a prostitute,' replied Maddie firmly, as if his assumption distorted the truth.

'So, what did you think she did?' asked Parish more cautiously, having been reprimanded for his previous supposition.

'She entertained men friends from the media, finance, business, and political arenas,' replied Maddie innocently.

'Entertained!' exclaimed Parish in disbelief. Maddie was obviously not going to set herself on fire as the only prosecutable accomplice to a criminal offence when the protagonist had permanently departed the scene. Parish wondered if maybe Maddie didn't know what Dhalia did but quickly dismissed that as highly improbable. But then again, he had no real evidence that Dhalia was being paid for sexual services.

'So, when did you last see Ms Vingali... alive?' asked Parish cautiously. Until now, Maddie had not displayed any apparent signs of emotion. But at the mention of the victim's name and the word *alive* in the same sentence, she instantly burst into a torrent of tears.

This threw Parish entirely off guard for a moment. The unanticipated reaction to his question only heightened his sense of detachment from the situation. That was when he realised just how much he had become immune to any meaningful sense of loss. It just wouldn't register anymore. This was understandable, even excusable under the circumstances. Nevertheless, he knew he should still be able to empathise with Maddie over the loss of another human life. Someone to whom she had obviously become deeply attached despite only knowing her briefly.

Delving dispassionately into sensitive areas of other people's lives was part of his job. But he still despised himself for his inability to feel emotion anymore. The light of his compassion was extinguished when he buried the remains of his wife and daughter. It had left him without the ability to grieve, cry, respond or react to death in any rational way. Instead, he felt bitter, angry, and resentful, sometimes plunging into the comforting dark oblivion of despair. But he also knew he must overcome all these feelings before moving forward, or they would eventually overwhelm and consume him. Only when he sat at home alone on the sofa with the gun barrel in his mouth and his finger stroking the trigger did he feel anything? Only then was he alive?

He moved around the table to where Maddie was sitting and put his arm around her shoulder to comfort her.

'I'm sorry,' he said quietly.

'Sorry? Why?' burbled Maddie quietly through her tears.

'That was a little bit blunt. It's just that I saw you talking with a techie earlier on, and you seemed to be entirely at ease, so I presumed you were over the shock.

'We were at school together talking about those days. He said he wasn't allowed to discuss details about the incident, so my mind was elsewhere for a few minutes, but when you…. '

Parish interrupted. 'Yes, yes, I understand. I shouldn't have jumped to conclusions.'

He pulled out a handkerchief and gave it to her, and she dabbed her moist eyes and smiled at him. He succumbed to normal emotions for a few seconds, something he had not experienced for a long time. She mouthed a silent thank you.

'We didn't talk about Dhalia,' confirmed Maddie

'Yes, I realise that.' He knew from experience and training that these valuable moments, when a person was emotionally charged and vulnerable, had to be quickly exploited. Once she had given her definitive version of events, she could never retell it differently, at some later occasion and preserve its integrity. Everybody responded slightly differently to murder. It was essential to differentiate between a genuine and a premeditated emotional reaction.

'Are you okay now?' he asked.

'Yes, yes, I am. I'm sorry, I don't know what happened.'

'It's quite normal,' replied Parish reassuringly. 'The shock is just kicking in now.'

'Yes, I think you're right,' said Maddie, wiping her eyes again.

'Can you carry on?' asked Parish.

'Yes, yes, I'm fine. I'll be all right now.' She blew her nose into his hanky and rolled it up. Parish returned to his chair.

'So, what time did you get here this morning?'

'About nine-fifteen. I went to a party yesterday. It was my day off, so I didn't stay here last night.'

'Is that normal?' asked Parish.

'Sometimes I get back late; sometimes I stay with a friend.'

'But you normally sleep here every night?'

'Yes.'

'Did you notice anything different when you came in?' asked Parish. 'Anything unusual, out of place?

Maddie thought for a few moments. Backtracking her movements since she had entered the house that morning.

'The kitchen light was on.'

'Is that unusual?' asked Parish, making a note.

'Dhalia never came to the kitchen. So if I'm not here, she makes tea upstairs.'

'Could you have left it on?'

'No. It was lunchtime when I left, so I wouldn't have switched it on then.'

'You leave through the kitchen?'

'Yes.'

'Not the front door?'

'No, that's for…' She paused for a second. 'That's for visitors. I use the back door.'

'Which is in the kitchen?' said Parish.

'Yes.'

'But you locked it?'

'Yes.'

'You are sure?'

'Absolutely,' replied Maddie, almost indignantly.

'Could anybody else have a key?'

'Not that I'm aware of.'

'Where does the back lead to?'

'There's a small private communal park, but it's fully enclosed by tall wrought iron railings, and there's a gate, which is kept locked. That leads to the main road.'

'But if someone had a key to that gate and a back-door key, they could....' He didn't finish.

'Yes, they could, but as I said, I am unaware of anybody else having those keys. I'm sure that Dhalia and I are the only ones. She never mentioned anybody else. She would have told me just in case they turned up unexpectedly.'

'Yes, I see that' said Parish. 'So, what happened when you came in?'

'I made some tea and toast, ate the toast and took a cup up to Dhalia. That's when I...' He could see a tear welling up in Maddie's eye, but she wiped it away.

'That's good. You're doing fine,' said Parish encouragingly. 'So, nothing out of the normal in the rest of the house?'

'No,' she replied, 'not that I've noticed.'

'Have you noticed anything unusual in the last couple of weeks? Anything out of the ordinary?'

'Like what?'

'Well, somebody you didn't know coming to see her. Maybe a client had an argument with her or something else that might have been troubling her that she may have casually mentioned. It may have meant nothing at the time, but now...?' Parish deliberately didn't finish.

'Not really.'

'Not really?' Repeated Parish enquiringly, noticing the slight hesitation in her voice. There was a gentle art to coaxing what appeared to be inconsequential details out of a witness, and Parish was a past master. He smiled at her sympathetically, which seemed to have the desired effect.

'Well, there was something odd... well, I'm not sure if it was odd. It was about a month ago. I was in the study when the phone rang. I took the call, and a man asked to speak to Rose.'

'A man?' replied Parish.

'Yes,' confirmed Maddie. 'He had a strange whispery tone - I remember that much. I could hardly make out what he was saying. I told him he must have the wrong number, but he insisted that he didn't.'

'Are you sure it was a man?'

'Yes, I think so.'

'Rose,' repeated Parish. 'He asked for Rose?'

Maddie nodded. He could see the name appeared to have little significance for her, so he pretended he didn't recognise it either. Small deceptions occasionally elicit unexpected results.

'Who is Rose?' he continued.

'I don't know. I tried to tell the man there was no one here of that name, but as I was speaking to him, Dhalia walked in. I put my hand over the mouthpiece and whispered, *'That it was someone asking for somebody called Rose, and he wouldn't go away.'* She asked me to pass her the phone and make us tea, so I did.'

'Then what?' enquired Parish.

'Nothing,' replied Maddie.

'Nothing?' asked Parish, in a way that he hoped might enthuse her to elaborate slightly.

'I returned with the tea about ten minutes later, and she explained it was somebody looking for the girl who had worked here before me.'

'So, that explains it.'

'Well, not quite. You see, the girl who worked here before me came by one day a couple of weeks after I'd started. She asked me whether I had come across a wristwatch she'd lost. She thought she might have left it here when she moved out.'

'And had you found it?'

'No, no, it wasn't here......'

'And?' added Parish, sensing there was a little more to come...

'Well, I remember when she knocked on the door, she mentioned her name, Collette.'

'Collette? Not Rose?' asked Parish.

'That's what she said.'

'Did you mention that to Dhalia?'

'That's just it, I did, but all she said was what a nice girl she was.'

'Did you mention her name?'

'Yes, I clearly said Collette had called.'

'And didn't you say anything about that when someone phoned for Rose?'

'No. I thought Dhalia may have had a few housekeepers over the years, and maybe she had just got a bit mixed up.'

'Maybe she did,' replied Parish. 'Is there anything else you can remember?'

'No, but I will let you know if I think of anything else.'

Parish took a card out of his pocket and gave it to her. 'Call me anytime, day or night.'

'I will,' replied Maddie. She smiled at Parish, and he got up and left the room, leaving her alone with her thoughts.

Chapter 10

Heart lingered for a few minutes outside Doctor Hackett's house, gathering his thoughts from the last few hours, trying to make sense of what he had seen before speaking to the doctor. It was an essential part of the detection process to give his brain enough time to absorb and objectively digest the vast array of information being generated. Of course, a certain amount of disinformation and irrelevant nonsense would always be thrown into the pot. All of which, had to be wheedled out and discarded to avoid future confusion and obfuscation. Part of Parish's philosophy, which had now become entwined with - and subtly ingrained into Heart's thought process, was that serendipity and gut instinct, both much maligned and misunderstood by some technical detectives (he considered himself to be of the cerebral variety), was occasionally the provider of apparently innocuous pieces of seemingly unrelated but profoundly important evidence.

The reluctance of Parish's fellow officers to accept the existence of chance and the part it played in life with each twist and turn was a fundamental flaw in the crime-solving process as far as he was concerned.

Something as obscure and seemingly insignificant as a miniscule change in cadence could play a surprisingly large part in solving a crime when reviewed in the context of all other available information. So Heart deconstructed, then reconstructed the chronological order of events to see if that would make any real difference, but it didn't appear to. Not at the moment, anyway.

He had attended many murder incidents during his career. But few, if any, were so enigmatically deliberate in their theatrical staging as this one. Surreal in concept, metaphorical in execution, a perfect marriage of art and death. Something that only Picasso or Dalí could have competently conceived and created. But theirs were disturbed minds, entirely under control, working in perfect harmony with nature and the emotive synchronicity of aesthetics.

This was the product of a severely disturbed and disrupted mind in mortal conflict with itself and entirely out of control. There had to be a reason and, therefore, accountability for the carefully staged tableau. If they could solve that riddle, that must point them toward the killer.

Why, thought Heart, would someone purposely drug a woman into such a subservient state that she would willingly consent, or more accurately not offer any resistance, to her own execution? It did not make sense. What bothered him even more, was the perpetrator's deliberate intention to display his power and control through the victim's apparent cooperation in the final act. He had not encountered this strange and troubling dimension before. Over twenty-five years on the job, he had become anaesthetised and immune to the graphical images of disfigurement each new crime scene offered. He was now accustomed to, though never entirely at ease with, the defence mechanism of incongruous flippancy bandied about at incidents of macabre dismemberment. He had become accustomed to the regular collection of strangely disparate plastic bags spread over his desk, each holding a tiny fragment of someone's life. Heart had come to terms with the emotional involvement. But often wondered whether this detachment from reality, which was essential if he wanted to keep his sanity, affected his ability to form any long-term personal relationship.

Many years ago, he had been married, but that relationship had collapsed after ten years of neglect, the inevitable malady of the dedicated but defective detective. In his limited experience, liaisons were not particularly dangerous, just precarious and invariably short-lived.

Having seen the various forms of gratuitous violence first-hand that one human being was capable of inflicting on another, he thought he had seen it all. But occasionally, something like this would come along and force him to re-evaluate his softening perspective on the depths of depravity to which some people could sink. He could understand intense moments of blind fury when the red mist descended, self-control temporarily disengaged. For a few brief seconds, sanity was abandoned, and a life was lost. That was instinctive, primordial, and impulsive, but premeditation was different in so many ways.

'Cigarette, sarge?' A uniformed constable held out a packet to Heart. Lost deep in thought, he was suddenly eased back into reality.

'Eh, no thanks,' he replied instinctively, looking around to see who had spoken. 'I've just put one out.'

The constable lit his cigarette and blew some smoke skywards, which he somehow managed to form into perfect little halos. 'Do you ever get used to it?' he asked thoughtfully. Heart stared up at the snowflakes that had started to fall again. Each one glistened for just a fraction of a second, reflecting the light from the streetlamps before descending to earth and instantly turning to slush - its short life over. He was presumably referring to murder, or maybe just death in general, thought Heart. But he could just as easily have been innocently reflecting on the metaphysical majesty of an idealistic representation of Christmas. Heart looked at him, thought for a few seconds, and then looked back at the sky.

'I thought I did.' He looked back at the constable. 'I no longer dream of dismembered bodies or rotting, maggot-infested corpses. I actually sleep quite well.' He managed a small smile. 'I can deal with all that. It's the total waste that I think about these days.'

'Time?' enquired the constable prosaically, a little uncertain about what he was referring to.

'Yes, time as well, I suppose,' replied Heart, 'but no, I meant life itself. She was in her prime, with everything to live for, and today, somebody decided to take it away forever. Somebody's dreams, all the things she had worked hard to enjoy, and in a split second, it's over. It doesn't make any sense, and sometimes I don't understand what it all means. When I was young, I thought life was easy. You got up each day, went to work, came home, went to bed, and on Saturday, you went out for a drink and a dance, and one day you got married and had children, that was all you had to worry about.'

'My mum used to say that life was easy...' said the constable. Heart noticed he had a broad Yorkshire accent. '...It was people that made it complicated.' The constable blew out more smoke rings, and they both watched them drift skywards.

'Your mum was a bloody genius,' said Heart. 'I hope you look after her.'

'Oh, I do, sarge, I do,' replied the constable.

'Good,' said Heart, in a patriarchal tone. 'Good. I'm glad to hear it.' A sudden gust of freezing wind whipped the snow into a flurry. Heart shivered briefly before pulling up the collar on his jacket to shield his neck. They

172

both continued gazing skywards for a few minutes before Heart decided to get on with interviewing the doctor.

'Right,' said Heart. 'I hate to break up our cosy little tête-à-tête, but I'd better crack on before my governor catches me skiving.'.

'No problem,' said the constable. 'See you next time.'

Next time, thought Heart? Yes, there will be a next time. There always would be, he mused philosophically. He smiled at the constable and wandered off towards number eighteen.

Hackett's front door was painted black, which was a little unusual, and there was no knocker or bell, which was even more so, so he tapped on the door with his knuckle. He waited for about half a minute and realised he was beginning to shiver in the chilly night air that was now descending. He wished he'd brought his overcoat, which was in his car. He was just about to knock again when the door opened. Doctor Hackett stood before him.

'Good evening,' said Heart. 'I'm Detective Sergeant Heart.' He showed Hackett his identity card. 'I'm here about the incident next door that....'

Doctor Hackett interrupted. 'Miss Vingali. Yes, unfortunate business. You had better come in.' He beckoned Heart into the hallway, which was similar to that of number sixteen but much warmer. The furniture was much older, mostly Victorian or Edwardian, he thought. There was the odd piece of reproduction that looked out of place, not that it mattered. Heart prided himself on distinguishing between something that was right and something that wasn't. He followed the doctor into his study. The log fire burning in the hearth lent a quintessential festive glow - but the room was oddly devoid of Christmas decorations.

'Would you like something to drink, Sergeant? I was having a snifter,' enquired Hackett, offering up a whisky glass from which he had evidently been drinking.

'Eh... no thank you,' replied Heart. 'Bit early for me, and I'm on duty.'

'Quite right,' said Hackett, nodding his head in approval and pursing his lips for a second. Then, he emptied his glass and wandered over to the open globe drinks cabinet.

'I'll just...' He removed the whisky decanter and replenished his glass, finishing it off with a tiny squirt of soda. He was obviously pedantically precise about his drinking habits and presumably much the same in his professional life. Heart stood by the fire, warming himself. When Hackett had replaced the whisky bottle, he turned to Heart and ushered him over to sit on the sofa, but he remained standing.

'I don't normally start this early, but as you will appreciate, it's been an unusual day, and it is Christmas.'

'Yes, yes it has, and it is,' agreed Heart, opening his tablet and getting straight down to business. 'So, you are Doctor James Hackett.'

'Yes!' replied Hackett firmly. 'Ex-major, Medical Corps retired,' he added sharply but politely, swiftly coming to attention for no reason. An old habit he had never quite gotten out of, thought Heart, and probably subconsciously used to impress lesser mortals when the need arose. It had no effect on Heart, who just made a cursory note. Hackett returned to an *at-ease* stance.

'And I understand you attended the crime scene before the police arrived.'

'Yes, I did. Maddie, Miss Vingali's housekeeper, came bashing on my door just after nine-fifteen this morning.

She was in a bit of a state. Blurted out something about a body, and could I come and have a look, so I did.'

'You didn't ring the police?' asked Heart, making notes and glancing at Hackett.

'No, I didn't. I presumed the girl had already called you.'

'But she hadn't?' queried Heart.

'No, she hadn't, but I didn't know that until I entered the bedroom.'

'Then what did you do?'

'I stopped immediately, realising this wasn't a natural death. That was pretty obvious.'

'And then what?' asked Heart.

'She asked me what she should do, and I asked her if she had rung the police. She said she hadn't, so I told her to ring them at once, which she did.'

'So why was that, do you think,' asked Heart?

'Why was what?' replied Hackett, not understanding the question.

'Why do you think she came to get you first instead of calling the police?'

'Don't know, really,' said Hackett. 'Maybe it was the shock. I suppose it would disorientate most people, finding a headless corpse.' He took a small sip of his whiskey and continued… 'There is an evil obscenity that contaminates the unsuspecting observer in situations such as this - I've seen it all before, replied Hackett glibly. 'I've seen a few decapitations in my career in the Army, but none since, that is, until today… it confuses you. It can change you forever. Maybe that's what happened to Maddie?'

'Yes, you're right, of course you are,' replied Heart. 'So, did you touch anything in the bedroom?'

'No, I didn't even touch the body. No purpose. Dhalia, well, I presumed it was Dhalia because… well… she was obviously dead. There was nothing I could do, nothing anybody could do for that matter.'

'No, there wasn't, was there?' agreed Heart, smiling politely at the doctor's trite comment. He made a further note on his tablet. It was recording their conversation anyway, so he only noted the doctor's reaction to the questions. For some reason, this seemed to unnerve Hackett. But then, that was partly the intention.

'How long had you known the victim?'

'Nearly five years,' replied Hackett a little cagily.

'But I understand she only moved here four years ago,' said Heart, referring to his tablet.

'That's right, but I knew her before she came here. I was her doctor when I was still working in general practice after I left the Army.'

'So, you've retired?'

'From general practice, yes, but I still retain a practice licence. I now act as a private consultant.'

'So, Miss Vingali was a private patient?'

'Yes,' replied Hackett.

'Did you treat her for anything specific?'

'I can't discuss a patient's medical records without her consent,' replied Hackett, with a tone of resentment which seemed to conceal an evasion.

Heart looked at Hackett with an expression of surprise and disbelief. 'That's not likely to be forthcoming, is it, sir? She is dead, and this is a murder enquiry.' Heart's tone was beginning to sound a little less friendly.

'But…' said Hackett.

Heart persisted. 'Look, I can get a court order if you prefer. It's up to you, but that could trigger an

176

investigation into why you were treating a possible prostitute, which is illegal in case you didn't know. That could affect all sorts of things, including your practice certificate.' He let that linger in the air momentarily, allowing Hackett sufficient time to consider all possible outcomes and consequences.

'I didn't know she was a…, but I'll tell you what I do know if that would help?' He replied, looking at Heart a little cagily. He had obviously reassessed his delicate position and concluded that intransigence was an inadvisable avenue to take under the circumstances. Having his practice certificate permanently withdrawn would seriously affect his lucrative consultancy sideline.

'That's very public-spirited of you, doctor. Thank you,' replied Heart, overemphasising the word doctor.

'So, what were you treating her for?' asked Heart.

Hackett didn't answer straight away and continued sipping his drink.

Heart thought he may not have heard the question clearly, so he started to repeat it. 'What were you…'

'AIDS !' mumbled Hackett sheepishly.

'AIDS !' exclaimed Heart. The sound of the word was still guaranteed to engender panic and concern, especially inside a Province. He took a deep breath that became frozen mid-air as he mentally reran his precise movements since he first arrived at the incident. Like many in the force, he secretly harboured a fear of accidentally contracting one of the new variants of HIV or AIDS. Which, despite the latest advances in drug development, was still the number one killer in the Ghettazone, though not so prevalent in the provinces. This was primarily due to the drugs only being available on a private prescription outside of a Province. This made them prohibitively expensive. Inside, they were free on the NHS.

However, that reassurance was insufficient to appease or diminish concerns over the possible infection as the drugs were only effective in 50% of cases. And, of course, contracting an infectious disease could warrant immediate expulsion from a province, no matter who you were.

The NHS no longer extended beyond the provinces. All Ghettazone hospitals and doctor's surgeries were now operated privately by SCOMTEL. Free medical treatment was a distant memory for a Glunde. If you lived in the Ghettazone, became ill, and had no money, you stayed home and recovered or died. It was as simple as that.

Had he come into contact with any of her blood, he asked himself? There was a lot of it splattered about, but no, he didn't think so. They were in isolation overalls, gloves, and masks, but he had removed his mask. Did he take his gloves off? He couldn't remember. The standard procedure was not to remove any protective clothing until the techies had cleared the area, but operating protocols had become a little slack since the introduction of the air scan technology.

Much of the evidence was collected, analysed, and collated well before he ever arrived at an incident.

'She had AIDS,' said Hackett, 'but it's not contagious.' He uttered the words slowly to reassure Heart. Heart, however, was displaying signs of being unsettled by the revelation. Hackett sat in the chair beside the fire and warmed his hands.

'Christ! I thought the government declared *"that"* disease had been virtually eradicated over ten years ago,' mumbled Heart disconsolately.

But then, nobody really believed anything published by the government that did not align with the general public's consensus of opinion. The more the government told you one thing, the more the people thought the opposite was the reality. Political propaganda had come full circle. With some highly contentious issues, the government would, with cynical forethought, broadcast the unadulterated truth, knowing the public would automatically assume the opposite was true. Telling the truth to confuse the issue was bizarre, but it worked. There were now Truths, Lies, Lying-Truths, Truthfull-lies and lying lies. A disturbing array of choices in which to secrete the true-truth.

'Is that what they said?' replied Hackett, expressing disbelief and surprise as he gazed into the fire.

'Yes,' said Heart, looking for affirmation from Hackett.

'Well, yes, to some degree. It has been controlled in gated provinces - the DNA security system saw to that. If you were infected, you would never get a permit to live in a province. So you were condemned to live in the Ghettazone, and it's thriving out there.' He pointed vaguely into the distance and took another gulp of his whisky.

'So how bad was she?' asked Heart, sounding slightly edgy.

'It was controlled by drugs, and I closely monitored her condition. Obviously, I was available day or night, living just next door, but it was terminal.'

'Terminal!' exclaimed Heart.

'Yes,' replied Hackett. 'She had maybe a year left.'

'So, she was going to die anyway?' asked Heart, a little astonished.

'Yes, ironically, she was. So, all that…' he shook his head then glanced upwards, 'was for nothing. It just cut short a life that was already effectively over.'

'I wonder if the killer knew that?' thought Heart aloud.

'Good question,' replied Hackett.

'That's why you didn't touch the body,' Heart suddenly exclaimed. 'You never even went close to her because you knew that….' Hackett said nothing and took another sip of whisky.

'So, was there any danger to other parties?' asked Heart. The implication was sexual partners, but he was obviously seeking reassurance on secondary indirect contact.

'Normal protected sex would not pose a problem, but any exchange of body fluids could be highly problematical.'

'Problematical?' inquired Heart, looking for further clarification on a word that sounded suspiciously like a political euphemism for "fucked" in this context.

'Not advisable then,' said Hackett, staring directly at Heart.

'So, could she have infected one of her clients?'

'I still don't know what she did.'

'Don't you,' replied Heart, sounding incredulous? Hackett was thinking more carefully about his answers, as he knew he could technically be an accessory to any potential death resulting from contact with Dhalia. As a doctor, he was legally obliged to alert the authorities about any patient with an infectious disease. This he had obviously failed to do.

'Could she have infected anybody?' asked Heart again.

'Yes, possibly. But only under certain conditions,' replied Hackett after some deliberation. He was now thinking very carefully about his answers.

'So, that could be a motive for murder by an aggrieved infected ex-client, couldn't it,' asked Heart with a smirking hint of righteous indignation? Hackett began to appreciate where Heart was coming from and where he was going.

'Yes, I suppose so,' he muttered somewhat reluctantly. He knew this was not going to end well for him.

'Sort of puts you in a bad place, doesn't it?' asked Heart, gently cantering towards the high moral ground.

'Why?' exclaimed Hackett defensively, sounding slightly outraged at what he thought was a direct accusation of intimacy with a patient, which was something he had completely misread.

'I didn't have sex with her if that's what you think. I was her doctor, for Christ's sake,' he rounded gruffly, incensed at Heart's less-than-subtle hint of unprofessional conduct. Heart thought his sudden attack of righteous indignation a little amusing but seriously misplaced in the circumstances.

'No, I wasn't suggesting you had sex with her,' replied Heart. He was discreetly grinning behind his teeth at the thought of a severely overweight septuagenarian with a lousy toupee and bad breath having sex with anybody. Let alone an attractive twenty-five-year-old woman, even if she was a prostitute.

'But whoever did... wouldn't be too happy if he found out you could have prevented him from being infected with AIDS .' He looked at Hackett with a knowing expression and a slightly censorious shake of his head.

'Oh, I see,' replied Hackett, who now sounded less agitated but slightly more apprehensive as the possible consequences of Heart's assumptions sank in. Heart got up from the sofa and wandered around the room, looking at the photographs in ornate silver frames. One was of an attractive couple on their wedding day. It could just be Hackett, thought Heart, but it must have been long ago.

'Did you know that wasn't her real name?'

'No,' said Hackett. Then, after a few seconds of thoughtful introspection, he corrected himself. 'Yes, yes, I did, actually.' Hackett was beginning to realise that the interview wasn't going quite how he had anticipated. Unqualified candid cooperation was the only practical lifeline left open to him. If he was going to extricate himself from the sticky mire into which he was slowly sinking.

'Rose Watson...' replied Hackett, pausing momentarily to consider his words. 'That was her real name.' The tone of his voice had dropped a semitone, now tranquil, indicating far more than his eyes would allow him to betray, but the humble stillness was real - and it was palpable. Hackett was a man who usually kept his feelings very much in check. But this situation, notwithstanding the unusual circumstances, had, for some reason, affected him far more than death usually did. There was a strange discernible air of contrition and expectation about him, an inevitability in his manner, which belied something. 'Rose Watson. She is... was a very nice lady.'

'Yes, everybody we've spoken to so far has said that, but then they would, wouldn't they,' replied Heart somewhat disingenuously? He tilted his head to one side as if he had some neck pain. He appeared distracted by something.

'And what else did you know about her,' continued Heart?

'Ours was a purely professional relationship, sergeant, I told you that. I didn't get involved in her private life.'

'But surely popping next door to administer drugs and to be on call any time of the day or night is being involved in her private life, isn't it?'

'I work outside normal office hours, that's all. I wager you occasionally work unconventional hours, sergeant?' He took another sip of whisky. 'I doubt very much if that's ever misconstrued as unprofessional conduct or inappropriate behaviour with your....' He paused for a few seconds, pondering over the choice of collective noun. 'Clients,' He knew the word wasn't quite right but couldn't think of anything more appropriate at that moment. The whisky was muddling his brain a little.

'Just victims and perpetrators,' corrected Heart, 'not clients.' Innocence and guilt that's all we deal with. It's as simple as that, right or wrong, no fuzzy middle ground,' but he conceded Hackett's point. 'But I don't work with live prostitutes. Mainly dead bodies, which is what this one has become.'

'So, conversation and relationships aren't your strong suit, sergeant,' asked Hackett condescendingly, drifting into an analytical mode? Heart realised this was becoming personal and uncomfortably introspective. So, he quickly steered the conversation back to the primary subject.

'So, you have no idea who any of the men that visited her were?'

'No. Why should I?' replied Hackett sanguinely.

'It's just that some of them were well-known figures. With your coming and going, I thought you might have recognised one or two of them. Neighbours tend to notice things like that.' Heart gave a half smile.

'As I told you, sergeant, I wasn't totally aware of what she did or who she entertained. That was her business. She was very discreet about it and never mentioned anyone specific to me.'

'Not totally aware?' repeated Heart, querying the qualification.

'I had certain reservations, but I didn't allow them to affect my professional conduct or detachment.'

'Right!' said Heart rather abruptly as he got up to leave. 'Well, I think that's all for now. But I will probably have to come back again if we have any more questions after the autopsy.'

'I understand. I'm nearly always in, sergeant.' Hackett placed the whisky glass, which he had been passionately cradling during the conversation, on an ornate ormolu occasional table and stood up to lead Heart to the front door. Hackett opened the door, and as Heart stepped out, he turned back with a pained smile and asked, 'You won't be leaving the province in the next week or two, will you?'

'No, I've nothing planned,' replied Hackett.

'Good,' said Heart. 'Good... I'll be in touch.' He walked out into the wintry night air and felt an instant chill. The snow had begun to settle.

After Hackett closed the front door behind Heart, he hurriedly returned to his study. He opened the filing cabinet in the corner of the room, where he anxiously flicked through the patients' folders, desperately looking for something. Finally, he found whatever he was looking for, quickly withdrew it, took it over to the hearth and threw it into the flames.

Chapter 11

Heart ambled back to number sixteen, reflecting on the conversation he had just had with Hackett. He was mulling over the details that had come to light, endeavouring to separate the relevant points from the inconsequential ones. Most of the techies had left the scene - scurrying off to their various laboratories to analyse their miniscule telltale fragments of someone else's life... and death.

Just as the house was beginning to regain its stolid composure, an eerie calmness suddenly descended. Two techies carrying a saggy black body bag carefully negotiated the last few steps of the staircase. They lifted the bag onto a gurney and pushed it across the hall to the front door. The body beneath the plastic shroud was evidently missing a head. That was somewhat less ceremoniously carried down the stairs in a black plastic bag by another techie. Behind him were two more techies carrying other smaller bags of evidence. Finally, a priest who had been called to give Dhalia the last rites could be heard mumbling incoherently behind the grim cortege. The procession, faintly reminiscent of a stilted Danse Macabre but without the music.

'That's about all we can do here for now,' said Parish. How did you get on with Doctor Hackett?'

'I'll tell you in the car, guv,' replied Heart. 'There are a few interesting details. How did you get on with the waiter?'

'He's in the clear. Dropped a dinner tray around at about eight o'clock, and that was it. He was working in the restaurant for the rest of the night. Didn't finish until past 2 a.m. How did you get here, by the way?'

'A squad car brought me,' replied Heart, unsure why Parish had asked.

'Right, we'll take my car. You drive. I need to think.'

'Where to?' asked Heart, with the solemn tone of resigned inevitability.

'Hawsley is a serious contender. So we're off to have a quiet little chat with him at Buck House.'

'Oh fuck,' muttered Heart under his breath. He knew this moment would come at some point during the investigation. However, despite his mental preparation during the past few hours, it still took him by surprise. Somehow, he thought it might be another day, possibly, hopefully, even another detective, but that was not to be.

'Sorry?' said Parish, waggling his earlobe with two fingers in Heart's direction. 'Didn't quite catch that.'

'Well, you do have to be joking, guv. We can't just turn up at CSP headquarters and ask the Lord Protector if he recalls shagging some unregistered foreign hooker. Then lopping her head off with a samurai sword, stuffing it down the bog and then having a piss on it. He'll think we're some kind of sick joke-a-gram. Anyway, we won't get anywhere near Buck House. Not with the security he has... *We are all but lowly mortals in the lap of the gods when adversity calls*,' he added as an afterthought. In times of stress, Heart was inclined to colour his language wherever possible, liberally pillaging and paraphrasing lines from literary classics or, occasionally, even Christmas crackers.

'Hmm, point taken,' replied Parish, deep in thought, wondering what the quote's relevance was. Heart felt a heavy load lighten. The imminent confrontation with Hawsley was now temporarily averted. He took a deep breath and pushed back into his seat.

186

The temporary reprieve was short-lived.

'You had better contact Control. Ask them to tell Hawsley that we will arrive within the hour.'

'Right,' said Heart. The load just got heavy again. He was still unconvinced it would be that easy or even advisable at this early stage to confront Hawsley. Heart rang through to the Scotland Yard control desk and spoke to the indexing team documenting the details of the investigation.

'Thank you for calling Scotland Yard control centre. My name is Yolanda, and I will be your contact today. How can I help you?' Her tone was pleasing and helpful, with a tinge of reluctant subservience.

'Hi, Yolanda, this is Detective Sergeant Heart. I'm with Detective Inspector Parish, and we're on the Malting Mews incident in Chelsea. The incident code is… hold on a minute,' he scrambled around for the note on the dashboard and read it back. '19776BB.'

'Hold on, please, while I get the details on the screen,' replied Yolanda.

'No problem,' replied Heart. A few seconds passed.

'She sounds nice,' said Heart, placing his finger over the microphone grill.

'Hmm,' said Parish.

'Right, I have you up now,' came the voice over the intercom. The operator sounded enthusiastic, almost exuberant, which surprised Heart. His previous experiences with Control receptionists had been closer to uncompromising obduration. 'What can I do for you?' she asked.

'Can you arrange a meeting with the Lord Protector in about an hour?' There was silence for about ten seconds;

muffled conversation could be heard on the other end of the line.

Yolanda came back. 'Do you mean the one in the CSP?'

'Yes,' replied Heart a little indignantly. 'How many more Lord Protectors do you know of?' She didn't answer, and the phone went quiet again. In the background, he could hear more muffled conversation, this time slightly more animated.

Yolanda came back on the line again. 'Well, it's just a little unusual. I've only been here a week, and I really do love this job.' She spoke with heart-warming sincerity, but her tone began sounding slightly edgy with a hint of concern.

'Why would you lose your job?' asked Heart, sounding a little short and confused. He looked at Parish, who could hear the conversation but was saying nothing and flashed him an expression of frustration. Parish smiled back in reply.

'Well, you could be a nutter for all I know,' replied Yolanda in a disarmingly apologetic tone. 'We do get a lot of crank calls.' Heart's eyes jumped upwards momentarily, and Parish smiled.

'Look, Yolanda, I told you who I was and the crime scene code. All that information is on the screen before you, isn't it?' Heart endeavoured to retain his composure but was drifting ever closer to the edge of belligerence.

'Yes, yes, it is, but…' agreed Yolanda.

'But what?' interrupted Heart sharply.

'Well,' said Yolanda, taking a deep breath.

'Well, what!' replied Heart.

'Well, I have to be sure, don't I?' Her guttural Essex accent began seeping through.

'And are you now?' asked Heart disparagingly.

'Yes, I am.' She paused, and Heart thought he heard her take another deep breath. 'I've been talking with my colleagues, and they told me you were the grumpy one,' she muttered as an afterthought.

'Grumpy! I'm not grumpy,' he replied grumpily.

'You sound grumpy to me,' replied Yolanda with newfound bravado, obviously gaining self-confidence as the conversation progressed.

'Look, Yolanda, I am a detective sergeant in the police force, and I am telling you that I am not grumpy.' Parish smirked at him again and nodded his head. That didn't help. Parish also wondered why being a sergeant could make any difference to his grumpiness.

'If you say so, sergeant,' replied Yolanda, now sounding mildly insolent. She was not going to be easily intimidated by a mere sergeant.

'Can you make the call then?' repeated Heart, sounding irritated.

'Yes, I will. I'll try and make the appointment for two hours from now, say six o'clock. I must give them enough time to arrange the LP's diary appointment. Is that okay?'

'Well, it won't take long to get there, but six o'clock is fine, thank you.'

'If there is a problem, I will call you back within fifteen minutes. Is that okay?' asked Yolanda politely, resuming her usual telephone manner.

'Yes, thank you.'

'Is that all?' asked Yolanda.

'Yes, that's all,' replied Heart curtly.

'Thank you for calling,' she paused momentarily, and everything went quiet. 'Have a nice day!' She slipped that in very quickly and then hung up.

'Ahhhhhhhhhhhhhh,' screeched Heart. Parish laughed.

'Have a nice day,' repeated Parish, smirking at Heart.

'Are you sure we should be interviewing Hawsley this early in the investigation?' enquired Heart, still concerned.

'Look,' said Parish firmly, 'this is the man who, in twelve years, has managed to virtually reduce immigration to zero. And also arranged for the relocation of the unemployable, the spongers, lawbreakers, religious cranks, and anybody else who was a drain on or threat to society into the Ghettazone. He has cut taxation to ten per cent and reduced unsolved crime to almost non-existent levels. We all live in nice houses in regulated provinces with lots of money, and it's all down to him. So, I'm reasonably certain he won't be remotely concerned about answering a few routine questions about our unusual air scan report. And about his connection, if any, to the victim. He will probably be only too happy to assist us in eliminating him from our enquiries.'

Heart almost believed what he was hearing until he glanced at Parish and noticed that he was pointing animatedly at the dashboard. Parish had occasionally expressed a paranoid belief that all police vehicles had surveillance equipment built-in to monitor private conversations. He smiled at Heart conspiratorially and raised his eyebrows slightly. But Heart didn't appear to share Parish's concerns about third parties eavesdropping on their conversation. He thought that would be going too far. This was probably another reason why he was still a sergeant.

'Some people... still think he's the new Hitler, Stalin, and Genghis Khan rolled into one,' replied Heart dryly. 'But without their more endearing qualities,' he added after a few moments of silence had passed. Despite his now solemn, measured, and resigned tone, it was patently evident to Parish that Heart was extremely underwhelmed at the prospect of interviewing Hawsley.

'Adolf bought his mother flowers every Sunday,' shrugged Parish with an anodyne flourish as if that one redeeming quality would excuse everything else. And he was kind to little children… German children that is….'

'Classic attraction by distraction ploy,' replied Heart.

'What,' said Parish?

'That's how authoritarian despots work. They do lots of endearingly nice things that everybody can see. Once you are distracted, they do lots of horrible things behind your back. Didn't you know that?'

'No, strangely I didn't,' replied Parish. He was pondering over Heart's rather spurious analogy, confident in his mind that it was apocryphal. He was not really paying any attention to the sudden diversion down banality road the conversation had taken. His mind had already drifted off elsewhere.

'It's an Orwellian nightmare coming to fruition, just a little later than expected,' mooted Heart fearfully. Sounding like some old Norse witch who had just cast her runes and conjured up some unpleasant predictions, which she was obliged to impart to her masters.

Thoughts of an unexpected, pensionless early retirement in the wastelands of the Ghettazone started playing on Heart's mind. Suddenly, the suburban utopia of quiet days spent fishing on the banks of the Thames, watching cricket on Sundays, and having a few beers with his mates was gone. His wife, he didn't have one at the moment but was hoping to rectify that shortly, would be at home preparing the roast dinner and humming slightly off-key excerpts from *The Sound of Music*. So happy would she be with her life. There would be occasional day trips to the seaside during the summer and maybe the odd game of bowls with a few friends. On frosty winter nights, he would tinker around with his 1966 Lotus Cortina restoration project.

All that would be gone in a trice if they got on the wrong side of Hawsley – well, the wife had gone already, he didn't like fishing, and he didn't have a Lotus Cortina come to think of it. He was as entitled as the next man to visualise his perfect fantasy, but that, too, was now in jeopardy.

Suddenly, a new vision appeared. One in which he could see himself sitting in a battered, striped canvas deckchair in the front garden of a dilapidated terraced house on an ex-council sink estate somewhere on the outskirts of darkest Leicester or, worse still, Milton Keynes. He had a shotgun resting on his lap, ready to fend off the giant, man-eating rats.

This doomsday scenario, always imagined with remarkable attention to detail, was regularly conjured up in Heart's mind whenever things were not going too well. Especially when the threat of imminent unemployment and expulsion to the Ghettazone reared its ugly head. Unfortunately, he had made the grave mistake of sharing this doom-laden prospect with Parish on one remarkably uneventful day when they didn't have much to do. So now, whenever he descended into one of these maudlin moments, Parish, who unnervingly always seemed to have an inkling as to what was going on in Heart's head, would abruptly interrupt.

'I bet you're thinking about your deck chair in Milton Keynes, aren't you?' said Parish, breaking the silence.

'No, I'm not,' replied Heart indignantly, but he was.

'There's a rumour he eats babies for breakfast,' murmured Parish with half a grin. Heart knew that's all it was. Propaganda circulated by malcontent left-wing extremists in the Ghettazone. Unhappy with their dismal lot after voting the Hawsley administration into power. Many urban myths and rumours that originated outside the gated Provinces had found their way into contemporary folklore, but natural declension eventually diminished their value.

'The question is, does any of that make him a bad person? Probably not,' said Parish rhetorically. Admittedly, it doesn't make him a saint either, but the system works, doesn't it? And that's what matters.' He sounded almost philosophical.

'Whatever you say, guv,' replied Heart, a little taken aback by Parish's patent admiration for Hawsley's accomplishments.

'Right, let's go and get something to eat, and you can tell me all about our Doctor Hackett. Then we can pop into Buck House for a nice cup of tea and a chat with the leader of the gang.' Parish sounded disturbingly avuncular.

'They don't call it that anymore. And, I don't think the Lord Protector would appreciate being referred to as the leader of the gang either,' remarked Heart drily.

'Whatever you say,' said Parish. He glanced at Heart and gave him an insouciant glare, clearly indicating his feelings. Heart said nothing and drove off. They found a café, and Heart told Parish all about Hackett's little secret.

'I wonder what other secrets he hasn't mentioned,' mused Parish, munching his way through a grilled llama and yellow cabbage baguette. 'Some people never tell you the whole story straight away, especially if they think they can get away with just telling you half of it.'

'I don't think there can be anything more,' said Heart confidently. 'He sounded very distraught when I left. I don't think he was holding anything back.'

'You don't,' said Parish, unconvinced? 'There must be more to the AIDS thing. I wonder how she contracted it. You would have thought she would have been extra vigilant, bearing in mind what she did.'

'Hmm,' said Heart, tacitly agreeing.

'You can be a bit too easy-going at times when you're not grumpy, that is,' teased Parish, 'I wager Hackett has a lot more he can tell us... we will have to go back and see him again and put the pressure on a bit.'

'If you say so, Guv,' replied Heart. He took mild offence at the disparaging comment but said nothing. He had worked with Parish long enough to know he didn't mean anything by it - he was just after a result. Sometimes, a well-timed silence can speak so much more than poorly chosen words. He had read that somewhere recently, so he thought he would give it a try. They were beginning to interact like an old married couple. Chiding each other over inconsequential details and disagreeing over trivialities. Oddly, and possibly more telling, neither of them had noticed it was happening. This was probably because it was part of their defence mechanism against the grim realities they faced with every murder investigation. And partly due to the grief they had both encountered in their private lives. They relied on each other far more than either would freely admit or possibly even know.

They strolled back to the car in awkward silence and continued their journey to the CSP headquarters. Nothing was said until Heart decided to break the silence by defaulting to the relative neutrality of banal chit-chat again.

'These Bluto cars are absolute crap!' he suddenly exclaimed.

'Sorry?' said Parish, whose wired mind was totally preoccupied with the forthcoming meeting with Hawsley. 'I missed what you said.'

'These Bluto cars are absolute bloody shit,' repeated Heart (Bluto being a derisory term Heart had coined for the Protton vehicle). Such ridiculous statements were a subconscious trigger through which they would slowly segue into a surreal conversational diatribe. This was a cerebral device Parish and Heart had inadvertently developed over the years. One they invoked whenever the complex realities of whatever they were currently involved in began to overwhelm them. A juncture when they urgently needed to clear their heads. It acted as a harmless safety valve and gave them time to retreat to a state of benign objectivity. However, during the brief duration of one of these tangential diversions, any third party who happened to accidentally overhear their ramblings could be forgiven for thinking they had both suddenly lost all reason. And had descended, irrevocably, into the realms of lunacy.

'They are not Bluto cars,' replied Parish quietly but with authority. This was how the conversation would continue, surreal in content and extrapolation. There was a hint of intentional, vaudevillian contradiction, apparently for its own sake. Not dissimilar to a Christmas pantomime, which was apt considering the time of year. 'Bluto was a much-revered character from *Popeye*, a sixties television cartoon. He was a big, ugly, clumsy, awkward moron who played the adversarial role to Popeye. Whereas Protton cars had none of those attributes. The derisive nickname was irrelevant.' Parish paused to glance at Heart to ensure he was paying attention. He had recently read a book by Professor David Reed, "Analysis of the Psyche of Cartoon Characters and their Relationship to Real People." So, he was well-versed in the subject.

'On the other hand, the Popeye character,' continued Parish, 'was a paragon of honesty, decency, chivalry and reliability, like our beloved Protton motor car.'   Parish half-smiled at his counter-argument.

Heart looked at Parish, a little stunned by this uncharacteristic outburst of righteous indignation in support of their mode of transport. Parish seldom took any notice of Heart's derisory haranguing of their method of transportation. On the other hand, Heart was stunned by Parish's almost encyclopaedic knowledge of a television cartoon character that, in all probability, he had never seen.

Parish continued. 'Prottons cost practically nothing to run, are environmentally friendly and exceptionally reliable.' Parish recited this mantra as if he were a car salesman. But then, he had fully embraced modern technology. Unlike Heart, an inveterate Luddite who still held on tenaciously to the past and his naïve misinterpretation of the cartoon series.

'Did you know...' continued Parish, pausing for a few moments to add a little gravitas to what was about to follow.

'That the idea for Popeye was originally devised by J. Edgar Hoover. He even supplied a few of the storylines as classic political propaganda, thereby surreptitiously embedding the danger of becoming too friendly with Russia into the American people's psyche. Bluto represented the ugly Russian bear, whereas Popeye stood for the good old US of A and all that was good and wholesome. With its superpowers (for spinach, read atomic bomb), he would always overwhelm and eventually defeat Bluto.' Heart was stunned by this polemic revelation. He had never really gotten his head around the concept of metaphorical analogy.

'The more subversive elements of the series revolve around the role of the unmarried Olive Oyl character. Initially, she appears to be a simple prostitute or, at the very least, a fallen woman of relatively low intellect who has lost her way. Interestingly, she is easily persuaded to trade her favours with both protagonists and allow herself to be used or misused as necessary to survive.

Here, the obvious metaphorical candidate is, somewhat embarrassingly, Great Britain. Who did try to bed both partners simultaneously. On various levels, we received many "treats" from the USA and Russia during the Second World War. However, Olive's lack of feminine guile, intuition, womanly features, and excruciatingly squeaky voice is more disturbing. She is painted as little more than a mentally retarded imbecilic woman with highly questionable morals.' Parish paused momentarily to ensure he still had Heart's attention. He did.

'There was also the matter of the baby, the last part of the puzzle. It probably represented Europe. The residue of a conflict fought over by the three parents. However, the baby's precise parentage is decidedly unclear and strangely ambiguous for a cartoon. For some reason, viewers are led to believe she is Popeye's child. But may also have been fathered by Bluto in some clandestine tryst. Possibly a forced liaison or, at best, without conscious consent. This element is hinted at during many episodes. Does that help you to understand?' He glanced condescendingly at Heart.

Heart was noticeably quiet for a few moments before answering. 'Absolutely. And remarkably interesting, too.' But he didn't sound overly convinced.

Parish was happy to plod along at this tranquil rate. Ironically, the vehicles' speed seemed to mirror the pace at which life now travelled. The cars were, without doubt, ugly, graceless, ungainly, and not particularly fast, only managing to reach a top speed of thirty miles per hour. But then, there was no longer any necessity to travel any faster inside a gated province. Time had ceased to be an issue. The A.M.G.S. controlled the pace at which you, and to some degree, life progressed. Protton's, or more precisely, the speed at which they travelled, appeared to have a soporifically calming effect on the residents and life in general. It was as if the province inhabitants had wholly embraced a less frenzied - less distracted lifestyle. The quality and enjoyment of life had returned. That was all that mattered now.

The manufacturing province of Redemption, the fourth largest gated province in the country, encompassed the old cities of Birmingham, Nottingham, Manchester, and Sheffield. All Protton vehicles, general manufactured heavy goods and residential power plants were produced in the province. It was now the only industrial area in the UK. An import embargo on all manufactured goods had been in place since 2017. Only essential raw materials that the UK could not produce were sanctioned for import. And only then when something of equal value was exported. This was enshrined in the Matched Trade Treaty of 2017 when large numbers of plutomarium products (mainly freestanding generators) were exported to other countries.

The Euro's collapse in 2016 had effectively thrown Europe and the surrounding countries into a financial depression from which they would never recover. The UK was no longer dependent on fossil fuels. It had no reason to negotiate for the importation of oil or gas unless the terms were acceptable to the Hawsley administration. Redemption produced the SunRay reactors that powered the electricity grid and the Protton vehicle system - now virtually the only motorised form of personal transport available.

The SunRay energy source was derived from the accidental discovery of a non-nuclear plutonium/amarium alloy named plutomarium. Amarium was discovered in enormous quantities in Wales but nowhere else in the world. Plutomarium, when exposed to surprisingly small amounts of sunlight, generates immense quantities of energy. One gram could vaporise a litre of water in 1/100 of a second, so with the use of condensers, it was possible to travel over 2000 miles before refuelling with water.

In effect, the definitive reusable energy source, the very elixir of existence, if not life itself. The vehicles worked in the dark with Sunray amarium batteries without any noticeable deterioration in performance.

Some experimental production models developed in 2014 ran on the alternative pressurised hydrogen fuel systems - but a problem with leaks led to a series of high-profile explosions. The vehicles themselves were also prone to explode under crash conditions. Despite enhanced safety measures, which also made the cars prohibitively expensive, their popularity waned and never recovered. You can lead a horse to water...

The SunRay technology had been further developed to power the Inter-Province Bullet train network and the aeronautical, space and defence industries. We had returned to the steam age with a stoic passion that would have made Stevenson ecstatic with pride. Saltwater needed to be combined with the plutomarium to create the cold fusion reaction, and Britain was surrounded by it. So, electrical energy was virtually limitless. Individual autonomous provincial power systems were much cheaper, safer, and easier to install. The national fossil fuel power network was rendered redundant by 2020. This incredibly affordable and efficient technology was a significant vote winner and guaranteed continuing support for the CSP for the foreseeable future.

'But they feel clumsy and awkward to me, and I feel like a moron when I'm being driven around in one,' mumbled Heart. They had returned from their brief diversion back to reality.

'Do you?' said Parish with a noticeable lack of interest. He was otherwise occupied rereading the air scan results again and not really listening. There were some odd discrepancies in the report that he would need to discuss with Gerry at their next meeting.

'I still prefer the old two-litre Mondeo.'

'Christ, it must be over ten years since they were last around,' exclaimed Parish with a pained expression.

'Still a classic. I've got one. I keep it in my garage,' said Heart, with a palpable sense of pride.

'What for? You can't drive it without petrol, and there's little of that about these days,' queried Parish.

'Don't need to drive it. I just polish it.'

'Do you?' said Parish, with growing concern. 'So, your Sundays are spent polishing your Mondeo?' he smirked, but Heart ignored the crude attempt at a double entendre.

'Yes, it's a part of our heritage,' replied Heart defensively, with a tangible sense of patriotism that Parish found quite touching.

'Is it,' replied Parish, with a caustic inflection? Heart took no notice.

'Petrol will come back one day when the water runs out.' Heart seemed almost troubled by the passing of the fossil fuel age and appeared to harbour heretical thoughts about a possible revival of leaded petrol. Parish found his apparent optimism profoundly misplaced and yet strangely endearing in equal proportions. He was also inwardly amused by the improbability. Considering the quantity of freely available seawater and that ninety-nine per cent of the water used in Protton technology was eventually returned to the atmosphere as rain. A truly sustainable source of energy. Current stockpiles of amarium were sufficient to last for 200 years, and estimates indicated that ninety-seven per cent of the precious ore was still in the ground in Progression.

'And you will be ready with your shiny Mondeo,' replied Parish, with a hint of sarcasm that he had failed to sufficiently suppress to avoid sounding disparaging.

'Yes. Yes, I will. Then we'll see who has the last laugh,' added Heart, sticking firmly to his old-fashioned beliefs.

'You don't really buy into the Hawsley thing, do you?' asked Parish.

'Yes, I do, but with reservation,' replied Heart, surprisingly unfazed by Parish's narrow perspective. 'You have to admit, though, it was a lot more fun before.'

'We've moved on, Heart, but you stood still. Maybe that's why you are still a sergeant at what? Fifty-three?'

'Fifty-one actually,' corrected Heart indignantly.

'And I'm an Inspector at thirty-nine,' replied Parish, as if to prove the point.

'Forty-two actually, guv,' muttered Heart with a smirk.

'Is it?' asked Parish. 'I don't keep count anymore.' Heart thought that a little odd but didn't pass any comment.

'You're probably right,' replied Heart, sounding reluctantly philosophical. He had to concede the obvious truth. He had not progressed in his career as far as he would have liked. The slippery pole of promotion always seemed much greasier whenever he tried to grasp it. And he wasn't that sure he wanted to progress any further anyway, what with all the radical changes that had taken place in the service. Satisfaction and contentment were achievable by enjoying what you were, not what you wanted to be.

'We would still have arrived here faster in the last century,' mumbled Heart.

'Odd you should say that,' said Parish. 'I seem to remember someone mentioning those exact same words back around the year 2000. He was referring to the time it took to get across London and how it took longer to travel a mile by taxi than in a horse and cart in 1900.' Heart thought carefully and mumbled something, but Parish couldn't make it out.

'Anyway, would it really make any difference?' queried Parish thoughtfully. 'We've still got to where we wanted to be, just a little slower and without any stress.'

'You're not stressed?' queried Heart, sounding incredibly surprised. 'We're about to interrogate Lord Protector Haw....'

'Not interrogate, corrected Parish. 'Interview. We're just going to ask him a few questions. We're not the secret police. This isn't a totalitarian state yet.' But it was…

'Just ask him a few questions,' parroted Heart. 'The man who can make people vanish off the face of the earth with just a click of his fingers,' mumbled Heart. He clicked his fingers to add emphasis, not realising how ironic that observation would eventually prove to be.

'That's an urban myth, old wives tales,' Parish unconvincingly replied.

'Well, let's hope he doesn't get too miffed with us,' replied Heart. 'If we piss him off, he might just prove you wrong.' Parish turned to Heart and glanced at him with a conciliatory smirk. They pulled up at the side security gate to the CSP headquarters. It had now been rehoused in the old Buckingham Palace building. They produced their ID passes to the security guard, who checked them against his tablet. He waved them through to the main parking area full of identical Prottons, all the same bland, utilitarian colour.

The car self-parked. Heart glanced at Parish, twitched his head and uttered, 'right, let's do this thing.' Parish winced at Heart's crass Americanism - he hated the phrase, and Heart knew it. They got out and started to stroll across to the main entrance, not saying anything more until they reached the bottom of the steps.

Two police officers stood guard by the door to the building. Both held Heckler and Koch light machine guns in a jaunty yet menacing manner. They looked very stern and intimidating. The sergeant seemed particularly obnoxious. Parish was beginning to appreciate how the gladiators must have felt when they entered the amphitheatre in Rome and were met by lions that hadn't been fed for a week. They were going to meet the most powerful man in the United Republic of Britain. And they were about to ask him, as diplomatically as they could, whether he had, on a crazy, psychopathic whim, beheaded a prostitute. The possible implications of their proposed line of enquiry and the probable nature of the ensuing conversation began registering on them. Aiden Hawsley was a social phenomenon, and they were about to question his integrity, honesty, and morality.

As the old BNP leader, he was consistently treated by the press and his political contemporaries as a social pariah. It was as if he existed only in the greyness of virtual obscurity. No more than a harmless figure of fun. Now, he had risen to the dizzy heights of power – as the head of the Christian Socialist Party. This was accomplished by an inspired change of name in 2010.

Hawsley had orchestrated a brilliant media campaign that changed the country's mindset, eventually leading to the most humiliating defeat of any government since the Tony Blair era. And the ultimate destruction of the triumvirate party political system that had existed in various forms since 1295 to the national elections in 2015. The other parties failed to take more than a handful of seats. The landslide victory eventually led to a complete overall electoral system. One of the world's oldest democracies was quickly and comprehensively dismantled and consigned to the history books as a footnote.

There was once a euphemistically titled three-party system. An egalitarian structure devised by the intelligentsia and political mandarins to perpetuate the enduring illusion of a freely elected democracy for the benefit of the proletarian masses. In a thrice, that was gone. In its place, the United Republic of Britain, with

Aiden Hawsley as Lord Protector of the Republic and leader of the new Christian Socialist Party.

What so many people had misunderstood for so long was that the existing system was not a system at all but just the flailing death throes of a diseased and corrupt bureaucracy.

Aiden had not been elected to office because he was a masterful and erudite politician (although, in fact, he was) but because he was a brilliant tactician. He had presented himself to the voters at the perfect moment and had managed to tap into the prevailing zeitgeist of the moment with impeccable timing. The country was drowning in austerity and hopelessness when he held out his hand. A messianic liberator, holding up the flame of hope. The pinnacle of the mountain of change had been reached, and he stood on the top looking down, the one man who could change Britain forever and make it a true autocracy.

Initially, people voted for him for one of three reasons. Out of a rebellious sense of frustration and anguish at the current administration. Or from an underlying fear of what could happen if things didn't change radically. Or in the desperate hope that he could alter the inevitable outcome that was becoming all too apparent with each passing day.

His natural charisma and silky orations quickly enraptured their minds, polarising their thoughts and focusing their voting fingers. He engendered loyalty, trust, integrity, credibility, and believability. So, the gathering storm of unrest made him appear even more electable than he really was.

During the election campaign, there was a defining moment when the tsunami of euphoric crowd hysteria began to overwhelm the nation. The electorate started to believe that not only could Hawsley make a difference but that he would make a difference in their lives. This hysterical adulation grew into such a thundering ovation that the people created, through this one moment of carefully orchestrated pandemonium, the enigma and paradox that was Aiden Hawsley.

Hawsley didn't immediately realise what was happening; events were moving faster than he could ever have planned or anticipated. He was swiftly elevated to an exalted position, and he embraced and controlled it. From this platform, he produced ideas that would continue to support and promote his godlike aura. Many millions of people even came to believe that he was the reincarnation of Christ. If you spoke out against him, it was tantamount to sedition, even treason, and you would be treated with biblical scorn. There were instances of people being beaten to death for disagreeing with his policies.

Like all significant phenomena of the last two thousand years, the figurehead was the ultimate creation of the people's imagination. Transmogrified into a life form. Absolute power and mass adoration make a person different.

The Beatles were probably the last great exponents of the process. A competent band of reasonably talented musicians with average creational ability but displaying no evidence of musical genius until after becoming famous. Then, they were suddenly adorned with the epithet of "the greatest band in the world" and musical prodigies. They were psychologically elevated to a position where it became incumbent upon them to produce music of a much higher quality than they had previously created. With that pressure and their self-belief - and possibly some assistance from Uncle Charlie and other assorted compounds, they produced the goods for many years. The band's quality as a live act in their early days of fame will never be known. When they were unknown and playing in Germany, their musical quality was comparable to hundreds if not thousands of equally talented groups. Many of whom never even made a living. Desperate to unshackle themselves from the cultural limitations of the past, the youth of Britain wanted something new - that belonged exclusively to them. They would have allowed any credible band to liberate them from the chains of post-war austerity. After the Beatle's first record became a moderate success, the masses found them. Such was the incredible sound generated by the screaming fans - the band could not be heard at a concert for nearly two years. The amplification equipment that was powerful enough to overcome the noise had not yet been built. Euphoric crowd hysteria had once again taken over - and would ultimately develop into the creative environment that would transform them into the musical geniuses they became.

Twenty-five years earlier, Adolf Hitler had done the same thing. He was a humble corporal with a burning ambition when he first trod the political trail. But he quickly discovered the panacea that could mend a broken nation, the underlying concern nearly every German thought about - but would seldom speak about. The fear that could and would unite a country and make them adore him for pronouncing in public the words and feelings that they dare not. He didn't excel at much, but he was a great orator with a pedestrian grasp of tactics. He didn't need anything else. It's easy to be great when everybody tells you that's what you are. All you have to do is go with the flow. Ride the crest of the opprobrium, which was his sneering scorn for the Jewish race. The masses wanted him, they needed him, and they would make him what he became. You can't kill a concept. He knew that. So, he planted the seed of hope and deliverance, and then all he had to do was be patient and wait for it to germinate and burst into life.

From a distance, Parish thought the police sergeant guarding the entrance looked a little officious, possibly arrogant. He surreptitiously whispered his thoughts to Heart before suggesting he might open the conversation.

'Good afternoon,' said Heart engagingly, craning his neck to engage the policeman's eyes while smiling courteously. The sergeant, standing five steps above them, approximately four feet higher from where they stood, looked down condescendingly as if noticing them for the first time. He must have been perfectly aware that they had been approaching the main entrance as they crossed the gravel drive. He sniffed the air as if something smelt unpleasant.

'Good afternoon to you, gentlemen,' the sergeant replied slowly in a monosyllabically dismissive tone. One you might use if you were passing the time of day with a couple of drunken miscreants sprawled out on a pathway in a park on a hot summer's day. You wisely wouldn't wish to antagonise them by ignoring them, but neither did you want to engage them in meaningful conversation. Nevertheless, you had to pass them to reach your destination, so it became necessary to acknowledge their existence with a discreet smile.

The sergeant, however, was perfectly aware this wasn't the case. Nobody passes by; there was nowhere else to go. Not a good start, thought Parish. Right on the first two counts, adding obnoxiousness to the mix. But he may still have misread the intonation, so he made no comment and allowed Heart to continue the conversation.

'I am Detective Sergeant Heart and this...' he glanced at Parish, who smiled discreetly, 'is Detective Inspector Parish.' They both offered their warrant cards, but the sergeant took no notice.

'We have an appointment for a chat with the Lord Protector.'

'I'm sure you have, son, but you must go through channels,' said the sergeant in a broad, slightly contemptuous Welsh accent. He finished with a supercilious smile.

Calling Heart son didn't endear him to Heart, who was much older anyway. Parish was now sure that his first impression was bang on the money.

'Scotland Yard has scheduled us to interview him at six pm. This is a murder enquiry, and we would like to talk to the Lord Protector as arranged,' replied Heart. He was more forceful this time. Assuming his full height and asserting his authority as best he could from the tactical disadvantage of being nearly four feet lower. He was still smarting from Parish's earlier comment about his unimpressive interview with Hackett. So he was making a special effort to redress that failing and appear more forthright and slightly more belligerent. It nearly worked. Any reservations he may have had about interviewing Hawsley were quickly dispelled. Swiftly replaced by a sense of pure loathing for the frustratingly supercilious sergeant.

'You may well have an appointment, laddie, but the Lord Protector is terribly busy now, and you ain't on the list.' He smiled authoritatively while tapping his earpiece. 'And if you ain't on the list, then you don't get in, savvy?'

'Busy doing what?' asked Heart indignantly.

'Well, it's not actually any of your business, really. But I understand he is discussing the issue of saving us from another invasion by the fuzzy wuzzies from bongo bongo land.'

'The what?' said Parish, who until that moment had been standing quietly, passively listening to the conversation, making mental notes and odd facial expressions.

'Fuzzy wuzzies, sir,' turning his attention to Parish. 'You know, nignogs, Sambos, wops, jungle bunnies, blicks, Muzzes, Micks, Ities, Gypos, Pykies and Krauts... Oh, and of course, we must not forget the fucking French. The heavens would open, and plagues of locusts would descend if we left them out.' Parish noticed his head appeared to pivot as if on a pole, not unlike the Mr. Policeman character in a Punch and Judy show. His body didn't move an inch. Parish imagined that he would produce a truncheon at any moment. Then adopt a strange twizzle tone and start repeating, 'How was I? – How was I?' He even considered the possibility of Judy turning up at any moment to top the show off.

'Can you say that?' enquired Heart curiously.

'I just did, didn't I? said the sergeant, smiling demonically. 'I can say what I like, sir. 'Because we live in a proper Republican democracy now. One man, one vote, none of your lefty, middle-class namby-pamby Arts Council veggie quango tish-tosh now, sir. We call a wog a wog, a spade a spade, and we don't want none of those Ghettazone, maggot-munching Glunde bastards creeping in here, do we now?'

But, of course, we didn't live in a democracy at all. That was Hawsley's most incredible illusion.

'One man, one vote,' queried Heart. 'Interesting concept.'

'That's right, Lord Protector Hawsley's the man, and he's got the vote.'

'I don't think that's quite what democracy means,' said Heart politely.

'It does to us, sir, and an excellent arrangement it is if I might say so.' Heart could see this was getting them nowhere.

'If you are not British, you're out. If you're muzzy, you're out, and any other pisspot-skiving scrounger is out. Britain for the British, sir, that's what the Lord Protector is doing, keeping all the thieving blacks and toerags out, and I am doing my bit, keeping you out.'

'But we're not black,' said Parish, still slightly stunned by the venomous diatribe he had just been subjected to.

'No, sir, and I am incredibly pleased for you,' replied the sergeant, smiling.

'If I ask you nicely, would you let us in to see him?' asked Heart in a humbling, contrite tone. He realised his initial forceful approach was not working well, so a more conciliatory approach might be more successful.

'You could try the passive non-confrontational method if you like. It might work,' replied the Sergeant accommodatingly, preparing himself for a revised request.

Heart took a deep breath to calm himself, counted to five, and then continued. 'Please... do you think it would be possible for us to see the Lord Protector for just a few minutes, please, thank you?' He spoke in the most obsequious tone he could muster while smiling politely at the sergeant.

'Absolutely not,' replied the sergeant. 'Are you fucking deaf as well as stupid?'

'Cunt,' mumbled Heart under his breath. He did a lot of that these days.

'What did you say, sir?' asked the sergeant, twirling the ends of his moustache with the one hand that was not on the trigger of his Heckler and Koch assault rifle. He did it in such a way that, for some reason, it severely irritated Heart. Parish said nothing, still waiting for the truncheon and the alligator to appear in this bizarre Punch and Judy parody.

'Constable, we will get a warrant if we have to,' replied Heart. The sergeant looked at him curiously.

'It's sergeant, actually,' said the sergeant, pointing proudly at the chevrons on his arm.

'My apologies,' said Heart with no conviction whatsoever. Parish wondered why it was that some people just didn't get on.

'So, do we have to get a warrant?' asked Heart with a subtle hint of intimidation, which had no effect whatsoever on the sergeant.

'You can get a dispensation from Jesus scribbled on the Turin shroud with a magic marker if you like, sir, but The L.P. still won't see you unless you have gone through channels, savvy?' The sergeant smirked at Heart.

'But we have. The Yard control centre arranged this appointment,' replied Heart, but his tenacity was beginning to wilt.

'Not according to my list, sir.' He mumbled something into his headset. 'Probably a cock-up in your office?' suggested the sergeant smirking yet again.

'Where is your list?' enquired Parish.

'It's inside, sir.'

'How do you know we're not on it?'

'You're not on it because my colleague and fellow patriot, who is inside, has just told me you're not on it.' He pointed to his earpiece again and then pointed his finger over his shoulder to a camera situated just above his head. The camera nodded slightly as if the man inside wanted to confirm he was watching the proceedings.

'And anyway,' the sergeant's eyebrows lifted slightly as if he were about to impart another stunning piece of useless information, 'there is another good reason you can't see him.'

'What's that then?' a now slightly deflated Heart ventured cautiously.

'He's not here.'

'Not here?' echoed Heart as if he had misheard.

'That's right. You really have got a hearing problem, haven't you, sir? I would get that seen to if I was you,' he added, raising his voice and accentuating the word 'hearing' for added effect. 'You should try Specsavers; I've heard they're pretty good.' He laughs, 'They have a special offer on at the moment for elderly gents.'

'No. I haven't got a hearing problem,' replied Heart indignantly, 'and I am not old.'

The sergeant nodded from side to side as if he disagreed with Heart's claim and that it was a matter for debate.

'Well, stay here much longer, and you might have, sonny.' He emphasised the "sonny" word.

'Is that a threat?' asked Heart even more indignantly.

'No sir, not a threat.' replied the sergeant, smiling. 'But it can get deafening and very fractious when the guns start going off. Which can happen if we think there is a possible incursion about to occur or an attempt on the Lord Protector's life is imminent.' He pointed at the armed constable on the other side of the steps. 'He can be a bit trigger-happy at times. He's also a bit prickly at the moment. He hates Christmas and being at home with his wife and kids. And he has just been told he has six days off for Christmas. So he is not a happy bunny.'

The constable nodded in agreement and smiled somewhat disturbingly.

'But you just told us he's not here,' said Heart.

'That's correct, sir, but that was a missive that I imparted to you as a token gesture of seasonal goodwill and to assist and maintain an amicable working relationship between you and us,' replied the sergeant. 'But I wouldn't let that minor detail affect any logistical decision I had to make regarding the security of the building and our leader.'

'Why didn't you tell us he wasn't here in the first place?'

'Because, my flat-footed friend, you never asked, and anyway, I enjoy a little intellectual badinage after my lunch. It helps with my indigestion.'

'We are police officers just like you,' replied Heart.

'Not like me, sir. I'm pleasant and accommodating. On the other hand, you are nasty and aggressive and a little bit on the grumpy side, if you don't mind me saying,' replied the sergeant, smiling disturbingly - not unlike his colleague. Heart could only assume that they had both attended the same charm school.

'I'm not grumpy,' said Heart, who was becoming slightly paranoid over this recurring theme.

'Yes, you are. And you're loud and aggressive and a little bit arrogant as well, if you don't mind me saying so... sir!'

'Where is he then?' asked Parish.

'In Scotland shooting peasants, probably having more fun than me.'

'Pheasants,' mumbled Heart under his breath.

'Peasants, pheasants, all the same to me, sir.'

'Why didn't you mention that before?' asked Parish.

'You didn't ask me,' replied the sergeant, sounding astonished. 'I told your sergeant that just now.'

'But...' said Parish.

'Channels, sir. I did mention it before. It must be your hearing playing up as well. You gotta go through channels, or you just won't get anywhere.'

'Channels,' exclaimed Heart stupefyingly.

'But this is a murder we're investigating,' interrupted Parish, 'not a bloody parking offence. You could have saved us a lot of time if you'd told us that in the first place.' He glared at the sergeant, emphasising the significance of their enquiry and his annoyance at the officer's time-wasting.

'It's no good going all gooey-eyed at me, sir,' said the sergeant. 'I'm sorry, but it has to go through channels. I am sure some Russian tart getting her head lopped off and stuffed down the bog is extremely exciting for you. But it ain't gonna bring him back from a few days' holiday shooting in Scotland, is it now?'

'How did you know that? It's confidential,' asked Heart indignantly.

'Know what?' said the sergeant in a dilatory manner.

'About the circumstances of the victim's death,' replied Heart.

'Don't be silly, sonny,' replied the sergeant. He smiled condescendingly at his unintended alliteration. 'We're the government. We know everything. We even know you don't like your little Protton car.' He looked at Heart intently as if expecting some swift rebuttal. Heart said nothing. He was completely thrown off guard by the sergeant's unnervingly accurate revelation. Parish must have been correct, after all, he thought to himself.

'How the fu…?'

'Leave it, Heart,' interrupted Parish, looking at Heart. He turned back to the sergeant. 'Okay, we'll go through channels… again.'

'That's the spirit, sir,' replied the sergeant smugly. 'Now you got it.'

'But we'll be back,' added Heart.

'Ooooh,' said the sergeant, mocking Heart's adversarial tone and pretending to shake with fear. 'I'm very frightened,' but Heart took no notice.

'Thank you for your assistance, sergeant,' were Parish's final words as they left.

'My pleasure. Do come again, any time. Ta ta,' replied the sergeant. 'Hope you enjoyed your visit. Oh, and a Merry Christmas,' he shouted as they walked away. He obviously enjoyed his job. 'Oh, Inspector,' he called out after they had walked a few more paces.

'Yes,' replied Parish,

'Don't bring the grumpy one next time if you return.'

'Don't say it,' responded Parish to Heart. 'Stay here for a minute.' He turned, and Heart watched him walk back towards the sergeant.

'I have one more question: can you tell me when Mr Hawsley left for Scotland?'

'Yes, I can actually,' replied the sergeant with a surly dismissive tone. He proceeded to smile at Parish. Parish waited for a few moments, half expecting the answer to follow, but it didn't. They stood looking at each other for a few moments before Parish realised he would have to ask the question again, more specifically.

'When was it then?'

'Oh, you want to know?' replied the sergeant. 'Sorry, I thought you just wanted to know if I knew.' He smiled discreetly at Parish.

'No, I would like to know the time if you could manage that.'

'Well, let me think… Yes, it would have been about midnight last night. He popped out for about an hour at about nine o'clock, returned at about ten, and left at about twelve o'clock for the airport. I was on duty from four to two, and he left a couple of hours before I finished,'

'Long hours,' said Parish.

'Dedication to duty, sir, and it is Christmas. Of course, the lads like to be with their families this time of year, but I'm not bothered.'

'You don't see much of that these days,' said Parish.

'You certainly don't.'

'Well, thank you.'

'No, thank you, sir,' replied the sergeant, curtly saluting as he left. Parish walked back towards Heart.

'Hawsley appears to have an alibi from early evening till he caught the plane to Scotland,' said Parish.

'So, he's off the hook?' asked Heart.

'Well, we need to check it out, but it's beginning to look that way,' replied Parish disconsolately.

'So, that only leaves Benny Maranno and the mysterious Mr. X with the unidentified air scan,' said Heart.

'So, it would seem,' agreed Parish. As they reached the car, Parish turned to Heart.

'Look, it's nearly seven. I will catch the tram home and study these reports a little more. Can you go back to the station and see what you can dig up on this Benny Maranno character? Send my car home. I'll see you at nine tomorrow at the station.'

'Right,' said Heart. 'See you tomorrow.' He drove off as Parish wandered through the security gates, walking up the road towards the tram stop. He jumped onto the next transit tram, swiped his travel card and tapped the destination button for home. The computer acknowledged payment and programmed his journey. Parish started reading the reports.

He would need to ask Gerry several questions in the next day or two, but most of it was as expected. The one unregistered scan was probably his most likely suspect. Avoiding registration required a great deal of effort and application. In fact, it was virtually impossible with the various security checks that were encountered almost daily. This gave rise to the possibility of some underlying secondary motive for avoiding their legal obligations and effectively rendering themselves invisible to the system.

Chapter 12

Parish arrived at his stop, stepped off the tram and walked the short distance to his house. He no longer called it home, merely referring to it as '*the place where I live*' if it ever came up in conversation. For him, it was just a building with beautiful furniture. A home was where a family lived as far as he was concerned. But that wasn't the case any longer...

He let himself into the hallway that led into the open-plan American-style lounge dining area encompassing most of the ground floor. It was a large room, almost too large for someone living alone. The automatic blue skirting lights threw a soft, almost eerie, luminescent glow across the hall and the lounge floor, lighting his way to another world.

When Catherine and Jade had been there, it seemed too small to accommodate them all. They were even considering moving to a larger house, but not now. There was no point. This was the time of day when he felt the most wretched. There would have been soft music playing quietly, probably some old jazz singer. Catherine loved Dinah Washington, Ella Fitzgerald, and Billie Holiday, as did he. There were so many things they had enjoyed doing together and a few they couldn't agree on, but these were the things that make a marriage work. They weren't even disagreements, just differences of opinion, which always made for a lively and entertaining conversation.

The smell of cooking food would be lingering in the air, the French doors would be wide open if it were summer, and the table was ready for dinner. Fresh flowers in a vase would be on the table: African lilies were Catherine's favourite. He always thought they smelt of cat piss but never mentioned it. But then he loved lavender, and she felt it smacked of little old ladies in their dotage.

It was winter now. The doors were closed, and the drapes were half-pulled. No music played, and the room smelt only musty and stale. The patio table was covered in its green winter jacket and sprinkled with snow. Everything seemed very grey and dismal.

The happy memories emanating from every corner of the house were still intense. Occasionally, they would reach out to him, and he would become entranced, almost captivated by unseen charms in this spellbound fantasy. It was as if the house was trying to absorb him, to draw him into its very fabric, and he was happy to let it do so. He edged off his shoes, pushed them behind the door, and walked over to the mini bar, moving slowly as if not wishing to unsettle the air too much for fear of disturbing the sound of silence. He poured himself a large Jack Daniels, pressed the ice button and watched the cubes chink into his glass. Finally, he wandered over to the sofa and sat down.

'Music on, please.' He spoke the words quietly and always said please and thank you. Old-fashioned etiquette the computer didn't require, but he did it anyway. He slowly swirled the ice around in the glass, watching the peculiar way it affected the bourbon, streaks of light and gold like olive oil mixing with water.

'Who would you like to hear, Mack?' asked the computer. The soft words were spoken by Catherine; he shut his eyes, and he could see her standing in the kitchen cooking ravioli or maybe spaghetti. He could smell her Penhaligon's Cairo perfume. She always kept some in the kitchen to spray herself whenever cooking to mask any unpleasant odours. Once again, he could feel the scent of her body slowly invading his senses and inveigling his soul.

Catherine had spent many hours programming their voices into the speech-activated entertainment system. It now responded personally to whoever issued commands, but all the replies were in Catherine's lilting, slightly husky voice.

'Play some Dinah Washington, please,' he asked.

'Thank you for your instructions, Mack.' There was a subtle hint of sexual promiscuity in the manner of her reply that only he could detect. It would appear entirely innocuous to Jade or to anybody else for that matter. You would have to have known Catherine intimately to understand the intonation.

This was Catherine's little play on subservience, something only they understood. They would often play games with words; it made them laugh together while confusing anybody else who might be listening. It was a secret language all their own, a language he would never speak again. The music started to play; Parish took out his revolver from the shoulder holster and carefully laid it on the table. This was his usual routine whenever he came home. At some point during the evening, Parish would pick up the gun, release the safety catch and point the barrel to his heart or his head. He would put his finger on the trigger and run it slowly up and down the cold steel. Just for a moment, he came as close as he could imagine to eternity with Catherine and Jade. For a few moments, he would be there.

One simple action and all his pain, anguish, and sorrow would be over... but he could be wrong. He might never see her again. That was the uncertainty that held him back.

'Tea in five minutes, darling. Can you open the wine?'

'No problem. Red or white?' replied Parish.

'Tonight...' she paused. She always paused to carefully consider her choice, seldom if ever, a rash decision; spontaneous yes, but never reckless. That's what made it even harder to accept the verdict. Death by misadventure. What does that really mean? Unlucky? Unfortunate? One tiny, innocuous decision – a bad one – made in a fraction of a second that would forever change their lives. It didn't take much. The Titanic captain said, 'I think we'll steam a little faster tonight,' and 1,500 people froze to death in the icy waters of the Atlantic. Was it that easy to change so many lives? That was something he would never fully understand: the serendipitous nature of life.

'I will try... the Merlot, yes the Merlot,' she uttered the words slowly, thinking carefully about every syllable, and then the decision was made. Thoroughly reasoned and meticulously considered. That was the way Catherine worked.

'Are you sure?' Parish asked, but he didn't really need to question her choice.

'Of course I am,' she replied with absolute certainty. 'Once a decision is made, it is done, so move on.' That was her maxim. She smiled at Parish, and he smiled back. Parish put his drink on the table, went over to the wine rack, pulled out a bottle of Merlot and began to open it. He thought about what she had just said. It kept running over repeatedly in his mind. Finally, a tear formed in the corner of his eye and began to roll down his cheek.

'Where's Jade?' asked Parish, wiping the tear away.

'Doing her homework in her bedroom, I think. Can you call her?'

Parish walked across to the foot of the staircase and called, 'Jade, dinner,'

'Coming, Dad,' she replied. 'Two minutes.' They would sit down together, eat dinner and talk about their day. Catherine worked part-time in a pathology lab, so they had many things they could talk about, which they both understood. Jade, in common with most teenagers, enjoyed the gory details. After dinner, she would clear up the dishes, and then it would be time for them to go. Before Catherine left, she would tell him not to be so 'bloody stupid' and to put the gun away, and he would, but he needed her to say the words. He needed to hear them before she left. If she ever stopped...

This was the moment he missed most. when they decided to go to bed... It wasn't the sex, not every night anyway. They had been together for nearly fourteen years and married for thirteen. The passion, vitality, and intensity of new love – physically demanding and often fraught, fractious, and occasionally emotionally draining – had, without skipping a beat, made the smooth transition to real, lasting love. It was now something that would endure the trials of a lifetime together. A passionate desire still existed, but now, to make each other feel happy, at ease, and secure. Just lying beside her, being able to reach out and touch her body and feel her response, this was something he couldn't put a value on... Always the simple pleasures.

To feel her turn over and reach out to touch his body – reassurance that what they had was real was all he needed to get him through each day. But now he was alone, and those moments were no more, and nothing could replace them. When they made love, sometimes in the middle of the night, not a word would be spoken as they lost themselves in the rapture of yearning ecstasy for each other. And after the caressing and kissing, when the moment was over, they would return to sleep. Both to rest in the knowledge that they were loved and always would be until…

Catherine and Jade had been gone for three long years. It felt like only yesterday when he had taken the call that informed him there had been a fatal collision between a lorry and a vehicle registered to Catherine. It was one o'clock in the morning, and Catherine had picked Jade up from a friend's house on the other side of Providence. Parish had arrived home late and decided to stay up until they returned, but they never did. He was told afterwards that the roads were almost deserted at the time. For some reason - never satisfactorily explained - the AMG system had malfunctioned, and their car had been crushed beyond recognition by a SCOMTEL juggernaut. The lorry driver - wholly exonerated from any blame - never fully recovered from the trauma and never drove again.

The enquiry found that Catherine and Jade were probably both asleep, which was reasonable for travellers on the AMG system, as collisions were fundamentally impossible. However, there had been an exceedingly rare electronic failure. Such was the extent of their injuries; the pathologist refused to allow Parish to identify the remains. His explanation was they were crushed so severely beyond recognition. It would have been impossible to determine what exactly Parish would be identifying, let alone who.

Parish searched his pockets for the little plastic box and retrieved the pin-chip, which he held close to the tiny chip bay behind his ear. The waterproof cover slid back, and the chip pin was automatically drawn in as if by a magnetic force. The cover closed again, and the familiar grey screen appeared. The on-screen options appeared. He guided the brain-activated icon to the fast-forward option. He didn't want to endure breakfast again. Once was quite enough for today. He found himself on the sofa in Loretta's parents' house. Perfect, he thought to himself. The screen, now transposed over reality, was reduced to a white dot in the lower right-hand corner of his vision with a miniscule cursor arrow just below it. With these two icons, he could control suspension, run, cancel, and fast forward, but he just needed to escape for now. So he activated the run option...

Chapter 13

'Come on, Mack, let's walk before your damn phone rings again.' Loretta sounded agitated, and I wished I'd purchased the more expensive VRS Zip-Chip option. At least I would have had a decent holiday without interruptions. As an inspector, I was always obliged to keep my mobile switched on, but I could normally expect an uninterrupted break of at least six hours over a weekend. This would generally be enough time to run the standard ten-day holiday VRS chip. I crossed my fingers and prayed to the heavens. Loretta, already dressed for walking, grabbed my hands and pulled me off the sofa.

'I've put some more suitable clothing in your bedroom,' said Loretta, smiling, 'so you go up and change.' I wandered upstairs to my bedroom. Sure enough, on the bed were some clothes. I stripped off - my clothes were a little conservative for Arkansas in winter anyway - and slipped on the blue Wrangler jeans and walking boots. They resembled something that someone might have worn to a line-dancing extravaganza. But had been rejected for being too ostentatious. This had to be some achievement, considering what some devotees wore. I picked up the bright red and black fleece-lined gingham shirt, waved it around a bit, toreador style, and then put it on. It was clearly from the same sartorial source as the boots. I slipped into an oversized bearskin jacket, threw a scarf around my neck to complete the ensemble, and made my way back downstairs.

'You look amazing,' said Loretta, flashing an enormous smile. But I couldn't be sure whether or not she was taking the piss. It was the sort of thing that Catherine would do. 'Come on. Let's go,' she said.

'See you later for dinner, Dad?' called Loretta, grabbing my hand.

'You be careful out there,' mumbled Jack, almost incoherent from behind his newspaper.

'I'm taking Mack to the forest,' said Loretta mischievously as she waltzed carefree out of the door, swinging my hand.

'Okay, sweetheart, you have fun. Keep her safe, Mack. She's all we have,' said Jack firmly but politely. I thought about that for a second or two...

'Will do, Jack,' I replied. Then, turning to Loretta, I asked, 'where are we going?'

'To the forest,' she replied with an enticingly mischievous smile. 'I just told you that.'

'The forest!' I replied. 'But aren't there monsters out there?'

'I don't know. Are there?' Loretta replied impishly.

'You're not leading me astray, I hope? My mum told me to be very wary of women who offer to take me into the woods.'

'You're a big boy now, Mack, and you've got your weapon to protect you, so I'm sure you can handle any demons and monsters we might encounter.' She smiled playfully as we walked down the path towards the forest, making fresh footsteps in the deep snow. But I had never entirely come to terms with my demons. I would have to face that someday, alone, in the future.

'How long have you lived here?' I asked.

'Forever, it seems,' replied Loretta wistfully.

'You're lucky. You wouldn't want to live where I live.'

'Tell me about your world,' asked Loretta, which, for some reason, surprised me?

'Isn't that a little dangerous?'

'Not really,' she muttered as if nothing mattered.

'But I thought that...'

Loretta interrupted. 'Every pleasure comes with a warning, so what's new. Whatever happens here stays....' She didn't need to finish the cliché and looked up at me, her eyes searching for something. 'I don't exist anymore when it's over, so nothing matters. In the end, nothing really matters at all. So, you have fun while you can, and then it's done. After that, all you have left is the memory.'

'That's the bit I never quite got my head around,' I replied. 'It all sounds too much like philosophical claptrap to me.'

'What? When a trip ends, everything disappears as if it never existed?'

'Yes.'

Loretta looked bemused. It was not a conversational aspect covered by the general chip design parameters. She had no long-term memory function to refer to – it wasn't necessary. Her ability to recall anything related entirely to the current experience. After that had been completed, the memory chip was wiped clean.

'You must understand that the location, duration and general content are your conscious selection. Those are the pre-selectable options available when you purchase the trip. The rest of the experience....' Loretta paused momentarily to allow me time to gather my thoughts '...that comes from your subconscious desires, which are created as you move through the journey.' It all seemed so simple to her. But then, her mind hadn't been scrambled by having to deal with reality and fantasy simultaneously.

It was all still relatively new to me, being only my third and most adventurous VRS experience.

'But where do you go?' I asked. I was deeply troubled by the transient nature of her virtual existence. In a way, it mirrored reality. It was an allegorical juxtaposition, in so much as her life ceased to exist at the end of the VRS trip. And in real life, it could also end very abruptly... These two imposters were beginning to segue into each other like swirling clouds of smoke from a woodland fire in the early morning mist. And in this murky atmosphere, I was hopelessly searching for clarity and understanding when there wasn't any to be found.

'We don't go anywhere. I don't exist. We never existed in the first place except in your imagination and the programmer's mind,' replied Loretta in a disarmingly blunt appraisal of her fleetingly ethereal existence.

~

It must have been just over a year after Catherine's death that Heart eventually persuaded me to have the Cyberon receptor implant. At first, I resisted. The thought of losing control of my mind filled me with dread. But I had mentioned several times that dark thoughts invaded my brain whenever I was alone at home. This had obviously troubled Heart, which was, presumably, why he persisted in suggesting I have the C.R.I. procedure.

I had once considered selling up and moving somewhere new, believing that might help ease the pain. But I found I couldn't do it when it came to making the call to the estate agents. I realised I hadn't yet managed to accept the final severance of the last tangible link I had with Catherine. I could still feel Catherine and Jade's presence in the home, and unsettling as that could be, it was also strangely reassuring and comforting. I preferred that to the nothingness that would exist if I moved to a new house.

I pondered for months over the sense of betrayal I might have to face before eventually agreeing to have the implant surgery. I knew I could access and relive unlimited experiences of joy, happiness, ecstasy, and contentment. Something Catherine and I would never actually experience again, not in the real world anyway.

My concern was whether infinite access to the virtuality experience would diminish and demean my real feelings and ultimately replace them. But that could never happen, or so I had been told. But how do VRS retailers know that for sure? They were selling a product and would say almost anything to close a sale.

It was completely unreal, nothing more than the new 3D... As the CyCo marketing people put it, Dreams and Desires on Demand. They were right in that respect because it was over the second you pulled the chip, and you were back to reality with no emotional involvement. It was the Virtual Reality Simulation chip's unique selling characteristic, but that still left a tiny nagging doubt in the back of my mind.

'Do you ever fall in love?' I asked Loretta. It was an odd enquiry because it related to a spiritual state in materiality. In contrast, she existed in a transitory form of illusion; therefore, it had no relevance. It could be compared to the chastity conundrum, *"was having sex in a dream considered adulterous behaviour?"* It possibly was in the eyes of papists, whereas other faiths tended to be more charitable. But as religion now played such a small part in society, even that consideration had become inconsequential.

'I can if you want me to,' replied Loretta, smiling. She had already explained that whatever I wanted to happen would happen; that was part of the appeasing sycophantic dimension, 'but the real question is, will you? When it's over, you're left with just a memory. I will be gone. Can you handle that?'

'I am learning how to deal with the memories, good and bad, but never falling in love? Doesn't that concern you?

'No!' replied Loretta bluntly. 'Why should it? She seemed genuinely surprised by the question, almost disturbed; it was as if she was beginning to doubt her convictions. 'It doesn't last anyway. That's an algorithmic parameter we're encoded with. Love is an anatomical anachronism. That's what we are programmed to think.'

'Who by?' I asked, intrigued at Loretta's uncharacteristically cynical observation.

'The Programmer, of course,' she replied, slightly surprised at my question. She grabbed my hand and pulled me forward encouragingly. 'Come on, it's not much further.'

'Who is the Programmer?' I asked curiously.

'I don't know,' she replied. 'I've never been asked before.' I didn't pursue the matter any further. There didn't seem to be any point.

We came to a clearing next to some fast-flowing white-water rapids, and I could see a traditional log cabin near the river edge. There was smoke drifting listlessly into the sky from the chimney. The smoke looked as confused as I was.

'Who lives here?' I asked, thinking somewhat naively that maybe we were here to meet somebody.

'Nobody,' replied Loretta reassuringly. 'I came up here before you arrived and lit the fire.'

'How did you know I would want to come?'

'Don't you?' Loretta asked knowingly. 'Isn't this something you've always wanted to do?'

'Yes, but that's not the point.'

'If you ask too many questions, you will ruin your illusion. Didn't they tell you that?'

'Yes, they did, but that doesn't stop me from being curious. I need to understand how this all works.'

'You have to let go. You do know that, don't you,' whispered Loretta almost rhetorically? She looked at me reassuringly, smiled very much as I remembered, kissed her forefinger, and gently touched my lips with it. I could sense a preternatural effect sweeping over my body like some medieval tincture or magic potion coursing through my veins. I knew the more I relinquished the reality of now, the closer to Catherine I could be.

'Yes,' I replied. I knew Loretta was making sense, and I was complicating something which was simple. 'Do you have problems in the real world?' she asked.

'No more than anybody else,' I replied, maybe abruptly. But I wasn't being completely honest. Of course, there was no reason to lie, but nothing would be gained from ruining the moment with dark matters.

'Do you want to tell me what it's like?' she asked.

'Maybe,' I replied. 'I'll think about it.' We entered the log cabin, which was warm and homely. In the middle was a hot tub set into the floor, burbling away with diaphanous clouds of vapour rising off the water. All around the edges were tiny red candles, which were alight and flickering... Some larger candles were positioned on tables and shelves but unlit.

'What do you think?' asked Loretta. 'I did it all for you. Is it good?'

'It's amazing. I always wanted to stay in a log cabin by a river, but….' I looked at Loretta and began to understand a little more, 'But then you knew that already, didn't you?

'Maybe,' she mused.

'But how? It's never happened before. I never had…'

'It's a CT modification being tested at the moment,' interrupted Loretta. So your trip can now be tweaked so you can experience your deepest hidden desires. I thought you would like it.'

Something else suddenly crossed my mind, but I quickly discarded the thought. That would be pushing the boundaries too far. Instead, I sat on the corner of the hot tub, trailing my hand in the warm water, watching Loretta as she began to disrobe. I was captivated by the technical perfection of her body. She was down to her G-string when she sat on the opposite corner of the tub to more provocatively remove the last vestige of clothing.

'This isn't a spectator sport, you know,' she purred as she slipped slowly under the water. 'You're supposed to join in.'

'I thought I would just enjoy the show for a moment,' I replied, smiling.

'Take your clothes off – come and fuck me,' whispered Loretta challengingly, blowing the soap bubbles dancing on the top of the water. Those were the same words, the same inflection, and the same beguiling look in her eyes that Catherine had used so many times when she was… She enjoyed teasing me - I could see that. Toying with my macho sensibilities, never in a hurtful way, just the way that lovers do.

'I thought I would make a coffee first. Would you like one?'

Loretta had other ideas. She leaned across the tub and grabbed my ankle; I overbalanced and fell into the tub, fully clothed - splashing water everywhere. The deluge immediately extinguished some of the red night lights. As we started to kiss, Loretta pulled off my shirt, which came away quickly despite being wet, but we had to scramble around to remove my jeans. It took a little longer, but we eventually managed it. Over the next two hours, we made love in the water in a varied and ingenious array of aquatic interpretations of the Kama Sutra. Sex was the only anaesthesia that could induce the total loss of sensitivity my body craved. When that avenue of distraction was temporarily exhausted, we sat back in the gurgling water and looked at each other, smiling with salacious indolence.

I had satisfied my physical desires and stolen a few hours of respite from reality in the bargain. This was the illusion, and it was mine to take or leave as I desired, and I liked that very much. But the memory inevitably drew me back to the misperception I had allowed to continue.

'So, is that what you imagined,' purred Loretta, letting her arms slowly snake out along both sides of the tub? I noticed that it had the effect of perking up her breasts slightly. Not that they were anything but perfect, anyway. Why wouldn't they be?

'Well, I did miss the coffee,' I replied drolly. Loretta impishly splashed water at me; I splashed her back, smiled, and then went quiet. My attention was momentarily distracted by the snow-covered idealistic view of the forest through the window and recollections of other golden days. A solemn mood had suddenly overtaken me, coming out of nowhere as it often did. For a few seconds, I revisited guilt, betrayal, and infidelity - this was all that was left. So I either took what I had and paid the tillerman whatever he demanded or settled for nothing but memories. I didn't yet know whether I was capable of making that decision.

'Are you okay? I hope I haven't worn you out?' asked Loretta mischievously, tempering the remark with a hint of genuine concern.

'No, I was just thinking about something,' I replied.

'Something or someone,' asked Loretta intuitively?

My attention returned to Loretta, and I smiled. 'You're very good, aren't you?'

'At sex or mind-reading?' she replied with a whimsical flourish of her hand, flicking soap bubbles into the air.

'Both,' I replied. 'You're good at both.' But she didn't need to be told; the Programmer understood these emotions and how to manage them.

'You can talk to me about her. I won't be the least bit offended. I know the part I play.' I suddenly felt the pain of unadulterated shame and embarrassment at my capricious and fickle infidelity. Loretta's frankness and candour completely overwhelmed me emotionally. She had done nothing wrong, and neither had I, a willing partner, but it suddenly felt all wrong, as if I was using her.

'This is not real sex, Mack. You do realise that? It's just two people making intimate mental contact for fun, and one of those people....' She slowly pointed her index finger at herself and flashed an elfin-like smile, 'doesn't exist. That's all this is – an illusion. It has nothing to do with love,' whispered Loretta reassuringly. 'It has no relevance to what has gone before and no bearing on what may happen in the future.'

'It seems real enough to me,' I replied harshly, almost berating her. 'Enough to make me feel like I've trashed her memory.' I cursed myself for being weak.

'But you haven't. You haven't done anything. This is just you making love to me mentally instead of her because…' she leaned over and stroked my cheek gently, 'because she can't be here, and you need to make love to somebody. But it's all virtuality. Your weapon is never fired in anger. It never leaves its holster during the whole experience.' I smiled at the cringe-worthy analogy she had obviously been preparing for some time.

'This way, there are no complications or commitment. Isn't that what it is?' she asked rhetorically. 'There can't be anything wrong with that, can there?'

I looked at her but didn't answer. I thought about her reasoning, as impartially as my mind would allow, but said nothing. I still wasn't entirely sure about the spiritual integrity of virtuality. The objectivity, discipline, and inquiring nature of being a detective were never that far from my mind. Subconsciously, I questioned most things, whether I was aware of them or not.

The sun began to slowly settle behind the cabin. The dappled light coming through the trees gave way to twilight. Evening shadows descended on the room. Loretta jumped out of the hot tub and strode over to the fireplace with deliberate, daring intention. She crouched down to pick up a taper stick and lit it on the fire's glowing embers. She turned her head momentarily to see if I was watching her. Apparently, vanity had been pre-programmed, or maybe it was a natural trait. I was watching her anyway, and I smiled. That was all that mattered to her right now.

Loretta meandered idly around the room, twirling her body in small pirouettes as she moved from one candle to another, lighting each one as she went. A whispery trail of glowing taper ash hovered in mid-air behind her as she passed. The flickering candlelight began throwing peculiar shapes around the room, which became more dramatic the more candles she lit. I watched her lithesome body move gracefully like a cat stalking its prey. Biding her time calmly, waiting for the opportune moment to pounce. When Loretta had finished lighting the candles, she sprang back into the hot tub, splashing water everywhere again.

'Let's make love by candlelight?' suggested Loretta, slowly lowering herself onto my lap - not for one moment did we lose eye contact. This gave her a psychological advantage. We were both aware of this, but I didn't care. Her eyes widened as she enveloped my manhood and drew it into her body. She smiled as she gracefully lowered herself further onto me. She had half expected some token resistance, but there was none. I had freely assented to losing control, losing myself again in the moment's pleasure. The aroma from the newly lit, heavily scented candles began to fill the room, seeping into my body. *The scent of her body invaded my senses, senses no longer as dependable as they once were, now bewildered - swirling around like centrifugal time. As she moved, she captured my mind, and I was lost in the vision.*

'You have a beautiful body,' I remarked. For a moment, I forgot that there was no necessity for euphonious superficiality in the world of virtuality. What was going to happen would happen, no matter what. Nothing could the inevitable.

'Then make love to me again,' whispered Loretta, slowly moving her body up and down.

'Why aren't you jealous?' I asked. Having made love to her for the last couple of hours, I felt embarrassed and strangely compelled to at least attempt some meaningful conversation. To try to understand her a little more.

'Jealous of what? The memory of your wife, who I know you loved and still do?'

'Yes,' I replied.

'I know what jealousy means. I know what it can do but don't know how to feel it. It was never part of my programming.'

'I don't understand,' I replied, not sure how I should respond to that.

'It has no relevance, and it is self-destructive,' Loretta replied matter-of-factly. 'It causes grief, heartache and unhappiness, so what good does it achieve? None. Hate feeds on jealousy.' She spoke as if she were quoting from some transcendental manual of life. Maybe she was, for all I knew.

'What good has jealousy ever done for anybody?' she asked.

'Well, nothing, put like that,' I replied. I was beginning to wish I hadn't started this conversation; maybe I should just enjoy the sex and keep my mouth shut. The major flaw in the VRS technology was the inability to develop a relationship beyond a certain point. The paradox was that there was never a relationship in the first place. Loretta didn't exist except in my head and only as a facsimile of Catherine, so any relationship would only ever be with myself... This further confused me. 'I was just trying to understand your feelings.'

'My feelings,' Loretta repeated, slightly bemused. 'What have my feelings got to do with anything?'

'But you're a woman, women have....'

But Loretta interrupted before I could finish. 'I'm a woman in your mind, but I don't have personal feelings, only what you expect me to have.'

'So why don't you feel jealousy?'

'Do you want the truth, or do you want me to lie?'

'I don't understand?'

'Well, the truth is I am what you want me to be, so I say what you would like me to say, and you wouldn't want me to say I was jealous or what my feelings are because that's part of the default pre-programming. That's not what you want to hear. You don't really want to know the truth; nobody does. So the real question is, could you deal with it if you did know?'

'And what if you lie?'

'I can't lie unless you want me to lie.'

'And what would you say if I wanted you to lie?' I asked. Loretta thought carefully about that. This was the question for which she had no direct access memory or pre-set default. So, it became necessary to utilise certain aspects of natural cerebral reasoning and the A.I. with which she was programmed. Profound philosophical arguments were generally outside the course of her everyday conversational requirements.

'Something different,' was her reply after careful deliberation.

'Will that be the truth?' I asked, becoming more confused.

'I don't know. I don't know what the truth is either. Only you know that.' I conceded that I was getting nowhere, so I kissed her, and we made love again. After we had finished, we got out of the tub, put on dressing gowns, lay in front of the log fire and cuddled each other for what seemed like hours. I didn't feel much like talking, and neither did Loretta. So, we just watched the flames making the shapes they had always made. The shapes that so many people had seen before and would see again.

A couple of hours later, I removed the VRS chip and went to bed alone again.

Chapter 14

'Morning Heart,' said Parish, peering round the door into his office.

'Morning, guv,' replied Heart, looking up from the stack of paperwork he was wading through.

'Any developments?' asked Parish, taking a sip from a paper cup of coffee.

'Nothing important. I was going through the initial report from Zac's office. There was no operational CCTV in the street. The internal security system had been disconnected - probably to protect her as much as her clients. Oh, and the lab came back on the DNA on the urine traces on the victim's hair. It belongs to an unidentified third person. So not much to help us there, but some interesting information about Maranno.'

Parish sat down opposite Heart, mulled over the two pieces of additional information, and took another sip of his coffee. He drank a lot of coffee in the mornings; the caffeine helped to kick-start his brain.

'So, what's the itinerary for today then,' asked Parish without any real enthusiasm? He surreptitiously smiled. His mind drifted back to the night before as he recalled the hot tub experience. His odd expression intrigued Heart a little. He was unaware of the reason, and Parish was disinclined to enlighten him. Ironically, it was Heart who suggested Parish had the interface transplant in the first place. The opprobrium levied at regular VRS users was akin to admitting you watched holavision soaps, afternoon game shows and talent competitions. Something for those too lazy to bother to interact with real people. Therefore, you didn't discuss it for fear of being labelled a Slart, a dubious-sounding acronym for Sad Loser Addicted to Reality Television.

'I've arranged a meeting with Maranno this morning and another meeting with Hawsley at five,' replied Heart.

'And the interesting information?' enquired Parish, with an ambivalently engaging expression intended to distract Heart's attention while he slyly picked up his sergeant's coffee cup and took a large slurp. Heart used a large china cup with his name, specifically brought into the office to stop others from stealing his coffee. Heart looked at him indignantly, but Parish smiled and tapped his shoulders, indicating that rank had privileges. A gesture he had obviously pirated from the recalcitrant sergeant they had encountered the previous day. He waggled the cup, signifying that one of them had the inalienable right to purloin the other's coffee. Heart half smiled and continued without comment.

'Well, firstly, he's one of the chief executives of SCOMTEL. So he runs the whole of the company's logistics operation, among other things.'

'Logistics,' repeated Parish curiously.

'Logistics,' confirmed Heart.

'What exactly is logistics?' asked Parish. He had always been fascinated by what he thought was probably another podgy corporate euphemism for something that was probably relatively mundane.

'The arrangement and planning of the overall transport and delivery policy of everything the SCOMTEL corporation sources and supplies across the country.'

'That's quite a job. Maranno must be terribly busy,' replied Parish, sounding slightly underwhelmed, adding derisively, 'but he doesn't actually drive all the lorries, does he?

'No, he just organises everything,' replied Heart, sounding slightly confused, 'Well, he probably just organises the people who organise the people who arrange the organising.' Parish looked at Heart with quizzical disbelief.

'So, he's important?' asked Parish rhetorically.

'You won't believe what his salary is,' said Heart.

'More than yours and mine put together, I imagine.'

'More than everybody in the department put together, twice over,' replied Heart. He was apparently impressed and possibly just a tad envious. 'How can anybody be worth that?'

'I don't know.' replied Parish, still unimpressed, taking another sip of Heart's coffee. 'So much for socialism and egalitarianism.' He mumbled. Parish glanced at Heart, bemused by his uncharacteristic proletarian whinge.

'He's also in charge of your favourite mode of transport.' Continued Heart.

'Legs?' asked Parish, a little perplexed. He always preferred to walk anywhere if possible.

'No, the Atlas Matrix Guidance System.'

'Oh, that,' Parish replied dismissively. His expression darkened slightly. He had little respect or admiration for the AMGS road control creation.

'And the Protton vehicle development programme.'

'He has been a busy boy,' remarked Parish, deep in thought. 'So, if Maranno makes so much money and is so important... how come he's only second in the pecking order to bang our vic? Can't he afford his own prostitute? And more to the point, why is Maranno sharing one with Hawsley and Christ knows who else?'

'We still don't have any evidence Hawsley had sex with her,' corrected Heart. 'We haven't found anything to prove that yet.'

'No, we haven't, have we?' mused Parish thoughtfully. 'And that's an interesting point. We are going to have to give this a lot more thought. It has to be more than a coincidence that they both knew her. Maybe she had something special the other girls don't have?'

'What like a detachable head?' suggested Heart glibly.

Parish was a little stunned by the quip. He thought it was in surprisingly poor taste, but he couldn't help but giggle quietly for a few seconds. Fortunately, he managed to hide his reaction from the rest of the team. Perversely, defensive mechanisms like this helped alleviate the repugnance of what they had to confront occasionally.

'Maybe she found out something, and someone was frightened she might talk?' queried Heart, not realising how close yet far from the truth he was.

'I always work on the assumption that everybody knows something they're not telling us,' said Parish. Heart retrieved his coffee cup, took a sip, and placed it back on the table, further away from Parish.

'I have arranged a meeting with Maranno at eleven today, at his private house, not the CSP headquarters.'

'Good. Maybe he will fess up on home ground, and we can have the rest of the week off,' said Parish, suddenly thinking of Loretta. Heart looked at him with an expression of premature expectation that quickly changed to disbelief. Which is tricky to pull off at the best of times, but he managed it.

They arrived at the front gates to Benny Maranno's mansion, rang the intercom and waited. Finally, after a few seconds, the gates began to open; the security guard was expecting them. They parked near the main door and were met by another security guard with a large Doberman Pinscher dog with big, angular, sticky-up ears. Parish remembered reading somewhere that they had to be specially operated on to make the ears stand up permanently in the intimidating, Batman-type posture. They flopped down in their natural state. However, some dog owners preferred the more aggressive stance of the cosmetically angulated erect version.

'You ask the questions, Heart,' instructed Parish. 'I'll just observe for now.' Heart pressed the bell, and an immaculately dressed doorman opened the door.

'Yes.' The doorman inquired in a sonorously reverberating but slightly effeminate manner.

'We have an appointment to see Mr Maranno,' said Heart. The doorman looked down at them condescendingly as if they were some lower-order pond life.

They held up their identity cards for him to read, but he didn't bother. Instead, he moved his head slowly in a peculiar circular motion before eventually returning it to the central position. Parish and Heart watched him perform, glanced at each other in bewilderment, and then returned their attention to the doorman. He had now completed the strange ritual he presumably performed for all visiting guests.

'Are you... from the press?' he queried scornfully, in a slow, deliberately affected tone.

'No, the police,' replied Heart bluntly, waggling his warrant card again. 'We arranged an appointment for eleven o'clock.'

'Oh, did you?' he responded as if they were stroppy schoolchildren asking for their ball back.

'Yes,' confirmed Heart, adopting an uncharacteristically belligerent tone.

'Well, I suppose you had better come in.' He nodded for them to follow him and led them into the main hall.

'Wait here. I will advise Mr Maranno you have arrived.' He made to walk off toward what they were about to discover was the conservatory. They both noticed he moved very slowly in an oddly exaggerated manner. Partly because he was moving his legs from the hips, more like a woman, and partly because he appeared to be using extraordinarily high lifts in his shoes. Presumably, he was under the misapprehension that the extra height would enhance his overall appearance. But as he was only a whisper away from a wobble, the visual effect was being severely undermined. He had height issues and obviously felt insecure about his deficiency. Heart and Parish glanced at each other, smirked, but said nothing.

Another man, apparently a security guard by his uniform and gun, closed the door behind them. He gave them a suspicious glare and grunted abruptly, 'Are you carrying weapons?'

'Yes,' replied Heart. 'Why?' Parish said nothing.

'Well, I usually insist they are left here before you can proceed any further.'

'Do you?' quipped Heart with a mildly derisive tone, 'That's very commendable these days.' That wasn't the answer the guard was expecting. Heart knew that but continued to glare at the guard with a disarmingly diffident expression, waiting for him to respond, but he didn't. Instead, he twitched his left eye, scratched his right ear, pushed his earpiece deeper into his ear, and readjusted his gun. It was angled across his chest in that jaunty manner most security men with an inferiority complex adopt when carrying automatic weapons. Then he turned and sauntered back to a position just behind the front door. He continued to observe Heart out of the corner of his eye as if he were a potentially subversive person. This was becoming a bit of a pattern, Heart thought to himself. It was the second time he had encountered a supercilious officious cretin in as many days.

He wondered whether a training academy existed that specialised in teaching these automatons how to be arrogant and patronisingly condescending. Maybe the government felt morally obliged to employ a token number under the Employment Act, as with the physically disabled. A symbolic gesture of support for the legislation, possibly, he thought. The light-footed doorman returned and glanced superciliously in their direction.

'Mr Maranno will see you now,' he announced. He beckoned them to follow him into one of the anterooms just off the main entrance hall. This was obviously a library that continued through to a large, decadently furnished conservatory leading into an atrium drenched in sunlight. In the centre, suspended three metres above the floor on black iron chains, hung a Victorian design cast-iron flower canopy trough approximately three metres squared. From this inverted garden, dangling down to a height of about two metres from the floor, were a large number of the rarest varieties of (as they would later learn) African Scented Orchids.

The floors were paved with Italian marble, which kept them cold. But the air was uncomfortably hot and damp with an artificially created tropical humidity, heavy with a strange, intoxicating scent. The whole glorious tropical illusion had obviously been carefully constructed by Maranno, presumably because he had experienced

247

something similar in an equatorial rainforest and decided to bring the concept home.

In the middle of the room, directly under the hanging canopy, the imposing figure of Benny Maranno was seated at an ornate antique oak desk, smoking a large cigar. A vice exceedingly rare these days and strangely incongruous in the current environment. The noxious smell of the cigar smoke intermingled with and slowly overwhelmed the delicate aroma emanating from the exotic flowers. It was a strange analogy, like spraying an expensive perfume on a turd..... what was the point? Benny stood up to greet them.

'I am Detective Sergeant Heart, and this is Detective Inspector Parish. We are...'

'Parish!' responded Maranno. He spoke well and carefully articulated the word, extending the second syllable further than was strictly necessary. It sounded like the ocean gently lapping over the sand in some exotic paradise. There was a deep reverberating resonance in his throat. 'I know that name from somewhere,' he added inquisitively. He thought for a few seconds, took another drag on his cigar, and blew out a cloud of smoke through a small hole he had formed with his lips. Possibly attempting but failing to impress them by blowing smoke rings.

'Doesn't that harm the orchids,' murmured Heart - referring to the cigar smoke spiralling upwards? Benny glanced up and pointed his cigar at a second ornate structure suspended just above the carved canopy but in the centre directly above their heads.

'Not at all. The air purification system draws in all the bad air....' Benny blew some more cigar smoke skywards towards the vent, where it was immediately sucked in. 'And blows it out clean and beautiful.'

There was the faintest hint of gutter twang in his articulation. And from experience, Parish knew that no matter how much money you spent trying to disguise a humble childhood, you would never fully succeed. You can't conceal the accidentally flattened vowel, dropped "h," or condensed diphthong you carry from the street despite years of expensive education. Perfect elocution was implacably enshrined from birth. It could never be mastered after the event without an occasional slip. In the beginning, people invariably despise that to which they ultimately aspire, so there was probably an element of inverted snobbery coming into play. Heart spoke with perfect clarity, with just a whisper of the Welsh valleys.

'Very nice,' replied Heart indifferently. His mind flashed back to Dhalia's bedroom, where a similar air extraction equipment existed. But that one didn't work.

'We don't want air pollution, do we?' stated Benny, with almost evangelical zeal. 'Anyway, gentlemen, what can I do for you?'

But before Heart could answer, Maranno suddenly turned to Parish and exclaimed. 'I remember now, wasn't your wife and daughter involved in that horrendous motorway tragedy three or four years ago? Unusual circumstances, as I recall.' Parish nodded, momentarily stunned by the revelation. His attention thrown entirely off-course by the apparently random reference to the accident.

'Some problem with the computer system or something, as I remember,' continued Benny, twitching a dagger in the wound. The statement delivered cold and lifeless, devoid of sensibility, emotion, or compassion, stunned

249

Parish into silence for a few more seconds, his breath temporarily stolen.

'Yes, you're right, it was,' replied Parish after a few more moments. Although it was seldom far from his mind, it had still surprised him to be suddenly reminded of it. This was a subject he had not expected to turn up during this or any investigation, for that matter.

'Unexplained computer malfunction with the matrix system,' said Benny. 'As I recall.'

'I'm surprised you remember it,' said Parish, still a little dazed by the mention of the accident.

'Doesn't happen that often,' replied Benny, 'but then you do also have that unusual surname. Hard to forget. I just put two and two together, and....'

'Still,' said Parish quizzically, 'to be able to remember the finer details....' His voice trailed off without finishing the question. The cogs in his head had started to turn; he was waiting for a few of them to align and stop moving.

'I was running that department at the time, but only in a non-managerial capacity, you understand.'

'Were you?' asked Parish, his mind hastily trying to recall Maranno's name from the accident enquiry.

'Yes.'

'I don't remember seeing you at the enquiry?' asked Parish, intrigued.

'No, I wasn't there; the head of the department was at the hearing. I was advising departmental heads on matrix system failsafe upgrades. Somewhat ironically, as it turned out.' His eyebrows went up and down very quickly, acknowledging the bizarre serendipity of the event. Unfortunately, Parish didn't see it in quite the same way. The casual, almost flippant nature of his reply hit a nerve, but he bit his tongue.

'To do what - exactly,' asked Parish? Heart was becoming a little concerned at how the conversation was veering a little off track. He glanced at Parish, seeking visual reassurance that this informal interview was proceeding as they had agreed it should. Parish gave him a comforting smile. He knew what Heart was thinking.

'Introduce an enhanced safety modification,' replied Maranno.

'So, was the system unsafe?' asked Parish.

'No, not at all, but you can never be too careful with health and safety, can you? And then there was that nasty accident, technically on my watch.'

There it was again, thought Parish. The questionable tenor of superficiality in his voice – that he couldn't quite put his finger on.

'We can't afford to become complacent just because something works perfectly, can we?' continued Maranno.

'Not that perfectly,' replied Parish, looking at Maranno fixedly. He seldom found himself taking an instant dislike to somebody. But he was prepared to make a notable exception on this occasion.

'No, I suppose not,' conceded Maranno apologetically. 'I believe they are still looking into the accident….'

'Are they,' asked Parish? He wasn't aware of that.

It was remote, thought Benny. I was miles away, pressing a few buttons and making a few adjustments on a computer screen. It didn't seem real. What eventually happened wasn't anything to do with me. It was the technology that killed them, not me. I was lucky that day, but it could never happen again. The entire system was changed afterwards… I had made sure of that.

'You killed them,' said Parish abruptly. 'It was your finger on the trigger.' He had no intention of letting the moment pass without dwelling a few moments longer on the gruesome details of the 'accident.' If only to reaffirm and quantify the level of Benny's direct involvement lest he should forget.

'All that mangled metal and blood and all those shredded body parts, bits of two people who used to live and talk and love each other, and other people. Now gone forever. Entangled and enmeshed with bits of steel, rubber, plastic, and oil, mashed up like a beef stew and splashed on the highway. That was all your work, Mr. Non-Managerial Capacity, all your handiwork. And all by just pressing a few buttons.'

Benny suddenly felt very nauseous, overwhelmed by the graphic depiction that Parish was describing. He had never given any thought to the autopsy's intimate details before, having made a conscious decision not to read the accident report. By not doing so, he had managed to distance himself from the event. Convince himself, somewhat naively, that the bodies were found intact, almost recognisable, instead of wholly deconstructed into their constituent parts. Around ten litres of blood (most of which had soaked into the road). Head and bones crushed virtually to dust - enmeshed within the gristle and muscle tissue—no more offensive than a small bin bag full of cow offal.

I wish that Parish would stop talking, thought Benny, and then maybe the horrible empty feeling in my stomach would go away, but he didn't ease off. He was actually enjoying this.

'Their lives are over,' Aiden had told him, 'over, but we go on. There's no option - we've come this far.' So there it *was, mea maxima culpa. 'We've come this far.' Aiden was right, of course. He always was. The only way to go was forward. There was never any going back. I was in too deep...*

'Are they,' repeated Parish, carefully studying Maranno, who appeared to have drifted off into a trance for a few moments and looked decidedly pale and sickly? Heart cautiously interrupted, delicately steering the conversation back to the enquiry.

'I understand you know a Ms Dhalia Vingali?' he enquired.

'Do I?' enquired Benny cautiously. He was saying nothing until he knew where this was going.

'We have a DNA scan report that places you in her apartment at approximately the same time she was murdered.'

'Oh, she was murdered, then! Not suicide,' exclaimed Benny? It was a pathetically crass attempt at sarcasm. Parish and Heart didn't respond.

'No, we don't think it was suicide. Pretty much certain it was murder,' replied Heart.

'Then I probably do know her then,' replied Benny surprisingly glibly, with no apparent concern at his proximity to the crime scene.

'What time did you visit Ms Vingali?' asked Heart.

'Well, let me see, it was last Saturday, wasn't it? He paused for a few seconds. His eyes drifted skywards, possibly to add a touch of dramatic tension for some inexplicable reason. 'Yes, now I remember. I had a meeting with some friends at around eight, left them about ten, so probably it was around ten-thirty... maybe.'

'And what time did you leave?' asked Parish.

'Ah, yes, I know that. It was eleven fifteen.'

'That's very precise,' replied Parish, surprised at Benny's exactitude.

'My driver picked me up. He's very punctual. I remember telling him what time to come for me. I usually like to be in bed at midnight, the same time each night.

'That still puts you at the crime scene in the right time frame,' replied Heart.

'Possibly it does, but she kissed me goodbye,' he paused for effect, 'on the doorstep, and my driver and a bodyguard saw us. So, she was alive, fit and well when I left. Well, I thought she was. But you could never tell with Dhalia, not for certain anyway. She could have been acting, I suppose.' He paused momentarily while his brain tried to assemble a suitably demeaning quip.

'Dhalia was never that lively afterwards - if you know what I mean.' That was the best disparaging witticism he could muster from his cerebral endeavours, lamely delivered with vainglorious contempt. 'I think I wore her out,' he continued, smirking at Parish, 'but her head was definitely still attached when I left, to her body, that is. That much, I do remember.' Benny's smirk morphed into a sanctimonious grin, an expression he had obviously perfected over many years when taunting subordinates. Benny was enjoying this little game of verbal gymnastics.

'We will need to interview them,' said Parish.

'No problem. Any time, officer,' replied Benny with a hint of self-righteous belligerence. That got right up Parish's nose. Benny had obviously carefully prepared them for that eventuality. That line of enquiry was unlikely to yield anything significant.

Parish got up from his chair to leave, and Heart followed.

'I think that will be all… for now, sir, thank you,' said Parish politely.

'No problem, officers,' said Maranno, picking out a fresh cigar from his desk and nonchalantly clipping the end.

As they reached the exit, Parish stopped and turned back to Benny to make one final comment.

'This has nothing to do with the enquiry…just idle curiosity more than anything else.' He paused momentarily, deliberating whether he should continue, 'a man-to-man question if you understand what I mean, but….' He lowered his voice almost to a whisper and adopted a guileless expression. It lent a complicit, conspiratorial dimension to the moment. Maranno nodded his tacit comprehension of the apparent change in temperament, lit his cigar and blew a few gentle puffs of smoke into the air before drawing closer to Parish in an almost benevolent fatherly mode.

Parish hesitated for a few more moments, deliberating whether he should continue. 'Just one other thing that has been troubling me, something that maybe you could help me with.'

'Anything to be of assistance, sergeant,' replied Maranno, who had *unintentionally* demoted Parish and now also spoke in a hushed tone.

'What I need to know is… what's it like having fourth helpings?' asked Parish quietly.

'Fourth helpings? I don't follow you, sergeant,' replied Benny, taking another puff on his cigar, uncertain as to precisely what Parish was alluding to.

'It's inspector, actually,' corrected Parish.

'Oh, my apologies, Inspector, but I'm still not quite with you.'

'Well, somebody was fucking her half an hour before you got there, and there were another two clients a couple of hours before that, so I just wondered what it feels like, you know? It must have been a bit like flopping a chipolata around in a bucket by the time you arrived. Not a great deal of friction, if you get my drift.'

Heart was surprised by Parish's crude but highly amusing analogy and couldn't help but snigger. Judging by Maranno's change of expression, it was a phenomenally successful attempt at antagonism. But was Benny Maranno a man you needed to provoke, thought Heart? Benny coughed as some smoke had apparently gone down the wrong tube. He spluttered for a few seconds before exhaling somewhat hurriedly - through what appeared to be an assortment of orifices.

'Fuck you, Inspector,' muttered Maranno with unrighteous indignation and a sneer that would have terrified a crocodile. Parish feigned shock and awe at Maranno's displeasure and apologised profusely. But with a conspicuously martyred air of total indifference. Maranno was plainly not pleased by Parish's crudely offensive comment. His body began to contort as he gasped for air. His face turned a curious puce colour, giving him the appearance of a lurching Hogarthian drunk. Parish thought he was about to have a heart attack but then realised he was merely blushing profusely with embarrassment.

'I really am sorry,' repeated Parish, but it lacked any degree of sincerity. 'Have I touched a nerve?' he ventured. 'Didn't mean to cause embarrassment. Thought you must have known you were just a lowly third reserve.'

By now, Benny had managed to recompose himself. The glowing redness was beginning to recede. His less bibulous manifestation was starting to return.

'I think you're wrong about that, Inspector,' said Benny, still recovering.

'No, I don't think so. Someone was definitely there before you. We have his DNA to prove it. So, we should have his name soon, but I wouldn't worry about it. Ms Vingali's not going to be telling anybody now, is she? Unless she has already. Which I suppose sort of gives you a motive, doesn't it?' Benny said nothing, realising he had walked into a trap.

'I have a witness, two in fact. So you won't disprove my alibi.'

'Not yet, we can't, no, I agree, but it's still early days.'

'Oh, and one other thing,' said Parish without changing expression.

'Yes?' replied Benny, half expecting another insult.

'She was HIV positive, so I suggest you get yourself tested for AIDS … quickly,' he added with a flourish and a smile.

Parish and Heart left the atrium, went through the conservatory, and closed the door behind them. A few seconds later, there was a loud crash as something disintegrated against the back of the door. Parish and Heart paused momentarily and, turning to face each other, smiling contentedly. It was not unlike some second-rate vaudeville act finishing their turn. Then, with a discernable extra spring in each step, they continued through the library to the front door, where they were met once again by the doorman. He appeared a little disturbed by the crashing sound in the background.

'What was that noise?' asked the doorman.

'Your master's just heard some tragic news,' replied Parish. The doorman looked mystified as he opened the front door, and they walked out.

'I don't think he's capable,' remarked Heart as they wandered back to the car.

'Probably not, but I tend to think that almost anybody is capable of anything under the right conditions. It's a bit like monkeys and computers,' replied Parish.

Heart didn't immediately grasp the point.

'Shakespeare,' Parish added to explain the analogy.

'Oh,' said Heart as the penny dropped.

'But we'll check his alibis anyway. He's another one who knows more than he is telling us.'

'I think you surprised him,' said Heart.

'Yes, he didn't take that well, did he,' replied Parish in a contemplative tone? 'I wonder why? He can't possibly be so naïve as not to know what was happening.'

'But love is blind, and lovers cannot see the pretty follies that they themselves commit, for if they could, Cupid himself would blush,' recited Heart in a sardonically poetic manner.

'Blind maybe, but surely not pathologically stupid?' queried Parish with a hint of a smirk.

'He did blush a lot, though,' added Heart.

'Flaky similarities to the central theme of a Shakespeare sonnet are hardly conclusive grounds for a murder charge,' replied Parish brusquely. (He hated Shakespeare)

'Many a slip twixt cup and lip,' continued Heart. Unabated by Parish's denouncement.

'He hasn't exactly slipped up either, has he- yet?' asked Parish.

'No,' replied Heart dispiritedly. Now wishing he hadn't bothered invoking the Bard in the first place.

'You've been doing that am-dram thing again, haven't you?' asked Parish in a slightly disparaging tone.

'Yes,' replied Heart sheepishly. 'I enjoy it.'

Parish mumbled something inaudible.

'Sorry?' said Heart. He couldn't quite make out what Parish had said.

'Good, good, I said good,' replied Parish. 'I'm going back to talk to Gerry at the lab about those air scans.' But that wasn't what he had mumbled.

'Gerry?' said Heart with a diffident, inquisitorial tone. Parish gave no response to the desultory enquiry as if he hadn't heard it.

'Drop me there. You can take the car and go check Maranno's alibi.' They drove away.

Chapter 15

'Afternoon Gerry,' said Parish, interrupting Geraldine, who was sitting at her desk deeply engrossed with something on a computer screen while scribbling notes on her tablet. She looked surprised to see Parish.

'Parish!' she exclaimed. 'Is it two o'clock already?' She glanced at the lab clock above the door. She'd got in early that morning to try and clear the backlog, but the day was three-quarters over, and she had hardly touched it.

'Afraid so.' He waved a McDonald's bag at her. 'Lunch?'

Gerry smiled; she was pleased to see him. He had always made her smile. Then, just for a few moments, her mind flashed back to their brief, very brief affair abruptly terminated by events almost beyond imagination. She still remembered the day so clearly. It was early morning when Parish telephoned to tell her what had happened. For one fleetingly selfish moment, listening to Parish pour his heart out, she couldn't think of anything other than the fact that they could now be together. As they spoke, her mind began making plans. She could now be with him, the man she loved. He had been utterly destroyed and was falling apart, and all she could think about was the two of them planning a life together.

Then, thank God, sanity kicked in, and she realised, just in time, what a pathetically sad person she must be. Was she really prepared to embrace any circumstance that would produce that end? No. She was not. Intuitively, she knew their relationship was destined to wither and die, condemned by circumstances beyond her control. As much as she hated to face reality, she knew the devastation of his loss would probably destroy any feelings he may ever have had for her. Despite knowing he was head over heels in love with his wife, she had made a play for him. It was contemptible, but an intrinsic part of the attraction, the challenge...

'Not for me, but you carry on. Do you want some tea?'

'Milk two sugars, please,' replied Parish. Gerry wandered over to the vending machine, selected a white tea and a black coffee for herself and touched the fingerprint identifier screen. The screen acknowledged her order and commenced the drip-feed into two paper cups. She took the tea over to Parish, sitting next to her desk, eating the burger.

'Thanks.' He took a sip and looked around for somewhere to put it down.'

'Anywhere is fine,' said Gerry, pointing at a scrap paper on the corner of the desk. She seemed distracted and took a sip of the coffee she was comforting.

'So how are you *now*,' asked Gerry as tactfully as she could? She wondered whether she should have left out the last word. The narrative implication was essentially an enquiry into someone's well-being after a particular event, which wasn't her intention – it was just how the words came out.

It was an awkward situation being alone together after all this time. Teetering precariously on the edge of a dangerous incursion into unchartered waters. Within the crime scene's confines, it was relatively easy to maintain a degree of professional detachment and objectivity. But together, with nobody else around, the dynamic changes. And personal feelings always come into play to one degree or another. Unanswered questions from the past hang listlessly in the air like helium-filled balloons waiting to be popped. But when they are, they deflate slowly, not with a bang. The intensity departed long ago.

She looked into his eyes, hoping he could see she was not prying into his grief - just expressing concern for him as a friend and colleague. This was, after all, the man she had once loved passionately, maybe still did – she just didn't know anymore. Gerry thought, no, she hoped, she could convey what she was not saying. But she had no desire to go tramping over old ground too much, in case he was still in a place – a place where other people were still not welcome.

'Fine, just fine.' He hesitated for a few seconds and looked back at Gerry. 'I still talk to her, you know.' Gerry hadn't expected that, nor had Parish. He hadn't spoken about this to anybody. Yet, here he was, blurting out details about his hallucinatory ramblings to someone he'd had a brief affair with at what now seemed a lifetime ago. Someone Parish hadn't seen since his wife died. Yet today, for some reason, he felt comfortable in her company, at ease with her.

'When?' asked Gerry, with no trace of disbelief.

'Most evenings, when I get in late,' replied Parish, gazing wistfully into his tea. Gerry chose her words carefully.

'What do you say to her?'

'We talk about the day, what's been happening. I suppose that makes me sound a little unhinged?' He looked up at her a little cagily, waiting for a reaction, but she just smiled, as always, and quickly put his mind in another place and a different time.

'I don't think so,' replied Gerry. 'You did love her very much. I know that much,' she paused. 'Probably still do; we were just sex.' She added this almost dismissively but without sounding indifferent. It was almost as if she wanted to diminish the act of making love to something as commonplace as eating a piece of cake. The spiritual and emotional elements systematically removed and eliminated from the metaphysical equation... But not really for her.

She hated saying that, and it really hurt. It was never just about the sex she kept telling herself. Honest lies sometimes burn in the mouth, but they must still be said. She had to keep the barriers up - for now - they were protecting her and Parish.

'Was that all it was?' he asked, sounding a little fragile, almost vulnerable as if he really didn't know.

'I think so. We haven't spoken for over three years. What does that tell you?'

'I don't know. What does that tell us?' Parish asked.

'That maybe you didn't love me. It was just physical, nothing more, not enough to build a life on.' It was a leading question, and Gerry knew it, but only by trawling for the tiniest hint of disagreement to her exacting appraisal of their relationship could she determine whether there was anything left to pursue. Just a shred of something, but simultaneously maintaining the façade of indifference while trying to sound mature, objective, and philosophical about their affair. Parish didn't really know what was going on.

'Maybe,' replied Parish. He thought about Loretta and how unreal that was but nonetheless enjoyable. And then Gerry in the real world and how emotions began to entangle and confuse his thoughts. At times, virtuality had some distinct advantages over reality. He took another sip of tea. 'Anyway, what have you got for me?'

Back to business, she thought, Maybe another time. They had returned to the safe haven of the working relationship.

'Well, to start with, as you know, her real name was Rose Watson. She changed it legally, so the DNA records followed her, and they checked out.'

'And she was HIV positive... AIDS,' added Parish, nibbling on his beef burger and casually glancing sideways at Gerry.

'How did you know that?' asked Gerry, sounding surprised.

'Got that from the horse's mouth,' replied Parish.

Gerry looked confused.

'Her doctor friend,' replied Parish, sounding just a tad judgmental. 'He was very accommodating, but then he's in a very tricky position, withholding information about a potentially contagious disease from the authorities, so he has to be.'

'Yes, she is, sorry, was HIV positive, and it had developed into full-blown AIDS. She appeared to have it under control with drugs, but she would die eventually, within a year at best, if not sooner. That would have been my prognosis.' She flipped over the page on her tablet.

'She was fourteen weeks pregnant. We have a DNA result from a foetus, but no familial trace or connection between Rose and anybody else on the record except her mother, who died in 2023.'

'So, the father is not on the Balingo database?'

'No,' replied Gerry. 'But then that only has the residents of the provinces on it.'

'So how did the person who gave her AIDS get into the province to have sex with her?' asked Parish curiously.

'Border Gate Security automatically scans all new arrivals for communicable diseases, so the simple answer is I don't know. Of course, she could have left the province and met someone…'

'But why would she do that, and how would she know anybody out there?'

'Sorry, don't know that either, but we all know someone who lives out there.' She looked at Parish. 'Don't you?' Parish thought about the question and looked at her as if to say, 'I see what you mean,' but didn't answer.

'Tell me something,' said Parish, finishing his burger. 'I am a little confused over one thing.'

'What?' asked Gerry, a little intrigued?

'Well, as she had AIDS, and you say nobody could bring it in, how did she manage to slip out through gate security? She must have left Providence at least once over the last few years to screw the person who gave her the HIV?'

'It's not really a problem. When you first register on the Balingo scan system, it retains your security record for life. If you leave a province, you only pass through a retinal scan. And it's the same when you return or enter another province. Just to check, it's the same person coming back. But it won't know if you've contracted a disease while you are outside. That would only flag up if you went to a hospital or a doctor and had a new DNA scan, which would then reveal the condition, and that would be updated to Balingo. Does that help?'

'Yes, it does. Now I know Dhalia could have picked up the virus in the Ghettazone and passed it on to a client, possibly unbeknown to either of them.'

'Yes, that's possible,' replied Gerry.

'And as our Doctor Hackett didn't see fit to report her condition to the authorities, she had free rein to continue as normal.'

'In theory, yes, but accessing the AIDS drugs he was treating her with without a patient's name is impossible,' said Gerry.

'Hackett appears to have friends in the right places.' Gerry didn't answer.

'So, we have no way of tracking the foetal father?'

'No, not unless you could access one of the old DNA registers they used to have before the gated provinces were built.'

'Who would have that?' asked Parish.

'Well, you - actually. It was a police PNC and DNA computer system they started to use around the turn of the century, mainly for criminals. Of course, anybody innocently involved in a crime was routinely tested to eliminate them from enquiries and to check they weren't involved in another unrelated incident. They started to solve quite a few crimes by accident that way. That's where the idea for the Balingo DNA scan security system originated. It used to be inadmissible in law to use evidence acquired in those circumstances, but that all changed.'

'But why weren't those old records incorporated into the new system?' asked Parish, sounding surprised.

'Why weren't they indeed?' reiterated Gerry philosophically. 'Twenty million DNA records, mostly for people now living in the Ghettazone, all lost.... My life, all our lives, would have been a lot easier if we had those. I could spend long lunchtimes in wine bars and go home at five every day.'

'So, they weren't,' conceded Parish, reading the expression on Gerry's face? He knew it would be unwelcome news and make his investigation even more arduous.

'Remember the civil riots of 2015?' asked Gerry gingerly. 'That was a tough time. Many innocent people were killed just for being in the wrong place at the wrong time. The police didn't come out of it particularly well and definitely not covered in glory.'

'Yes, sadly I do,' Parish replied with a tinge of remorse. He was not particularly proud of that period of his career. It was the nearest the country had ever come to a second civil war.

'Well, you've obviously forgotten about the terrorist attack on the IT bunker in Winchester where the DNA computer system and records were stored. Completely zapped the entire system and wiped the backup as well. Really well organised, that one.'

'I do remember it now you come to mention it,' replied Parish.

'Hawsley kept it incredibly quiet at the time - didn't want that to get out. That's why they initiated the new system. The old one effectively didn't exist any longer.'

'So, there's no way it's any help to us, then,' asked Parish.

'Well, that's what I would have said,' replied Gerry, 'but she hesitated for a few moments. 'I did hear something not long ago about some records that had been partially reconstructed by a boffin working in the Central Intelligence Research Centre in Deliverance. Something to do with the university, I think. Some innovative technology this guy has developed. It can restore whole data from partial data on an IPA. Sorry, I'm always talking in acronyms. I mean Intelligent Probability Analysis basis, but I don't know anything more about it, and I haven't heard anything since.'

'What exactly does Intelligent Probability Analysis mean?' asked Parish, slightly confused. 'It sounds a bit like an oxymoronic euphemism to me.

Gerry smiled. 'No, not quite. In theory, the program works in a similar manner to the human brain. Given a small amount of data, it theorises by statistical probability what the quantum of the missing element might be. It's an ingenious algorithm, so I understand... the basis of all artificial intelligence.

'Oh,' said Parish, still sounding suitably unimpressed. 'So, strictly speaking, it's still little more than a guess?'

'I think it does slightly better than that. It's a bit like a detective's intuition.' She smiled at Parish. 'What's that based on?'

Parish thought for a moment. 'I suppose experience and the ability to discount the immaterial details.'

'Precisely what IPA does: it learns to distinguish facts from fiction based on previous experience. The more data you feed in, the more accurate the information it produces.'

'I see,' said Parish, taking her point.

'I could look into it if you want me to,' said Gerry. 'If we could trace the father, he could be your killer, especially if he found out she'd infected him and their baby with AIDS. It's a possible motive.'

'Still doesn't explain the ritualistic slaughter,' said Parish, 'You would have thought he would have tried to help her beat the AIDS instead of killing her.

'No, that part of it is still a bit of a mystery to me,' said Gerry.

'Anything else on the air scans?' asked Parish while making notes on his tablet.

'The scans and DNA trace have been checked, and they confirm what I've already told you: she had sex with two different men before seven o'clock and then with Mr X, and last but not least was Mr Maranno.'

'Definitely that order.'

'Yes,' confirmed Gerry. 'Semen deteriorates rapidly but at a linear rate, depending on temperature. So, it's easy to assess the rate of degeneration and work back.'

'You see, we have a problem,' said Parish. 'Maranno has an alibi, two in fact, for when he left her, and he appears to be the last one there.'

'Last one having sex with her,' qualified Gerry. 'Still, Mr X was there and had sex with her, so it could still be him. He could have gone back. Has to be the last person to see her alive that killed her, not necessarily the last to have sex with her.' Parish acknowledged the point.

'Then we still have the problem of his DNA being on her body, but no air scan DNA to place him there. So somehow he had sex with her but didn't bother breathing for ten minutes?' Parish smiled at the absurdity of that option, and Gerry went to say something but changed her mind.

'Maybe he was so over-excited while having sex – that he forgot to breathe,' suggested Gerry drolly. 'It wouldn't have been for long,' she added disparagingly. Or maybe he sent her his semen by post?' That was Gerry's final derisory observation; she was evidently not taking this line of investigation very seriously.

'Or she went out to meet him,' suggested Parish thoughtfully, 'but that doesn't tie up with our other information. Then, there's Aiden Hawsley's positive air scan, so he was there but didn't have sex. Where does he fit in? It doesn't make any sense.'

'Well, he's out there somewhere, maybe in the Ghettazone,' added Gerry phlegmatically.

'Yes, he is, isn't he?' replied Parish. The thought of trawling around the Ghettazone didn't exactly fill him with joy. The final repository for the rejects from Aiden Hawsley's Social and Criminal Reform Act of 2016 and the reconstruction of the social system. There are a lot of severely depressed people out there now.

'Oh, one other thing,' said Gerry. 'She had a strange drug concoction in her bloodstream. I think it was some hybrid variation of Rohypnol combined with revamped Lysergic Acid Diethylamide. But I will have to do a little more work before I can confirm that.'

'LSD,' said Parish curiously.

'Something like that,' said Gerry, looking a little surprised, 'but more specifically, in this case, a highly refined variant, an entheogen, in fact,'

'Which is what exactly,' asked Parish looking puzzled?

'It's a semisynthetic psychedelic drug of the ergoline family, well known for its psychological effects. This can include altered thinking processes, closed and open-eye visual synaesthesia, an altered sense of time and occasionally, strange spiritual experiences. It's an illegal recreational drug, but more commonly, it's used as an agent in psychedelic therapy. Remarkably similar to the LSD used back in the nineteen-sixties, but the formula has been tweaked. They call it Benacane now.' Gerry made some uncharacteristically 1960s hippy-type movements with her hands. It looked highly ambiguous and incongruously erotic. Then she started rolling her eyes in an unfamiliar, somewhat demented, but nevertheless engaging manner.

This was all the more extraordinary because neither had any living memory of the period. These retrospective gyrations must have been based purely on information gleaned from binge-watching old holavision shows of hippie festivals from the 1960s.

The pros and cons of the flower-power make love, not war ethos of that period was a constant topic of dinner party conversations in an age when staid conformity was the order of the day. But the allure of political rebellion and sexual freedom still existed as a smouldering undercurrent. In these modern times, opportunities for free expression on a communal basis were extremely limited within a province but not so restricted in the Ghettazone, where Panzanoid and other recreational drugs were freely available, and open-air festivals were attended by up to a million people.

On several occasions, Parish had toyed with the idea of a retro VRS chip experience from the 1960s. If only to evaluate the perceived academic opinion that it had been one of the most culturally enlightening and artistically creative periods of the past 100 years. But he hadn't gotten around to it just yet. Maybe, he thought, now would be the appropriate time.

'It's basically a hallucinatory drug combined with a muscle relaxant. That could explain why there was no evidence of any defence wounds on the victim.' Gerry stopped gyrating, realising that Parish was watching her with some obvious concern for her sanity. 'What I don't understand is the necessity for such a drug.'

'So, what you're saying is he could have drugged her with this concoction, got her to pose naked on her knees for him while he sliced her head off?'

'It's a possibility, but I will have to recheck the veracity of the drug just to make sure.'

'How long will that take?'

'The lab guys will probably turn it around in a day if I beg them.'

'Can you ring me as soon as you have the answers?' asked Parish.

'No problem,' she paused. 'If it's what I think it is, she would have been receptive to almost any proposition with that amount of junk swilling around her brain.' Gerry was still rolling her eyes, but now for her own amusement.

'Oh, and it's reasonable to assume that she was probably conscious when it happened. In fact, she probably looked the killer straight in the eyes as he, or she, sliced her head off, as you so nicely put it, and she wouldn't have flinched at the critical moment. She would have known precisely what he would do but totally incapable of comprehending the outcome.' Gerry stopped rolling her eyes and resumed normal service.

'Christ, that's horrific!' exclaimed Parish as his mind conjured up the killing scenario, slowly shaking his head in disbelief. The thought of her tacit compliance with the executioner's act was almost too disturbing to contemplate.

'I've never heard of anything like that, not even in the riots of 2015.' *Some awful atrocities were carried out in the name of patriotism. The insurrection was eventually put down, but only after an extraordinarily significant loss of life. The final numbers were never released, but various*

272

estimates were never put at less than two million dead in less than three months.

'Odd you should mention that,' said Gerry, 'because that's the last time I encountered something not so dissimilar to this.'

'You've seen this stuff before?' queried Parish, sounding surprised.'

'Oh yes,' replied Gerry, 'back during the riots you were just talking about.'

'So how did you first come into contact with it?' he asked.

'Well, that was a mystery to start with. Lots of our soldiers were complaining of mild lethargy and disorientation. We thought the rebels were using some fentanyl nerve gas, the stuff they use in sieges to neutralise personnel. But it turned out the water supply system, regulated from inside the gated compounds, was intentionally contaminated with this drug concoction. It was being introduced into the water somewhere near the perimeter walls. The rebel forces in the Ghettazones were still drinking the water, so they were covertly being fed the drug. However, a small quantity had managed to find its way back into the internal province water supply. But it only affected the areas close to the perimeter walls, where the police and soldiers were in barracks. So, they accidentally consumed tiny amounts of it, but it was highly diluted.'

'So, it was being used to subdue the rebel forces?' asked Parish, still a little confused.

'Exactly,' replied Gerry. 'That's the unique feature of the drug. It makes killing easy when the enemy doesn't resist. They smile at you and give up. Make love - not war. A bit like the Swinging Sixties again.' Parish didn't respond to her last comment for fear of another drug-related retro hippie dance routine.

'So, it was all carefully planned?' he paused momentarily... 'on both occasions?'

'Possibly, if it's the same drug,' replied Gerry. 'Particularly this one, and very carefully planned for some reason. I mean, you don't wander about with a flask of this shit in your back pocket on the off chance of a revolution happening; at least, I hope not.'

'No, no, you are right,' said Parish thoughtfully. 'So, is there anything else?'

'No. That's it,' said Gerry. 'Everything else in her body, besides the drugs, is as expected. If I find anything else, I will let you know.'

'That's been really helpful, thanks.'

'That's what we're here for,' replied Gerry, smiling. Parish went to kiss her on the cheek but changed his mind at the last moment, unsure where that might lead.

'I'll be in touch,' said Gerry. She had noticed the sudden change of heart but didn't react; she, too, was unsure where casual contact might lead. After any betrayal, there will always be mistrust and caution, and love cannot flourish where apprehension prevails. They would have to learn to trust each other once more before moving on to a different level.

'Yes,' replied Gerry, 'do. I would like that.' Parish smiled and left. Wandering up the corridor to the exit door, he thought about what had just nearly happened, where they had been before, and whether it was a place he wanted to revisit. Most of all, he remembered Gerry dancing erotically in her white overalls. That vision would remain in his memory for some considerable time to come.

Chapter 16

The phone rang in Parish's office, and Heart picked it up.

'It's for you, guv.' He passed the phone over. 'It's Gerry from the path lab.' Parish listened intently while looking at Heart with a quizzical expression.

'And that's certain, is it?' asked Parish. He listened for a few more moments, thanked Gerry and replaced the phone in its cradle.

'Something more to go on, I hope,' asked Heart expectantly?

'Not really. There is nothing much we didn't know. Apart from confirmation that Dhalia was drugged with a highly concentrated version of the drug Benacane, which renders you incredibly lethargic. I imagine Dhalia would have been wide awake during the incident, fully aware of what would happen but physically incapable of doing anything about it.

'Emm,' commented Heart, who appeared horrified by the explanation.

'Possibly of more importance to us though,' continued Parish, 'is where the killer would have sourced the drug and why this particular variant. It's a spectacularly cruel and sadistic way to kill someone. He must have really hated her to do this. She must have really pissed him off.'

This form of barbaric violence smacked more of the mid-twentieth century when the old East End London gangsters would derive many happy hours of psychotic joy inflicting physical pain rather than the subdued, almost torpid environment in which they now lived. Back in the Swinging Sixties' heyday, there was sex, love, peace, flower power, pot, and unbelievably gratuitous violence.

People were nailed to a floor in crude East End crucifixions for minor transgressions of gangland etiquette. Swords were used by the notorious Kray brothers in highly creative and ingenious variations of DIY cosmetic surgery to make you laugh with a much broader smile.

After six years of world war, killing and torture were an everyday occurrence, a psychological by-product. People had become anaesthetised to horror. But this gratis torture instilled the reverence and respect necessary to control gangland territories.

'But why would someone want to do that,' asked Heart?

'Revenge!' suggested Parish, 'I think he was very annoyed about something.'

'But from what I have heard about Dhalia, she wasn't malicious or vindictive, and yet somehow she managed to provoke him enough to make him do that to her. It could have been blackmail, I suppose....' but Heart was grasping at straws. 'Either way, it looks like she knew her killer.'

'Possibly,' replied Parish thoughtfully. 'Well, I hope she did. Otherwise, we have a sociopathic homicidal maniac roaming around out there with a bag full of catatonic stupor-inducing drugs and an urgent desire to randomly dismember people. And he appears to have no traceable DNA, which means he's virtually undetectable... and very dangerous.'

'Maybe it was just a one-off. Maybe he or "*she*" had personal reasons, a grudge possibly,' suggested Heart, always conscious of the politically correct environment they now lived in? Parish smiled at Heart's addition.

'A grudge,' replied Parish, looking slightly stunned at Hearts theory? 'Bit over the top for a grudge, I think. No, people like this never stop at one. There will always be more. This, unfortunately, means we may have to pay a visit to Deliverance, possibly even into the Ghettazone.

'Visit the Ghettazone? Why?' reiterated Heart with some trepidation. 'I'd rather have all my teeth pulled out through my arse if it's all the same.' He smiled sardonically at Parish.

'It's not that bad,' said Parish, who knew that Heart hated the Ghettazone. Heart looked at Parish in stunned disbelief.

'Not that bad?' I had to shoot somebody the last time we were there. We'd only been there a couple of hours.'

'He was shooting at us,' replied Parish casually. 'Anyway, that was three years ago. It's more peaceful now.'

'Is it?' replied Heart curtly, without any real conviction. 'Anyway, why out there?'

'That call from Gerry. She also gave me the details of a Professor Grimes. He's been working on retrieving the data from the old Criminal Records Office files destroyed during the riots. He might just be able to help us crack the DNA problem with this case. He works in an old IT bunker at Portsmouth University in Deliverance.'

The province of Deliverance covered an area from Bournemouth to Newhaven, following the old A31, M27 and A27. The perimeter walls were built on the motorways and major roads. They afforded quick and easy access and delineation between the province and the Ghettazone while incorporating all the major south coast commercial ports. Security gates were positioned every thirty miles along the route.

'Why do we have to go there?' asked Heart, palpably reluctant to venture outside the province.

'To see if they can identify the DNA of our Mr X,' replied Parish.

'And if we do, how are we going to find him. There's no straightforward way of tracing someone out there any longer.'

'We'll find a way. Anyway, we don't know for sure that's where he lives yet. How did you get on with the techies and Rose's computer?'

'Hard drive was destroyed. I don't think the Techies will get much from what's left, but they are still trying. Bank accounts appeared normal – no untraceable income.'

'So, nothing,' said Parish, resigning himself to another dead end.

'No, not quite,' said Heart, with a sufficient degree of enthusiasm to lift Parish's spirits slightly.

'What did you find?' asked Parish.

'Well, it was in her personal records. It's her mother.'

'What's she got to do with anything?' asked Parish.

'Well, I thought I would just check out her family in case they knew anything, but the only relative I could find was her mother.'

'Is that good,' asked Parish cautiously? He couldn't bring himself to be any more enthusiastic. He could see there was something else coming.

'Not really. She's dead,' replied Heart, sounding oddly sanguine about her demise, which didn't surprise Parish for some reason.

'Not so good,' replied Parish, a little deflated. He picked up his coffee cup from his desk and took a sip. His eyes winced as if he'd encountered something unpleasant in the coffee, but he swallowed it anyway and placed the cup back on the desk. Parish took out a hanky and wiped the corners of his mouth while pondering over what Heart had just told him.

'Not necessarily. She died in unusual circumstances,' continued Heart.

'Go on,' prompted Parish, fully engaged but endeavouring not to become overly excited. This was turning into an emotional rollercoaster, like everything connected to this investigation. Two steps forward and one step back into the shit seemed to be the pattern.

'She used to work for…' He didn't go any further but took a sip of his coffee. 'Guess who?'

Parish stared at him; he was a little annoyed. He hated puerile guessing games. 'I don't know,' he replied. Slightly exasperated by Heart's procrastination, but Heart had to play his little game.

'Go on, have a guess,' he said smugly.

'I don't know,' replied Parish, now losing patience and obviously not interested in playing games. 'Surprise me.'

'Aiden Hawsley.'

'Hawsley,' repeated Parish, conjugating his thoughts into a logical arrangement as the revelation sank in. His expression changed completely.

'Hawsley.' He repeated the name again, and his eyes squinted a little. 'That has to be more than a coincidence.'

'Yes, I thought so too,' said Heart.

'Well done, Heart. That really could be important.'

'Could it?' asked Heart, thinking it might just be an odd coincidence, but Parish didn't believe in them.

'What time have you arranged for us to meet him?' asked Parish, now freshly invigorated by this information.

'Five o'clock,' replied Heart.

'Excellent.' replied Parish. He was beginning to see a few small pieces of the puzzle fall into place. 'You'll make inspector yet.' Heart didn't respond to that, as he wasn't sure how to react. Not once could he remember Parish ever indicating any thoughts or opinions in this direction.

'I'll be happy to make it back from the Ghettazone,' replied Heart more prosaically, still dwelling on his misgivings about their forthcoming journey.

'I'd like to see that arrogant little shit again,' muttered Parish.

'Who, Hawsley?' asked Heart, a little confused as they hadn't spoken to him yet.

'No, not Hawsley, that bloody sergeant.' There was a distinct hint of dark pleasure in his voice. As it was just after three o'clock, Parish decided they would make their way to CSP headquarters.

They could take a leisurely drive; they had no option as the matrix system reduced traffic speed during "rush hour." A term that had now become perniciously oxymoronic. The very last thing the rush hour was - was a rush. It was more of a gentle meander and would take much longer than an hour. Eventually, they arrived at the main gate and, as before, produced their identity cards and were directed to the side of the building, where they parked. They walked over to the main entrance, where the same sergeant was back on duty.

'Good afternoon, gentlemen, and what can I do for you today?' asked the sergeant, still arrogant, still bombastic.

'We have an appointment with the Lord Protector,' replied Heart. 'We came yesterday; I don't know if you remember?' Heart knew he remembered.

'Ahhh, let me think...' The sergeant made an appalling impression of someone deep in thought, gazing skywards with his thumb and forefinger caressing his chin.

'Nope, can't say I do.' He was evidently lying merely to aggravate them.

'We had a very lengthy conversation,' prompted Heart, 'surely you can't have forgotten already?'

The sergeant continued with his pained impersonation of someone scrabbling around in his brain for something while slowly sucking air through his teeth, but eventually just shook his head. 'Nope, can't say I remember that at all. The old memory must be playing tricks.'

'Something is,' muttered Parish under his breath.

'Never mind,' said Heart. 'Can we come in today? We do have an appointment.' Heart did his best to remain calm and polite despite the sergeant's sudden amnesia.

'Let me see.' He turned slightly to one side and spoke furtively into his throat mic.

'I have a...' He turned to Heart. 'Sorry, what were your names again?'

'Detective Inspector Parish and Detective Sergeant Heart,' replied Heart, endeavouring to restrain himself from commenting further.

'Paris, Heart, very romantic,' quipped the sergeant, smiling oddly. 'Sort of conjures up a balmy night on a riverboat cruise on the Seine, secret assignation, misty moonlight, chilled champagne, pink roses, two people besotted with each other, love in the air....' He lingered there for a few moments while Parish and Heart looked at each other quizzically, not knowing how or if they should respond. It was as if the sergeant was recalling some long-forgotten memory, enraptured by the bucolic scene he had conjured up in his head.

Heart thought it was a little disturbing.

'It's Parish,' corrected Parish, enunciating each letter. 'P-A-R-I-S-H. Parish with an H.' He emphasised the H.

'Is it now? Right, my apologies,' said the sergeant a little sternly. 'Parish and Heart.'

The sergeant repeated the names into his throat mike once again.

'May I?' He gestured to see their identity cards, which they dutifully handed over and which he carefully checked.

'That all appears to be in order. Go straight through.' He smiled sanctimoniously for a split second. 'A security guard will meet you inside and take you up.' He smiled again, somewhat disquietingly, and stepped aside. Heart stood back to allow Parish to enter first. As he passed immediately behind Parish, he muttered something quietly under his breath, which the sergeant didn't quite catch.

'Sorry, I missed that. Could you repeat it?' asked the sergeant.

'Didn't say anything,' replied Heart. 'Just clearing my throat. Bit of shit, I think.' Heart pointed at his throat and coughed pathetically.

The sergeant flashed him a sceptical glare, and his nostrils flared like an angry bull. 'Maybe your ears are going the same way as your memory,' suggested Heart? The sergeant squinted, but Heart just smiled and continued walking until he had drawn level with Parish, who was busy admiring the splendour of the hallway.

'Not antagonising the nice policeman, are you?' asked Parish acerbically.

'No, not me, guv,' replied Heart. 'Wouldn't dream of it.'

They followed the guard through security and handed over their weapons. They were directed to follow another guard who guided them to an elevator and ushered them in. He followed them and pressed the button. The lift mechanism whirled quietly as the elevator moved swiftly to the third floor, where the doors slid silently open. As they stepped out of the lift, the guard pointed to a pair of tall, ornate oak-panelled doors a few yards away. He nodded toward the doors and smiled politely but said nothing.

They thanked the guard, who politely nodded his acknowledgement. The elevator doors closed softly, and the lift was gone. Parish and Heart crossed the cavernous, galleried landing towards the two large doors. The Lord Protector's name had been embossed on them in gold lettering, which seemed a little pointless, but no doubt, there was a reason. Maybe he became confused with all the offices, thought Parish.

Heart was about to knock when one of the doors suddenly opened. A man they immediately recognised as Aiden Hawsley appeared before them.

'Good afternoon, or is it evening,' asked Hawsley? There was a sense of bewilderment in his question as if he really didn't know. He spoke softly, with a lyrical resonance more in keeping with what you might expect to hear from a well-educated, gay vicar than a politician infamous for his ruthlessness.

'We are…'

But Hawsley interrupted Heart. 'I have never been sure quite when the change actually happens.' He smiled disarmingly with an exaggerated, almost theatrical hand movement and beckoned them into his office. 'Please come in.'

It was decorated with surprising simplicity. With none of the ostentatious vulgarity of which they had previously been misinformed. Hawsley directed them to a large oak desk piled high with books and files, around which were five utilitarian chairs placed randomly. The immediate impression was a ladies' book club discussion group rather than a tenacious autocrat's control centre. Half a dozen or so oak filing cabinets were just behind his desk. Some were half-open. The cabinets also had many files stacked on top of them. Several large but not particularly impressive oil paintings depicting nondescript country scenes hung on the walls. Various sofas and armchairs were scattered about the room, many laden with more files and books. Oddly inconsistent and out of kilter with all they had been expecting. It was more the quintessential study of a university academic preparing for another lecture on something or other... not a politician.

'Take a seat, please. Would you like tea or coffee?' Hawsley pointed towards two of the chairs around his desk that were not covered in books.

'Tea, please,' replied Heart. 'Milk and one sugar, or sweetener if you have it.' He suddenly realised how crass that sounded and apologised - but Hawsley just waggled his finger as if to say he understood and took no offence.

'Me too, thank you,' added Parish, radically adjusting his preconceptions of how he had anticipated this interview might play out. Aiden pressed an intercom on his desk and asked for tea, some digestive biscuits, and 'some of my favourite sandwiches, the....'

The girl taking the instruction had obviously pre-empted Hawsley's request.

'Yes, those, thank you,' he confirmed, then sat down to face his inquisitors.

'I'm terribly sorry,' he continued, apologising profusely for his oversight, 'would you like some sandwiches?' he enquired politely. 'They do a delicious yak cheese and cherry tomato here with sweet onion relish.' Parish thought this was all a little unnerving. It began to feel as if Hawsley had invited them for afternoon tea and a cosy chat at the Ritz. Not the headquarters of a notoriously ruthless despot to answer some questions about a murder where he could quickly become the prime suspect.

Parish began to warm to Hawsley but still clung tenaciously to his initial reservations.

'Ah no, thank you,' replied Parish.' Yak cheese somehow didn't appeal to him. His brain had conjured up a laboured vision of long-haired, oddly shaped, straggly animals and matted hair falling into pails of the freshly squeezed milk, slowly extracted by ladies with triangular hats sitting on three-legged stools chanting slightly out-of-tune extracts from the *Sound of Music*. Heart shook his head, politely declining the offer, which was unusual. Normally, he would eat almost anything placed before him. But he, too, was finding this surprisingly affable encounter a little surreal.

Parish was still half expecting the doors to be flung open at any moment with the arrival of several intimidatingly bulky secret service agents brandishing guns and making threatening... threats. Christ, he thought, even my brain has stopped working rationally. However, that concern slowly receded as his fears were swiftly consigned to the waste bin along with the memory of the yak sandwich.

'I'm sorry I haven't introduced myself properly,' said Parish, 'I'm Detective Inspector Parish, and this is...

'Detective Sergeant Heart,' said Heart. They both offered their warrant cards for inspection, but Hawsley just brushed it away as if to say, *I know who you are.*

'You've got this far, so I think it's reasonable to assume you are who you say you are,' responded Hawsley with a scholarly flourish of his hand. So, they slipped their warrant cards back into their jackets. 'And anyway, your reputation precedes you....'

'Does it?' asked Parish, not aware he had one.

'Nearly twenty-three years with the police force, fastest ever elevation to DI, an almost flawless record for solving major incidents, possible chief super material even.' He had obviously been well briefed, although the last remark hinted at vacuous flattery.

Suddenly, Hawsley changed direction. 'I was sorry to hear about your wife and daughter.' He lowered the pitch of his voice a couple of semi-tones to enhance the gravitas. 'Tragic, tragic affair. It's still sort of unsolved, though, isn't it?' This was a classic oratorical tactic but enhanced with a Machiavellian twist. Parish had not been involved in the original accident investigation for obvious reasons. Hawsley obviously knew this and had taken the opportunity to specifically refer to the incident as unsolved. In contrast, Parish had always been led to believe it was an unfortunate tragic accident resulting from an electronic malfunction in the matrix system.

The seed of doubt had now been delicately planted in his mind, but for what reason, he wondered. The unexpected and unwelcome introduction of a personal dimension into the conversation took Parish a little off guard. It threw him off balance momentarily, and he couldn't decide whether this was a genuinely empathetic remark or some kind of psychological mind game. It had the timbre of a challenge about it, so Parish took his time carefully considering how to respond and made a mental note to listen more attentively to the nuance and inflection in every word that Hawsley uttered.

Something was going on, but he didn't know what. Of more concern was this was the second time in as many days that the circumstances of the car crash that had claimed the lives of his wife and daughter had been mentioned. Each time by someone he had never met before and, as far as he knew, wasn't connected to the accident in any way. It made him wonder...

'It was a motor accident,' replied Parish abruptly, 'so there wasn't anything to solve.' He answered with expressionless disdain, fighting back the welling emotion that threatened to overwhelm him.

'A malfunction with the AMG system, I understand?' said Hawsley. Although phrased as a question, the nuance indicated something entirely different. Hawsley shook his head empathetically. 'So incredibly sad.' He paused for just slightly longer than was absolutely necessary. 'I don't have any children either,'

That was uncalled for, thought Heart. Words designed for effect rather than empathy. He was already displaying aspects of his actual disposition but still cleverly concealing it under the cloak of a faux Pavlovian response.

Hawsley picked up a tumbler on his desk and took a sip. 'That's something I miss. I don't know how you carry on with the burden of that every day; you are an incredibly courageous man. If that...' He paused to take another sip that somehow, at that particular moment, completely devalued the currency of his words, '...if that happened to me... I think I would just put a gun to my head and....' Without taking his eyes off Parish and without expression, he made a crude gesture with two fingers shaped like a gun pointed at his temple.

That was completely unnecessary, thought Heart; you're an even bigger cunt than I first thought. Like so many people, he had formed his opinion about Hawsley from the news, rumour, vague innuendo, and occasional appearances on holavision. That view had not been mollified one scintilla during their brief time together. In fact, the tone of the conversation had only fortified his initial assessment. He was painfully aware of Hawsley's verbal pyrotechnics. But he could do or say little about them as he wasn't sure what Parish was thinking. Hawsley had done his homework, but his initial apparent admiration for Parish, bordering on cloying sycophancy, now began to sound more like a threat.

His underlying self-righteous authority was beginning to seep through the masquerade of sincerity. Now stencilling the darkness with an outline of who and what he really was.

'You have been much braver than I could ever have been in the circumstances, Inspector,' said Hawsley.

'You flatter me, sir,' replied Parish, who was still pondering the subtext of Hawsley's previous statement. 'I don't think I have.' Suddenly, he felt uneasy in Hawsley's presence. The battle lines had somehow been imperceptibly drawn. When this was done, would his career be left in ruins, or Hawsley's? What troubled him most was whether Hawsley would be so ingenuous as to challenge him if he were guilty?

'I do hope your loss doesn't affect the outcome of this case, Inspector?' muttered Hawsley casually. He glanced at Parish with dead-fish eyes, and for the first time, Parish glimpsed the steely ruthlessness and cold-blooded streak deeply embedded in Hawsley's soul. A man equally impassioned and imprisoned by the bloodied chariot of flesh that he now inhabited. Parish knew one thing for sure at that precise moment: he didn't know what this man was capable of. But of more significance was Hawsley didn't appear to understand either what he was capable of. It was as if he were under the control of another.

'Why should it? That was over three years ago,' Parish replied. He couldn't immediately see how Catherine's death could have any bearing on the murder they were investigating. But Hawsley's demeanour was as if he alone had access to a slender thread of connectivity between the two events.

'Why should it indeed,' agreed Hawsley contemplatively? 'So why are you here?' he asked after what seemed like another inordinately long pause.

'We're investigating a murder,' replied Heart, who decided this was probably an appropriate time for him to take over the conversation. 'And we have information that you....' he paused for a second to take a breath. The slightly charged, semi-convivial atmosphere could change dramatically with the statement he was about to make. '....you may have been at the crime scene during the period when we believe the victim was killed.'

There, he'd said it. He had effectively accused the most powerful man in Britain of possibly murdering someone. Now, he could only wait for the inevitable fallout, for which he was fully prepared... But nothing happened.

Hawsley hardly batted an eyelid and sipped from his glass without drawing breath. There was no response or indication of his connection to the murder. He placed the empty glass on the desk and carefully wiped the corners of his lips with a napkin.

'So,' said Hawsley, pausing for a second, 'who is this woman, the one you obviously think I have knowledge of?'

He conceded nothing, not the slightest change in his expression. The first point to him thought Heart. Cool, almost casual under fire.

'Her name is Dhalia, Dhalia Vingali. She lived in Chelsea.'

Hawsley didn't say anything immediately but rose from his chair and sauntered over to the French windows. He stood there gazing up at the Mall. A flurry of snow started falling again, adding a graceful charm to the beautiful scene outside.

'Do you know....?' He hesitated briefly, scrutinising every tiny element of the glorious view. It was as if his whole life had been waiting for this moment. 'This is the very same balcony the *family* used to stand on when they presented themselves to the public after a wedding or a coronation, but never after a death?' His voice had an underlying, undeniable suggestion of antipathy but not enough substance to convince anybody listening of genuine conviction. He was obviously still in awe of their ability to engender love, loyalty and true patriotism, a feat he had never been quite able to achieve.

'No, I didn't,' replied Heart, who thought it an odd comment.

'Must have been an incredible sensation, all those people cheering.' Hawsley seemed carried away by the past euphoria that once inhabited the room and the balcony. Parish wondered if maybe he secretly craved some of that adoration for himself.

'It's what they used to believe in, who they trusted, who they loved,' remarked Heart almost panegyrically. 'That was the zeitgeist of that moment, the belief in the Royal Family. The thread of commonality that held it all together.'

'Until Diana,' added Hawsley. 'You remember Diana, Sergeant? The Roman Queen of Heaven, but never Queen of England?'

'Yes, indeed,' replied Heart.

'That's when it all changed,' said Hawsley. 'The crowds didn't roar quite so loudly after that. They still cheered, oh yes, they cheered, but their heart wasn't in it anymore. William and Harry getting married helped restore the faith a little, but not enough, and one marriage didn't last very long. It's hard to be loyal when you can't afford to eat because the kakistocracy has emptied the coffers. Wasting all the money supporting criminals, aliens, immigrants, city parasites and corrupt third-world countries.

'Do you know, it's less than thirty years since that fateful day, the day that marked the beginning of the end, and here I am standing where they once stood.' He paused, obviously relishing the thought of that moment.

Heart went to say something, but Parish gave him a glance that he instantly interpreted as an instruction to keep his mouth shut. *He was on to something... let's run with it.* Parish had detected a tiny penitential note in Hawsley's intonation. He wanted him to continue unimpeded by unnecessary interruptions that could divert him down a less illuminating pathway. Hawsley's speech intrigued Parish; it could be a priceless insight into how his mind worked.

'It wasn't their fault,' Hawsley continued. 'They were just the collateral damage from a series of flawed, weak, spineless governments; administrations corrupted by greedy institutions.' Hawsley paused for a few moments before continuing. 'Council house upbringing, well, housing association, adequate middle-class euphemism, sort of smacks of possession but not quite. It doesn't quite scan the same, does it? State school education, now that sounds better, adequate once again, but nothing particularly outstanding. Public school... now that's a strangely ironic title. Just about anybody can go there, except, would you believe, the poor Public. I scraped through university by the skin of my arse, unemployed until I joined the National Front. And now....'

Parish was enjoying the self-enlighting socialist tirade. Maybe this investigation would not be as challenging as he first thought. Hawsley might even disclose something relevant amongst the diatribe if he continued long enough. He appeared to have a massive chip on his shoulder.

'....I told them what they wanted to hear, that's all. It wasn't hard,' continued Hawsley. 'I gave them back their self-belief, a backbone after they had been filleted by the pretenders, and I gave them back pride in their country. I'm a patriot, you know. I love this country and will do anything to protect it, so I have done what had to be done. There are no spongers here any longer. Nobody bleeding the lifeblood out of us, just the good honest people who have always made this country great.' Hawsley seemed genuinely astonished by his own achievements.

'Rose,' he turned around and looked at his inquisitors. 'Her real name was Rose Watson.' Heart glanced at Parish, surprised at the admission as if to say, *Is this all really going to unravel so easily?* But Parish said nothing, and Heart turned back to face Hawsley.

'How did you know that sir?' queried Heart.

'I knew her. That's why you found my DNA with the air scan.'

'How did you know that?' exclaimed Parish, who had not mentioned anything about the DNA evidence. He was displaying signs of being slightly disturbed that supposedly confidential case evidence had once again been leaked out to a third party in such a relatively short time.

'They, the ubiquitous they...' he said with emphasis and nodded nonchalantly to the air, 'keep me advised of anything relevant that happens.'

'They?' queried Parish, 'who are they?'

'Oh, the security people are always looking for troublemakers. They probably knew I visited Dhalia and even installed the air scrub unit. They're very protective like that. Funny thing, security. I have always thought of it as being a bit like silk stockings. It hides nearly everything: all the varicose veins, the nasty scars of life, all the horrible bits you don't want anybody else to see, and it makes the legs look beautiful and tanned. But it can't hold in the blood and pus that starts seeping when the leg turns gangrenous and begins to die.'

'It wasn't working, though, was it?' remarked Parish curiously, ignoring the strange analogy.

'No, so I understand. It's a little odd that: - it makes me wonder if....' Hawsley seemed genuinely surprised but not overly concerned. There was a knock on the door, and a girl entered, pushing a trolley into the room with tea, biscuits, and sandwiches. Hawsley beckoned her to bring the cart over to his desk. She poured out three cups, asked Heart and Parish how they wanted theirs, and then placed their cups on the desk in front of them and Hawsley's on the other side. Hawsley returned to his chair, and the girl brought over the plate of sandwiches before removing his empty cup.

'Is there anything else you need,' she asked politely, looking at each of them in turn? They all declined her invitation, and she left the room. Parish picked up his tea and took a sip; he always liked his tea hot, almost boiling. It would burn the throat of lesser mortals but didn't seem to affect him.

'When did you last see her?' enquired Heart.

'Two nights ago, the night she was murdered.' Hawsley spoke in a cold, matter-of-fact tone without inflection or emotion and made no attempt to hide the fact.

'What time were you there?' asked Heart.

'Got there about nine and left about ten. Had to be back here to meet someone, then I was driven to the airport just before midnight.'

'Why were you visiting her?' asked Heart.

'She had some personal problems that I was trying to help her with. She was a friend of a friend.'

'Benny Maranno?' asked Parish.

'Yes, I think it was actually, now you come to mention it.'

'Did you know she was a prostitute?' asked Parish.

Hawsley thought carefully about the question for a few moments before answering, but just a fraction of a second longer than was essential for it to sound unconsidered and spontaneous.

'Was she?' he replied, looking unconvincingly surprised.

'Did you know?' repeated Parish insistently.

'Well, that's a problem, isn't it?'

'Is it? Why?'

'Well, if I say I did, then surely that would constitute a breach of the morality law?'

'There's no evidence you had sex with her, so maybe you didn't know?' Parish put this as a question that required an answer, but it also gave Hawsley an escape route.

'I don't think I did,' replied Hawsley cautiously.

'So, what was the personal problem you were helping her with?' asked Parish.

'Is that relevant?' asked Hawsley.

'Well, it could be. You went to see Miss Vingali about something, not sex, as I understand, and a few hours later, she's found dead. What do you think?'

Parish watched Hawley's face, looking for anything that might indicate a flicker of panic passing through his brain - but there was nothing.

'I see,' replied Hawsley. He paused for thought for a moment, carefully considering his answer. It was a bit like playing chess: you make a move, and once committed, once you have removed your finger from the piece, you have temporarily lost control. There is no going back, even if you have made a gross tactical error. You must stand by your decision and defend as best you can from what could now be a severely weakened position. So, the trick was always to think three moves ahead. 'Her mother was killed over three years ago, and you – the police, not you personally...' he emphasised the 'you', 'never found the killer.'

Parish glanced at Heart. This was becoming even more embarrassing as Hawsley appeared remarkably well informed, far better than they were, so it would seem. 'Dhalia contacted me. Asked if I could help her find out what happened to her mother, Janice, as the police had failed, so I said I would look into it.'

'And did you?' asked Heart.

'I spoke to the P & C Commissioner, who told me she'd been found incinerated almost beyond recognition in a car in the Ghettazone just outside Providence. Apparently, she was dead before the fire started. Shot in the eye, I believe. They said she was probably kneeling at the time, possibly begging for mercy... something to do with the body's position and how it had shrivelled up in the heat. Those pathologists are very clever.'

He looked at Parish for a moment with a complete absence of expression. 'I passed those details on to Rose, but that's what she'd already been told, well, most of it.'

The coldness with which he delivered these details sent a shiver down Heart's spine. Hawsley seemed to enjoy saying the words.

'Did Rose know why her mother was murdered?' asked Heart.

'Thought she was killed because she found something out. That's what she told me.'

'You have no idea what Janice found out?'

'No. As I said, it was just an idea that Rose had. Possibly just something to give some meaning to her mother's murder. I suppose it's easier to deal with an unexplained death if you can come up with a conspiracy theory to explain it away. Rather than accept that it was a random attack and there was no reason. It was just fate.' He looked at Parish but said nothing.

'So, you think it was just a random killing?' asked Parish.

'I don't know. That's what the police told me,' replied Hawsley.

'I see,' said Parish. 'Did you ever have sex with Rose Watson?'

'No,' replied Hawsley diffidently, 'and I presume you haven't any evidence to prove otherwise, or you wouldn't have asked.'

Parish smiled at Hawsley. 'No, we haven't. It's just that she was an attractive, unattached woman and someone in your....'

Hawsley looked at Parish disdainfully and barked tersely. 'Are you insinuating that I would take advantage of my position to intimidate vulnerable women and force them to have sex with me, Inspector?'

'No, not at all, sir. It was just an observation... one which was plainly incorrect, but some lesser mortals might think differently.' Parish took another sip of tea...

'Did you know another member of your inner cabinet was having a sexual relationship with her?' asked Heart.

Hawsley considered the question before concluding, 'So Maranno was fucking her?

Heart didn't respond immediately, but his expression was enough to antagonise Hawsley. Parish noticed an almost imperceptible change in his temperament.

'He's weak, you know. He can't control his thoughts, bladder, mouth or dick, and sometimes they all get the better of him, which can be a little disagreeable.' There was little chance that thoughts and deeds would ever get the better of Hawsley. They wouldn't dare.

'Are there others?' asked Heart.

'Women?' suggested Hawsley. 'Yes, he screws anything. That's his Achilles heel, well maybe not with his heel, but....' Hawsley smiled with cheery condescension at his joke.

'Is it?' asked Heart, making a mental note.

'We all have our weaknesses, sergeant. Just as we all believe, somewhat mistakenly, in my opinion, that we also have at least one redeeming virtue, which we tend to keep to ourselves. Even you.' He looked at Heart as if he knew something unpleasant about him, making him feel a little uncomfortable.

'Well, I think that will do for now,' said Parish. 'I think you've answered all our questions, so we'll leave you in peace for today.' They all got up and walked to the door. As they reached it, Parish turned to Hawsley.

'I understand that her mother, Janice Watson, used to work here?'

'Did she?' enquired Hawsley, sounding surprised. Heart referred to the tablet he was holding.

'She was a researcher for you?' confirmed Heart.

'A researcher,' repeated Hawsley, making a poor impression of somebody delving into the depths of his memory, searching for something he had absolutely no intention of recalling. Heart noted the odd similarity to the sergeant outside. Maybe it was something in the tea?

'The name doesn't spring to mind,'

'You didn't know her, then?' asked Heart.

'I don't think so.'

'Yet she worked for you for quite a long time.'

'Well, I'm sorry, you have me at a disadvantage, Inspector,' replied Hawsley. 'I don't know anybody... Oh,' he suddenly exclaimed. 'You mean Janni – but it sounded like Jenny.'

'That's right, sir, Janice Watson,' confirmed Parish. 'But you knew her as Janni?' he asked.

'Yes, I do remember Janni. I believe she did something on the ground floor. It's not an area I often visit. I think she did come up a few times to see me, but I can't remember what for, precisely, and anyway, I haven't seen her for at least two, maybe three years.'

'That's because she was murdered three years ago,' said Heart.

'Yes, of course, I forgot,' replied Hawsley whimsically, but he hadn't.

'Quite a coincidence, don't you think?' said Parish.

'What? That we worked in the same building? Not really. Over a thousand people work here. I don't know all of them. In fact, I hardly know any of them.'

'No, that's not what I meant. I was referring to the fact that you work in the same building as somebody who was murdered, who you say you didn't know. You also visited that same person's daughter, who was also murdered. What do you think are the chances of that happening?'

Hawsley considered the question briefly, 'I've no idea.'

'Remote, almost non-existent, I would have said, wouldn't you?' asked Parish.

'I suppose you could say it's a bit like winning the lottery then,' replied Hawsley glibly. 'That's extremely unlikely, isn't it? Even a small win.'

'Yes, you could say, but still, it happens to someone...' said Parish.

'And quite often, so I understand,' replied Hawsley.

'But in your case, you would have to win the jackpot twice, wouldn't you? said Parish, smiling cynically. Hawsley didn't reply immediately.

'Twice? Why twice?' Curiosity was getting the better of him.

'Well,' replied Parish, 'once for knowing two people who were both murdered in very unusual circumstances. And once for them being mother and daughter and probably being murdered for the same reason. One in a billion chance that, don't you agree?' Hawsley smiled but didn't reply.

'Oh, and there is even a third chance at the jackpot, but I won't go into that right now. I'll leave that for later.'

Hawsley looked intrigued but not particularly disturbed by this revelation. He was always a good poker player. He knew when to hold and when to fold.

'Thank you for your time, Mr Hawsley,' interjected Heart after a few moments, glancing at Parish to see whether he had finished asking questions.

'No problem. Any time,' replied Hawsley. Parish nodded, and they left the office, making for the lift - Parish deliberately left the door open. Hawsley walked across the room to close the door and stood momentarily, looking across the hall to Parish and Heart, waiting at the lift doors. They both turned and smiled politely at him before entering the lift.

'Mack,' said Heart, but before he could go any further, Parish put his index finger to his lips, and Heart went no further. The lift reached the ground floor, and the doors opened. They were greeted by a guard, who took them back through security and returned their weapons. As they left the building, they passed the sergeant they had encountered the previous day.

'I do remember you now,' he said, waving his finger ominously at them as if he were about to make a dramatic announcement. 'You came when the Lord Protector was out, didn't you? Tried to get a little bolshie with me, as I remember. You see, I never forget a face.'

'I don't think we did,' replied Heart. 'I think you were the one being pompous and arrogant.'

'There you go again,' said the security sergeant. He turned to Parish. 'You'll have to keep that one on a leash,

Sergeant. He could be a bit dangerous let out on his own. Shouldn't feed him meat if I was you. Affects some people that way.'

'It's Inspector, Sergeant,' corrected Parish.

'Of course it is. My apologies. I always get a little confused with you two. What with him (the sergeant nodded imperturbably at Heart) being nearly retired, I thought....' He didn't finish the sentence as Heart moved closer to the sergeant, but the sergeant cautiously took one step back.

'Goodbye, Sergeant,' said Parish as he started to walk away. Heart stood still for a few seconds, glared at the sergeant, then turned and followed Parish to the car.

'You weren't going to hit him, were you?' asked Parish.

'No,' replied Heart shortly. 'Why would you think that?'

'No reason,' replied Parish.

'So why did you shush me in the lift?' asked Heart.

'Hawsley seems to be getting most of his information faster than us. I thought maybe the lift was bugged. Everything else seems to be.'

'Oh, I see,' replied Heart, acknowledging the possibility.

'So where to now?' Parish stood by the car momentarily and looked up at the window adjacent to the balcony of the room where they had just been. He could just make out a solitary figure looking down.

'Back to the Yard. I want to talk to the techies working on Dhalia's computer. See if they have found anything else. Then home, I think. We have a long day ahead of us tomorrow in Deliverance.' When Heart opened the car door and sat down, the computer asked him where he wanted to go.

'Scotland Yard,' replied Heart.

'Thank you,' said the computer and the car sedately moved off through the gates and into the matrix system.

'So, what do you think,' asked Heart once again? Parish put a finger to his mouth and gestured towards the onboard computer. Heart pursed his lips and laid his head back to catch forty winks. They arrived back at the Yard after an uneventful journey.

They took the lift to the first floor, where the technicians and forensic departments were and made their way to the IT section. Zac had promised to hang on until seven o'clock to see them. Most of the staff had gone home, but they could see the light still on in Zac's office at the end of the corridor. They knocked and entered.

'Evening, Inspector, Sergeant,' said Zac, looking up from the bench where he was sitting.

'So, what have you got for us?' asked Heart, looking around the surprisingly bare worktops. Conspicuous by their absence were the usual trappings of a laboratory: bottles, samples, wires, and sundry other paraphernalia. He expected to see more than just a single laptop with two leads snaking out from the back, plugged into the wall behind. The room was impeccably neat, which, in his experience, was highly unusual for a techie's office. It emanated the impression of an area of exquisite precision under the control of someone who was anally retentive with a severe OCD issue. However, on the end of the desk was one item that defied the general impression: a large, straggly bunch of African lilies, their slightly pissy odour permeating the air. Parish remembered Catherine used to like Lilies.

Zac picked up some paper printouts neatly piled on one side and started to flip through them until he reached one particular page. 'To be honest, there wasn't much here. I have some personal details, quite old. It must have been copied from another older computer because it was held in an archive file we no longer use. It mainly relates to when her mother was at university from 2005 to 2007.'

'Which university?' asked Heart, making notes.

'Oxford, studying English and Politics, but she didn't finish. I contacted them, and all they could tell me was she dropped out suddenly after her mother died in 2007.'

'That's a coincidence. I think Catherine was at Oxford during that period,' commented Parish, a little surprised they were both there at the same time.

'So was I. It's a small world,' replied Zac, 'but I was there a bit later.'

'So, no salacious details about clients then, telephone numbers, mailex correspondence… sexual preferences?' asked Parish, 'nothing that could help us?'

'No, nothing like that. There were some odd references that I am still working on, but nothing else. That's about it. Sorry there wasn't more. I'm returning to the apartment tomorrow, so if I discover anything relevant, I'll ring you.'

'Any time,' added Parish. Zac nodded.

'She must have kept a diary of some sort. Otherwise, her clients would have been tripping over each other,' suggested Heart, slightly puzzled.

'Well, if there was one, it wasn't on the laptop. Maybe Dhalia kept a little black book. Probably a lot safer these days,' suggested Zac, smiling. 'The spooks are everywhere. But she may have had another computer or a tablet, and we still haven't found her phone. It may still turn up.'

'Maybe,' said Parish. They thanked Zac, left the lab, and wandered off to the lift.

'I wonder if Janice knew Catherine,' asked Heart, with a hint of discernible hesitation? He knew mentioning her name would be an emotive topic, but it was an odd coincidence that he thought was still worth mentioning.

'Why do you ask that,' asked Parish with a curious expression?

'I don't know. Maybe I'm just picking up on your serendipity vibes.'

Parish thought about that for a moment. 'Oddly enough, I had already considered that as well,' said Parish. He smiled at Heart. 'Could make a detective out of you yet...' it was a throwaway quip in good heart. 'But even if they did know each other, I can't see how it could be connected to the case. Catherine was training to be a doctor, and Zac said Janice studied English. It is a big university.'

'Yeah, I guess you're right,' agreed Heart, 'but...' he rocked his head as if to say *you never can tell.*

'Well, I think we'll call that it for today,' said Parish. 'Can you pick me up from home at nine o'clock tomorrow?'

'Nine o'clock, then,' said Heart. He pressed the call button for the lift.

Chapter 17

On his way home, Parish's mind drifted back to what Zac had said about Catherine and Janice studying at Oxford University during the same period. On the balance of probability, it was very doubtful they knew each other. The Oxford campus covered a vast area and included more than thirty-eight colleges. With twenty-two thousand students on different courses, attending at different times, there was no apparent common ground. Yet, for some inexplicable reason and against what seemed like highly unfavourable odds, Parish knew they had to have met.

He remembered one lesson at school when his maths teacher had explained that in a class of thirty students, although statistically, you would think that everybody would have their birthday on a different day, there was a remarkably high probability that two of the students would share the same birthday. This meant that apparent odds of 365 to 1 were, in fact, closer to 30 to 1. This reflected the hidden law of probable outcome. Something that Parish often referred to for guidance - in circumstances such as this. *As Sherlock Holmes said, once you have discounted the impossible, whatever you have left, however improbable, must be the solution.*

He tried to reason that even if Catherine and Janice had met, it could not have any bearing on the Dhalia Vingali murder. But deep down in a tiny corner of his mind that never slept, something was niggling away at him, trying to attract his attention. Something had always bothered him about the serendipitous synchronicity of life. How seemingly unconnected events could become inexorably intertwined. It didn't make any sense; these things shouldn't happen, but they still do. Deep down, and despite there being no tangible evidence to prove a relationship existed, there could still have been one. He had never really come to terms with the concept of pure coincidence, which undoubtedly had some bearing on his decision to become a police detective.

The car arrived at his house and parked in the layby just outside. Parish jumped out, clutching some files he had brought to read later. The computer spoke, as it always did when he opened the door. But the biting east wind cut so deeply into his eyes and ears that he overlooked, or maybe just chose to ignore it, as he quickly made his way to the front door. The wind gusted fiercely for a few seconds. As it swirled around, it lifted flecks of snow off the bushes high into the air before they slowly fell back down to earth. Parish remembered the snowflakes in the hemispherical glass-domed snowman ornament that his grandmother used to display every Christmas. She knew it fascinated him. He often wondered what had happened to the purposeless curio that fascinated him so much as a child.

It was always quiet in the street at this time of night. Nearly all the houses had their ground-floor curtains pulled tightly together, keeping out the demons of the night - maintaining the illusion of neighbourhood morality and respectability. Here and there, however, he could see a few chinks of light peeking out from half-closed bedroom curtains, which seemed to belie the propriety of the ground floor. It was as if the prospect of mutual sexual gratification via voyeuristic access to the nocturnal predilections of the bored middle classes was being tantalisingly placed on offer to other like-minded devotees but from the comfort of their own bedrooms. A sort of home dogging club (with the aid of a decent pair of binoculars), but perhaps his brain was just being overly imaginative.

When he allowed his mind to roam freely, it had a habit of drifting off on strange, fanciful tangents. But he didn't know his neighbours well enough to make that kind of disingenuous judgement. In fact, Parish and Catherine had never really got to know their neighbours at all, probably because of Parish's job.

On one occasion, four years previously, they were invited around to the Smythe-Andersons at number 14 for Christmas drinks. It had been an uncomfortably stilted evening. They both agreed afterwards that they would make an excuse the following year if another invitation arrived. He and Catherine spent the next few days at home, devising the most ridiculous yet plausible reasons they could think of. Catherine came up with the best one, but she was dead by the following Christmas, so they never got to use it. No further Christmas drinks invitations ever arrived.

One of their other neighbours called round to offer the street's condolences. Other than that, Parish had not spoken to any of the other neighbours since. Apart from the occasional pleasantries - if they happened to pass one another while walking- that didn't happen often.

The only lighting in the street came from the lamp-posts, casting their ethereal glow onto the snow and slush, most of which had now been swept into the kerb. As Parish approached his front door, a plump little robin swooped across the garden and settled on an old flowerpot by the porchway. Parish instinctively looked to see if it was the same robin he had encountered at Dhalia's house but realised almost immediately what a ridiculously stupid thought that was. If it were the same bird, how would he know? The bird carefully watched him as he put his key in the door as if to ensure that he was safely home, a sort of guardian angel. Then it flew away. Parish turned around to see where it had gone and watched as it settled on the wall at the end of the pathway, still standing guard. Maybe it was the same bird, after all.

As he opened the door, the soft Tanzanite glow of the skirting lights automatically illuminated the floor. Taking in the first breath of the warm, inviting air, he could still detect traces of Catherine's favourite Penhaligon's Juniper Sling perfume and other fragrances of Christmas. Holly leaves jasmine scented candles, pine needles and cinnamon. After all this time, they shouldn't have still been in the air, but they were... it was as if...

Dinah Washington was singing 'September in the Rain', his favourite song. Before he had left that morning, he had pre-set the music system as the house felt a little less desolate if he came home to music. It was an illusion, but he was happy with that.

Another night of possible joy followed by anguish beckoned, but he couldn't talk to her tonight. She came less and less now. He knew it was only his imagination, some cruel trick of the mind. He was just fooling himself into thinking that anything would ever come of it. Soon, he would have to take control of these moments. Before the illusion completely consumed his mind and carried him away to a place from whence he could never return, but not just yet. There were times when the wretchedness of solitude dragged him to the very edge of despair, but he knew he must never give in. Despair is the solace of fools who mistake the clouds for gloom.

Tonight, he just wanted to escape for a few hours. So he dropped the files on the hall table, hunted around in his pockets for the little box, removed the VRS chip and slipped it into the interface behind his ear...

'Welcome back,' said Loretta, standing by the old deep oak French chiffonier that Jack had lovingly converted into a mini-bar - complete with fridge. She had just started to pour two glasses of wine, but she put the bottle down and crossed the room to greet me. She held up her hands to my cold face and kissed me gently on my lips. I didn't say a word but just put my left arm around her waist, settled the palm of my hand into the small of her back and pulled her firmly into my body. She didn't resist; she never did, and as I leaned my head slightly to one side to kiss her neck, I slid my right hand down to her waist and then a little lower and pulled her closer still. We kissed passionately; I almost crushed her. I couldn't help it.

Loretta's tongue began exploring my mouth, and I could feel the tension in my body slowing ebbing away. Gradually being replaced by the intensity flowing into our embrace. Loretta knew I wasn't kissing her, but she didn't mind. Her symbiotic programming had prepared her for such situations. She instinctively knew precisely how to act and react with the right degree of passion and reserve to maintain her lover's interest. After a few minutes, we parted slightly to take in some air, and she began to explore my lips with the tip of her tongue. Her sensuality excited me. All the other thoughts running around in my head seemed to melt away as I pulled her back closer to my body and kissed her again.

'Whoa, tiger, don't break me. I'm very fragile,' Loretta whispered playfully after a few more minutes spent kissing and caressing. She could tell I'd had a stressful day.

'Hi Loretta,' I said, smiling at her as I absorbed every tiny detail of her face. She held me tightly again as we embraced, and our bodies began to entwine. Slowly, we descended to the rug in front of the fire and started carefully undressing each other before eventually making love on the floor. All without saying another word... it wasn't necessary. Loretta knew I now understood how everything worked. Any earlier reservations, uncertainties or misgivings I may have had were set aside and of no further relevance.

When we had finished, she took my hand and led me to the shower, and we washed each other, still without saying a word. I made love to her again, this time against the tiled shower wall. Loretta could sense that I was using her to help unwind from my day - I felt guilty about my shallowness, but she understood that and was okay with it. That was what she did. After showering, we put on bathrobes and returned to the living room. I sat on the large black sofa in front of the log fire while Loretta poured out two glasses of Segla Margaux. She knew I liked Bordeaux red... of course she did.

'It's a little warm now. Is that okay,' asked Loretta? I nodded. Loretta brought over the two glasses and sat down beside me. We cuddled tightly, gazing into the roaring flames while sipping the wine.

'So, what have you been up to today to get you all fired up?' she asked, sensing the hint of pent-up frustration when I had first arrived, but which, to some degree, she had now helped to alleviate.

'I had a meeting with a suspect,' I replied, still slightly preoccupied.

'Was it to do with that horrible murder case you mentioned?'

'Yes, yes, it was.'

'Tell me about him?'

I hesitated momentarily – considering whether it was wise to mix business with pleasure. Then I remembered this wasn't real, so why not? What did I have to lose?

'He's powerful and clever, and he knows far more than he is telling us or ever will,' I took a sip of the warm wine. 'I don't have a shred of evidence to prove he did it. All I know is - he was there, that's it. And yet I hear this little voice telling me that....'

I didn't go any further. I knew deep down that as much as I wanted to believe Aiden Hawsley was responsible for the murder - possibly just to give me the personal satisfaction of being able to arrest him - that wouldn't make it so. And it was becoming increasingly unlikely that I would ever be able to prove he was guilty without some compelling new evidence. My dislike for the man did not justify charging him with murder. I had been doing this job long enough to know that incontrovertible proof was essential to convict. Without that, I wouldn't be able to submit a case to the National Prosecution Inspectorate for their consideration, let alone obtain an agreement to proceed with an arrest.

'Sounds like you need something else to confront him with, something that might even things up a bit. There has to be some tiny detail that he's overlooked,' suggested Loretta. 'Guilty people always miss something. They always make one tiny mistake.'

'Yes, but what?' I replied, looking at her for inspiration, but none was forthcoming.

Loretta was trying to be helpful and supportive. I knew that. Lovers always are, but there was nothing she could suggest that I had not already considered.

'I don't know,' she replied, not taking her eyes off the flames, 'I have never met this Mr Hawsley and never will.' When she said things like that, I realised just how strange it was that Loretta only existed temporarily in a virtual existence, a suspended animation of life that had no relationship to reality. I wondered whether I would prefer to stay here permanently, away from my other life - but instantly, I knew that would never be possible. That made me feel wretched for a few moments. I couldn't have the life I once had, and I couldn't have the life I had right now, as I was only a virtuality tourist. All I had left was the material remains and a memory of something good that was gone forever. Losing Catherine was something I had never ever been prepared for - not in my wildest nightmares.

Loretta broke into my thoughts. 'Jack has invited some friends over tonight for dinner. Would you like to meet them?'

Why not, I thought. It would take my mind off things for a while, not that Loretta hadn't already done that. 'Yes, that sounds good. What time?'

'They're coming about eight.' I looked at my watch.

'Well, it's just after five now, so we have nearly three hours before we have to get dressed.'

'Yes,' said Loretta, smiling. I kissed her again and started to remove her dressing gown. We began making love once more in front of the roaring fire. A fiery splinter burst free from the flames, forging its tiny orbit high into the air before crash-landing on my back and burning my skin. For a moment, I could feel this excruciating burning sensation, but I didn't flinch as it perfectly balanced the ecstasy of the moment. I found myself actually enjoying the pain. I smiled at the irony of the moment, the symbiotic pleasure. Then I thought about the similar antibiosis between Hawsley and me... I knew the more significant it became, the less harm it could do to me and the more damage it would cause him. Therefore, eventually, it would destroy him... that was my only consolation.

I turned my head to look at the hearth where the flames raged. The log needed to burn to enjoy a brief but exhilarating life. The fire created a warmth that benefited people's lives and occasionally inflicted immense pain. Eventually, the log would turn to ashes and be gone, but the other entity, now warm and thriving, would live on. So, the log had lived, died, and served a purpose. Hawsley was my log; I just needed to find a way to ignite the fire that would eventually turn him to ashes. I knew this was an odd analogy, but it made sense. At this moment, it did anyway.

Chapter 18

Heart arrived at Parish's house a few minutes early at eight forty-five the following day, as always. Punctuality with a margin for error was something his father, Frank, had instilled in him as a boy - a prerequisite of good manners. Nothing infuriates people more than someone who arrives late. *'Tardiness bouggers up plans and fooks up decent grub'* was his father's favourite aphorism, which he always enunciated with severely flattened Northern vowels and explosive "B's." This was a little unusual, as Frank had lived most of his life in a tiny village in Sussex where he and his wife ran the family ironmongers. The growling rumble of his father's words often sounded more like a heavy smoker early in the morning, clearing the grime from his clogged-up throat - than an attempt at conversation. Life tended to be like that for Heart's father, a series of astute observations, philosophical opinions, and opportunities to vent his spleen. He was never one to spend his time idly.

As he grew older, Frank could be heard quietly mumbling the curse under his breath whenever someone broke his life mantra. Russell and his younger brother Peter would wait months for someone to turn up late for some family gathering just so they could wander around the house, mumbling the maxim in close harmony. Much to their fathers' amusement and their mother's mortification.

Their preference would be a birthday party or, better still, a funeral because they both enjoyed cucumber sandwiches with salad dressing, which only ever appeared at funerals.

On days like today, when it was freezing outside, Heart wondered whether he had made the right decision in life. A career in the Navy would have guaranteed him the opportunity to travel the world and visit all the warm, exotic places he had read about in stories by Kipling and Hemingway. Instead, the furthest he ever ventured with his wife Victoria and sons Peter and Paul had been a regular two-week camping holiday in the Dordogne every summer.

When the boys left home, this suddenly changed for reasons never fully explained by Victoria. Their annual holiday became two weeks in a self-catering bungalow in sunny Salcombe on the Devon coast, where it nearly always rained. This is where they started playing bowls, a game he hated. She made all the arrangements as he was usually too busy, so it was partly his fault. Victoria eventually left him for a self-employed butcher with a squinty eye, who still had his own shop in the Province of Deliverance.

For some reason, Heart had always imagined life would have been more exciting, but it wasn't to be. Not that it was boring. The day-to-day challenges of the police force saw to that. Seldom were two days the same. Occasionally, the administration became a little tiresome as it had increased immeasurably since he had joined the police nearly thirty years ago. That aside, he enjoyed the work - most of the time.

He tooted the car horn as gently as he could, wincing as he did so. It was a quiet neighbourhood, and he always felt guilty about using it while parked. He would have gotten out of the car and knocked on the door, but it looked freezing outside. Parish came out after a few minutes and gingerly made his way up the icy pathway. The snow had frozen overnight. He climbed into the car.

'Morning, guv,' said Heart, sounding a little too sprightly for Parish at this time of day.

'Heart!' mumbled Parish curtly. He was rarely communicative this time of day.

Parish was wearing a heavy overcoat and black fedora hat with the front right edge sloping downwards at a slightly rakish angle. Loretta had made a complimentary remark about his hat the night before, and it had stuck in his mind. It would stay there for a long time. Some compliments do that; some even change how you live your life from that moment onward. Casually, he threw the hat onto the back seat.

Heart thought he looked a little how he imagined Raymond Chandler's Phillip Marlow may have been. He smiled in admiration at Parish's attire. Heart had always been an avid reader of classic detective stories, and just for a moment, he was actually immersed in one. He wouldn't mention the whimsical comparison he had just conjured in his mind; that would be wrong, wholly inappropriate and a little strange.

Once the computer had detected that a second person had joined Heart in the car, it spoke:

'Where would you like to go?' Heart looked at Parish for instructions.

'Deliverance,' stated Parish. It sounded more like a profound statement of religious intent than a destination.

'Deliverance,' repeated Heart, for the benefit of the computer. The computer started the car, and the Protton moved off automatically and locked into the AMG system.

'Why Deliverance,' asked Heart curiously?

'It's a bit of a long shot, I know, but I thought we should have a chat with this Professor Grimes that Gerry mentioned yesterday.'

'Right,' said Heart. He guessed that was why they were going there, but he still needed to make sure.

'Thought we would take a couple of samples down for him to look at....' He produced a small crime evidence bag from his inside pocket containing two phials. Placing it on the back seat alongside his Fedora, he turned to Heart, '...just in case he can come up with a name.' Heart didn't say anything.

'Do you have any specific requirements today?' asked the computer with a hint of condescension? Parish glanced at Heart, scrunching his eyebrows oddly to see if the computer's haughty inflection had registered with him. Heart hadn't noticed anything and looked back at Parish with a puzzled expression.

'What?' Heart asked, unsure whether Parish had asked him a question.

'No, nothing,' replied Parish, 'I just thought that....' He turned back to face the computer screen. He was inclined to ignore it most of the time. All it usually displayed was a continuous flow of mundane news updates about trivial local issues. Most were of little interest to him as they disrupted his thought process.

'No specific requirements right now, thank you,' replied Parish dismissively.

'Thank you,' replied the computer, now sounding disturbingly cheerful for this time of day, incapable of grasping the scornful inflection in Parish's voice.

'Please feel free to contact me at any time,' replied the computer, with what now appeared to be a faintly detectable acerbic edge. Maybe it could recognise the subtleties of tonal nuances after all.

'I will,' answered Parish, giving the screen a distorted grimace. He despised this technical intrusion and was convinced the computer had the Machiavellian ability to interpret what he was thinking by how he addressed it. For this reason, Parish was cautious about how he spoke in the car but less guarded with his mannerisms, which the computer couldn't understand, or so he thought.

The car progressed slowly towards the outskirts of Providence into one of the main security zones near the perimeter wall. As they reached the main gate, the vehicle slowed down, and the front windows descended automatically as the car came to a halt alongside the security booths. The retinal scanners perched on the end of telescopic arms slowly moved towards each passenger.

'Please look directly into the lens,' asked the computer. The scanner edged closer to scrutinise Parish, and Heart's eyes then withdrew.

'Retinal scans complete for....' there was a small delay as the information was collated. 'Mr Mackenzie Parish,' there was an odd pause before it confirmed his rank, 'Detective Inspector, and... Mr Russell Heart... Sergeant. Thank you,' advised the computer, its harsh, staccato tone sounding almost alien. 'You may now continue to the Ghettazone,' it went on. 'Please proceed with caution.'

It seemed a strangely considerate remark, thought Parish when couched in the computer's dispassionate voice. It was so cold compared to his home computer's lilting, mellifluous tone. Like many domestic systems, it had been customised with the owner's voice to recreate the social intimacy of a family friend rather than the harsh tones of a disembodied stranger. His mind immediately flashed back to another disembodied stranger...

They moved off onto the slip road towards the motorway that would take them to Deliverance and Professor Grimes. The highways were less congested these days as anybody embarking on a journey between provinces would typically take advantage of the bullet train, which was fast, efficient, safe, and comfortable. Once on the motorway, their vehicle took up its allotted position for the journey and automatically disengaged from the AMG, reverting to manual drive. Protton vehicles occupied the nearside lane, maintaining an orderly procession at their maximum speed of forty miles per hour. In contrast, the centre lane was reserved for the SCOMTEL public logistics company. They transported a continuous stream of high-speed pantechnicons carrying all the replenishment stocks between the provinces and the Ghettazone. The outside lane was utilised mainly by public utility and emergency service vehicles. They travelled the fastest of all, along with the occasional fossil-fuelled relic meticulously maintained by an enthusiast who still yearned for the thrill of throaty acceleration. Something sadly unavailable in Protton vehicles.

Sunday was generally a quiet day on the roads. This was when a surprisingly large number of these old fossil-fuel cars could be seen driving for pleasure at high speeds. Unfortunately, the motorway's lack of matrix control meant that overtaking in the fast lane could become a life-or-death decision depending on when space became available in the centre lane.

It would be over two hours before they reached Deliverance, and with his lifelong aversion to travelling long distances by car, Parish decided to put his seat back and go to sleep as best he could under the somewhat less-than-ideal conditions.

'Wake me when we get to the outskirts,' he mumbled as he tried to make himself comfortable in the reclined position.

'Yes, guv,' replied a slightly resentful Heart. He was driving, so he couldn't sleep as well. One of the disadvantages of travelling outside of a province was the matrix system hadn't been extended to the Ghettazone, so traditional hands-on driving was necessary. Although Protton vehicles were fitted with anti-crash technology, there was no defence against a high-speed pantechnicon in a decontrolled driving zone without any enforceable legislation. The perilous antics of the drivers of these juggernauts were notorious. They seldom displayed anything other than utter contempt, scornful arrogance, and total disregard for other road users.

Glancing out of your car window and seeing the wheel hub of a lorry can be a very humbling and intimidating experience. Prottons still benefited from satellite communication and navigational assistance, but Heart found it incredibly tedious now that he had become accustomed to being driven everywhere.

Occasionally, they passed through what were once major industrialised areas - now deserted ghost towns. Creeping vegetation had regained control over that which it once had dominion – along with the wild creatures that had made the steel and concrete canyons their home. Thousands of empty factory units, stripped of their valuable base metals, stood as rusting skeletal relics, monuments to an industrialised society now wholly contained within the province of Redemption. The eerie early morning sunshine flashed stroboscopically through the stanchions, creating an apocalyptic light show rivalling anything man could devise. These abandoned areas became more prevalent as they drew closer to the outskirts of Deliverance.

In the early years of the new century, there had been accusations of a monopoly by the big four supermarket chains. Not only had a cartel pricing system made food exorbitantly expensive, but the retail chains had purchased all the largest parcels of land on the outskirts of every major town and city in Great Britain. They were planning massive perimeter gigadrome developments. Many towns were effectively one-shop towns. The big four were already planning to dominate the shopping experience. The realisation that the Christian Socialist Party proposed significant changes to the planning agenda was an inconvenient but not insurmountable setback to their plans, or so they thought. However, the formation of SCOMTEL and the compulsory purchase of the four major supermarket chains gave the government essential control for their plans to succeed.

There would be hundreds of SCOMTEL shops strategically positioned in every province. In the Ghettazone, gigastores were built to satisfy local demand but seldom less than forty miles apart in any direction. Each store was highly fortified to prevent incursion by the rebellious hordes that roamed the open land. There weren't any DNA scanners, and social registration was not a prerequisite to gaining access to these monolithic monuments to consumerism. However, strict security was enforced to prevent armed customers from entering. Everything had changed. Thirty years ago, busy, densely populated towns that had existed for hundreds of years attracted large superstores. Now, gigadromes in the middle of the countryside attracted vast numbers of customers, and new Ghetto cities grew up around them.

Traditional high streets abandoned and deserted, looked strangely reminiscent of the old main streets in abandoned mining towns in American Westerns. Even stranger was the sight of horse riders trotting through the middle of what was once a bustling metropolis. The horse had returned as one of the most reliable, affordable means of long-distance transport. Protton vehicles were available but prohibitively expensive for most people - especially those living in the Ghettazone.

Impressive buildings that once housed large corporations, town halls, schools and shops were now crumbling, a visual metaphor for what the old society had become. The Glundes who inhabited these ghost towns had managed to create their own micro-economy. It was primarily based on trading drugs, sex, people, horses, organic food grown on allotments, and farm animals.

'Almost on the outskirts, guv,' advised Heart after driving through deserted wastelands for what had seemed like days. Parish slowly opened his eyes to see Deliverance's soaring perimeter walls and guard towers looming up in the distance. It was probably how Camelot would have appeared to King Arthur when he returned from the Crusades - but without the searchlights.

La Morte d'Arthur was one of Parish's favourite books; often, he would see life through the eyes of different characters. For some strange reason, Morgan la Fey, King Arthur's sorceress, came to mind today. Maybe he would require her healing powers soon. Perhaps he had needed them for a while.

'*This world is all nonsense; how long must I endure it?*' He remembered what she had said and wondered what she meant. In sleep, the body would rest, but the mind could play devastating games with your dreams.

'That didn't take long,' muttered Parish, rubbing his eyes as he woke up. He adjusted his seat to the upright position, 'not as bad as I thought it would be.'

'No, guv,' replied Heart ambivalently, smiling to himself. It had taken over two hours, but Parish had slept through most of the journey. Heart took the slip road to the province and followed the snaking line of SCOMTEL lorries, all making for the same destination. They went through another retinal eye scan at the main security gate. Then, their vehicle locked back onto the AMG system.

'Where would you like to go today?' asked the computer.

'Central Intelligence Data Centre in Portsmouth,' replied Parish.

'Programming route... You may continue. Thank you.' The car moved off, and the arrival time clicked up to thirty-two minutes. They both sat back and admired the scenery, what little there was of it on the outskirts of Portsmouth on a freezing, miserable, grey day. They passed the strange sailing sculptures on the bridge as they entered the city, a dedication to a bygone age.

'Where did I put those samples?' asked Parish.

Heart waved at the plastic crime scene bag lying on the back seat. 'In there, guv,' he replied chirpily, but Parish seemed distracted. 'Why two anyway?' asked Heart curiously.

'Gerry wanted me to check out something else while we were there.'

'Related to this enquiry, I presume?' asked Heart.

'I don't know, to be honest. Just something Gerry thought of. Women's intuition and all that.'

'Oh, I see,' replied Heart, still not entirely placated by the answer. 'You seem preoccupied today?'

Parish didn't answer for a few moments. 'Would have been our sixteenth wedding anniversary today if....'

Moments like this were always a little tricky to handle.

Heart could remember his sixteenth anniversary, spent drinking with some old French friends in a restaurant in Bordeaux. Their summer holiday in France always coincided with their anniversary. Those were happy times.

Now, it would be just another uncelebrated anniversary. This one spent working on a cold, bleak day in Deliverance on another murder investigation. Not much to mark an occasion that had once been the epicentre of his existence.

'Sorry, guv. I didn't realise,' apologised Heart, with as much compassion as he could muster. It also prompted him to reflect a little on his own life. He had been divorced for nearly eleven years and had made little headway with any new relationships. He now also relied on VRS trips for his pleasure.

'Nothing to apologise for. You wouldn't know. Why should you?' shrugged Parish.

'What are we going to do if we don't get any joy here today?' asked Heart, changing the subject.

'I'm sure they'll come up with something,' replied Parish, sounding reassuringly positive. 'They have been working on the data retrieval stuff for quite a few years, as I understand. Wouldn't have wasted all that time for nothing, would they?'

'I wouldn't be so sure about that. The university has been doing most of the work, and they wouldn't knock themselves out to finish anything if it's a government-funded project.' Heart sounded uncharacteristically cynical.

'Maybe,' muttered Parish. They arrived at the main entrance to an impressive rambling complex. On one of the gate pillars was a large sign: "Portsmouth University I.T. & Research Department."

'Professor Grimes's office must be in there somewhere,' said Heart, pointing at a tall grey building with reflective mirrored windows. It looked decidedly austere and utilitarian.

The car slowed down to pass through a security gate, and they had to stop for another retinal scan. They continued driving towards the central parking area, and the Protton automatically parked in a restricted bay. They walked towards the main entrance, where a constable waved them through without asking for identification. Heart paused just as he passed the guard.

'Atlas parked us in a restricted zone. Is that okay?' he asked.

'No problem here. We don't stand on ceremony here. It's all very casual. I'll keep an eye on it for you.' He smiled disarmingly. Heart felt a little more at ease.

'Don't you want to check anything?' enquired Heart.

'No need to,' replied the constable. 'You've been through two eye scans, so you must be meeting someone by prior arrangement, or you wouldn't have got this far.'

'Hmm,' mumbled Heart, acknowledging the simple logic.

'How did you know we had been through two?' asked Parish casually.

'Providence plate,' said the constable, smiling and pointing at their Protton car. 'So I presumed you drove here today, which means you must have come through two perimeter gates. And, if you don't mind me saying so, you look a bit tired, probably from sitting in that…' he nodded derisively at their car, 'all day.'

'Very observant, Sherlock,' replied Parish, smiling in quiet admiration. 'You're wasted here. You should come and work with us in Providence.'

'Thank you very much, sir, but I like it here. Very peaceful, with no stress. I can walk home every night, see the wife, play with my children, meet my friends and generally enjoy life, and I don't have to sit in a bloody Protton all day.'

The constable probably didn't appreciate the unexpected thundering poignancy enshrined within those few simple words. They weren't intended to be derisory or contemptuous. They were simply an expression of his personal satisfaction with his lot. Nevertheless, they found an empty spot to settle into and left a deep impression. For a moment, Parish thought about the humble, sound, philosophical counsel he had just received from an unassuming police constable. On so many levels, it was probably one of the most profound statements he had heard in a long while. He would not quickly forget those words.

'Point made,' acknowledged Parish. 'It would mean lots more money,' he added half-heartedly. He wasn't really making an offer of employment; it was nothing more than friendly badinage. The constable smiled.

'We are looking for a Professor Grimes,' asked Heart?

The constable pointed out a building in the distance. 'Dinger's office is in that unit. You won't miss it.' He smiled again.

They carried on as directed and found the office of Professor Dinger Grimes on the third floor. Parish noticed a large hand-painted sign above the door:

DINGER'S BUNKER
We try to save some dead data and solve most problems. But first, abandon hope,
all ye who enter here,
(just in case)

Parish gazed in admiration at the blithe, insouciant nature of the message. The final lines could so easily relate to their current assignment.

Heart knocked warily on the door.

'Coooooome!' a sonorously booming voice commanded. The word seemed to resonate for ages. They entered a large laboratory where they could just make out a giant figure in the distance, whom they presumed to be Professor Grimes, sitting alone at a desk. On drawing closer, the first impression that immediately formed in Parish's mind was that of an infamously bibulous Dickensian character with uncanny prescient talents. Someone who would respond with little interest to the pressure and demands of his contemporaries.

As they approached his desk, the professor eyed them up and down and smiled heartily. And then, with overtly boisterous enthusiasm, gracefully rose and began rumbling slowly towards them.

Up close, this gregarious leviathan with masses of grey curly hair, rosy red cheeks, a brightly glowing nose, and a massive bushy beard (*Parish was sure he could see something living in the middle of it*) was even larger than life. The ponderous vibrations of his movements were clearly detectable through the old oak floors of what was evidently an ex-naval establishment. Ropes and hawsers dangled down from the lofty ceilings, and rope ladders were slung between the oak beams. Various pieces of maritime history were scattered around the walls, including what appeared to be an intact Exocet missile hanging from two girders.

'Digby Grimes,' boomed out Dinger as he held out his enormous hands to greet them, 'but call me Dinger; everybody else does. Welcome to my world.' Life was what you made it, and he had obviously made his life exactly how he wanted it to be, and he was happy about that. The room emanated serenity despite its cavernous dimensions; it had seen two hundred years of active naval service, but now, at last, it was at rest. Digby conveyed the rarest of traits: an immediate sense of inerrancy. The unshakeable belief that you could never die with Digby close at hand because he was courageous and stood firmly on the side of righteousness. He was probably also precocious and annoyingly confident as a child, and he would have infuriated everybody because of it. But with age, he had mellowed and grown into the man he had become.

He epitomised everything that Parish used to think was good about life. Too much of what he encountered these days was systematic, formulaic, mundane, uninteresting, and uninspiring. Dinger gave no indication of suffering from any of these woefully saccharine conditions. Nearly everybody, to one degree or another, harboured fears of being replaced by a computer. But there was no possibility that the Dingers of this world would entertain such concerns; they needed him, not the other way around. He had shrewdly negotiated a unique position repairing severely damaged computers. That was the one thing they couldn't do yet. The benches in the lab were cluttered with machines, screens, and hundreds of internal parts of something. All apparently connected by a mass of wires. It was a far cry from Zac's clinical environment. Dinger shook both their hands warmly as he welcomed them into his kingdom.

'So, what can I do for you, gentleman? I understand you have some DNA samples that don't match any regular members of the club.'

'The club?' queried Heart.

'Oh, just my little euphemism for the registered residents, the in-crowd, so to speak. We are all in rather than out if you see what I mean,' said Digby. He smirked at Heart. It was apparently a reference to the province's containment geography.

'Oh, I see,' said Heart, but he didn't. He hadn't fully embraced the eccentric nature of his host, not yet – Parish, however, was on board from the start. Heart gingerly offered up the samples.

'Rightio, so what have we got, then?'

'Well, Professor…'

'Dinger, please call me Dinger,' interrupted Digby self-effacingly. 'Professor sounds so bloody pretentious.' He sighed a little despondently. 'It makes me sound old and decrepit.' Heart thought that a bit odd because that was precisely what he was. He must have been seventy-five if he was a day; maybe not decrepit, but on him, 'Professor' was most definitely not pretentious.

'Well, Dinger,' a word Heart used cautiously as he held up the first sample. 'It's the semen DNA from a crime scene. It's from someone who managed to enter

Providence completely undetected and possibly murder our victim - but the DNA doesn't turn up on our database.'

'And this one?' He held up the second sample, turning to Parish for an explanation.

'It's the DNA of the victim, Dhalia Vingali. We need to know anything you can tell us about her.'

'Unusual name,' queried Dinger.

'It's not her real name,' offered Parish by way of a partial explanation.

'I see,' said Dinger contemplatively. His mind was already working on that slender piece of information. In his experience, people changed their names for one of three reasons. The most obvious was to avoid being found, which probably meant they had something to hide. Second, they simply didn't like their birth name. His middle name was Dirk, and at school, for reasons unbeknown to him, he was called Dirk Grimes, which had the unsavoury ring of a porn star about it and which he hated with a passion. He had consigned Dirk to history once he arrived at university and resumed using his preferred Christian name, Digby. But this was promptly superseded by a new nickname, Dinger, after he portrayed, to great acclaim, the Australian cattleman crucified by the Japanese in a footlights production of *A Town Like Alice*.

This was partly his own fault, as he had so convincingly encapsulated the very soul of the central character, Joe Harman. The authenticity and immersive realism he managed to channel into the character were due, in no small degree, to him being methodically coached in the vagaries of the Aussie twang by an Australian Stanislavski fanatic. Who, fortuitously, was also attending the university at the same time and had been selected as production director.

The third reason people changed their names was to make them sound like something they were not - to influence people for various financial or commercial purposes. Dinger fell into the second category. So, what were the circumstances,' asked Dinger?

'Well, as far as we know, he... *and we are reasonably certain it was a "he."*' Parish added this assumption as a guarded qualification, '...entered Providence, passing through all the security systems. Then the perpetrator accessed the victim's house, raped and killed her, leaving virtually no evidence, and left. We do have some DNA, but it doesn't match anybody on our database, so it's not of much use to us. Technically, he doesn't exist? We need to know if what I've presumed so far is possible, and if so, how did "He" circumnavigate the security?'

'To be honest, I don't know how I can help?' said Dinger, slightly confused.

'We understand you have been reconstructing the old police DNA database, which was blown up in the riots in 2015.'

'Yes,' Dinger answered warily.

'I was hoping you might be able to identify the DNA from your records,' asked Parish.

'How far have you got?' asked Heart in a decidedly earnest but detectably pessimistic tone.

'Is it finished,' added Parish slightly more enthusiastically? Dinger looked at them and smiled - his face lit up the room. Everything else seemed so grey and subdued, but amongst all the dullness was Dinger Grimes.

'Well, as you obviously know, I've been reconstructing - in my spare time, I would hasten to add - the data records from the mainframe police database that was blown up.

And in answer to your question, Sergeant... and to be perfectly honest, no! It will probably never be completed.

Almost simultaneously, dejection swept over Parish and Heart. Dinger smiled at the visual synchronicity.

'Not related, you two, are you,' asked Dinger?

'No! they both replied firmly in tandem,' surprised at the question.

Dinger flashed an odd expression.'

'Let me explain... The ceramic discs are in thousands of pieces, and you must bear in mind that each hard drive has around a hundred stacked ceramic discs. There were forty computers in the hosting centre, so roughly speaking, I have about four million pieces to patch together. A foolish endeavour, some might say, in fact, quite a few, but I feel compelled to complete my task however long it takes, or until I snuff it, of course.'

He laughed aloud, and for a moment, Parish's mind went off on a tangent, and for some reason, he tried to imagine Dinger being dead and lying in his coffin, but he couldn't. His energetic and gregarious presence could never be effectively contained within a simple box. The sound of him laughing and bellowing would linger in the air long after they fed him into the furnace.

'Oh,' said Parish, his optimistic expectations shattered by the gargantuan nature of the task that lay ahead and the distinct possibility that it might never be completed.

'Couldn't happen today, of course,' retorted Dinger, dispelling the haze of despondency that had suddenly descended over the conversation.

'Why not,' asked Parish, grasping at the thread of hope entwining itself around every word that Dinger uttered? He was a half-full person, and it would always be nothing less for him. Oh, to be that courageous and with such conviction, Parish thought. This man would take a setback, failure, or disaster and stamp it down until it became firm enough for him to clamber up and stand on top of it. Just so that he could reach up for even higher ground.

'It's all different now,' continued Dinger. 'No moving parts, and anyway, everything is dumped on, or should I say up to, the old cloud as a backup,' replied Dinger, pointing upwards. Unbelievably, they both looked up. 'So, you can't destroy the information anymore. Once you commit it to Barty, it's automatically copied onto a central cloud database.

'Barty?' interrupted Parish, a little confused.

'Sorry,' said Dinger. 'That's my abbreviation for Balingo and Artemis. First letters, see BA... ART? Bart Simpson?   Clever stuff, hey?' he said self-mockingly. 'You do watch *The Simpsons,* I hope?' he said sternly. 'Vitally important social/ecological thesis. Not what it seems, you know. There are still some seriously misguided people who actually believe it's a cartoon series for children.'

He laughed, and the whole room reverberated. 'CIA propaganda, of course, from beginning to end, subliminally brainwashing every American generation into believing they are technically and intellectually the superior nation. Having an incompetent idiot like Homer working in a nuclear power station is a subtle attempt to assuage any fears Americans might have about having a nuclear power plant on their doorstep.'

'Yes,' replied Parish, agreeing enthusiastically but feeling a bit stupid as he had never watched it, believing it to be a banal children's programme. Heart looked at Dinger in dismay at this surprising revelation. *He never knew, either.*

'Of course,' continued Dinger, 'the corollary is that any damning information is also stored on BARTY somewhere.' Dinger tapped the side of his nose and pointed his index finger towards the ceiling. 'Had that system been in place in 2015, we would have everything we want without all this palaver. You can't destroy anything on that system. You can hide it...' he paused to add a little gravitas, 'but it's always there... somewhere.' Dinger added the final quantifying word with a glowing expression of pride and achievement, a *knowing* shake of the head and a nonchalant wink of an eye.

'I've managed to complete the reconstruction of the primary database, which means I should be able to at least give you a name if his DNA was ever recorded. What I can't tell you is his last known address. So you may still have some work to do even if we do find a name. And, of course, I am only up to the letter D with second-stage reconstruction. So, there is still some way to go.

'Anything will be more than we have now,' said Parish.

'I would have had much more to give you....' replied Dinger apologetically. 'But Hawsley's anally retentive inbreds drastically cut the funding budget. So, to keep the project going, I do this in my spare time. In fact, I haven't received a single penny in funding over the last two years. It's as if he's no longer interested in accessing all that old information.'

'So why do you bother carrying on if you're not being paid for it?' asked Heart curiously. 'I wouldn't.'

'Good question,' replied Dinger, pausing thoughtfully while looking Heart squarely in the eye with a monastic, almost biblical gaze suffused with passion and emotion. Then he tapped his forefinger gently on his lips. 'I suppose...' He paused yet again and brought himself up to his full height. With his head tilted histrionically skyward - having made sure that he had arrested the attention of Parish and Heart, he began speaking with a strangled evangelical tone.

'It's... out of a sense of... duty loyalty and commitment. An act of selfless...unflinching dedication. To say thank you to our beloved Lord Protector *(he coughed to clear his throat)* for all the great and wonderful things he has achieved. And for which we all are eternally thankful and from which we all will benefit, one day, Amen.'

He closed his eyes as if about to pray.

You could almost hear the dulcet strains of 'Land of Hope and Glory' seeping through and teardrops splashing on the floor; such was the majesty of Dinger's gushing paean. Parish and Heart didn't quite know what to make of it.

Heart's eyes widened in disbelief as he digested Digby's rousing words. Dinger held the histrionic pose for as long as was absolutely necessary to cement the desired effect. Heart was coming to terms with the realisation that he may have wholly misread Dinger's true political allegiance when Dinger's expression suddenly morphed into a sardonic smirk.

'Absolute bollocks!' he exclaimed loudly, collapsing into hysterical laughter, his entire body reverberating with merriment.

'He had you there, Heart,' said Parish, beaming the smile of the co-conspirator.

'I'm sorry, Sergeant,' said Dinger. 'I couldn't resist a little theatricality. It's in my blood now. It lends a certain elegance – and eloquent piquancy to the proceedings, don't you think?' Heart smiled acquiescently, only too pleased to find his gut instinct hadn't entirely deserted him. He was further comforted to find himself in the company of somebody who didn't trust those in control of the system any more than he did. Someone who also had a wicked sense of humour.

'No, the real reason is I enjoy doing it. It's as simple as that, and that's the real challenge.' It's the old "touch and grasp thing."

'Sorry?' said Heart, unsure what he meant.

'Never let your touch exceed your grasp.'

Heart was still a little confused.

Dinger continued... 'I can just touch it with my fingertips - I am that close. But I can't quite grasp it yet, but soon, I will have it in the palm of my hand.' Dinger clenched his mighty fist tightly and shook it to make the point.

Heart smiled with quiet admiration at Dinger's tenaciously defiant mindset.

'So why have they cut the funding,' queried Parish? 'That just doesn't make any sense.'

'Well, that's what I would have thought, but *they*' – he held his fingers up to place air quotes around the word – 'say it serves no purpose. All province residents have been rescanned now. And as they don't worry too much about solving crime in the Ghettazone, where most people on this database probably live, why bother? Anyone with a criminal record - claiming social benefits or a member of certain religious persuasions was ejected from the province when the walls went up. That is why the DNA criminal records computer was targeted for destruction by the rioters. Had they got there just a few minutes earlier, all the records would have been destroyed, and they would all still be in here today.'

'But they didn't,' said Parish.

'Correct.' said Dinger. 'And anyway, all the hard copy records had already been downloaded and printed. So the police knew exactly who they were going to throw out. Once they had completed the expulsions, they recorded the DNA and retinal scans of everybody left on Balingo. Artemis backs up the latest information to Balingo each day.

As you know, Balingo is used by security services to check anybody moving in or out of a province. So, if you break the law, it's recorded on Artemis first, then backed up to Balingo, and then if you try to gain access to a province, it denies you entry. There is no way somebody not on the system can avoid or bypass it.

Artemis monitors internal crime and is used exclusively by your lot. It allows them to check things like DNA without disturbing the integrity of the Balingo system, which is purely for security. Do you see?'

'Sounds extraordinarily complex having two systems instead of just one,' said Heart. 'Why is that?'

'That's obvious,' replied Dinger without a moment's hesitation, 'Hawsley doesn't trust your lot. You're too bloody honest for your own good, so he has to keep you as far away from him as possible.' Parish and Heart were bemused by the obtuse irony of the statement.

'But why?' asked Parish, surprised by this heretically damning condemnation of Hawsley's integrity.

'I've just answered that one, haven't I?'

'Have you?' asked Parish, sounding slightly puzzled.

'Well, why else would he run two systems, one of which you can't even get close to? I understand only Hawsley and Maranno can access Balingo to change anything. Whereas almost anybody working for the government can access Artemis. Even I have access.'

Dinger glanced at them, expecting a response, but there wasn't one. The ramifications of his frighteningly simple extrapolation began to crystallise. It was starting to make some sense. 'I would say he was hiding something,' added Dinger with a smile.

'So, the Balingo system wasn't there to protect the good people from the bad people; it was there to protect Hawsley and his cronies from everybody else,' suggested Parish?

'Maybe, or maybe just you?' Dinger smiled again. 'And his idea works, doesn't it? I bet you are hardly ever called to a major crime scene now unless it's a complicated murder. They don't need you sniffing around, not with a computer system that records everybody's...' He paused. 'Well, nearly everybody's DNA.'

'Only works if something is left behind,' suggested Parish.

'There's always something,' said Dinger, smiling with the reassuring confidence of a scientist used to working with minuscule scraps of information. 'Even in this case, you have three suspects, all from the DNA. All you have to do is decide which one did it.' Parish thought back to something Loretta had said the previous night.

'The one with no name,' said Parish.

'Yes, an interesting one, that,' mused Dinger with a hint of a smirk.

'You could have had an amazing crime detection system if Hawsley had continued funding the reconstruction work,' said Heart. Wonder why he didn't?

'We could probably have solved this murder much quicker if it had been completed,' said Parish.

'Very true, but only if the culprit lives inside a province,' said Dinger, 'if he's from the Ghettazone, you'll never find him. The police will say it's so infrequent that it's not worth bothering with. Or they will just send someone dispensable...' he glanced at Parish, 'out into the Ghettazone to investigate it, which has to be more cost-effective.'

Dinger smiled and raised his bushy eyebrows in mock consternation.

'I see,' said Parish, a little disheartened by Dinger's crushing hypothesis. It touched on his uncertainty about the system as it had a ring of truth about it.

'Still, let's see how we get on.' Dinger held out his hand for the plastic containers and took them across to a sealed unit with glass sides. He opened a sliding shutter at one end, pushed the two containers in, and closed the shutter. There was a purring sound as the air was extracted from the holding area of the unit.

'What is that doing?' asked Heart.

'It's cleaning any alien DNA from the external areas of the containers before I open them.'

'Is it a sort of air scrubber, by any chance,' asked Parish curiously?

'Yes, it is. It's a bit crude, but it functions well. Tell me something, how do you know about scrubbers?' Dinger immediately broke out into reels of laughter at the innocent innuendo.

The whole room rumbled with his joviality again. 'Sorry, didn't mean that quite as it sounded,' continued Dinger.

Parish and Heart laughed.

'We've seen one before, two days ago, in fact, at the crime scene,' replied Parish.

'I thought you said it was a private residence?' asked Dinger.

'It is,' replied Heart.

'But air scrubbers are only fitted in government buildings. It's illegal to have one fitted privately, apart from the obvious problem of finding a supplier and an installer.'

'Yes, we wondered about that,' said Heart.

'So, you haven't actually got any DNA air scans from the crime scene?' asked Dinger, looking slightly confused.

'Yes, oddly we have,' replied Heart. 'The scanner wasn't working. Some electrical fault.' Dinger's face lit up again, and his nose glowed a little brighter. The happier he was, the brighter it became.

'That was a bit of luck,' he replied with a sigh of relief.

'Yes, we thought so too,' replied Heart, with a certain amount of satisfaction at the realisation that good fortune hadn't wholly deserted them. 'But we will need much more of that before this ends.'

'It's almost as if...' But Parish didn't finish.

'What?' enquired Heart, intrigued.

'No, nothing. Just thinking aloud.'

'Oh,' said Heart empathetically. He was going to push Parish a little further to finish what he had started to say but changed his mind midway.

When the air extraction cycle finished, Dinger put his two arms into the box's flexible glove sleeves. He lifted an internal shutter and moved the containers into the adjacent compartment of the unit. Here, Dinger removed the first container's lid, took the sample and placed it into another small, cylindrical container connected to the chamber. He closed the cover to this container and withdrew his hands from the gloves. He pressed some buttons on a panel next to the box, and the analyser began its hum.

Parish gazed into the analysing unit, 'How long will it take?'

'About half an hour,' replied Dinger.

'Can we get a coffee somewhere,' asked Parish, looking at his watch?

'There's a coffee shop across the square if you want a proper cup or a vending machine just down the hall,' replied Dinger.

'That'll do fine. Would you like one,' asked Parish?

'Not for me. Prefer tea, thank you,' replied Dinger, pointing to a sizeable elephant-shaped teapot on the worktop, 'made in a china pot. You're welcome to a cup of my homemade special.'

'No, it's okay,' replied Parish. 'I could do with some fresh air anyway. Helps me to think.' He looked at his watch again. 'We'll be back in about thirty minutes then.'

'Okey-dokey,' replied Dinger, picking up the elephant teapot and rumbling off toward the sink. Heart and Parish left the lab and walked contemplatively up the hallway towards the coffee machine.

'Bit odd cancelling his funding. I would have thought all that old data would be invaluable,' said Heart.

'Yes, I wondered about that too,' said Parish, 'but then I suppose they have to make cutbacks where they can. Nothing much changes there.' They arrived at the drinks machine, and Heart punched in the code for two coffees and waited for them to dispense. They picked up their drinks and walked across to the corridor's glass side overlooking a Japanese-style ornamental garden surrounded by university buildings. There were a dozen or so small Acer trees, mostly devoid of leaves, some wooden benches, and a little wooden bridge over a pond - that was now frozen. The narrow gravel pathway, only just wide enough for one person to walk alone - erratically wove its way around the garden as if lost in a swirling maze. Trying desperately to find its way out. The fairy-tale scene was covered by a light dusting of sparkling, unblemished snow.

They drank their coffees in silence, looking out over the quixotically designed garden - a foible, or perhaps a designer's momentary whim—a creationary folly reminding observers of the past but of no relevance in today's world.

Parish presumed the park was purely for staff occupying the surrounding buildings but wondered if they ever bothered to use it.

He thought back to when Jade was younger, and the three of them would go to the park close to where they lived. That was unless it was raining, but sometimes, even then, they would still go. They used to like walking around the lake and playing silly games with Jade, making plans for all the things they would do and all the places they had yet to see.

'Can I have an ice cream, Daddy,' asked Jade, gazing up with the same big brown eyes as her mother? How could he resist her simple request? Already, she could see into his soul, just as Catherine had always been able to. These were the only two people in the world from whom he could hide nothing and from whom he didn't want to. Jade sat down on the grass to eat her ice cream, and he sat down with Catherine on a bench. Catherine flicked her long dark hair backwards, gazed up at the sun and licked her ice cream. He couldn't take his eyes off her. She looked so beautiful today.

A drop of melted ice cream fell onto her decolletage and started to run down her breast. Parish moved to lick it off but suddenly stopped, realising they were in a public place. Catherine looked at him and smiled. She pushed up her cleavage provocatively, challenging him to continue. She didn't appear remotely intimidated by their surroundings or concerned that someone might see them engaged in an innocent act of intimacy. However, despite the evident frisson of sexual familiarity, he still felt embarrassed. He wiped the ice cream away with a swipe of his finger instead.

'Chicken,' she whispered. 'Don't you want me?' She flashed her eyes and looked up at him through her long lashes. He smiled back. Catherine loved to play these little games in summer; something about the warmth of the sun released her from all inhibition. She was like a beautiful butterfly coming out of her winter chrysalis and showing off her body.

The first few weeks of sunshine had already bronzed her skin. She accentuated this change by carefully choosing her clothes, wearing white cotton blouses and long flowery dresses. As the summer wore on, Catherine's skin would become darker, and the blouses would appear even paler.

She would appear as a wayward gipsy dancer from some travelling production of *Carmen* or even a captivating Fiona from *Brigadoon*, enticing him to stay forever in an enchanted place. A place from which they could never escape. It was as if she had become a different person. Someone possessed, even enchanted by the summer, and just for a few months while the sun shone, she would smile in a way that he had only seen once or twice before in his lifetime. The naive innocence of a child, as yet unaffected or burdened by reality. Her smile could light up the world, and then, in an instant, she would look at him, and the warmth would soak into his soul, alone, to the exclusion of all others.

She understood him in a way that he wanted to be understood, and he didn't have to explain anything to her. She just knew. Catherine loved to dance to Spanish flamenco music. Sometimes, when the weather was warm and they were alone, she would dance naked. Those nights would always end the same.

Catherine had never been to Spain, yet she managed to embody the passion and the erotic pulsating, stamping rhythms of the dance. When summer ended, the dancing would stop, and the gipsy would fade away till the following year. Come spring, the enchanted carnival would return, and the wheel of magical illusion would begin to turn again.

When it didn't return, he couldn't be sure whether it had ever been there at all. Everything became jumbled in a topsy-turvy cloud of summer memories and winter rain. The bitterness of regret for what would never be and the sadness of being alone - left behind while they had travelled on ahead, still stretched out and touched him nearly every day.

He could handle it better now, but the memory was always there, waiting to eviscerate his heart. He wanted to return home once more to be with them again. Only there could he find the solace and consolation he hungered after.

'We'd better get back. It should be finished by now,' suggested Heart, interrupting Parish's thoughts. He woke from his daydream and looked at his watch. He thought they had only been gone for five minutes, but they had been standing there for nearly an hour. Heart knew better than to interrupt too early when Parish was like this. This was the understanding they had, something that had developed since Catherine's death. They never spoke of it; they didn't have to. They wandered back to the lab in silence and made their way towards Dinger, who they could see was deep in thought, reading some printouts and smiling to himself.

'Must be your lucky day,' said Dinger, looking up. Parish felt a small buzz of elation. Maybe the journey had been worth the effort after all.

'Drummond Cleaver, that's who you brought me. Well, he's your sample A and your third suspect.'

'There's no mistake?' queried Parish, sounding surprised.

'Just to confirm, where did that sample come from?' asked Dinger.

'Vaginal swab from our victim, Dhalia Vingali,' replied Parish.

'Then there's no doubt about it, Drummond Cleaver raped, or let's say had sex with your victim, on the night in question. It's incontrovertible evidence. So, he could have killed her….'

Parish felt a palpable sense of self-satisfaction for taking the long shot and pulling it off. These moments didn't come too often, so he savoured each one joyously when they did.

'So how do you know sample A is Drummond Cleaver?' asked Parish, trying not to sound too negative.

'Let me explain…' said Dinger in a quasi-tutorial tone. 'I checked the BARTY records to see how the original DNA record was obtained. Apparently, nearly twenty-five years ago, a girl called Janice Watson, aged fourteen….'

'Janice Watson!' exclaimed Heart, looking astonished and turning to Parish, who didn't respond immediately. Dinger noticed their instant recognition of the name.

'Is this important?' Dinger asked quizzically.

'I don't know,' said Parish. 'Maybe it's just a coincidence. Please continue.'

'Right, well, she was raped at a party. But the police had nothing to go on except for a semen sample. She appeared to have been drugged with something because she had no clear recollection of the incident. The police investigators carried out a block screening of all the potential candidates in the area, including the students from the local university. But nothing came of it, and the case was never solved. But the police were a bit naughty. They never destroyed all the DNA samples. They were left on the system - the system I am rebuilding. One of the guys they screened was a Drummond Cleaver, and it turns out to be good news for you because it matched the DNA semen sample A you brought me from Dhalia Vingali.'

'So, he was interviewed about the rape of Janice Watson twenty-five years ago and then has sex and kills Dhalia Vingali twenty-five years later,' summarised Parish. 'Bit of a pattern emerging. Maybe there were others?'

'Well, no, actually,' replied Dinger tentatively. 'The records don't show he was ever interviewed about the Watson rape, just that his DNA was taken in a block DNA test. It didn't match the semen taken from Janice Watson at the time.'

'It didn't?' said Parish.

'But the DNA sample from Mr X from the Dhalia Vingali murder is definitely Drummond Cleaver,' repeated Heart.

'Absolutely,' confirmed Dinger. 'As I said, it's your lucky day. Hopefully, that should save you a bit of time.' He handed Parish the computer printout.

'So,' said Heart, 'that makes Cleaver a definite suspect.'

'Maybe,' said Parish contemplatively.

'There is a little more,' said Dinger.

'More?' said Heart, unsure what else there could be.

'The other DNA sample you brought for Dhalia-Rose....'

'Yes,' said Parish cautiously.

'Well, they're very closely related, possibly father and daughter. I can tell that much from DNA.'

Parish looked surprised. 'Related? How do you know they're re…'?

But Dinger interrupted. 'Related?.... A considerable number of familial consistencies clearly indicate a close relationship. The patterns show a male, possibly a brother or the father, which is the most likely. It's as simple as that.'

'So, he raped and possibly killed his own sister or daughter,' asked Parish, stunned by the revelation?

'That's how I see it, and there's one other thing,' said Dinger.

'What?' said Parish.

'I found Cleaver through one of the retrieved records of his DNA from....'

'Yes, you told us that,' interrupted Heart abruptly.

'If you let me finish,' said Dinger, gently chastising Heart for his impetuosity.

'I'm sorry,' said Heart, looking a little like a schoolboy who had been admonished by his teacher.

'Well,' continued Dinger. 'Janice Watson's DNA indicates that she is also related to your murder victim. Dhalia Vingali is probably her daughter.'

'Yes, we had more or less worked that one out,' said Parish, 'but it's good to have it confirmed. Nothing is quite what it seems in this case.'

'Oh, said Dinger,' a little deflated. 'So, do you want me to check against other records?' he asked.

'I thought that's all you could check?' said Parish.

'No, I only checked the sample against the original Janice Watson case, not against any other crimes.'

'How long will that take?' asked Heart.

'Could be a week.'

'Well, we know who it is now, so I don't think it's worth worrying about, but please do it if you have the time, and please let us know if anything else comes up.'

'No problem,' replied Digby.

'But we've got him now,' exclaimed Heart jubilantly.

'Well, we have a name and a matching DNA sample. It's just a little odd that there was no air scan evidence to place him there as well,' replied Parish cautiously. 'Balingo should have confirmed that much and told us where he lived.'

'Everybody had to register on Balingo, didn't they?' said Parish. 'So why not Cleaver?'

'Don't know the answer to that one,' said Dinger.

'This guy always seems to be one step ahead of us,' said Parish.

'Yes, he does, doesn't he?' said Dinger. 'Maybe his records have been deleted.'

'Maybe,' said Parish. 'And that tells us something else, doesn't it?'

'What?' asked Dinger.

'Well, if someone has his records erased from BARTY and manages to arrange for the original database to be destroyed under the pretence that rioters were to blame, it indicates that he must have known the full extent of the risk to himself from the information on the original DNA computer records. Hopefully, he doesn't know you are rebuilding the files. Could be a bit dangerous for you.'

'Good point,' said Dinger, suddenly looking a little uneasy.

'So,' said Parish, 'Cleaver must have had inside information from either the police or the security service. That information would never have been released to the public, would it?' He looked at Dinger, who was nodding in tacit agreement.

'Absolutely. The miscreants would have to carry out a damage limitation exercise. And to do that, they would have to have kept it secret – very secret,' said Dinger.

'So, Drummond Cleaver has to be connected,' said Heart?

'Somehow, he must be,' replied Dinger.

'To Hawsley or Maranno?' asked Parish.

'Possibly both,' said Dinger. 'But then anyone in the higher echelons of the new government or the security service would probably have known. And as it was well over ten years ago, it will be hard finding out who.'

'Maybe,' mumbled Parish, 'but there could be another way.'

'How,' asked Heart?

'I'll think of something.'

'If you could find Marshall Hayden, he could help you,' suggested Dinger.

'Who is Marshall Hayden,' asked Parish curiously? 'I don't recognise the name.'

'Well, he was a Chief Superintendent at the Guildford nick back before the Hawsley administration took over, but there was some scandal about ten years ago. There was something about backhanders and bribery, and he was kicked out. All a little unpleasant, as I remember. I worked in their I.T. forensic department back in those days before they put me out to pasture over here. He lost his job and his pension. It's all a bit sad. He was a nice bloke, honest as the day is long, it left a bit of a nasty taste.'

Dinger paused for a moment. 'I liked him a lot. They shouldn't have treated him the way they did.' He spoke like a man who carried a guilty secret, but not for what he may have done, more for what he didn't do. One day, he would have to atone for that failing.

'How can he help us?' asked Parish.

'Well, he used to run the serious crime incident team, and I'm sure he also had something to do with the unsolved crime unit. He might remember the Janice Watson rape case. As I recall, it was something to do with an unsolved case that caused his downfall, that and the alleged bungs.'

'Do you know where he is now?' asked Heart.

'Last I heard, he was still in the Guildford area,' replied Dinger thoughtfully. 'One of the little villages just outside. Compton seems to ring a bell.'

'That's deep in the Ghettazone,' said Parish gingerly.

'It's not healthy asking questions out there,' warned Dinger with a wry shrug.

'But if that's all we have. We will have to speak to him,' replied Parish.

'I think he was doing something in security for what it's worth, but he's probably retired by now,' added Dinger. 'I don't think I can be much more help than that.'

'You have been more than helpful,' said Parish, shaking Dinger's hand.

'Glad to be of assistance. Makes a change from talking to myself all day.' He smiled. 'Good luck. You'll need it.'

'Thank you,' said Parish. Heart shook Dinger's hand, and then they both left his world. Back in the car, Heart and Parish deliberated over what they had learned that day.

'We can drive back to Providence and come back to Guildford tomorrow,' said Parish, 'or we could take the old road back and pop in today. Might turn up something?'

Heart said nothing at first but took out his automatic and carefully checked how many rounds of ammunition he had. He felt like a sheriff from the old Wild West, setting out to find the bad guy. He counted thirty-six in two clips and put the gun back in his shoulder holster and the spare clip back on his belt. Parish looked at him with a curious gaze. They both knew the Ghettazone was a lawless environment and extremely dangerous. Two strangers asking questions about the whereabouts of one of their own would not exactly endear them to the locals. But he didn't think it warranted that sort of concern.

'Let's get it done with,' said Heart. Now's as good a time as any, and we are already halfway there.

'Right,' agreed Parish. There was no need for further discussion. Heart started the car and drove out through the university security gate into the province street network.

Chapter 19

It was nearly four o'clock when they reached the province's main exit gate for the A3, having stopped off for a late lunch at the Churchillian pub on the top of Portsdown Hill. They passed through security without incident and headed towards Guildford on the motorway. They continued for nearly an hour before seeing the first signs for the old A331, where they left the highway's relative safety and continued for the rest of the journey on the old road to Guildford. It was getting dark now, and the streets no longer had the benefit of overhead lighting. They drove for another hour before reaching the outskirts of the town.

As they drew closer, rain began to fall, adding an extra layer of apprehension. The roads were now only maintained to a rudimentary level. After nearly ten years of neglect, they were little more than a mix of loose shale, hoggin, broken tarmac, remnants of the original concrete substructure and sundry indefinable detritus. This was all compacted by the traffic, making it just serviceable when dry but turning it into a quagmire after a downpour. The pavements had all but disappeared and were now more or less part of the road. It was almost impossible to see where one ended and the other began. Not that it mattered much anymore. What traffic that did use it were either the occasional Protton vehicle - SCOMTEL articulated pantechnicons delivering supplies to the local gigadrome - and horses with or without carts. Pedestrians were a rarity.

In the retro-development cycle, the horse had once again become the dominant form of transport for the masses living in the Ghettazone. They required little maintenance, were cheap to feed, and were inherently reliable. Their numbers, somewhat serendipitously, had increased dramatically over the last ten years. Best of all, if starvation should suddenly and unexpectedly come calling, you could eat your horse and steal another later.

Nature had come to the rescue, as it often does in times of need. It had sensed an increasing demand and dependence on horses and had responded accordingly. In truth, of course, most of this was due to the increased breeding activities of farmers and Romany horse traders who had identified a new and lucrative business opportunity. Driveway tarmacking had lost its financial attraction outside of a province. Humankind was no longer evolving - natural evolution sat quietly weeping in the corner - all hope now lost forever.

Horseshit was now a significant health problem. At one time, it had been actively sought and collected for horticultural purposes, usually as a fertiliser for roses and rhubarb. In the past, piles of steaming dung on pavements and roads had been tolerated for some unfathomable reason. It was acknowledged as an anachronistic by-product of a long-forgotten bygone bucolic era. Today, under profoundly different conditions, it was a severe health hazard. Copious quantities were continually being trampled into the roads. This created a firm but crispy surface when dry but an odiously repulsive sludge when it became wet, which encouraged the return of a vast assortment of rare and extremely unpleasant diseases. Many, were long thought to be extinct. Pedestrians were generally advised to avoid the roads altogether. New footpaths were beaten alongside the main roads but sufficiently far away not to be splattered by passing vehicles throwing up their slurry of stinking, disease-infested sludge.

'Christ, this hums a bit,' grumbled Heart.

'Healthy tang of the country, lad. It's good for the lungs,' replied Parish, adopting a distinctly ineffectual rural tone. However, even he thought it was a lot stronger than he remembered. 'It will clear the tubes out a treat.' Heart glanced at him in disbelief.

'That smell,' replied Heart, clearly unimpressed by Parish's clichéd homily, 'is rotting horse crap and a few other unsavoury bits. It will clog your lungs and choke you to death, and it's definitely not healthy.'

'I'll turn the air recirc on if you can't handle it,' replied Parish unsympathetically.

'Please do,' said Heart, his face a little paler than usual, 'before I throw up.' Parish turned on the recirculation unit, slightly improving the air quality, but the toxic tang lingered.

'How do people live with that, asked Heart, now partially recovered?

'Did you never live in the country,' asked Parish?

'No, I did not,' mumbled Heart ungraciously, 'and that is why.' He pointed to the air, waving his finger erratically.

'It's not really that bad. You do get used to it.' replied Parish. Feebly attempting to placate Heart's grumbling by pretending to sniff the air again, rapture in its bouquet, and appear not to notice any discernible difference. 'It could be a lot worse,' he added. In fact, it was a lot worse.

He was beginning to wonder why he was trying to defend it. He was also beginning to feel a little queasy but doing his best not to show it. He didn't want to give Heart the satisfaction of winning another psychological point in their routine daily banter. Parish enjoyed short interludes of mindless banality. They solved nothing and served no rational purpose whatsoever, but they helped pass the time on arduous journeys.

Maybe that was precisely why he enjoyed them so much. He found the subtraction of intellectual stimulation from their simpleminded repartee strangely addictive. Probably because, just for a few precious minutes, it allowed him to switch off entirely and escape from the dark memories that constantly haunted him. Heart probably derived a similar therapeutic benefit from these short diversions from reality. Not once did they ever discuss why they engaged in these absurd routines. To do so would have broken the spell - the dark cloud of reality would return and, with one sweep of the cloak, overwhelm them, possibly forever.

'And that's supposed to make me feel better, is it?' asked Heart.

'It could be a lot worse. Be thankful it's not,' Parish chanted, almost chastising Heart for complaining.

'I was choking to death a lot, and now I'm only choking to death a little, so I should be happy? Whoopee!' mumbled Heart, smiling disparagingly. Parish ignored Heart's ranting as he had just noticed some lights in the distance.

'There's a SCOMTEL store coming up,' interrupted Parish, swiftly changing the subject. 'We'll pop in for a cup of tea and some nice clean air.'

'That'll be nice,' replied Heart, still struggling with the stench.

The car rumbled slowly over the broken road until it reached the flat concrete of the parking perimeter. They parked as close as possible to the store and then made their way on foot towards the monolith that towered above them. The gigastore was surrounded by a four-metre-high concrete wall similar in design to that which surrounded each province. The primary reason was to prevent the armed marauding gangs of thieves and killers from entering the complex. Security barriers were less sophisticated than those used in a province. It would have been pointless using a retinal security scanner here. It would have prevented almost everybody from entering the store.

Once relieved of weapons, gang members and other unruly elements were of little threat to the prolific numbers of heavily armed security guards inside. Parish and Heart had to enter through a separate gate as they carried weapons - which they were reluctant to part with. Eye-scan identification confirmed they were detectives from Providence, and they passed through security and made their way over to the restaurant.

Chapter 20

'Before they started all this....' Heart was alluding to the monolithic edifice in which they were eating. 'My dad used to have an ironmonger's in Horsham High Street. Been the family business for nearly a hundred years until it closed in 2016.'

'Burnt out during the riots, I suppose?' enquired Parish idly while munching on his sandwich.

'No, surprisingly not,' replied Heart, sounding distracted. 'He struggled through that period and continued for another year. No, it was screws that finished him off.'

'Screws,' repeated Parish with a hint of curiosity. He thought he had misheard Heart for one moment but decided not to question the reference. Heart now had his undivided attention.

'Couldn't get any,' replied Heart wistfully. 'They'd already started to restrict the supply of goods to smaller shops in discreet and subtle ways after the nationalisation of the large multiples. One of the first things that SCOMTEL did was buy every screw the factories produced. Didn't matter how many they made. SCOMTEL bought them all and then sold them cheaper than we could buy them, the bastards!'

There was venom in his voice as he uttered the words. 'Screws, for Christ's sake, why screws? Can you imagine going into a hardware shop and not being able to buy screws? It made him look ridiculous, but that was their plan – total humiliation.'

'At one stage, my dad used to go to a SCOMTEL store to buy his stock, but that didn't last because customers just stopped coming in. We were obviously more expensive.

Then electric power tools became impossible to source, followed by plastic goods, you know, dustpans, buckets, kitchen bins, that sort of product. That's when he decided to call it a day. Shut the shop one night, went back home, picked my mum up, and went for a drive in the country. He connected the last piece of flexible 75mm plastic tubing he had in the shop - it used to be a couple of quid a metre, as I remember - anyway, he connected it to the exhaust pipe and fed it into the back window of the car. They drank several bottles of wine, swallowed thirty diamorphine tablets, injected each other with a lot of insulin, held hands, and watched the sun go down and... well, you know the rest.'

Parish was stunned into silence by the story Heart had just recalled. Not hugely dissimilar from his own father's choice of departure from Mother Earth.

Never before had Heart mentioned how he felt about the SCOMTEL conglomerate and how it had affected his life. And this, despite the fact he obviously held them totally responsible for the death of his parents. What was more telling was the overwhelming sense of emptiness and detachment Heart conveyed while recalling the event. He appeared devoid of any emotion. It was as if he were retelling a story about somebody else he had never met. During the whole of his recollection, his expression never changed.

Parish was stunned into silence by this sudden, unsolicited revelation.

'I often wonder what they thought about in those last few hours, just sitting there gazing out as the sun slowly dropped over the horizon for the last time. Did they say anything as the drugs and exhaust fumes slowly overwhelmed them? Probably said they loved each other -

might have mentioned me... I suppose.... But what do you think about when you arrive at that point in your life? Maybe nothing at all.'

Parish realised that that incident must have had a devastating effect on Heart at the time. Strangely, there was no visible evidence of that now. In fact, he didn't even look up for a few moments as he continued reading something on his tablet and eating his meal. When he did eventually look up at Parish, he smiled.

'I cried for a whole week after that. A forty-year-old man crying for his parents. Ridiculous, but I got over it eventually.' But he hadn't; Parish could see that.

'Do you know why I cried?' asked Heart. Parish didn't give an answer, and Heart wasn't expecting one. 'Because it was all for nothing, the whole bloody thing was a complete waste of time. None of this really matters... In the end, nothing really matters to anybody.' It was a towering existential proclamation, a condemnation of humanity and all its kind, delivered with a cold, dislocated innocence.

'A waste?' ventured Parish cautiously, unsure what Heart was alluding to.

'Well, why bother when...' But he didn't finish. There was something there, lost deep behind his eyes, a steely coldness Parish had never noticed before, not once in all the time they had worked together. Parish took another sip of coffee.

While Heart lingered with his thoughts about his parent's final days, Parish had been half-heartedly gazing into the vast shopping complex. His attention held by one of the till supervisors who was gliding majestically around the aisles on roller skates, effortlessly navigating a path from one till to another, sorting out one problem before streaking off to another section with her tablet in her hand to sort out another.

She was entirely in control of her destiny and everything around her and still spontaneously performed a freely choreographed fantasy on concrete. A routine that would have received rapturous applause had she been performing at Covent Garden. Or, more aptly, in some radical rehash of a Matthew Bourne production of *Lawrence of Arabia* on ice at Sadler's Wells. Instead of which, she was working as a day shift floor supervisor in a SCOMTEL gigadrome.

Suddenly, Parish's attention was brought back to what he had just heard, trying to backtrack on any salient point he may have missed. There was no drama in Heart's voice, no sense of the bitter regret that you might expect, just the empty words spoken in an uninflected, impartial monotone. Heart carried on eating his meal, apparently unmoved by the recollection. But Parish knew the total lack of emotion in Heart's voice conveyed far more about how he felt than any histrionic breast-beating would have achieved.

'He left me the business in his will,' continued Heart. 'But ironically, the shop was looted and burnt to the ground on the same day they were cremated. So, the opportunity of a new life as an independent shopkeeper simultaneously went up in smoke - along with my parents. So, I carried on being a policeman. Still, it would have been a hell of a struggle to survive much longer anyway. So, I suppose SCOMTEL did me a favour in a roundabout way.' The irony of his words was not lost on either of them.

At times like this, Parish was, unfortunately, prone to utter some glib remark making light of the matter, but today, he couldn't find anything to say that seemed suitably appropriate or even inappropriate - so he said nothing. He had worked with Heart for over nine years. Not once in all that time had he ever mentioned that his parents committed joint suicide. In one respect, he thought it must reflect on him in some small way for never having bothered to inquire about them. Having only scant memories of his own parents, the subject had never come up in conversation.

'So how will we find Marshall Hayden?' asked Heart tentatively while finishing his tea.

'Hopefully, the local police might know where he is. We'll try there first.'

They left the confines of the gigadrome and returned to their vehicle on the far side of the car park. Parish touched the search icon on the computer screen.

'Good evening, Inspector,' asked the computer. 'Where would you like to go?'

'Local police station.' The voice didn't reply for a few seconds as it searched back through the satellite link to the central database.

'Are you sure you want to continue after dark in the Ghettazone?' enquired the computer in an overly protective, maternal fashion. It did this from time to time if it considered an instruction unwise.

'Yes,' said Parish.

'Guildford police compound is nearest to your current location. Do you want to select this option?'

'Yes,' replied Parish, a little abrasively.

'No matrix guidance available. Reverting to satnav guidance. Thank you for your enquiry.' The satnav screen lit up with the route to the police compound. Heart followed the instructions until they reached the police station's main security wall. At the first security gate, a woman with a Liverpool accent, which was somewhat unusual for a computer, spoke.

'What is the purpose of your visit?' Even with a slightly jovial scouse tone, the impersonal nature of this greeting irritated Heart. He felt like immediately asking for a double whopper and fries but thought better of it. His last annual review statement adversely reflected flippant verbal badinage with public computer systems. It had included sundry end notes under the section marked 'Areas for Improvement.' It expressly referred to Heart's flagrant disrespect for government property in caustically disparaging terms,

'We would like to see the senior police officer in residence if possible. It relates to an ongoing Investigation in Providence province.' There was a slight delay before the voice returned.

'Chief Superintendent Drysdale is available to see you. Please proceed to Office 44, Block A.'

At the second security gate, a retinal scanner probe slowly approached the passenger window - the window automatically lowered. The security system had already detected that Heart was driving and that he was not the superior officer. The probe slowly entered a few inches into the car, allowing Parish, now turning his head ninety degrees, to engage his eye with the robotic probe. The scan took a few seconds, and then the probe slowly retracted.

'Scan complete for... Inspector Parish. You have a passenger in the vehicle?' it asked rhetorically.

'Yes,' replied Parish, a little brusquely, 'Sergeant Heart, he's the driver.' The computer went quiet for a few seconds. 'Retinal scan not necessary for Sergeant Heart. Heart... low priority... You may proceed... Thank you.'

'Low priority,' replied Heart indignantly. 'What the fuck is that supposed to mean?'

'I think they're talking about the current security status,' replied Parish, attempting to assuage what sounded like an insult but probably wasn't. Why should they insult him? They didn't know him. But then again, did they need to know him if they just wanted to humiliate him. Parish wondered about that as Heart drove to the parking area for visitors to Block A.

They made their way to the fourth floor and, halfway down the corridor, found the office door marked Chief Superintendent D. Drysdale. The partition walls were half-glazed, and they could see someone, whom they presumed to be Drysdale, sitting at his desk. He was looking out of his window while talking animatedly on the telephone. Heart knocked, and Drysdale swung round on his chair and smiled. He pointed to the phone he was holding and made a gesture indicating he was having a conversation he didn't want to have. He beckoned them to come in and pointed to a couple of chairs. When Drysdale had finished his telephone call, Parish started to introduce himself.

'I'm Inspector McKenzie Parish, sir, and this is….'

'Oh, I know who you are,' said Drysdale. 'That's what that was all about,' pointing to the phone. Parish looked more than a little surprised. 'Your reputation and your quest precede you, Inspector.'

'Who was it, sir? If you don't mind me asking,' said Parish.

'Not at all. It was Assistant Chief Constable Daniels at Scotland Yard.'

'But they don't know we're here. No one knows. We haven't told anybody. This was a spur-of-the-moment thing,' said Heart, sounding slightly alarmed.

'Well, sergeant, he knows you're here and wants to be kept informed of any material developments.' Parish looked at Heart, stunned by the revelation but not altogether unsurprised.

'So, what can I do for you, Inspector?' Drysdale was surprisingly at ease and unconcerned about the telephone conversation he had just had, passing it off as nothing more than two old coppers exchanging pleasantries.

'We are looking for an ex-Chief Superintendent Marshall Hayden,' said Parish. 'We understand he ran the serious crime division in Guildford in 2001.'

'Yes, he did,' confirmed Drysdale. 'He was a Chief Inspector then. That was before he was promoted. He left around 2023. That's when I took over.'

'That was when he was accused of taking bribes and lost his job, wasn't it?' asked Parish.

'You're very well informed, Inspector. Yes, he was thrown out of the force. Lost everything, including his pension.'

'What happened to him, sir?' asked Parish.

'Don't know for certain,' replied Drysdale cautiously. 'I believe he moved to one of those small villages just outside Guildford, somewhere in the Ghettazone.'

'Compton,' suggested Heart.

'Yes, I think that was the place,' replied Drysdale, a little surprised again. 'But he may have moved by now. Why do you ask?'

'He worked on the rape of a fourteen-year-old girl in 2001,' said Heart. Her name was Janice Watson. She was drugged, possibly on Rohypnol. Identification of the assailant was never established.'

'Sounds like thousands of other cases, and it was twenty-five years ago, so I doubt whether Hayden would remember it.' Drysdale sounded oddly blasé.

'Yes, I can appreciate that, sir' said Parish sympathetically.

'Why are you so interested in the case now?' asked Drysdale, becoming more curious.

'The man who raped her was never found,' continued Parish. 'A lot of supporting evidence went missing... Then, the case just seemed to fade away. Janice Watson eventually moved away with her mother. Nothing more was heard of her until about three years ago when her body turned up in the Ghettazone, shot and burnt almost beyond recognition.'

'Still can't see where this is all going,' said Drysdale.

'At the first rape in 2001, they took DNA semen samples, but they were never matched to any of the suspects, and after that, it all went quiet.' Parish paused momentarily before continuing, 'Until last week, that is when the same DNA turned up on the body of another murder victim. A girl called Dhalia Vingali, whose real name is Rose Watson, and who we now know was Janice Watson's daughter.'

'Odd coincidence... but I'm still not sure how I can help you, inspector,' replied Drysdale, still unsure where this was all going.

'Well, Chief Superintendent Hayden...'

'Ex!' corrected Drysdale sharply, making it sound like the accompaniment to an act of defenestration.

'Ex-CS Hayden,' repeated Parish, 'may know more about what happened at the original investigation than was in the report. Maybe even more than he realised, and as we are trying to find the whereabouts of a suspect who has now been identified from the DNA, I think he may be able to help us.'

'And you've matched the DNA on the Dhalia Vingali/Rose Watson murder and the Janice Watson rape from twenty-five years ago to the same person?' said Drysdale.

'Not quite,' said Heart, 'but possibly the Janice Watson murder three years ago.'

'Oh,' Drysdale paused momentarily, 'and what's this suspect's name?

Parish's mobile phone began to ring.

'Sergeant,' he said, 'could you...?' Parish got up and went to the corner of the office to answer the call.

'Drummond Cleaver,' continued Heart. Drysdale didn't seem to recognise the name.

'Does he have a criminal record?' enquired Drysdale.

'No,' replied Heart, 'that's why we want to talk to ex-CS Hayden to see if he remembers anything from the original rape enquiry. Something that was never put on the record. And we also need to know if he had ever interviewed a Drummond Cleaver during his investigation.'

'So, Sargeant, tell me something. Why is there all this activity over a twenty-five-year-old unsolved rape case, a three-year-old unsolved murder and the death of a prostitute.' asked Drysdale with a dispassionate flourish?

Standing on the other side of the room, Parish heard the word 'prostitute' and glanced quizzically towards Drysdale, hoping to catch Heart's attention. He failed, so he turned back and continued with his telephone conversation.

'There must be a few whores that still manage to operate, even in Providence?' continued Drysdale cynically.

'Probably, sir,' agreed Heart.

'Anyway,' continued Drysdale. 'I thought whores were traditionally murdered by an outraged evangelistic zealot on a moral crusade to purify the world and rid us of sin. Or a pissed-off punter whose blow job went wrong.' There was a scornful, angry tone to his words that Heart found oddly disturbing. We are what we are, and we do what we have to do to make a living, he thought. That didn't mean it was open season on prostitutes.

Still standing in the corner of the room and still on his mobile, Parish heard the word prostitute once more and glanced at Heart again, but he still didn't see him.

'We don't know she's a prostitute, and she was still murdered,' replied Heart, emphasising the last word as it didn't appear to have made any impact on Drysdale. 'Decapitated, actually,' he added.

'He chopped her head off!' exclaimed Drysdale, sounding contemptuously unmoved and only mildly surprised. 'Sounds like the act of a very disgruntled punter. More the sort of thing I would have expected to encounter here in the Ghettazone rather than the big city, Sergeant.'

'Is it, sir,' replied Heart?

'Knives and swords are the weapons of choice here. Bit of a shortage of conventional weapons.'

'Is there,' said Heart, making a brief note on his tablet?

'Something sexual about a beheading, though, isn't there,' queried Drysdale in an oddly glib tone? Heart looked up for a moment, surprised at his remark. He couldn't imagine how decapitation by any stretch of the imagination could be considered a sexual act.

'I don't know, sir. Is there?' Heart hoped that Drysdale might expand on that observation, but he didn't.

'Look,' said Drysdale, 'you will have to excuse me if I sound a little ...' He hunted around for the right word, 'indifferent, Sergeant, but out here, murder really isn't a big deal. I suppose I've become immune to it, over-conditioned, you might say.' He sounded almost smug but in an angry, self-loathing way.

'I understand, sir,' replied Heart, but he didn't.

'I'm sorry,' said Drysdale contritely. 'I've not been particularly helpful, am I? It's just that working out here for years and suddenly having you turn up brings home just how dreadful things really are. And they're not getting any better. You're here trying to solve a good old-fashioned murder in a province. But here, it happens every day. The difference is I no longer have the resources to investigate any of them. Even if we did, the killer would be long gone, and there's little chance of finding them with the technology we have available. That's what I used to do, proper policing. Now, I'm reduced to being a human resource manager in a feral cesspit. You have no idea how much I'd like to investigate a murder properly - but it will never happen, not here anyway. My job is shite, and my life is shite, and that's how it will stay until I get out of this place or die....' The last few words hung in the air for a few moments.

Drysdale sounded deeply disappointed with his lot; definitely not a man enjoying his job, thought Heart. 'I'm sorry about that, sir,' said Heart empathetically. The reality of life in the zone was becoming more apparent by the minute. He was beginning to realise how lucky he was, never having been seconded to the Ghettazone.

'No need to apologise. It's not your problem,' replied Drysdale, waving his hand as if to dismiss any misunderstandings.

'So, is it just Cleaver you are after,' continued Drysdale?

'Drummond Cleaver is our main suspect, but there are also two other potential suspects,' replied Heart.

'And they are…?' asked Drysdale, lighting a cigarette and offering one to Heart. Heart declined. Drysdale took an exceedingly long drag, which apparently gave him great satisfaction. Heart was surprised at what appeared to be a blatant disregard for the anti-smoking laws. Drysdale smiled at Heart and took another drag.

'You look surprised, Sergeant,' remarked Drysdale, alluding to the cigarette he was holding.

'I am, sir. In Providence, you could lose your job for smoking in a government building.' The legal implications of smoking didn't so much concern Heart. He occasionally smoked a cigarette when permitted, but Drysdale's total disregard for the law being so deliberately flouted surprised him.

Heart had long ago come to terms with the vast disparity in jurisprudence interpretation inside a province and out in the Ghettazone. But the ambiguity displayed by Drysdale's cavalier attitude could only further muddy the guidelines for the officers under his command.

'One of the consolations of doing a ten-year stint out here in shitland,' explained Drysdale with a sardonic smirk, 'is you can smoke all you like, Sergeant. Back in Providence, nobody gives a fuck what we do as long as we keep the Glundes under the cosh.'

Resigned acceptance of the inevitable was sadly evident in the tone of his voice, burnished with a tinge of desperation, bitterness, indifference, and regret. It wasn't Drysdale's fault things were the way they were; that was just a consequence of circumstances he could no longer control.

Presumably, he, too, once had aspirations of working in a quiet office in one of the provinces until early retirement beckoned. Instead, he had been hastily and somewhat unexpectedly transferred to the Ghettazone. Retirement was no longer a remote possibility until he was sixty-five. It was unlikely he would ever be transferred back to a province.

'Good old-fashioned policing, then,' said Heart, smiling with just the tiniest hint of acerbity in his voice.

'Beginning to understand why you're still a sergeant, Sergeant,' replied Drysdale disparagingly.

Heart didn't reply. Rather than antagonise him further, he would let the comment pass without further comment. 'Aiden Hawsley and Benny Maranno,' said Heart abruptly, 'are the two other suspects.' The matter of the cigarette issue had now passed.

'Our esteemed leader and his bagman Benny Maranno. You don't do things by half, do you, Sergeant?' replied Drysdale, smiling subtly.

'DNA Air scans placed them at the crime scene, sir,' stated Heart matter-of-factly. The acrimony of the past few minutes seemed to fade away.

'So why haven't you arrested them if you have the evidence,' asked Drysdale? He sounded confused but, at the same time, was giving the impression of knowing more than he was letting on. Heart felt a twinge of apprehension in how the question had been phrased; a sixth-sense instinct for self-preservation had served him well in the past and was now sending him odd signals. He would have felt more at ease if the question had been phrased in a more passive-aggressive tenor instead of the defensive tone Drysdale had chosen to use. It was only semantics, but the colour of words sometimes makes all the difference.

'Air scans placed them both at the Dhalia Vingali incident, but the DNA evidence on the two bodies was....' Heart hesitated. He wondered whether now was an appropriate time to adopt a more cautious approach with the information they had collected so far, '....inconclusive.' And that was his final word.

Parish completed his phone conversation and returned. 'Sorry about that. Somebody we've spoken to has just given me some more information. As I was saying, the DNA evidence on Dhalia and Janice is from Drummond Cleaver,' said Parish. 'Maranno admits to having sex with Vingali, that is, Rose Watson, during the evening, which explains why there's a positive DNA air scan. But then you knew that, didn't you, sir,' he added?

'Yes, Heart mentioned some of it,' replied Drysdale.

'No, I meant you knew that before we arrived, sir?'

'Did I,' asked Drysdale?

Heart looked a little confused.

'You did make a comment just now about Dhalia being a prostitute. We never mentioned that,' said Parish.

'It was in the telephone call I was taking when you came in.'

'From ACC Daniels,' asked Parish?

'Yes, I told you that just now,' replied Drysdale.

'But why was he calling you about the case?'

'Just wanted to make sure that I gave you every assistance in the matter. ACC Daniels filled me in on the background and some of the delicate dynamics of the... situation.'

'Dynamics,' queried Heart?

'Hawsley called him, didn't he,' said Parish intuitively?

'I don't know.' Drysdale paused for a second or two. 'He may have done, but ACC Daniels didn't say. But then he wouldn't, would he?' He paused again. 'That's what I meant by dynamics. He just suggested that you should be advised to tread very carefully and not make any mistakes.'

'That sounds more like a veiled threat than friendly advice, sir,' suggested Parish.

'No, not at all,' replied Drysdale, sounding slightly edgy.

'So, am I to assume that we are supposed to pull back on our investigation?' asked Parish hesitantly. 'Has it become too sensitive?' He was searching for a small chink of light in the darkness as he was now unsure what the unspoken agenda was.

'No, absolutely not. Carry on as usual,' said Drysdale. 'Look, this is to be treated just like any other murder - murders, so I think the gist was to help you all I can with your investigation. Hopefully, you will tidy it up as soon as possible.'

'It was a serious crime, sir,' interjected Parish. 'The murder of Dhalia Vingali was particularly horrific, and....'

'Yes, I understand, in Providence, murder is probably still a serious matter.... but out here, in....' He stopped talking and looked at them pensively for a few moments. First at Parish, then to Heart, then back to Parish. It was as if he were a thoroughbred racehorse trainer weighing up the prospects of two colts at a horse auction. He made his decision and rose from his chair.

'Can you come with me? I need to show you something.' Drysdale's mood seemed to change; it suddenly became less confrontational, more amenable, almost friendly. They followed him into the lift and descended five floors into the basement without a word passing between them. When the lift doors opened, they stepped into a dimly lit hallway and were immediately overwhelmed by the warm, damp, airless atmosphere and the unmistakable stench of advanced human bodily decay. The air-conditioning system was not working as efficiently as it should have been.

Parish's first instinct was not to breathe. Heart was already there, his sense of smell now highly tuned after his previous nasal experience in the car.

They were only taking in air when it became absolutely necessary. Parish wanted to ask a question but decided against it. Heart gagged, and he almost threw up for the second time in twenty-four hours; he was not having a good day. It was fortunate that neither of them had eaten anything substantial that day. It would have probably considered making an unscheduled return journey.

Drysdale, who didn't seem significantly affected by the stench, walked over to a battered grey metal cupboard in the corner of the room. He prised open one of the doors and took out three face masks, each sealed in a plastic bag. 'Put these on. They might help a little.' They hurriedly complied with his instruction. The heavy aroma of camphor and sandalwood slowly permeated through the mask, partially alleviating the overpowering nausea and the almost uncontrollable inclination to gag.

'Follow me, gentlemen,' said Drysdale, beckoning them forward. 'Please,' he added, as they appeared a little disinclined to oblige immediately.

'Where are we going?' asked Parish, his voice muffled by the mask.

'Please,' repeated Drysdale in a desultory, imploring manner. Apparently, he didn't want to endure this any longer than they did, but something was driving him forward. Whatever it was, it compelled them to follow. He led the way further down the dimly lit corridor. Their footsteps on the once shiny green concrete floor echoed ominously off the bare walls. They reached two large, battered white doors, one of which Drysdale pushed and held open to allow Parish and Heart to pass through. The lights were even dimmer in this room, and they had to wait a few moments for their eyes to adjust to the strange pinkish glow. The room was cold but not cold enough. The oscillating whooshing sound of several enormous fans could be heard in the distance.

Despite the masks, the stench from the decaying bodies still managed to seep through the protective filters and into their nostrils. Their breathing became shallower as, once again, they became less inclined to inhale. As they became accustomed to the low-level lighting, the enormous hall and its contents slowly began to slip into focus.

They could now clearly distinguish hundreds of gurneys in neat rows stretching almost to infinity. Each was neatly draped with a white sheet. Some were smeared with dark crimson stains, but the unmistakable shape of a human body underneath each one was clear to see—each a small ripple in a continuously undulating sea of death.

In the middle distance, some of the overhead fluorescent tubes were flickering and cracking. It was as if they were deliberately attempting to fail, ashamed of what they were illuminating and forced, against their will, to witness.

'Our dead bay,' announced Drysdale, with a discernible hint of failure in his voice. 'I apologise for the smell, but we don't always receive the freshly dead. Sometimes, they can be a few weeks old or more before we get them. Nearly four hundred bodies in here, all victims of some form of violent death, and all of them will return to dust soon, forgotten forever.' He stopped talking, and just for a fraction of a second, his eyes, eerily peering over the top of his mask, suddenly plunged into the depths of complete and utter desolation. He quickly recovered from the momentary lapse and continued his explanation.

'The natural cause cases go to another department a few miles from here. They are the lucky ones.'

'Lucky ones,' enquired Heart, sounding curiously intrigued by the expression?

'The staff, not the bodies; they have refrigerators over there... that work.'

Heart wandered around the shrouded bodies, noticing a peculiarity about the shapes. Upon closer inspection of the first dozen corpses, Heart saw something unusual, something he had not encountered on this scale before.

'You seem to have what I would have thought was a disproportionate number of bodies with limbs and heads missing?' he queried casually.

'Very observant, Sergeant,' replied Drysdale, who had walked over to the first gurney and taken hold of two corners of the sheet covering the body. He looked at Heart and, with a grandiose flourish of his hands, reminiscent of a matador tormenting the dying bull in its final throes of resistance, he whipped away the sheet in one theatrical gesture. It revealed the remains of a woman's decapitated body, with a head and a hand, presumably hers, carefully placed between her thighs. "O*lay,*" whispered Drysdale.

Heart gasped. He felt his stomach lurch, and for a moment, he thought he would be sick again. The sudden reaction involuntarily forced him to inhale air, some of which, unfortunately, had not benefited from his face mask's filtering properties.

There was little respect for the dead here, only contempt. It was almost as if Drysdale despised these people for allowing themselves to be killed. This was not the clean cut of a single sword stroke, noted Heart on closer inspection, but the fevered hacking of a maniac. There was visible evidence of at least two off-target attempts, possibly defensive wounds, as her body swerved to avoid her attacker.

'They're not actually missing,' qualified Drysdale, 'just not attached. He waited for that revelation to sink in before continuing. 'We keep their heads and limbs there for safekeeping, just in case you are wondering.'

'That's the way that...' but Heart was interrupted.

'Your victim died,' finished Drysdale. 'Yes, I know, and that makes it even more unusual. Several nicer options are available inside a province for ending someone's life. He smiled when he said, *"nicer."* Parish and Heart didn't respond.

'But out here,' continued Drysdale, 'it's understandable. People defend themselves with whatever they can. Guns are a luxury and surprisingly hard to obtain, so the weapon of choice is a knife, machete or sword. Easy to manufacture by any decent blacksmith, and there are plenty of them around these days. They make all manner of things for carts and the like. And anything else when there is a demand.' He made a theatrical slashing gesture.

'Why do you keep the murder victims here for so long? Haven't you solved any of them, sir?' asked Heart with such reproachful innocence that Drysdale couldn't help but chuckle.

'How long do you think we keep them here, Sergeant?' He replied without emotion apart from the almost undetectable hint of derision subtly enshrined within the tone of the question.

'Well, I presume until you've completed the post-mortem examination, determined the cause of death, and completed toxicology and DNA reports if necessary.' Heart was referring to the usual practice in Providence. 'Then possibly you keep them on ice for a week or so before releasing the body to the next of kin.'

'Very urbane,' replied Drysdale, who would have been amused by Heart's naivety had it not reminded him of just how much the process and procedural aspects of a suspicious death had deteriorated over such a short period and how much it had changed him. He looked at Heart and Parish, who were both physically shocked by what they could see but felt nothing. Drysdale had become immune to the level of human butchery conducted daily in the Ghettozone, but he knew that was wrong. He should have been able to feel what they were feeling. He should have felt despair but did not - he felt nothing.

'In a civilised society,' continued Drysdale,' maybe, but we do it differently here. We don't keep them that long, just a day or two. We don't carry out autopsies or try to determine the cause of death because it's not within our working parameters. It's usually patently obvious how they died. And anyway, we no longer have the resources to carry out post-mortems on every victim.'

'So how do you solve the murders, sir,' asked Parish? He had been listening intently but had said almost nothing up to this point? He was a little intrigued by the odd terminology being used.

'We don't!' replied Drysdale abruptly. That's the point, and these...' he pointed to the bodies in the room, 'these came in over the last few days and will be incinerated tomorrow. The crematorium is a bit overloaded right now. They're running a bit behind. Otherwise, most of these would be gone by now.'

'Working parameters?' asked Heart, querying the phrase that Drysdale had used.

'It's a political euphemism,' replied Drysdale, half expecting a response from Heart, but nothing was forthcoming. 'In the Ghettazone, death is not the issue anymore. Containment and disposal – that's the problem.' He paused to let that point sink in and await a response, but none came. 'Our operational mandate is precise: clear the bodies and control civil unrest. How the inhabitants treat each other is not our problem anymore, or concern, for that matter. The *law* is no longer our responsibility.'

'But that means you're essentially condoning murder. You can't ignore law and order just because somebody tells you it doesn't matter anymore.' Parish was becoming frustrated by Drysdale's seemingly obdurate stance but was still painfully aware he was talking to a senior officer.

'Inspector, this wasn't how I would have planned it.' Drysdale spoke firmly, almost aggressively, vainly attempting to reassert his authority.

'We are overwhelmed by mediocrity. That's the problem. I can't fight it alone, and we don't have enough officers or resources to change it. What would you suggest I do?'

Parish said nothing for a moment. He was slowly becoming aware that this entire process of social degeneration was ultimately being planned and controlled from a place far beyond Guildford. He could sense a complete absence, not of the responsibility - the passionate desire to do something was clearly evident - but of the ability to wrest responsibility from parties unseen.

'So, you think this is all part of Hawsley's master plan?' asked Parish.

'You tell me,' replied Drysdale acerbically. He was calmer now. 'I understand you're on a social footing with him. Maybe you should ask him next time you pop around the palace.' There was a hint of mildly acidic sarcasm in his tone, but it wasn't really being directed at Parish, and Parish knew that.

'You seem remarkably well informed about my movements,' said Parish.

'Jungle drums still work, even out here,' replied Drysdale with a smirk.

'We were interviewing him during our enquiries,' replied Heart, by way of an explanation for something he realised afterwards he didn't need to explain.

'Are you sure it was that way round?' asked Drysdale, looking at Heart with an expression that immediately planted the seed of doubt in his mind.

'So why did you bring us here to see this?' asked Parish.

'Because...' Drysdale paused for a second or two to think about what he would say. 'I wasn't sure whether you understood what happens... what is happening here? And down here, nobody can hear what we say.' Drysdale slowly looked around the room and up at the ceiling before continuing....

'You seem like a couple of decent officers, so I can be frank. You came looking for information to help you find someone who may have murdered a prostitute....'

'We still don't know she was a prostitute,' interrupted Heart, echoing his earlier comment.

'Maybe not. But because it happened in a nice, clean, law-abiding gated province, and you have all your DNA technology, laboratories, and lots of motivated policemen perched on the moral high ground, keen to find the killer, all the stops are pulled out. But out here, if that happened, she would be dumped onto the next body cart that passed by, cremated in a day or two, and that would be it, finished, complete, game over, job done.'

Drysdale's detached, insouciant manner was not lost on either of them.

'We don't have the inconvenience of having to solve crime anymore. We can't afford that luxury.' His pallid, expressionless features flattened by the low-level lighting matched the soulless tone of his voice. 'We just deal with the body bags. Now, do you see what I mean?'

'Hmm,' replied Parish disconsolately.

'Let's go back up to my office,' said Drysdale. 'The air is better.'

'So, you can't help us?' asked Parish, who had resigned himself to expect little cooperation.

'Au contraire, Inspector, I will help you all I can. I don't like what is happening here, and I despise what I have become. I'm not a policeman anymore. I'm just a bloody mortuary assistant. I can't do anything about it, but you might be able to. It's not likely, but it's more likely than me doing something.'

Parish was taken aback by Drysdale's candour. Maybe he had misjudged him after all. They arrived back at the lift, dropped the face masks into a container by the door, and stepped in. The doors closed, and as if in sympathy with the departed - the whine of the motor began. They didn't speak a word as they ascended from the bowels of the Dead Bay - accidental tourists absconding from hell. Seldom had Heart felt happier to leave a room. Something was deeply depressing about the dead bay; it wasn't just the stench of rotting corpses. It was the pervasive, inescapable sense of absolute desolation, hopelessness and despair. In some strange way, a venal analogy was being played out—the morality of the dead against the immorality of the living.

'So, can you tell us where we can find ex-Chief Inspector Hayden,' asked Parish cautiously?

'I can, but you must understand he keeps a low profile just to stay alive. Ex-force living in the Ghettazone are still vulnerable targets, and we can't afford him any protection.'

'I can see that,' replied Parish.

'I'll give you his address when we get back to my office,' said Drysdale, 'then it's down to you. I can't let you have anybody to help; I wouldn't want his whereabouts to become common knowledge.' He looked at Parish for confirmation of the unspoken agenda. 'You understand?'

Parish acknowledged his tacit agreement.

Drysdale took out a small notebook from the wall safe in his office, jotted an address down on a notepad, tore off the sheet, and reluctantly handed it to Parish.

'Please destroy that when you find him,' asked Drysdale. Parish thought the request was a little out of character for a man who appeared weary and disheartened with everything and everyone that surrounded him. A man who had evidently case-hardened himself against his environment and yet was still capable of showing signs of compassion and concern for another human being.

'Why are you still concerned about him if he is a bent copper?' asked Heart.

'Hayden bent? Bullshit. I never believed that. We went to police college together, and I would stake my career, if that's what you call this, that he didn't take a bung. He was fitted up, but I can't prove it. One day, it could be me. I might need him to protect me.' He looked at Parish. His expression was that of someone who felt vulnerable. Someone who might well need protection one day, but it was unlikely to be Hayden who would be able to assist when that day came. He would probably be long gone by then.

'Thank you,' said Parish. They shook hands and started to leave. But Drysdale called them back.

'I do have one final question, Parish,'

'Yes, sir?' replied Parish with respectful courtesy.

'How did you check the DNA from your murder against a twenty-five-year-old rape case when virtually all criminal records were destroyed in 2015?'

'That one's easy, sir. We found a university scientist rebuilding the old computer records in his spare time… he found the match. Chance in a million, but there it is.' Drysdale was stunned.

'A match to what exactly?' asked Drysdale.

'They took DNA samples from everybody who knew her at the time,' replied Heart 'for elimination purposes.'

'So, was somebody arrested?' asked Drysdale.

'No. None of the samples matched the forensic evidence from the victim… but for some reason, the elimination evidence was never deleted from the police database,' replied Parish, 'and that's what he is rebuilding.' Drysdale's face went strangely pale.

'That's amazing,' replied Drysdale. 'Rebuilding the computer files,' he mumbled quietly to himself.

'Will be if he ever finishes it,' added Heart.

'So, most of the evidence you do have was technically obtained illegally?' Drysdale's mind was still sharp. Years working in the Ghettazone hadn't dulled his tentative grasp on the PACE (Police and Criminal Evidence Act) fundamentals. However, it was unlikely that he would be called upon any time soon to use his knowledge of the act.

'Yes, I suppose technically you could say that,' replied Parish, a little taken aback by the question.

'So, if you aren't allowed to use it in a court case, what can you use?'

'I'm sure we will find more evidence now we know who we are looking for,' replied Parish.

'I hope you do,' said Drysdale, 'and don't forget what I said about that.' He pointed imperiously at the note in Parish's hand. 'We still protect our own when we can. We have little else left but self-respect. There but for the grace of God, blah de blah…' were his closing words as they left, a polemic of despair and self-loathing that would linger in Parish's thoughts throughout the coming days.

Chapter 21

'I never realised just how bad it was out here,' said Heart, settling down into the driving seat of the Protton. Realising that the rules, regulations, and laws in provinces didn't apply here was hard enough to comprehend, but coming face-to-face with the reality of a brutally feral and primitive society was terrifying.

Before the province walls were constructed, no-go zones had mushroomed in all the UK's major cities. Crime had flourished, but it had been tolerated and, to some degree, contained within accepted boundaries. These lawless areas were not dissimilar to the Ghettazone of today, just much smaller. Murder in those zones had still been considered a serious crime and had been rigorously prosecuted. These no-go areas had disappeared within the gated provinces, and the troublemaking elements were quickly and efficiently expelled. This left one vast, uncontrolled area outside the wall - the Ghettazone.

'Neither did I,' replied Parish. The full impact of the last few hours was only now beginning to take effect.

'Sort of makes you wonder what is really happening when they can keep that sort of thing under wraps,' mused Heart.

'Do we ever really know what a government is up to,' asked Parish in reflective mode?

Where would you like to go... Sergeant Heart,' asked the computer? Heart glanced at Parish enquiringly. Parish looked back at Heart, deep in thought for a moment.

'Put her in free drive,' said Parish.

'Free drive? Why?' asked Heart, who hadn't driven without computer assistance for years. Parish said nothing but just pointed to the relatively innocuous FD control.

Heart selected Free Drive, and the computer responded. 'You have selected free drive. Are you certain you wish to disable the computer system?' It spoke with an odd, staccato inquisitorial tone. The inflection on the last word was wrong.

Heart looked at Parish again for confirmation. Parish nodded.

'Yes,' said Heart.

'All satellite communication will be untethered, and computer assistance suspended until free drive is deselected,' advised the computer. 'Are you sure you wish to continue?'

'Yes,' answered Heart firmly.

'Use of free drive is a breach of communications protocol. Do you still wish to continue?' The computer was conversing with unusual caution, adopting a bold, pedantic tone to its questioning.

'Yes,' replied Heart abruptly.

'Who is the authorising officer?' The computer was now being officious.

'Inspector Mackenzie Parish,' answered Parish.

'Do you have the authority to disengage?'

'I am self-authorising,' replied Parish.

'Disconnecting satellite communications....' There was a short pause. 'Disconnection complete. Computer system now shutting down.' There was another brief pause before the screen went blank.

'Is that it?' asked Parish.

'That's it. We're on our own.'

'Right,' said Parish. 'This is where we are going,' handing Heart the piece of paper that Drysdale had given him.

'But why without the computer system? It's going to be murder....' He stopped for a second, considering the unfortunate choice of word. 'It's not going to be easy to find this place without a map.'

'I just thought it might be safer for all concerned if our every movement was not being tracked and relayed back to Hawsley.' He pointed at the computer console.

'Ah,' said Heart. 'Good idea, but how will we find where we are going without a map?' Parish rummaged around in his pockets and produced an old, battered iPhone.

'These still have sat nav, don't they?' he queried confidently, holding the mobile up for Heart to see.

Heart smiled, 'Yes, probably, but the user is still logged in, so they could still track it back to you and know where it's going.'

'Not my phone,' replied Parish sanguinely. Heart looked at him as if to say, *Well, who the hell does it belong to?*

'It's Catherine's,' he replied without any visible emotion. There was still a tacit reluctance to fully consign her to the past; hanging on to a few personal belongings was his way of dealing with it. 'I just kept her contract going for some reason. Couldn't bring myself to cancel it. It's my last tangible link. Sounds a bit stupid, but....'

'I don't suppose they would be tracking that, then, not when...' interrupted Heart, but he stopped short of finishing what he was about to say.

'That's why I held on to it, just in case. Thought one day it might come in handy.'

'And it has,' said Heart. 'So which way?' Parish fiddled around with the sat-nav app until he had downloaded a map and directions.

'Right,' said Parish. 'Straight ahead up the old A287 to Camelsdale. Just follow the signs.' Heart started the car, and they began their journey to find Marshall Hayden...

Like all the roads they had used recently, this one was almost indistinguishable from a mediaeval horse track. All semblance of the original magnificent concrete and tarmac arteries of commerce and civilisation was gone. The infrastructure that had once supported nearly seventy million people's existence was now reduced to shattered remnants. The illustrated embodiment of a disintegrating and dissembled society.

Ironically, the major road signs, lampposts, footbridges, and gantries stood as monuments to the recent past, oddly incongruous in a countryside slowly being consumed by nature in its unforgiving, relentless march to reclaim that which it once owned and would own once again.

The Ghettazone, which stretched from the South Downs of southern England to the Scottish Highlands, was now inhabited by over eighteen million unemployed, semi-illiterate people eaking out a meagre existence. Two-thirds of them between sixteen and forty-five had never been formally employed.

These were the lost generations who would never know the pure pleasure of arriving home after a hard day's work to find their partners waiting for them in a beautifully warm house. Dinner cooking in the oven, and their children playing in the garden. For them, all that beckoned was a short, miserable, painful life and the constant struggle to stay alive and to make enough money to buy food. Darwin's theory had come full circle. Once again, only the fittest, the strongest, the meanest and the shrewdest, would survive.

Many people had gone back to growing their own food, and small cooperatives had already begun to spring up to facilitate the trading of produce. A new ecological age was evolving.

The total number of Ghettazone inhabitants had dropped considerably over the past ten years. Rare diseases were rife; AIDS, cholera, typhoid, diphtheria, whooping cough, smallpox, Weill's disease, and tuberculosis now thrived unabated. The mortality rate was further increased by the open accessibility of a legal hybrid variant of the recreational drug that used to be known as skunk, now rebranded as Panzanoid.

The Hawsley administration made the drug freely available to all non-residents to reduce dependency on illegally imported stimulants. It was also an expedient chemical cosh, producing indefinite periods of hallucinatory euphoria. It was a welcome alternative to reality in a society devoid of pleasure. Unbeknown to the users, it was also slowly but permanently destroying major cognitive areas of their brains, leaving them incapable of making rational decisions. Panzanoid users could perfectly comprehend the necessity to protect whatever they had within their immediate vicinity, but they could not grasp the concept of a broader community.

This meant they were slowly becoming less of a threat to province society. To a significant degree, they no longer realised it existed. For most of them, the perimeter wall was the world's end. In fact, the Ghettazone was a genetic engineering paradox that would eventually destroy all its inhabitants, thereby cleansing the UK of all undesirables... If you weren't hacked to death by some psychopath high on Panzanoid, then the air you were breathing or the water you were drinking would probably do for you. The perfect plan, in fact. Hitler would have been proud of what Hawsley had achieved without the disagreeable negative media coverage he had attracted.

It was nearly dusk as they approached Camelsdale. Parish noticed some of the houses appeared to have lights, but as they drew closer, he realised it was only the flickering of open-hearth wood fires. Electricity was still available for those who could afford a plutomarium generator.

Those choosing to steal the power, which was more common, would never openly display the fact for fear of a visit from a R.E.P.A. (Revenue Energy Protection Agent.) These quasi-police officers methodically roamed the streets at night, looking for the tell-tale signs of illegally connected energy supplies. They were merciless in the execution of their duty.

'Where to now?' asked Heart, struggling to see the road. Without streetlights, there was only the moon to show the way as it reflected off the patches of frozen water by the roadside.

'There should be a church called St Veronica's. It's on the left-hand side,' Parish was reading from his phone screen. Heart drove on for about another quarter of a mile but much slower than before. There were large ruts in the road covered in ice, and there was no way of knowing how deep they were. They could hear the ice gently cracking like a ringmaster's whip, and they flinched each time it fractured.

Whispering as if the noise of the car wouldn't be noticed, Heart exclaimed, 'There's a church,' pointing to a spire in the distance, 'That must be it.'

He slowed down and stopped to check the name on the weather-beaten wooden sign on the front wall.

GOD WELCOMES EVERYBODY TO Sᴛ. VERONIC...
PLEASE COME IN TO PRAY OR FOR QUIET REFLE...

The end of the sign had rotted away and fallen off. Heart presumed the last word was "reflection." Parish wondered what there was to reflect on.

'This must be it,' said Parish with some apprehension, unsure how Marshall would react when approached by two strangers who inexplicably knew who he was. 'In we go.' Heart turned the car into the courtyard and parked opposite a cottage next to the church. They noticed some flickering flashes of firelight emanating from tiny chinks in the threadbare curtains of the front room. As they drew closer, it became even more noticeable as near-total darkness had descended. The only other light was from the moon's misty glow piercing through the yew trees, highlighting the church's steeple. A giant bird's dark, eerie shadow slowly rose from the ground and appeared to fly towards the moon.

Heart instinctively took his gun out to recheck it, then replaced it in its shoulder holster. He knocked on the door of the cottage. When there was no response, he knocked again, a little louder. This time, he heard a sound from inside. A small hatch about ten centimetres square opened in the door at eye level. Heart could make out the withered features of an elderly lady's face lit by a candle.

'Yes?' she said bluntly, obviously not used to visitors and definitely not after dark.

'I'm Sergeant Russell Heart, and this is Chief Inspector McKenzie Parish from Providence Police Department,' said Heart. They both produced their warrant cards for inspection - but there wasn't much light for her to inspect them. So Parish held up his phone with the torch application to illuminate the cards. 'We've spoken to Chief Superintendent Drysdale at Guildford. He told us we could find ex-Chief Superintendent Marshall Hayden here. We need to speak to him about an old case he worked on.'

The elderly lady continued to inspect the warrant cards for what seemed like an inordinately long time. 'Why so late,' she whispered abruptly? 'Why didn't you come during the day?'

'We were returning to Providence from Deliverance,' replied Parish, for some reason answering in a whispered tone. Heart could see that the old lady was having a problem believing this was on their way to anywhere.

'Wait a moment,' she mumbled, then closed the hatch. Heart could hear some faint mumblings from inside. The hatch opened again after a few minutes. 'There's nobody here of that name. You must have the wrong address.' She went to shut the hatch again.

'This is the right address,' insisted Heart. 'We need to talk to Mr Hayden about Drummond Cleaver.' The lady didn't reply immediately, and they could hear more incoherent mumblings in the background.

'Let them in, Grace,' said a muffled voice from deep in the cottage. The lady reluctantly closed the hatch again and unlocked the safety chain, slid back a couple of what sounded like extremely cumbersome bolts, and then opened the door to let them in. She slowly led them through to a small room near the back of the cottage. Marshall Hayden sat in a wheelchair with a broken shotgun on his lap. As they walked in, he snapped the gun together for effect but didn't point it at them - he just let it lie on his lap.

'So, Drysdale sent you, has he?' Hasn't been sacked for shagging sheep yet, then?' he asked, speaking very slowly.

'I don't understand,' said Parish.

'He's Welsh,' said Heart. 'Drysdale, he's Welsh and....'

'Oh, I see,' said Parish. He turned back to Hayden, who was smiling.

'No, he's still hanging on.'

'It's surprising,' said Hayden, sounding a little bitter. 'They normally get rid of the honest ones,'

'Do they,' asked Heart hesitantly? Hayden looked at him but didn't respond immediately. He coughed again into his handkerchief.

'Don't I know you, Sergeant, from a few years ago?' said Hayden, peering quizzically at Heart. He couldn't place him, but the face seemed familiar.

'No, I don't think so,' replied Heart. 'I don't recall serving under you. I'm sure I would have remembered.' Heart appeared a little agitated by the question.

'Oh, maybe not, then. I've known a lot of young bobbies in my time.'

'I'm sure you have, sir,' replied Heart. 'I imagine we all look much the same at that age.' Hayden looked at Heart again, still searching his memory.

'So, what do you want to know,' asked Hayden, wheezing? He was having trouble breathing and took a long, deep rasping breath.

'You were in charge when a girl was raped nearly twenty-five years ago,' said Parish.

Hayden looked surprised by the statement. As if it were bordering on the incredible (which it was), but he made no immediate comment. He went quiet for a few moments, searching the annals of his mind for any details of cases that he could remember.

'Lots of girls get raped. Jesus Christ, I don't remember every case from that far back.'

'But you must remember this one. Her name was Janice Watson; she was found dead in 2023,' said Parish.

'Janice Watson? Oh yes, I remember that name. She's the real reason they got rid of me.'

'Who got rid of you?' asked Heart.

'That's just it,' he replied. 'I don't know. I know I was fitted up on some ridiculous charge of taking bribes while I worked on that case. It was to stop me.' He coughed a couple of times. 'I'm sure that was the reason.'

'But why?' asked Parish.

'We found DNA evidence for a suspect, a....' He was searching his memory.

'Drummond Cleaver?' suggested Parish.

'Cleaver, yes. That was his name, Drummond Cleaver....' Hayden seemed to drift off for a few seconds. Maybe recalling past events, or possibly the cancer was taking another small step towards its final objective. Suddenly, he was back. 'Anyway, we found some DNA that matched him on her body, so we knew we had him,' said Hayden.

'So why didn't you arrest him?' asked Parish.

'Don't know. Suddenly, it all became very confusing. Witnesses changed statements, evidence mysteriously disappeared, and I was blamed, but I didn't remove it - they just removed me. Said I was taking bribes and corrupting evidence, would you believe?'

'We have the same DNA on a murder we're investigating, a Dhalia Vingali,' added Heart.

'Very odd name,' he coughed.

'That's not her real name,' said Heart. 'Rose Watson, that was her name.'

'Watson? Were they related?' asked Hayden.

'Mother and daughter,' said Parish.

'Strange coincidence,' said Hayden curiously; you could see his mind beginning to whirl as it would have done in his younger days.

'And we now know the person who probably murdered Dhalia Vingali was Drummond Cleaver,' added Heart.

'Christ!' said Hayden. 'And you haven't been fitted up yet?'

'We've been gently warned to be careful,' said Parish.

'I bet you have,' said Hayden. 'I bet you're getting awfully close to where I was. Be careful. You're dancing in a different language now.' He stopped talking as he took a couple of deep breaths from an inhaler.

'I don't understand,' said Parish, intrigued by Hayden's warning.

'It's not just a murder. It was never about murder. There's more, much more,' rasped Hayden, his eyes widening as he looked at the two of them. He wanted to see their faces clearly, the faces of the two men who might unravel the puzzle that had used him up and cast him aside. It would give him something to hang on to and think about before he died. A final act of defiance against those who had conspired to destroy him. Maybe all was not lost after all... and perhaps his life hadn't been entirely wasted... if only they...

'But what else is there,' asked Heart, who had been listening but not saying much?

Hayden turned to Heart and smiled. 'How old was Rose Watson?'

'Twenty-five,' replied Heart, almost immediately realising why Hayden had asked the question.

'So, Drummond Cleaver could be her father?' said Hayden. Parish acknowledged the assumption. Hayden's health may have been failing, but his brain was still razor-sharp.

'That would also mean he was fucking his daughter and possibly murdered her,' suggested Hayden.

'Marshall!' exclaimed his wife from the kitchen.

'Sorry, dear,' he replied. 'My wife doesn't like me to curse in company. It's all right when we are alone, though,' he whispered quietly. 'Christ knows why. We don't have the vicar round for tea anymore. The Glundes ate him.' He pointed to the outside and smirked to himself at his little joke. Heart and Parish didn't laugh. 'That's motive; maybe she was going to expose him?'

'But why kill Janice?' asked Parish.

'Maybe she found out first,' suggested Hayden.

'Doesn't work for me somehow,' said Parish.

'I've known people murdered for a lot less,' said Hayden, coughing into his handkerchief again.

'So, where is he?' asked Parish.

'Don't know for sure. He worked in the pathology department for us, surprisingly. That's how the guys working in the DNA department found him. He hadn't been with us long.'

'How exactly did they find him?' asked Parish.

'Well, to avoid cross-contamination, the department kept a record of the DNA of everybody working there. They automatically eliminate those people if they turned up on any evidence they may have accidentally handled.'

'So, what you are saying is, anybody in the DNA department could murder someone. And if their name cropped up in the pathology lab, it would be automatically discounted?' asked Parish.

'Well, yes, sort of, but there are safeguards. There would have to be a good reason for their DNA turning up on the murder victim in the path lab, especially if the original DNA was taken from the crime scene. They do wear gloves and plastic suits, you know,' replied Hayden sarcastically, 'so it's highly improbable that a lab technician contaminated a body in the lab and then contaminated the same body at the crime scene. Lab technicians don't go to crime scenes.

The only person who normally turns up at both is the pathologist. When Cleaver disappeared during the investigation, they did another check. That was the same time I was suspended on the bribery charges, and then the file and all the DNA evidence from the station went missing. Somehow, the case got completely side-tracked and was lost in all the confusion.'

'So, you're still not sure he did any of this?'

'Well, I wasn't until I received an odd phone call from a woman about a week after Janice was murdered. She refused to identify herself. All she would say was she had been talking to Janice a few weeks earlier, and Janice had discovered something the police didn't know. Drummond Cleaver's DNA must have been switched to throw the police off the scent during Janice's original rape investigation. Then this DNA turned up on Janice's body, a minimal trace, but enough. So, I thought we were on to something.'

'I wonder who the woman was,' said Parish. 'Can you remember anything else she said?'

'Not much. As I remember, it was a relatively short conversation; she kept repeating the same phrase, *"It's in the DNA. Check the DNA. The answer's there."* Something like that. That's all I remember. Short and sweet. "The answer's there."'

'And nothing else?' asked Parish.

'I asked her how she knew; she just said, I'm a doctor; that's how I found out.' I asked her for a phone number, but she just hung up. I was a bit preoccupied with the bribery allegation at the time, so I had a few other things on my mind. But it confirmed what we had already worked out. So I made a note about the call but never took it any further as I was suspended the next day.'

'She could really help us,' said Parish.

Hayden agreed with a nod, 'I know.'

'Don't know how we'll find her after all this time,' said Heart.

'And there was no record of the phone call,' asked Parish, turning to Hayden in quiet desperation?

'I don't know, probably not now,' he coughed again. He was obviously becoming exhausted, 'after I was suspended, I never knew what happened to the investigation, only that it was shut down a few weeks later.'

Parish had a little more information than before but was still no closer to finding Drummond Cleaver. He noticed that the room had suddenly become much colder while they had been talking despite the wood fire crackling away in the hearth. On the mantle over the fireplace, Parish could see two red twelve-bore shotgun cartridges standing upright next to a photograph of a married couple. He presumed it was Grace and Marshall. Next to the wedding picture was another picture of a young man in a police uniform.

'That's our son Nathaniel. He was killed in the riots.'

'I'm sorry,' said Parish.

'Wasn't your fault,' replied Hayden tersely. 'You didn't start them.' He said it in a way that indicated he had someone in mind but didn't want to expand further. Hayden struggled to get to his feet and leant his shotgun against the wall before hobbling unsteadily over to Parish while holding out his hand. Parish stood up as Hayden drew closer.

In the light, he could see his skin was bluish in colour, almost cyanotic, like the mucous membrane of a jellyfish. The veins and finger bones were clear to see. Parish put his hand out to clasp Hayden's and gently shake it. The definitive gesture of trust and friendship and one of the last physical vestiges of civilisation and communication. One handshake overcomes all barriers.

'Look, I haven't got long for this world, but I'd be grateful if….' He coughed again and wheezed. Every breath was a struggle. He began whispering so Grace couldn't hear what he was saying. 'If you could sort out what happened to me, it would be greatly appreciated. We have a little money left, but I don't know how Grace will survive after I'm gone - when it runs out. The pension would have made a hell of a difference.' He looked Parish in the eye and smiled. 'Didn't take a bribe, never took a penny in my life I didn't earn honestly. Can you believe that?'

'I'll do what I can,' replied Parish. Heart took Marshall's hand and shook it gently. Their eyes met for the last time, and Parish and Heart made their way back to the front door, where Grace stood. Marshall settled back down in his chair and coughed once more.

'I'm sorry for being so abrupt when you knocked,' apologised Grace, 'we don't get a lot of visitors anymore, especially in the evening; we have to be so very careful. It's dangerous around here after dark.' She paused for a moment... 'Not much better during the day...' she quipped reluctantly, attempting a humorous aside.

She paused again and smiled, 'I always imagined we would end our lives together somewhere warm, somewhere safe after Marshall worked so hard all his life, but now, well....' Her voice trailed off. 'He's a good man, you know.' She went to open the front door. 'I do hope you find what you're looking for.'

'So, do I,' replied Parish, 'maybe then we can sort all this out.' Grace smiled in dignified resignation, and Parish shook her hand warmly. He vowed that one day he would return but said nothing to Grace in case he didn't manage it. This was not a moment for conveying false hope. The odds were still heavily stacked against them solving this case, and he knew it. Whatever the conspiracy was, it was holding firm.

Grace closed the door behind them, and they heard the heavy bolts slowly sliding across, securing the house for the night. Parish pulled his collar up; it had become bitterly cold and desolate outside. They settled back down into the car and drove away. Thinking quietly about what had been said, who to believe and what to do next.

Chapter 22

Parish arrived home late, well after 2 a.m. and tapped in his security code to open the front door. The house was still, very still. Inside, the skirting lights automatically phased in, emanating their soft blue glow across the hallway and into the living area. He thought back to Marshall and the egregious disparity between the two of them - despite both being policemen who had served their communities. It felt so very wrong.

He removed his jacket and threw it onto one of the armchairs. He was feeling tired, which was to be expected. Travelling back to Providence had taken the best part of three gruelling hours. Driving at night down unlit broken roads had taken its toll. He felt every pothole as it reverberated through his body and pounded the back of his head. Protton vehicles were not built for comfort.

He unclipped his shoulder holster, taking out the Smith and Wesson revolver before dropping the holster on the floor and collapsing on the sofa. He held the gun briefly before releasing the safety catch and putting the barrel to his temple. Slowly, he moved it up and down, caressing the slight indentation, closed his eyes and began thinking about where he could be. He could feel the tension building in his index finger, the tiny muscles tightening; the desire to increase the pressure and ease the pain was overwhelming. But his finger, seemingly governed by an unseen force, just glided slowly up and down the trigger, gently caressing the cold steel but unable to make that final leap into eternity.

Anibal Arias began to play 'Por Una Cabeza' on the sound system. Something deeply evocative about that simple, haunting melody always held him back. It transported him to a different time and place. He knew what it meant.

'You're late tonight, darling,' enquired Catherine as she descended the staircase. 'I've put some music on - thought you might be a little stressed.'

'How do you know that?' enquired Parish, sounding bemused and slightly intrigued.

'I just do. I can't explain. I just knew.'

Parish smiled... 'you won't believe the day I've had, running around the Ghettazone getting cold and damp and very depressed, and I don't think I smell too good either.'

Catherine smiled. 'I'll run you a bath if you want.'

'I'll have one later. I'd like to talk to you just for a while.'

'That sounds ominous,' said Catherine playfully.

'No, not at all. I just want to hear your voice. I can forget the world and all the crap in it when we're talking. That's what you do to me....'

'Would you like a drink?' she asked, smiling at his compliment.

'Uncle Jack on the rocks,' replied Parish. 'Thank you,'

'Coming up,' said Catherine, moving to the drink cabinet. 'I've heard it's not nice out there.'

'It's not,' he replied, looking at the floor and still thinking about what Drysdale had said. There was something he'd missed. It was there, in plain sight - Parish just couldn't see it. What was it, he wondered?

'So why were you there?' asked Catherine, casually breaking his train of thought.

'Looking for answers, always looking for answers.' Parish sounded weary.

'Did you find what you were looking for?' she asked. She placed the drink on the table and walked back towards the kitchen.

'Sort of,' he replied. He thought about what Grace had said as he left her house; almost the exact words...

'Tell me about it. Maybe I could help. I'll start on the dinner,' replied Catherine from the kitchen.

'Do you really want to know,' asked Parish? It's just the same old business.'

'Of course, I do,' replied Catherine. 'We share our problems, don't we?'

Parish lay back on the sofa and stretched his arms out along the back.

'Everything we have so far points towards this one man murdering our victim, maybe more, but we can't seem to find him or any trace of where he's been for ages. He doesn't appear to use a mobile phone or credit card, and nothing turns up on security scans. He's almost invisible, yet he's out there somewhere.'

'And that's why you went to the Ghettazone?'

'Yes.'

'So, tell me everything that happened,' said Catherine wistfully. She was still in the kitchen preparing dinner, and he couldn't see her face.

'It started out with a charmingly eccentric professor up in Deliverance. He has a box of tricks assembled from the remains of hundreds of computers blown up in the riots. And with this remarkable piece of equipment, he was able to confirm that the unknown DNA we had was from our elusive Mr Cleaver.'

'That was good news, then, wasn't it?' asked Catherine.

'Yes, it was,' replied Parish. 'Then we went to see a seriously demotivated Chief Superintendent at Guildford.

His workload mainly comprises collecting the bodies of hundreds of murder victims daily and arranging for their prompt disposal. Did you know they don't even bother to investigate murders out there anymore because they have so many?'

'No, no, I didn't,' replied Catherine, sounding genuinely surprised.

'That was an eye-opening experience, but he couldn't help us much. He did, however, steer us in the direction of a retired ex-policeman, a man called Marshall Hayden, and his wife Grace. This couple lived just outside Guildford. Marshall was investigating a murder three years ago, which is sort of connected to the current murder case we are investigating. But then, out of the blue, he was suddenly kicked out of the force on bribery and corruption charges.

Then, a large part of the case file disappeared a few days after he was sacked. All a little conveniently coincidental. Oh, and then he had this mysterious phone call from a woman just before he was sacked. She told him the answer was all to do with the DNA, but he never spoke to her again. So there, that's it. It feels like the circus has come to town, and I've been abducted to join as one of the idiot clowns. We're dancing around in the spotlight, and everybody's laughing at us because we can't see what's happening right in front of us. They can see us, and they can see what's in front of us, but we can't see them.'

'The thought of you and Russell dancing together? Now that does paint a disturbing picture,' commented Catherine, sticking her head around the corner of the door and giggling. She stood in the doorway and swirled around erotically for a few seconds to the tango music playing in the background before disappearing back into the kitchen.

'Not literally, darling,' said Parish. 'Anyway, his beard's too rough for intimate dancing....'

Catherine paused and smiled before continuing the conversation in a calm, inquisitorial tone, 'So who was this woman who spoke to Hayden?'

'Don't know, no record of the call, all the details have been lost, so no change there.'

'You could be just looking in the wrong places,' said Catherine. 'He's probably right in front of you, hiding in plain sight, but you just can't see him, probably because you're looking too hard.'

'Looking too hard,' repeated Parish. He thought about that for a few moments. 'Maybe you're right. You normally are. Maybe we are looking too hard. Anyway, enough about me. How was your day?'

'Same old thing, helping sick people get better and consoling those I can't,' replied Catherine.

'Almost as depressing as my job,' said Parish.

'We could always swap jobs,' suggested Catherine with a smile, 'but I'm not sure about your bedside manner. It's a big part of what we do, just talking to people, reassuring them when all hope seems to have gone. That's why I love doing the job.'

'So where does that come from?' asked Parish, ambling down a philosophical side road.

'What, the bedside manner,' asked Catherine, poking her head around the corner of the door again and smiling at him? He wasn't usually so interested.

'No, love! What I mean is, you love what you do, and you love me, and I love you, but where does that actually come from?' Catherine returned to the lounge and leaned against the doorway to the kitchen.

'It doesn't come from anywhere. It's just there. All you have to do is let yourself go, gently fall back into the wind, and it will find you. You can't search for it because you will never find it; it just happens.'

'Like death. That just happens,' said Parish prosaically and a little sadly.

'Yes, yes it does,' said Catherine. 'Tragically, that just happens as well.'

'How do you get over that? How do you get over losing somebody you've loved so much?'

'You don't. You think about it every day, for years sometimes, and then one day, you find you only think about it every other day. Then, one day, you realise you've gone a whole week and not thought about it, but nothing has changed. It's just slipped a little further back into the shadows, but it's still there; it's always there. It may not seem as clear and vivid as it once was, but it never disappears.'

'Catherine, I'm afraid,' said Parish, looking up, tears slowly running down his cheeks. 'I'm afraid that I'm never going to get past this. I need to find a way to hide it away, to make it not happen.'

Catherine wiped the tears away with her fingers and, holding his face with both hands, gently kissed him on his lips. Parish closed his eyes.

'You can't resect the fear, Mack. It's part of what happens. It will fade in time, like all the other sad things.'

'Not until I've found out why,' said Parish, clenching the gun. He felt so frustrated with life at times. The tears still rolled down his cheeks.

'Put it down, please, darling,' she said quietly. 'Would you like another drink?'

'Yes, that would be good.' Parish put the gun on the table, and Catherine went over to the drinks cabinet, poured another glass of bourbon on ice, and gave it to Parish.

'Where's Jade?' asked Parish.

'She's staying over with a friend tonight. I'm going over tomorrow night to pick her up.'

'What time? I thought we could go out for dinner?'

'About nine. Will you be in early?' asked Catherine.

'Hopefully. Where is Jade staying?' asked Parish idly.

'Over the other side of town, with Natasha from school.'

'Hmm,' replied Parish.

'But I'm also popping in to see Jenny,' said Catherine. Parish didn't recognise that name. 'I don't think you know her. She's an old friend from university. We've had coffee a few times over the last couple of months, but she rang me yesterday to say she urgently needed to see me, all a bit of a mystery. So I'll be killing two birds with one stone.'

That comment hurt Parish more than she would ever know. With that thought, he slowly fell asleep on the sofa, listening to Dinah Washington singing 'September in the Rain'.

Chapter 23

Parish arrived at the Yard at just after eight o'clock. He had awoken early that morning and didn't want to hang around the empty house with so much going on in his head. Heart greeted him as he entered his office, which surprised him a little, as he wasn't due in until ten.

'I thought we said ten?' said Parish.

'You did, but I knew you would be in early, so what the hell.'

'Coffee two sugars?' Heart offered Parish his cup.

'Thanks,' he smiled. Heart knew him too well. He went to the vending machine, dispensed another coffee, and sat opposite Parish's desk.

'So where to today,' asked Heart? Parish thought about last night, and a vision of dancing the tango with Heart sprang to mind. His smile unnerved Heart a little.

'Why are you smiling?' asked Russell.

'Oh, nothing, just something I remembered. I am allowed to smile, you know.'

Russell didn't reply but just shrugged suspiciously.

'I think we should go and see Mr Hawsley again. Can you ring his office and set up an appointment?' Heart scratched his neck and lifted the telephone receiver.

'I thought Drummond Cleaver was our number one suspect now?' said Heart.

'He is, but as we can't seem to find him, I thought we could have another chat with Hawsley. I know he's not telling us everything.'

'Does anybody,' replied Heart, sounding uncharacteristically cynical? Heart made the call to CSP headquarters and got straight through to Hawsley's secretary when he told them who he was. Obviously, Hawsley had instructed them to cooperate in any way they could.

'Eleven o'clock today,' muttered Heart, holding his hand over the mouthpiece. Parish nodded his agreement, looking a little surprised, as did Heart. He confirmed the time and replaced the receiver.

'He must be getting to like us,' said Heart.

'And why shouldn't he?' We're very likeable policemen,' replied Parish, sardonically looking at his watch. 'Look, I've just got to pop over to the techies' department. I'll meet you back here at ten, and we'll go over to see Mr Hawsley.'

They arrived at CSP headquarters just before eleven o'clock, passed through security, and made their way to the same front door as before. This time, the sergeant smiled and greeted them with a cheerful, if slightly servile, 'Good morning, gentleman,' before opening the door. They followed another security guard through the hall, where they were directed to the same lift as before. When they arrived at Hawsley's floor, the lift door opened. To their surprise, they were immediately confronted by a stunningly attractive woman smartly dressed in a pinstripe business suit, black high-heeled shoes, and strangely incongruous bouffant hair. She was also very tall, intimidatingly so, radiating confidence and lethal acuity from every pore. For some inexplicable reason, the woman immediately reminded Heart of an American country and western singer, but he couldn't recall which one. She greeted them with a generous but carefully contained smile.

All Heart could remember was that the singer always appeared to be a little top-heavy. Which seemed to be par for the genre, and she was in constant danger of toppling over. Whereas the paradigm of elegance standing before them most definitely was not. Many women inwardly aspire to this level of self-assurance but paradoxically despise others for displaying the same quality.

'Please follow me,' she requested politely and then almost appeared to swivel around on her heels like a dancer. With a slightly exaggerated hip movement, she led them slowly across the hallway into Hawsley's office. The door was already open, and she directed them to Hawsley's desk, where two chairs had been strategically placed. Hawsley rose to shake their hands and sat back down again. The woman sat down in a fourth chair to one side of the desk, facing Parish and Heart, and crossed her legs.

'My name is Olivia Makepeace... Ms.' She accentuated the title to enforce her singular credential, more as a badge of honour than a clarification of marital status. For some inexplicable reason, Heart immediately thought lesbian - any previous thoughts of her breaking into song instantly vanished.

'I am a lawyer representing Mr Hawsley, and I've been asked to attend this interview. May I see your warrant cards?' She was very precise in her manner, not someone to tangle with unnecessarily. Heart and Parish handed over their warrant cards. She took a few notes and passed them back.

'This isn't an interview,' corrected Heart. 'We just have a few questions regarding a murder enquiry. Mr Hawsley isn't under...'

'His correct title is Lord Protector Hawsley,' interrupted Ms Makepeace, making a note on her tablet precariously balanced on her knee.

'I believe he should be addressed accordingly in deference to that position.' She looked at the two of them for an acknowledgement of her point of protocol. Parish wondered what the note said.

'Lord Protector Hawsley,' said Heart, adopting a formal manner, 'is not a suspect. But of his own free volition, he confirmed that he was in the victim's apartment approximately the same time she was murdered.'

'Can you prove that?' Makepeace asked inflexibly while carefully inspecting her nail varnish for chips. Parish wasn't sure if she was just making noises to justify her undoubtedly exorbitant fee or whether she was just going through the motions for Hawsley's benefit.

'We don't have to. The Lord Protector has admitted being there,' replied Heart, sounding slightly bemused at what appeared to be a direct contradiction of an earlier unsolicited declaration by Hawsley.

'That remains to be seen,' said Makepeace. 'He may have been mistaken?'

'He wasn't,' replied Heart abruptly, looking slightly stunned at her declaration. 'We have a positive DNA air scan which perfectly matches his security DNA record.

During this lively badinage, Hawsley listened carefully to what was being said and smiled but never said a word. It reminded him of the satisfying pleasure medieval kings must have derived when sending their personal knights into jousting tournaments on their behalf. Usually, to settle minor squabbles. Meanwhile, they would sit back and enjoy the theatre of death played out before them while drinking a cup of tea…. And all without the threat of being maimed or killed.

'So, you do have proof, but it hasn't been independently verified,' asked Makepeace in a sceptical tone?

'No, but an independent lab would still have to access the main security database. That is the only record available.' replied Heart.

'We may have to consider carefully rechecking your DNA scans for integrity.' She made this statement with surprising intractability. There was obviously no doubt in her intention.

Parish immediately knew where she was coming from and where she was heading.

'So, what exactly are you saying?' asked Heart.

'There could be a mistake with your evidence,' replied Makepeace.

'So, you think the crime scene may have been unlawfully contaminated with Lord Protector Hawsley's airborne DNA?' asked Parish, with just a hint of disbelief.

Makepeace turned to Parish. 'It is a possibility. He is a high-profile, vulnerable politician with many enemies, many of whom might go to great lengths to discredit him.' She smiled discreetly. But with a subtle hint of condescension, bordering precariously on the edge of contempt.

'Yes, it's a possibility,' agreed Heart, 'except that Lord Protector Hawsley admitted he knew her and was there that night.'

'As I've said already, that remains to be seen,' replied Makepeace.

Heart was a little flummoxed by that assertion. 'Remains to be seen? What the hell does that mean,' he asked with palpable exasperation? Smart-arse lawyers with verbal diarrhoea are the bane of my life, thought Heart.

'Nothing is ever quite what it seems, Inspector,' replied Makepeace, as if her words had some deep philosophical meaning.

'Sergeant,' corrected Heart, smiling at the irony of her words. Makepeace slowly moved her surprisingly long forefinger. First pointing to Heart than Parish, then coming to the sudden realisation she had accidentally juxtaposed their ranks, something that happened all too frequently for Heart's liking.

'My apologies,' said Makepeace, smiling feebly at Parish. It was then that Parish noticed that beneath the ice-cold, calm, rock-hard exterior was an attractive woman with maybe just a little too much makeup for that time of day.

'Anyway,' said Heart. 'We didn't come here today to question Lord Protector Hawsley about his movements, but for any information he may be able to give us about a possible suspect – a Mr Drummond Cleaver.'

'Cleaver,' interrupted Hawsley, who up to that point had remained perfectly content to indulge his pet Rottweiler while she went on a mild rampage. 'So, how can I help you?' Makepeace looked at him with consternation, but Hawsley smiled back at her with casual indifference, which appeared to put her mind at ease. She was evidently not accustomed to clients speaking for themselves.

'Well, we understand you knew him?' asked Heart.

'Cleaver, yes, we both did,' replied Hawsley.

'Both?' queried Parish.

'Yes, Benny Maranno and I knew him from when we were at university. In fact, we joined the BNP together.

'Then what?' asked Heart

'When the party was elected, he became a minister in my government for a few years. After that, he headed up our security research establishments, which was up to about six years ago. Then, one day, he had some kind of breakdown, and after that, he was transferred to a less strenuous job, I believe. I don't know where... then we lost touch.'

'What did he do?' asked Heart?

'He's a chemist, the only one of us that finished university.'

'So, what did he do in this research establishment?' asked Parish.

'He headed up the team working on developing a harmless substitute for cocaine and cannabis. Part of our election manifesto was to eradicate the proliferation of illegal drugs and find a suitable safe alternative for addicts.'

'Like Benacane?' asked Heart

'That's hardly harmless,' replied Hawsley, 'but I believe it was along those lines.'

'But it is manufactured, not organic, isn't it?' said Heart.

'Yes, I believe it is, but Benacane has no legitimate medical use,' said Hawsley warily. 'I believe he was working on Panzanoid.'

'So how easy is that to manufacture?' asked Parish.

'I'm not a chemist, so I wouldn't know.'

'But wasn't something similar used during the riots to suppress the....' Parish stopped for a second to carefully consider what word to use. He landed on 'dissenters?'

Hawsley looked at Makepeace for guidance; almost imperceptibly, she shook her head. She glanced at Parish with an expression of mild admonishment for attempting to entice her client into some vague admission of association. She achieved this by doing little more than lowering her eyelids by a fraction of an inch. Her expression then slowly segued into a decorously subtle smile. Her mannerisms said so much more than her words. Parish always learnt far more from what people didn't say than they did.

'I don't know,' replied Hawsley innocently. 'Was it?' He knew that Parish knew little about the extremely sensitive tactics used during the troubled period. Any assumptions he might make would have to be based on nothing more than vague rumours and anecdotes. Parish was now delving into a giant black hole without any illumination, carefully feeling his way around the edges to avoid falling into an abyss.

'I have information that a drug remarkably similar to Benacane was used to pollute the water supply to the Ghettazone during the riots. Would that have been authorised from the highest level,' asked Parish? He looked at Hawsley for some sort of reaction, but none was forthcoming. It was clearly an indirect accusation against Hawsley.

'I have absolutely no idea,' said Hawsley, obviously caught a little off guard by Parish's mention of the drug but not showing it. 'Maybe it was a decision taken by the police and the military. An expedient measure to lessen the loss of life, possibly?'

'Maybe,' said Parish. He went quiet for a moment. 'So, you don't know where Cleaver went after he left you?'

'No idea,' said Hawsley.

'And he never contacted you during the last three years?'

'No, not that I can remember.'

'Didn't you find that a little odd?' asked Heart.

'I'm a busy man,' replied Hawsley. 'I can't spend my days speculating what happened to somebody I used to know. Wasting time on something like that would be a

414

gross dereliction of my responsibilities. Anyway, he never tried to contact me, so why should I bother taking time out looking for him?'

'But you were such good friends, and you all started together. And now here you are, Lord Protector of the country. And Benny Maranno's in charge of the Ministry for Distribution, Security and Transport, and the third member of this glorious triumvirate destined for such great office is....' He paused, hoping that the pregnant void would be filled by Hawsley. Conversation abhors a vacuum, a quirk of social behaviour that he had cultivated to his advantage on many occasions. But it didn't quite work on this one.

'Where?' asked Hawsley, seemingly interested. 'Where is he?'

'I don't know. That's the point,' said Parish. 'I thought you might.' Hawsley smiled.

'And yet,' Parish paused for a second, 'this phantom person managed to have sex with someone you knew within hours of you seeing her, and you never ran into each other.'

'No, I didn't. Strange, isn't it?' replied Hawsley. 'Maybe...' But Makepeace glanced at him, and he didn't proceed further. She knew the value of economy in conversation. Less said now, less to explain later.

'Yes, that's what I thought,' replied Parish.

There was little more they could do, so Parish decided to call it a day. He got up to leave, and Heart stood up to follow him.

'If you think of anything else, you will call us, won't you,' asked Heart? He handed Makepeace a card.

'Yes, of course, but I really don't think there is anything else I can add,' replied Makepeace. Parish nodded to Makepeace and turned to leave before turning back to make a final comment.

'I understand Cleaver worked in the police Pathology Department until three years ago.'

'Did he?' said Makepeace. Hawsley looked a little disturbed at that disclosure.

'Yes, we found that out by accident. Apparently, Cleaver was there during the Janice Watson murder case... in some capacity.'

'He was a very restless soul. But I didn't know that,' said Hawsley.

'Why should you?' said Parish. 'You have no need to concern yourself with trivial police matters, do you?' Hawsley didn't reply.

'If I come up with any more questions, is it okay to call round?'

'I look forward to it,' replied Hawsley. His expression betrayed nothing, but the consummate orator and manipulator almost appeared disappointed he couldn't talk more. Makepeace had managed to rein in any further outbreak of garrulousness.

'As long as you give us some warning, so I can be here too, Chief Inspector,' added Makepeace with pertinacious insistence.

'Just Inspector,' corrected Parish. 'Not been promoted yet.'

'I'm sorry, my mistake,' said Makepeace dismissively. 'Still, if you sort this out satisfactorily, you may receive something extra in your Christmas stocking you weren't expecting.' She smiled with a subtle trace of recklessness not evident up to that point - but Parish had no intention of reading anything more into her blatantly transparent gesture. He remembered what his mother once told him

416

about the *tangled web that people weave when first they practise to deceive.* It wasn't quite the same situation as here... but it was close, very, very...

'I'll ring you first,' said Parish as he left.

'You do that, Inspector,' replied Makepeace, smiling capriciously.

'I wonder what they're saying right now?' said Heart as he pressed the lift button.

'Probably just that,' replied Parish, smiling.

'Why did you mention Cleaver's job?' asked Heart.

'Just wanted to unnerve him a bit, see his reaction. I don't think he knew we knew that.'

'There isn't much he doesn't know,' added Heart.

'No, not much,' replied Parish thoughtfully.

Chapter 24

'We could revisit Maranno, rattle his cage,' suggested Heart. There was a hint of mischief in his voice. 'No doubt Hawsley will have rung him by now.'

Parish thought about Heart's suggestion for a moment and smiled. 'Ring the Yard to see if they can arrange an appointment. We'll sit here until they ring back. That should give Hawsley something to think about.'

'Can he see us,' asked Heart, who was unsure exactly how they were positioned geographically? Parish pointed up the Mall just through the main gates.

'Hawsley's favourite view, isn't it?' said Parish, referring to their previous meeting with Hawsley and his comments about the balcony and the ex-Royal Family. 'If we can see that - he can see us. I'm sure he's looking down at us right now, wondering why we're still sitting here.'

After about fifteen minutes, the Yard called back to say Mr. Maranno was in, and they could go straight there. Heart gave the onboard computer instructions for their destination, and the car moved out through the courtyard side entrance security gates. They arrived at Maranno's house about half an hour later and were greeted by the same security guard as before.

'Back again, lads.' He asked with contemptuous ambivalence while surreptitiously scratching his arse. He evidently had a problem, probably haemorrhoids, thought Heart from personal experience.

'Like a bad penny,' replied Heart, smiling.

'Bad penny,' queried the guard? He didn't appear to have heard the phrase before.

'Oh nothing, just a turn of....' But he didn't bother to complete the sentence. Inside, the doorman ushered them through the library into the atrium.

'He's watering his plants,' the doorman mumbled. 'He was terribly upset after you left last time. He has a very delicate disposition, you know?'

'Has he?' enquired Parish, displaying little interest in his welfare. 'Well, I'll try not to upset him, then.' He smiled economically as they made their way to the atrium. They couldn't see Maranno and stood for a few seconds to see if they could hear him moving around. Heart became impatient and shouted, 'Mr Maranno, it's the police.' There was no reply. They could hear nothing except the rustle of a breeze through the plants. There must have been a door open somewhere. Maranno suddenly appeared from behind a large palm tree, holding a watering can.

'No need to shout, officer. I'm just here looking after my orchids. They must be watered very sparingly, you know. Not too much, or they will drown, too little... and they wither and die.' He seemed to hang on to his last word for what appeared to be an inordinately long time.

'Is that so?' said Parish glibly. 'Bit like people then?'

'Very droll, Inspector,' replied Maranno, who carried on watering his flowers. 'Please take a seat.'

Benny gestured for them to sit down at his desk. Parish sat in a rather old, badly stained chair with a few small, ragged holes in the back.

So, what can I do for you gentleman, this time?' asked Maranno, but not with any conviction.

'Drummond Cleaver,' said Heart.

Benny stopped watering for a few seconds, then resumed. 'Cleaver. Yes, what about him?'

'We're trying to find him,' said Heart.

'Haven't seen him for years,' replied Maranno abruptly. He continued watering the plants.

'Strange, that,' said Parish, 'because he had sex with Dhalia probably about half an hour before you did on the night she died.' Maranno put the watering can down on a small, ornate Victorian table and turned to Parish.

'Did he indeed? Well, he can't be too far away then, can he?' He smiled scornfully at Parish, wandered over to his desk, and sat down.

'So, you haven't had any contact with him?' said Parish.

'No, I haven't,' Maranno replied.

'Despite being in the same building as him, at the same hour probably,' said Parish, 'visiting the same woman.'

'I don't know how we missed each other, but then Dhalia was always very discreet.'

'Was she?' said Parish.

'She was obviously more popular than I originally thought.' He didn't respond in quite the same way as the last time they had spoken to him about her.

'And you have no idea where Cleaver is?' said Parish.

'None at all, Inspector,' replied Benny.

'Could you call us if he does contact you,' asked Heart, handing him a card with his telephone number on it?

'Of course, Sergeant, but I don't think it's very likely, do you?' He smiled a little disturbingly.

'If you could,' said Heart, pointing at the card as they both got up to leave. Parish innocently ran his hand along the back of the old chair he had been sitting in. Maranno watched contemplatively, resisting the temptation to make some quip.

'Is that it?' asked Maranno.

'Yes, why?' replied Heart. 'Was there something else you had in mind?'

'No, not particularly,' replied Maranno, 'but you could have asked me those few questions on the phone.'

'It's not the questions that matter,' interrupted Parish. 'I already know the answers. I just wanted to see what your face said when you answered them, and anyway, we like to make that extra special effort, you know, that little personal touch with our inquiries.'

'Oh, I see,' said Maranno. 'And what did my face tell you?'

Parish gave just a hint of a smile and sauntered back towards Maranno with a fixed gaze as he did so. He stopped a few inches from Maranno's face, smiled and quietly muttered, 'That you are a fucking lying retard, and you probably killed or arranged for someone to kill Cleaver.'

The stunning display of invective caught Maranno completely by surprise. He immediately took a step backwards. His face started to change colour, much as before, and he started shaking with rage.

'How do you know that?' he shouted with sneering arrogance.

'Actually, I didn't,' replied Parish, smiling. 'Well, not until now, that is.'

'But you have nothing to prove that, do you?' said Maranno indignantly.

'Not yet, but we will find something,' replied Parish.

Maranno smiled and, looking past Parish, spoke to Heart. 'Oh, how did you get on with my alibi, Sergeant? You never said.'

'It checked out. Dhalia was alive and well when you were picked up,' confirmed Heart with an expression of disbelief.

'So, you won't be arresting me for that one, will you?' He gave Parish another supercilious smirk.

'Not yet, no,' answered Heart, 'but it's still early days.'

Maranno smiled. 'You really don't have a clue, do you?' he added disparagingly.

'We are fairly sure Mr Cleaver could help us with our enquiries,' said Parish.

'If he's alive, that is?' replied Maranno, unable to resist baiting Parish a little.

'If?' said Parish. 'Have you any reason to think he's not?'

'None at all. It's just that Cleaver appears to have disappeared. And with all the security and surveillance services watching us all the time, I'm just a little surprised that anyone could just dissolve into thin air. Maybe he doesn't want to be found; maybe he has gone on holiday.'

'Maybe,' replied Parish. They stared at each other, mordacious loathing versus clinical contempt, the latter just pulling ahead by a short head.

'Goodbye, Inspector,' said Maranno, grinning again, effectively ending their short conversation. They both started to leave.

'He knows much more than he's telling us,' said Heart.

'They both do,' replied Parish. 'Everybody does come to that. Getting them to tell us is going to be the trick.'

'Odd phrase to use, "dissolve into thin air," wasn't it? Asked Heart.

Parish glanced at Heart with a curious expression but didn't reply.

They drove back through heavy traffic, and Heart dropped Parish off at his house just after nine o'clock.

Chapter 25

Parish poured himself a large bourbon and water, dropped some ice cubes from the dispenser, and collapsed on the sofa. He had a headache, probably caused by all the unresolved issues running around in his brain and bumping into each other. Parish took out his handgun and put it on the table, something he always did when arriving home. He slowly pushed the gun barrel around the table with the whiskey glass, stopping every time the barrel pointed at him. He nudged the pistol again to set it spinning in his version of solitaire Russian roulette, but Catherine didn't materialise tonight. She appeared less and less these days. After another couple of glasses of bourbon, he fell asleep on the sofa. The thoughts of what he had seen and heard over the past few days continued swirling around in his head, still not making any sense.

Sometime later, he was awoken by the ringtone of his phone. He glanced at his watch, but his eyes were still blurry, and he couldn't focus on the dial. The only illumination in the room was the blue skirting lights, but this wasn't enough to see his watch. It felt like the middle of the night, of that much he was certain because everything was so quiet. He had a disgusting, acidy taste in his throat and a banging headache. He didn't feel that great. He wondered who the hell would be calling him at this time of night before cautiously pressing the speaker button on the mobile and scrabbling across to turn on the table lamp. The light brought reality abruptly back into focus. He squinted briefly while his eyes became accustomed to the brightness. It was ten past three in the morning.

'Hello,' he said cautiously. 'Who's that?'

'Inspector, is that you? It's Zac.' It was an odd question, thought Parish. The voice sounded strained, squeaky and slightly effeminate in the way that some men project when they become overly excited. It was as if he couldn't hear the words he was saying.

'Zac?' questioned Parish. The name didn't register immediately, and his mind started whirling around. 'Zac? Zac, who?'

'It's me, techie Zac,' replied Zac. There was a lot of noise in the background, possibly a nightclub, thought Parish and Zac did sound a little drunk, which might explain the squeakiness.

'Oh Zac, Christ, it's a bit late for you, isn't it? It's... It's after three in the morning. Are you still at work?' He knew he obviously wasn't and wondered why he had asked, but Parish's brain was still not fully functional.

'I'm not at work. I'm with some friends in a nightclub,' replied Zac.

'Oh, I see,' replied Parish, reaching for the whisky glass on the table. His throat felt parched. Only warm water was left in the glass, which must have been from the ice cubes that had now melted. It had a very distant hint of whisky, which tasted ghastly when diluted to that degree. He drank it anyway, replacing one unpleasant taste with another.

'I did try earlier, but there was no reply,' said Zac apologetically.

'I was asleep, I think,' said Parish.

'Sorry, didn't realise,' said Zac apologetically. There was something not quite right with the way he sounded.

'No problem,' replied Parish. His head was a little clearer now, but the headache remained. 'What can I do for you?' He was beginning to sound just a tiny bit more affable. He rubbed his eyes again.

'Well, I thought you would want to know this immediately,' he paused briefly. Parish could hear him talking to someone at the club - then he came back, 'I've checked out Dhalia's computer, and there's nothing on it to help you.'

'Oh,' replied Parish. Now sounding a little disappointed, having been woken up to be told that Zac had found precisely nothing. 'Surely that could have waited till the morning,' he was going to say, but Zac continued before he could get the words out of his mouth.

'But something else did turn up.'

'Oh,' said Parish, now trying to sound enthused as he wandered over to the drink's cabinet.

'Dhalia had been investigating her mother's disappearance about three years ago, and, well, this is the odd thing. Did you know that...' He paused for a few moments. Maybe this would have been better done face to face, but it was too late to stop now.

'That what?' asked Parish, who was becoming impatient. He would prefer to go back to sleep rather than have this conversation at this time of the morning, but... He leaned down to the bedside cabinet, took out an emergency bottle of bourbon and poured himself a drink. He needed something to take away the disagreeable taste of the water.

'Well, Catherine and Janni knew each other.'

'Catherine?' repeated Parish. 'Catherine, who?'

'Your wife Catherine... who died... I'm sorry, but... I think they knew each other....'

There was the distinct hum of a nightclub disco in the background, and Parish wondered whether, in his hazy

426

state of consciousness, he had misheard what Zac had just said, but he hadn't. Just the sound of her name sobered him up almost immediately, and his headache disappeared almost as fast. His eyes opened wide, his brain kicked into gear, and the wheels started turning.

'Janni?' queried Parish, wiping the sleepy dust from the corners of his eyes and taking another sip, 'who's Janni?'

'Janni, that's what Dhalia called her mum, Janice.'

'And Catherine?' asked Parish, trying to get his head around what Zac was saying. None of this seemed to make any sense. The puzzle pieces were flying around inside his head, totally confused, each trying to fit into the wrong place. 'She knew Catherine?'

'Yes,' replied Zac. 'That's what I think.'

'But how, why?'

'Well, they went to university together, so Catherine might have known something about Janice's rape. I think they may even have lived together in the same flat for a while. They probably talked about it. That's what girls do, talk about things.'

There was a direct implication that men didn't talk about things, not the things that mattered anyway. He was probably right. Zac communicated better with women than men; he slipped under the invisible alpha barriers and fraternised on equal terms with them.

'How do you know all this?'

'Dhalia kept a journal with all the information she had discovered since her mum disappeared. There were various references to her university days.'

'But I thought you said there was nothing on the laptop?'

'There wasn't, but she was a very clever girl, our Dhalia. She kept all the details in a notebook. You know, one of those things where you can tear pages out, throw them away, and put new pages in. It wasn't on her laptop at all, would you believe? She handwrote it with a fountain pen. So, all my amazing computer skills weren't a lot of use on this one.'

'Notebook!' exclaimed Parish.

'That's it,' said Zac. 'Haven't seen one of those for years, not until today, well yesterday.'

'So how did you know she had one?' said Parish.

'The powers of deduction, Holmes,' replied Zac.

'Just tell me, I'm tired,' said Parish. He was not in a good mood and was becoming a little frustrated at Zac's overly exuberant enthusiasm and misplaced theatricality in the middle of the night.

'Found a bottle of ink.'

'Ink?' repeated Parish. *Is that what he said? He* thought to himself? *Or am I just going mad?* It was the middle of the night, after all. Maybe all this was just some weird dream… But it wasn't.

'Yes, it's exceedingly rare these days,' confirmed Zac. 'Nobody would bother buying ink unless they had a reason. So I surmised there must be a fountain pen. And if there was a pen, which there was, but nobody noticed it except me, then maybe she used it. To write something down.'

The simple logic of Zac's explanation was a little unsettling. It was something Parish should have picked up on. Something he should have noticed much earlier. He wondered whether he was beginning to lose his edge.

'How did you know this?' asked Parish, who still had trouble absorbing this convoluted extrapolation. His mind was working overtime, evaluating what possible scenarios might exist if Catherine did know Janice.

'I went back to the apartment and found the book. It was there all the time, tucked in with all Dhalia's other books, hidden in plain sight, you might say....' Those words jarred for Parish. Hidden in plain sight. Hidden in plain sight. Where had he heard that before? It went over and over in his brain...

Zac continued, 'But nobody noticed it because nobody was looking for a book. We were all looking for information on laptops and mobiles.'

Parish's mind jumped back for a second.

'But she never mentioned Janice.' He couldn't recollect Catherine ever mentioning a Janice, and then the penny dropped.

'Oh, and there's a note about three years ago: "Mum meeting CM",' said Zac, but Parish didn't absorb that detail; he was still thinking about something else. 'I thought that might be...' continued Zac, but Parish interrupted.

'You said, Janni?' inquired Parish.

'Yes,' replied Zac.

'I do remember something about a Janni, but what?' He was racking his memory, but nothing immediately came to mind.

'Anyway, just thought it was a bit of a coincidence, and you should know about it immediately. For what it's worth, Catherine and Janice definitely knew each other.'

Parish thought about those last words. They stuck in his mind. Zac had found something relevant, but what did it mean?

'What was Catherine's maiden name?' asked Zac.

'Mandleton,' replied Parish curiously. 'Why?'

'CM,' said Zac. 'That could be Catherine, Catherine Mandleton?'

'Yes,' said Parish, 'it could be.' His head was spinning again. 'I appreciate this, Zac. Thanks for calling.'

'No problem. Sorry it was so late. Sorry to wake you.'

'That's OK. Oh, where's this book?' asked Parish.

'I've put it in an evidence bag and sent it to your office. It will be there in the morning. We've finished with it for forensics. Oh, the ink matches and Dhalia's prints are on the file and the fountain pen.'

'Okay, thanks.' Parish put the phone down and thought again about what Zac had said, then took another swig of bourbon. Janni. Janni Watson! He said her name repeatedly in his head; there was still something he had missed. Eventually, he fell back to sleep. At five o'clock in the morning, he woke with a start.

'It's over the other side of town, but I'm also popping in to see Jenny.' That was it. Catherine was going to pick Jade up on the night she died, but she was going to Jenny's first - but it wasn't Jenny, it was Janni. He had simply misheard what she said. He was just not paying attention. Catherine did not know, as she travelled through the night on the last journey she would ever make - that Janice had already been murdered a few days before. And that she was destined to die that night. Now, he knew something which nobody else knew. But was it relevant, and, more importantly, why had they been secretly meeting? Why had Catherine never mentioned Janice to him? And why had Catherine been going over to see her that night? Those seemingly disparate thoughts repeatedly turned over in his mind as he desperately tried to fall asleep again. But there was little chance of that.

Chapter 26

Parish arrived early at the Yard to read the notebook and reread all the information so far collated on the murder enquiry. Heart came in at nine with two coffees as usual.

'Morning, guv.'

'Morning, Sergeant,' mumbled Parish, deeply engrossed in what he was reading.

'Something unusual turned up last night.' Heart continued sipping his coffee.

'There's not a lot that's usual in this case,' said Heart glibly.

'Zac rang me at some ungodly hour to tell me about a notebook that Rose kept.' He threw it over to Heart, who only just caught it with one hand.

'It turns out that Catherine knew Janice Watson. In fact, they went to university together until Janice's mother died. That was when Janice had to drop out because there was nobody to look after Dhalia-Rose. According to the diary, Janice disappeared about three years ago before turning up dead in the Ghettazone. I've checked Barty this morning, but there is no record of her ever living in Providence. She seems to have been completely erased.'

'That's odd considering she worked in Hawsley's office,' mused Heart.

'We need to find out how that happened. I'll ask Zac to look into it. According to the diary, Rose was conducting her own investigation to determine what had happened to her mother. She knew she was the product of the rape, and according to this, she thought her mother was getting close to finding out who her father was. In fact, Janice had somehow acquired the DNA records from the rape incident. And had been hawking them around, trying to get somebody to check them against the police DNA computer. That could be the reason she was murdered.'

Heart stopped drinking his coffee and slowly sat down in his chair. The blood seemed to drain from his face. He had turned a peculiar shade of reddish grey, but Parish didn't notice.

'Does the diary mention who gave Janice the DNA file?' asked Heart sounding uncharacteristically sheepish.

'No, it doesn't. Why?'

'Well, that might have been helpful,' replied Heart, relieved.

'That's another job Zac could do. The trouble is, I don't think many records still exist from that period. Janice was incredibly fortunate to have acquired those DNA records.'

Parish looked up and noticed a distinct change in Heart's normally cheery disposition. 'You okay? You look like you've seen a ghost.'

'No, no, I'm fine. Just juggling the pieces around in my head to see how they might fit.'

'We may just have it all wrong,' said Parish. 'Try this...'

He got up and went to the incident screen, where Dhalia's name was top. He rubbed her name out and wrote Janice's in its place, then drew a line down to a new position where he put Rose. Sideways from Janice, he drew a line to the right, wrote Cleaver's name up, and then drew another line down and back across to Rose. Then, another line over the top from Cleaver to a new position where he drew in Catherine and Jade's names. Parish stood back and stared at the changes he had made on the board.

Heart was surprised to see Catherine's name now on the screen and waited for an explanation.

'They were working together to find out who raped Janice. We now know that much, and if, let's say, Cleaver found out that Janice was getting close to him and had some inside help, then maybe he panicked and killed her. And then somehow, he found out that Janice may have mentioned his name to Catherine, so he would have had to kill her as well.'

This was beginning to sound a bit fanciful for Heart. It was stretching credibility a bit thin. But he dared not say anything because it could be possible, especially with the information he had not told Parish. He would have to say something about the DNA file soon... but not yet.

'But she died in a car accident. I thought that was indisputable?' said Heart, cautiously prodding to find any possible weakness in Parish's theory.

'Maybe it wasn't?'

'But it was,' said Heart cautiously, not wishing to dwell too much on this emotive subject. A disturbing thought suddenly crossed his mind. By giving Janice the DNA file all those years ago, had he unintentionally handed her a death warrant and possibly condemned Catherine and Jade to death by proxy... Heart felt an icy shiver run down his back.

'But,' said Parish, deliberately taking his time to carefully think it through, 'what if somehow somebody had tampered with the matrix control system? Her car did cross over the electronic barrier into an oncoming juggernaut. They said then that it was a computer malfunction, but was it?'

He gazed at the incident screen with all its scribbled corrections and alterations. Heart could see Parish's back and neck muscles beginning to tense up. He was starting to feel the same tightening sensation in his stomach... but for a different reason. One that he'd dare not consider possible - but neither could he dismiss out of hand.

'All right,' said Heart, 'assuming that is what happened, then what you are also saying is Cleaver did all that. Then, he starts having sex with his own daughter, and then, three years later, he decides to murder her in some bizarre ritual. That's where I have a problem: why did he wait so long if all the witnesses were dead and the evidence was gone? Dhalia didn't have anything to go on.' Parish didn't say anything but continued to stare at the screen.

'It's there, but something is not right. Something is missing.' He continued glaring at the screen. 'Dhalia knew something, enough to get her killed.'

'Drummond Cleaver. That's all that's missing. He could explain everything if we could find him,' said Heart. 'I think Maranno or Hawsley have him hidden somewhere.'

Parish turned around and looked at him quizzically. 'Maybe you're right. Maybe they have him stashed away somewhere, or maybe he is just plain dead.'

Chapter 27

2023: *The morning sky was grey and overcast, and it was raining. The north wind raged in the Greek port of Aulis on a day like today, but not in the right direction for King Agamemnon as he waited to sail with a thousand ships to attack Troy. But the God Artemis was angry and would not send the southern wind, so they could not sail, and the warriors grew restless and angry, for they were eager to do battle.*

King Agamemnon had slain one of Artemis's beloved creatures, a wild hare, to feast upon, and now Artemis demanded payment before she would turn the wind: the sacrifice of Iphigenia, King Agamemnon's daughter.

On the appointed day, the king's warriors carried her and her hopes and dreams of a beautiful life to the temple of Artemis. For her father had told her that she was to marry Achilles. At the temple, she was bound shrieking to the altar, and all the soldiers looked down in shame as the priest pulled back her hair and laid bare her slender neck, and Agamemnon looked down upon his beautiful daughter who cried out...

'Why me? Father, why me? What have I done to deserve this?'

And he could not answer, for he was ashamed. He looked up to the heavens, searching for the gods, before plunging the dagger deep into his daughter's pure white throat. Her eyes watched him as the lifeblood spurted from her neck, splashing onto his robes. And he looked down in shame for the life of his virgin daughter had been taken, but he didn't curse the gods for the bargain had been made. As she passed into another world, the harsh northerly winds died, the southerly wind blew, and the ships sailed out of the port with billowing sails. Hoping for glory, but the sacrifice had been in vain. It took another ten years before Troy eventually fell, and then only by the subterfuge of hiding warriors in a wooden horse.

Janice Watson would never learn the whole story or understand the tragedy, for she had never read the Iliad.

~~

Janice awoke earlier than usual, feeling uncomfortably warm, damp, and tense. She always left the bedroom window slightly ajar to allow a breeze to flow through the room, but that had made no difference. She was soaked with sweat despite only wearing a sheer silk negligée, still clinging uncomfortably to her body.

Although she slept alone and had done so for many years, she still preferred to wear the more attractive night attire of a much younger woman. It made her feel sexy and confident about herself. The time would come soon enough when less than alluring flannelette two-piece shapeless pyjamas would inevitably become the sensible option, but not just yet.

All night, she had tossed and turned her febrile body as her mind subconsciously rearranged the fragments of information she had gathered so far. Carefully fitting them together in strange Picasso-esque patterns. But each one made no sense because she was being denied the vital missing pieces of the puzzle.

While she showered, she decided that today she would try to speak to Hawsley, share her thoughts and notions and ask him for help. As she sat at her dressing table gazing into the middle distance, she pondered over what she should say. Carefully, she began applying her makeup today with just a little extra attention to detail. She began formulating the questions she would need to ask and what information she would need to convey to him. Most of the crucial elements were in the old file on her dressing table. Careful preparation of the questions she needed to ask was critical. She assumed she would probably only have a limited period to explain why she was there and what she was hoping to achieve.

She dressed as usual in her dark blue business suit and blue Louboutins. The one extravagance she had allowed herself the previous Christmas and which she only wore on special occasions. This was one. She popped a piece of bread into the toaster and made black coffee. The toast popped up, and she buttered it, ate half, threw the rest in the waste bin, and walked out the door at eight-fifteen.

It would take her about thirty minutes to get to CSP headquarters from her flat in Bayswater. Probably a little longer today because it was raining. It always took a little longer in the rain; everything moved slightly slower, more circumspectly. Time was so important. From an early age, clocks and timepieces fascinated her. How they measured life in seconds and hours. Slowly ticking away from one point in time to another. With total disregard for all the consequences. She was intrigued as to how a man could build something that didn't require a battery or electricity and depended entirely on the controlled release of suppressed tension in a piece of high-tensile sprung steel to make it work.

Some of the people she knew worked similarly. Starting the morning thoroughly wound and… she did not know quite how to finish that thought - but her fascination with the technical accomplishment never waned.

It was for this reason she had collected many antique timepieces over the years, all of which she kept fully wound and synchronised. They were placed on various shelves and ledges around her apartment, each slowly ticking away her life's hours, minutes, and seconds until the tension had almost run out. Then, miraculously, she would revive them just in time before the ticking ceased. Even on holiday, she would arrange for a friend to come to her flat and wind the clocks. She agonised continually over this strange compulsive obsession - convincing herself, somewhat irrationally, that if, by chance, one day they were to stop, then...

Janice finished her work at lunchtime. She pulled her security card from the computer, opened her bag, and put the card into her purse alongside the old yellow file she had been carrying for days. She stood up - took one last sip from the lukewarm coffee on her desk, and then began the long journey to cover the short distance to Hawley's office on the fourth floor.

With some trepidation, she made her way slowly along the thickly carpeted, hushed corridors towards Aiden Hawsley's suite of offices. The furnishings on this floor differed from the utilitarian décor of the general administration area below. The opulent grandeur of a bygone era still existed, but only in the furniture and fittings. All other vestiges of the Windsor dynasty were gone.

The towering carved oak doors, silent guardians to every room, portals to the enclave of power, loomed ominously overhead, carefully scrutinising all those who passed below. They instilled a sense of reverence to the daily proceedings conducted in each dominion. At the central office door, she was met by a security guard who only gave her internal security badge a cursory glance. Then, surprisingly, she was ushered straight into Hawsley's outer offices without any questions being asked. She walked over to the secretary's desk in the centre of the room. The room was deserted, so she stood for a few anxious minutes, waiting for someone to appear. On the wall, she noticed a painting of the taking of Troy.

'Can I help you?' said an eloquent voice from the other side of the room. Janice turned to face a smartly dressed man who had just entered the room through another door. She thought she recognised him but strangely could not immediately place him.

'I wanted to make an appointment to....'

Hawsley interrupted, 'I'm sorry, but Suzanne had to leave early today. Is there anything I can help you with?' She realised she was speaking to Hawsley. Not quite as she had expected.

He was charming and self-possessed, with a soft, lilting voice. There was no hint of the arrogance she had previously been warned about. He was far more attractive in the flesh than his media pictures or even holavision appearances made him look. His skin was darker and tanned, possibly from a recent holiday. He smiled at her, and she suddenly felt the sensation of butterflies fluttering in her stomach.

'Well, yes, there is, but it's...' she took a short breath; she had forgotten to breathe for a moment and felt a bit heady. 'It is a bit complicated, and I don't know how to....' Hawsley held his hand up to stop her falling, realising she looked slightly uncomfortable and might faint, but she didn't.

'Come on through and sit down. Suzanne keeps this room far too hot for my liking.' He appeared very friendly, not what she had expected. He gently ushered her into his private kingdom. Not actually by touching her back, but by holding his hand just a few inches behind her, which, somehow, she could sense. He shut the door behind him and directed Janice to a chair, but she did not sit down immediately. This room was a lot cooler, and she felt her headiness begin to recede.

'I am so sorry,' mumbled Janice.

'Please don't apologise. Would you want a drink?'

'No, I am okay, thank you.'

'You're from research, aren't you?' Asked Hawsley, sounding genuinely interested and cleverly putting her mind at ease by referring to a neutral subject. He walked over to a filing cabinet and started to look for something.

'Yes. I'm surprised you know that,' replied Janice.

'I've seen you around the building. I do try to understand what everybody does if I can.' He turned and smiled chivalrously, 'and you have been mentioned a few times.' She smiled back, a little too coquettishly, she thought afterwards. He probably thought she was a gawky simpleton. He turned back to the filing cabinet.

'All good, I hope?' she replied, instantly wishing she hadn't asked. Questions like that have only one positive and one negative response – there is nothing in between. There is no middle ground in which to hide under the masquerade of polite diplomacy.

Her expression was noted by Hawsley, who, without a moment's hesitation, replied, 'Absolutely.' He knew the value of timing. Hawsley turned and smiled again to reassure her and beckoned her to sit down. 'I won't be a second. I'm just looking for something. Only Suzanne seems to know where anything is. Look, would you like a coffee or tea?'

'A coffee would be nice, thank you. No milk or sugar,' Janice added as an afterthought. Hawsley walked over to the coffee machine, placed a sachet in the top and closed the chute. The machine sprang into action and started making that curious hissing noise when percolating coffee. He turned back to face her.

'Please do take a seat.' She walked over to the chair he had pointed to but hesitated momentarily, unsure whether she should sit down before he did. He wasn't royalty and did not technically command the same propriety. But in her mind, his position and status more than made up for this distinction. He gestured with both hands for her to sit down. The coffee machine finished, and he brought the two cups over to the desk and sat down.

'Now, tell me how I can help you.' This wasn't quite how she had expected the meeting to proceed, and she began to imagine that she might, after all, make some headway in her quest for answers.

'It's to do with something that happened to me many years ago when I was only fourteen.'

'Don't know if I can be much help with something that happened so long ago, but I'll try.' He seemed genuinely concerned about a problem that was obviously troubling her.

'I went to a party at...' Hawsley picked up his coffee, took a sip and nodded for her to continue.

'And I was drugged by somebody and...' she hesitated. Janice had spoken to so few people about that night, except the police. Now, in the cold light of day, when the opportunity had arisen for her to recall the event, she found herself wanting. Janice was beginning to doubt whether it had ever really happened at all. Was it all perhaps a figment of her imagination conjured up out of her loneliness and insecurity? Suddenly, she was unsure. Was it just a puerile cry for attention that she had carried around for so many years and had unknowingly slowly embellished and transformed into something it was not? She became agitated, unsure whether she should continue, but the moment of indecision was taken out of her hands.

'You were raped?' Hawsley suggested, almost intuitively avoiding unnecessary prevarication and embarrassment. He spoke the words without any emotion or unnecessary inflection.

'Yes,' she replied, sounding a little stunned. Hawley's unambiguously accurate summation of the event sharply refocused her attention and instantly re-established her self-belief.

A cold chill ran down her spine, and the hairs on her body became alive and sensitive, but the moment quickly passed.

'It wasn't uncommon, as I remember. A little different now, though, I hope?' Hawsley posed this as a question, but she did not respond.

I was later told that I had been given some kind of drug in a drink, probably Rohypnol. I don't remember anything that happened, just waking up the next day at home still bleeding,' Janice looked down at the floor for a moment, embarrassed by her admission.

'I don't know how I got there, but the state of my clothes left little doubt in my mind about what had happened. My mother called the police, and they took me to the hospital, but they never found him, although they did find his DNA from my....'

'I understand,' Hawsley graciously interjected to avoid any further embarrassment.

'I just want to find out who he is.'

'But why now, after so long?' Hawsley appeared genuinely concerned.

'Various reasons... In just a few minutes, he changed my life completely and forever, and I never got over it. I have lived with it all these years, and now, I need to know what became of him. I want to know if what he did in those few minutes made any difference to him at all. Or did his life continue as if nothing had happened and nothing had changed?'

'You're not looking for justice or revenge?' queried Hawsley cautiously, presuming that maybe she was just looking for some sort of atonement from the man who raped her.

'Justice? What is justice,' replied Janice abrasively? 'Just another rich man's toy to control and destroy ordinary people and settle old scores?' She muttered the words in a cold, unfeeling tone. It was as if every trace of warmth and compassion had been sucked out of her soul.

'Like everything in this life, you only get what you can afford or are prepared to steal....' Hawsley was somewhat taken aback by her heartfelt yet scathingly vitriolic damnation of social inequality in the judicial system.

'No!' Janice continued, 'I'm looking for absolution for me... and the sacrament of reconciliation and contrition. I feel as if I have sinned - not he and my soul needs to feel there is some recompense – some reparation for what happened to me, and for this, I need to be able to face him just once and ask him why and then maybe....'

'Well, I don't know if I can help with that,' replied Hawsley, 'but I will try if I can. What about the police? Surely, they would help. Have you asked them to reopen the case?'

His kind demeanour and soft, reassuring tone put her further at ease. She felt she could trust him, and she could tell him everything, and, more importantly, he would listen. It was almost as if he were a priest, and this was her confessional... but it wasn't.

'That's the problem,' Janice was looking a little sheepish. 'You see, because the case was unresolved in 2002, they closed it, and after all the problems in 2014, the records disappeared along with so many other files.'

'Yes, that was a very disruptive period. I'm glad it's over, and things have settled down now,' replied Hawsley, sounding just a little sanctimonious. 'But of course, that means there is nothing for the police to work on. Even if I did ask them to have another look at it.'

'Well, actually, there is,' said Janice cautiously. 'I went back about five years after the attack to see one of the policemen who had helped on the case. I was nineteen by then, and he had been promoted to sergeant. I asked him if the case could be reopened, but he said that as nothing had changed, and there was no new evidence, it was unlikely that it ever would be, so I asked him if he could get me the police file.'

'What for?' asked Hawsley, now slightly more attentive. Janice's story was beginning to interest him on another level.

'Well, I didn't know, to be honest, but I thought if I had the file, then one day I might be able to hire a detective or somebody to look into it again as the police didn't seem that bothered anymore.'

'And?' asked Hawsley, now sounding intrigued. 'What happened?'

'He got it for me eventually, or part of it anyway.'

'Did he?' replied Hawsley tersely, surprised at the casual breach of police evidence convention.

'What did he actually give you?'

'Just the police DNA report.'

'The DNA report!' repeated Hawsley. 'You do realise that it was illegal.' He didn't say it as if he were reprimanding her, more in the tone of a piece of friendly advice, which encouraged her to divulge more. He even managed to smile.

'Yes, I know that now,' she replied quietly, 'but then it seemed as if nothing was ever going to be done, and I was clutching at anything that....'

'I understand,' interrupted Hawsley sympathetically. He took another sip of his coffee. 'Anyway, it happened long before my watch. So, I won't be doing anything about that little misdemeanour.' He smiled at her.

Janice relaxed a little more and smiled back. 'Thank you,' she muttered quietly.

Hawsley thought for a moment. 'That information could still be of assistance now as everybody's DNA is on the security system computer. However, a successful prosecution could now be severely jeopardised. Its integrity is flawed because of the controversial way the DNA evidence was obtained. It could be claimed in a court of law that it had been tampered with after leaving the police filing system. Of course, if the person lives outside a province, we probably won't have his DNA on record anyway.'

'But if I hadn't asked for it, it would have probably been destroyed,' replied Janice, desperately pleading a defence for her actions.

'Possibly,' nodded Hawsley, 'and I can understand your dilemma, but it still doesn't change the fact that I doubt very much whether it could be used as evidence in court now.'

'I was afraid you might say that. I had already been told the same thing by somebody else, but as I said, I only wanted to confront him now. That is all.'

Hawsley remained silent for a moment, thinking about what Janice had said. 'You say somebody has already told you there is not much chance of a prosecution,' replied Hawsley?

'I discussed it with an old uni friend, Cathy Parish. She is married to a police inspector, but she only confirmed what you said. I tried to get her to discuss it with her husband, even let me talk to him - but she said she would rather not unless there was no other alternative.'

'She gave you good advice,' replied Hawsley.

'And then she suggested that maybe there was somebody else….' She paused.

'There was?' asked Hawsley, intrigued by what Janice was saying.

'Yes… you,' she replied, looking slightly embarrassed.

'Me? Oh, I see,' replied Hawsley, surprised, 'But I don't know what I can do after all this time.'

'Can you help me have the DNA file checked out?' asked Janice cautiously. Hawsley did not answer immediately but mulled over the possible beneficial media coverage of helping solve a twenty-five-year-old rape case. He slowly rubbed his left temple in little circles with his forefinger as he thought about the request.

'Why not?' he eventually answered confidently. 'It's the least we can do to sort out a problem that the last administration couldn't. He smiled. 'Do you have the file?' he asked quietly.

'Yes.' Janice gingerly removed the crumpled, well-worn yellow file from her bag and handed it to Hawsley.'

There was a faint glimmer of hope in her eyes. At last, the possibility of finding the closure she had been seeking for so long. She also felt a tinge of embarrassment.

'I feel like a thief returning something they have stolen to its rightful owner?'

'Rightful owner,' queried Hawsley?

'Well, the file does belong to the police, and you are....'

'Oh, I see what you mean... yes.'

'You'll look into it for me?' she asked.

'Of course, I will. Leave it with me,' said Hawsley. 'I'll do what I can and let you know as soon as I have any results.' Janice got up and held out her hand to thank him. But he walked around the desk, pulled her towards him, and hugged her, which she found oddly uncomfortable, almost embarrassing. But she responded accordingly and then left his office. After leaving the room, Janice experienced an odd sensation, a metaphysical connection with Hawsley. She had never expected or felt it with anybody else except her mother.

After Janice left, Hawsley read the file, paying close attention to the minutiae. He extracted the single-sheet DNA report and gave it to one of his assistants. He requested that she take it to the police data centre and run it through the BART database. The following day, the assistant returned the DNA evidence results and placed them on Hawsley's desk. He was out of the office at the time.

When he returned, he did not immediately notice the file on his desk among all the other documents accumulated in just one day. Eventually, he cleared some

447

paperwork away and came across the file marked "HIGHLY CONFIDENTIAL DNA Report." He opened the file, and inside was the original yellow DNA file and a new report. He read the contents and then fell back into his chair. It was as if all the air had suddenly been sucked from his body. He sat there, not moving for three to four minutes, contemplating the ramifications of what he had just read. Then he picked up the telephone and asked the operator to put him through to Benny Maranno.

'I need to see you right now!' said Hawsley. Benny mumbled something by way of a lame excuse - but Aiden did not appear to hear what he said. He repeated his request more firmly as if speaking to a belligerent child.

'No, right now! It's important!' There was a real urgency in his tone, which slightly unnerved Benny. It was unlike Hawsley to be alarmed about anything, but that was precisely how he sounded today.

Hawsley slammed the receiver onto its cradle and walked across to the French doors leading out onto the balcony. For a few moments, he stood and gazed up the long, dark red road leading to the Republican Arch, just visible at the other end of the Mall.

Half an hour later, Benny arrived at CSP headquarters and went straight to Aiden's office. He walked straight in without knocking. Seldom did he knock when entering a room. Over the years, he had learnt many valuable things by arriving in mid-conversation at an unexpected moment. Today, however, the room was empty, apart from Aiden.

'Morning, Aiden,' said Benny chirpily, walking briskly over to the desk and sitting down. 'What's the problem?'

Hawsley did not reply but handed the DNA file to him. 'Read it! Now,' said Hawsley sharply.

'Oh fuck,' said Benny after a few minutes.

'Oh, fuck indeed,' replied Hawsley. 'So, what do we do?'

'I don't know,' replied Maranno. 'It's not my name in there.' Hawsley glared at him with incredulous, fiery contempt but said nothing at first. These days, he seldom acted hastily, and this was not the time to change the habits that had served him well for the last fifteen years. One rash, impulsive act in a lifetime was enough.

'No, it's my name, and that's my DNA on the rape report,' shouted Hawsley, 'and it's a match for my Artemis DNA file, and she could have been hawking this about to anyone for years. Christ, she even tried to show it to a police officer but didn't manage it, fortunately. Why the hell wasn't it destroyed with everything else?'

'I don't know. Where did you get it from,' asked Benny, cowering in his chair at the unexpected outpouring of vitriol from Hawsley? He began to see visions of everything suddenly unwinding rather badly.

'I was given it by one of my staff who asked me to look into her rape twenty-five years ago. The case was never solved. So, I had the DNA checked against the BART database to see if it could match the sample, and hey, presto, guess what... it's me, and I'm fucked.'

Maranno smiled at the bizarre irony of what Hawsley had just told him, but not so Hawsley could see it. That would have been more than his life was worth. 'So, where did she get this file from?' he inquired casually.

'A copper... who I'll have thrown into the sewers for the fucking rats to eat once I find him.'

Aiden was not a happy bunny, thought Maranno. 'What's his name?'

Hawsley looked at Maranno incredulously. 'I don't know his fucking name. It's been erased from the file she gave me. The little bastard wasn't that stupid.'

'Do we have any records going back that far?' asked Benny.

'No, not many, that's why it was lucky for her that she managed to acquire it....' he pointed at the file with a venomous glare. '...before the riots,' he emphasised the words for Benny's benefit, '...and the destruction of the old police files.'

'Well, it's hardly conclusive evidence,' replied Maranno, attempting to mollify Hawsley.

'Apart from the blindingly obvious, you mean,' replied Hawsley.

'Let me think about this for a moment,' replied Benny. 'All she actually has is a DNA file that matches your DNA?'

'But any reinvestigation into the incident could bring all our names up from the original rape enquiry. It wouldn't take someone long to work out that my DNA mysteriously matched the unknown suspect and that I had swapped my DNA for Cleaver's and then adjusted my DNA record to match.' Hawsley chose his words carefully.

'Burn it,' squawked Benny with a faginesque smirk.

'She's probably got another copy,' replied Hawsley with an expression of total disbelief at Benny's crass suggestion. 'She would have to be pretty stupid not to.'

'She brought it to you,' replied Benny imperiously, with a glance that seriously questioned the wisdom of her action.

'That wasn't particularly astute.'

'She thought I could help,' replied Hawsley, 'so if I destroy the file, she will know we had something to do with her....' Hawsley was strangely reluctant to finish the sentence.

'It was rape! And not "we",' exploded Benny defensively. 'That is what *you* did, Aiden. I had nothing to do with it. I knew it would come back to haunt you. Cleaver told you it would. I'm glad I had nothing to do with it.'

'Jumping ship already, you treacherous little fuckwit,' shouted Hawsley.

'No need to shout or call me names, just stating a fact,' replied Benny, who remained remarkably calm.

'I wasn't shouting,' replied Hawsley, trying to contain his rage.

'Whatever you say,' mumbled Benny.

'This isn't helping,' replied Hawsley after a few moments, now slightly calmer. 'If it gets out, we're all finished. Whether you indulged or not, you're tainted by association. Just remember that. If this becomes public knowledge, the whole bloody party will be over, and we'll all be swinging by our bollicks.

Benny flinched.

'This is all Cleaver's fault. He gave her the bloody drug in the first place,' said Hawsley, slamming his fist down on the desk and making his cup jump and splash cold coffee over some papers.

'But he didn't rape her,' replied Benny bluntly, endeavouring to ensure that the facts did not become blurred or muddled up with the fiction in Hawsley's mind. Keeping a clear mind and not panicking was essential at this critical juncture. 'Drummond covered up for you last time by giving a false DNA sample. Maybe he could do that again?'

Benny spoke quietly and was apparently thinking aloud, for he knew where this might lead. Usually, he would only prompt Hawsley with a vague suggestion and allow him to come to the obvious conclusion. The trick was all in the psychology as far as Benny was concerned.

'No, we need more than that this time,' said Hawsley, with a quiet menace that sent a chill down Maranno's spine.

'How is that going to work?' Benny did not sound particularly enthusiastic about that proposition.

'I don't know. Can't you think of something? You usually do?' replied Hawsley.

'We could just switch the DNA records again,' suggested Benny. Hawsley stood up and thought about that for a few minutes, pacing his office several times. He looked out onto the Mall and suddenly realised how beautiful it was. How everything he could see and everything he had achieved could so quickly be undone. All he had built could come tumbling down, all because of one fleeting moment of alcohol-induced madness. He could not allow that to happen. Surely, all the good he had done must count for something. It probably would, but not enough to save his position. That would become untenable if the truth were ever revealed. By his own decree, he would be sentenced to live out the rest of his days in the Ghettazone. At best, ostracised from society. At worst, he would be a target for anyone with a grudge for being sentenced to live there. That would be quite a few people.

'It worked last time,' implored Benny.

'Until now, that is,' retorted Hawsley, 'But this time, we have to do something more permanent.'

'So, what do you suggest?' asked Benny hesitantly.

'You can access Bart, can't you?' asked Hawsley.

'Yes,' replied Benny.

'So, you can switch the DNA records on Artemis?'

'Yes.'

'And you could wipe Cleaver's file?'

'That's no problem either, but why?' said Benny, unsure of the reasoning behind the suggestion.

'If my DNA is found anywhere, it will show up as belonging to somebody unknown. You will have to leave Balingo as it is. My air scans and retinal security scans are being read all the time. The only problem will be my Balingo DNA record won't match my Artemis DNA record, so if they carry out a cross-match it….'

Benny interrupted. 'Not a problem,' he said, smiling effusively.

'Not a problem?' asked Hawsley, mystified by Benny's sudden elation.

'They never cross-match DNA on the two computers.'

'They don't!' exclaimed Hawsley. 'Why not?'

'There's no need to. Artemis automatically uploads data to Balingo every day,' replied Benny.

'So that idea won't work?' asked Hawsley.

'Yes, it will,' replied Benny. 'You see, the upgrade file parameters specifically preclude any DNA changes. So, as long as we manually switch the DNA file on Balingo, any DNA you leave anywhere will always present as unknown on Artemis. Once I have deleted Cleaver's file. It will never be checked against Balingo because they will assume that Balingo has already been updated with the same information. That's part of the system's integrity to prevent police misuse and tampering.'

He smiled at the irony of the statement. 'Only the security service can check unknown DNA with Balingo, so unless you become involved in an attempt on your own life, that is a relatively unlikely scenario.' Benny smirked at that little quip, but Hawsley's expression didn't change.

'So, all we have left to deal with is Janice and Cleaver,' said Hawsley, who had settled down a little and was now thinking more rationally.

'Deal with,' queried Benny cautiously? Hawsley looked at Benny, and he knew what he meant.

'The only question is, how do we do that,' asked Hawsley almost rhetorically? He started to pace up and down the room.

'I could get someone to…' started Benny, but Hawsley put his finger to his lips and interrupted Benny before he could finish.

'We don't want to involve anybody else.' He thought about it for a few moments. 'We will have to do it ourselves.'

'I'm not sure about that,' mumbled Benny, visibly wavering a little. He was aware that radical action was necessary but had no desire to become intimately involved in the act of extreme physical violence. All his life, Benny had managed to avoid confrontational situations. Even as a choirboy in Wells Cathedral, where he had been repeatedly and sadistically sodomised by one of the priests, he had said nothing. Never once did he raise his hand in anguish, never once did he resist, a subconscious act of acquiescence, a surrender that would haunt him for the rest of his life. Had he attempted to repel his assailant just once with a simple token gesture of defiance, this would have lessened to some degree the burden of self-loathing that overwhelmed him so comprehensively at times of indecision. This was one of those times.

The thought of killing someone while you were close to them was abhorrent. So close that you could smell the body odour, the stench of urine, and loose excrement as they uncontrollably emptied their bowel and bladder. The realisation that they were suddenly struck incontinent by the thought of what was about to happen. This is what he feared most: the victim's terror. The condemned man standing on the trapdoor looking into the executioner's eyes, knowing that any second, he would pull the lever that would dispatch him to hell.

'Not going all squeamish on me, are you?' asked Hawsley.

'Either we destroy them, or they will destroy us.'

He looked at Benny for a reaction. So much more could be garnered from carefully studying people's reactions and how they moved - not just listening to them speak. The way they delivered the words was so often far more revealing than the narrative alone. If you read the signs, a tiny facial gesture, or the flicker of an eye, it could almost tell you what is not being said. Sometimes, he found people conveyed information when they were unaware they were doing it. He put this down to some prehistoric self-preservational instinct, something we were born with but didn't know we still had. Something controlled from deep inside our brains, way beyond the parameters of everyday human behaviour. It could be compared to receiving an unexpected electric shock. No one ever taught you to let go – it was an instinctive and spontaneous response to pain but controlled from where? Self-preservation was controlled by something. This was what Hawsley always looked for.

Animals, and to a lesser degree, humans, sense fear, but how did they do that, he wondered. Suddenly, he could smell the sweet tang of fear on Maranno.

'I'll deal with Janice,' said Hawsley in a matter-of-fact way, as if he was putting some rubbish in a dustbin. 'She already thinks I am helping her, so I can take her somewhere under the pretence of having found her rapist – which won't actually be a lie.' Hawsley thought that was quite amusing and smiled to himself. His expression and demeanour changed suddenly. 'You will have to deal with Cleaver.'

'How?' said Benny.

'I'm sure you'll think of a way,' said Hawsley, tapping the gun on his desk.

'What! Kill him?' exclaimed Benny.

'Yes, of course, you have to kill him. What were you expecting to do, take him to a fucking tea party, make him eat too much fruit cake and hope he dies of a heart attack?' Benny felt a little disorientated, shell-shocked by Hawsley's histrionic outburst. 'We can't have him wandering about with my DNA, can we? That would give the fucking game away, wouldn't it?' Hawsley spoke quietly and disparagingly, with an alarming sense of detachment.

'No, I suppose not,' replied Maranno, slowly coming to terms with what they would have to do but, more importantly, what he would have to do.

'So, yes. You will have to kill Cleaver.' It was so matter-of-fact for Hawsley, thought Benny, but then he was never one to hang about languorously on the sidelines waiting for something to happen.

'And Janice?' asked Benny, mindful of the lengths Aiden was apparently prepared to go to protect what he had.

'I can take her to the Ghettazone; she's bound to go along with that.'

'You still need to get that file off her if she has copied it,' said Benny, tidying up the details in his mind. 'I'm not happy about killing Cleaver. He has always been one of us.'

Hawsley looked at Benny but said nothing for a few seconds. This was all becoming very tiresome.

'Okay, you get rid of Janice. I'll deal with Drummond,' suggested Hawsley.

'What! Kill someone I've never met?' exclaimed Benny, who appeared to think that was far worse.

'Well, it's either that or someone you have met; it's your choice,' replied Hawsley. Benny didn't answer.

'Look, do you like your life with all your bloody orchids and nice houses, expensive wine and Cuban cigars,' asked Hawsley? The question seemed to hang listlessly in the air as if it didn't need an answer.

'Yes,' replied Benny eventually, in a reluctant murmur.

'Well, he's the one who is about to make it all disappear unless you can think of something else.' Benny thought about it for a few more moments, then somewhat unenthusiastically nodded in approval.

'So, we're agreed, you take Cleaver, and I deal with Janice.' Benny reluctantly nodded his head again, resigned to what he must do.

Benny stood up, and as he did, Hawsley crossed the room and stood in front of him, staring into his eyes. Benny felt a little anxious, unsure about what was about to happen - then Hawsley held out his arms, took hold of him and embraced him as tightly as if he were a long-lost brother. Benny was a little shocked by the uncharacteristic gesture of camaraderie. For some reason, he spontaneously hugged Hawsley back. It was an odd few moments in Benny's life. In fact, it was something Benny had never encountered before - a sense of comradeship.

He could feel tears in his eyes as the emotion overwhelmed him. He felt much stronger, inwardly reassured, loved even. Then, suddenly overwhelmed by the joyous sensation that everything was going to be okay, such was the confidence that Hawsley's words instilled.

'We can do this,' whispered Hawsley. 'Together, we can do this. I love you, Benny, my friend.' Hawsley pulled away and smiled again at Benny, who quickly wiped the tears away. Benny smiled back at Hawsley, turned, and left the room. Hawsley smiled as he went.

The phone rang on Janice's desk, and she picked up the receiver. It was a simple response that would change her life forever.

'Janice, Janice Watson?' said the voice quietly.

'Yes,' replied Janice cautiously.

'It's Aiden, Aiden Hawsley.' He purposely made himself sound obsequiously inconsequential, trivialising his position.

'We spoke the other...' But Janice interrupted him before he could finish,

'Yes,' replied Janice. 'Yes, we did.' She felt an anticipatory fluttering in her stomach. Could this be the news she had waited so long to hear?

'Can you come to my office at lunchtime today?' He phrased the request delicately, almost affectionately, carefully avoiding any hint of instruction.

'Yes, yes, of course, I can. Do you have some news,' Janice asked expectantly?

'I will tell you what we've found when I see you if that is okay?'

'Yes, yes, of course.' She was repeating herself and beginning to sound a little tense. She was possibly one step closer to finding out who had raped her but unsure how she should feel. Trepidation, exhilaration, panic, all these emotions raced through her mind, playing their part. But the worst feeling of all was fear - the fear of anticipation and resolution.

After so many years, she had almost come to terms with what had happened. But having a daughter whom she dearly loved - a direct consequence of the rape - left her forever confused about how she should feel.

'Don't say anything to anybody. Just come to my office, and I will explain what I learned. Can you come at, say, one o'clock?'

'Yes, one o'clock is fine,' she replied, replacing the receiver. The rest of the morning passed very slowly until the appointed hour when she made her way up to Hawsley's office. She knocked gently on the door, and Hawsley opened it.

'Come in, come in.' He ushered her to a chair by his desk and sat down opposite.

'I have found somebody who matches the DNA sample you gave me, but just to be certain, have you got the original report? I presume the one you gave me was a copy.'

'No, that was the original,' Janice replied, 'I never bothered to make a copy; I didn't see any reason to.' Hawsley smiled demurely, carefully hiding the elation and relief he felt inside.

'In that case, it definitely must be him. I can take you to where he lives. That, of course, is if you want me to take you.'

'Yes, of course, I do,' replied Janice effusively, suddenly overwhelmed by how fast matters had progressed in so short a time. After waiting patiently for so many years, the sudden realisation that, at last, she might meet him was beginning to sink in. The aphorism about cats and curiosity never crossed her mind.

'I suggest we observe him first, and then you can decide what to do. He lives in the Ghettazone, so it could be dangerous.'

'I'm not worried about that,' replied Janice, 'but what about you? Don't you have some kind of protection squad?'

'It's not a problem, but I don't want all my security people tagging along. They might frighten him off. We will have to do this without too much fuss. I will take one of the fleet cars and pick you up if that is convenient.'

'That's fine,' replied Janice, still a little overwhelmed by how helpful Hawsley was being.

'Say tomorrow at seven o'clock. We can meet at your house, yes,' asked Hawsley?

'Yes, seven is good,' said Janice. She stood up and leaned across to shake his hand. He stood up, took her hand, and she smiled. 'Thank you, thank you very much.'

Hawsley smiled. 'It's a pleasure to help. Till tomorrow then.'

'At seven,' she smiled and turned to leave. 'Oh,' she said, turning back. 'Do you know where I live?'

'Of course, I do,' he replied, smiling. 'It's on the system.... it knows everything....' Hawsley felt a slight twitch in his neck, and a flash of pain seared through his brain.

'Of course, it is, silly me.' She smiled again and left.

After a few minutes, Hawsley dialled Benny's number - Benny answered.

'We are leaving Providence around eight pm tomorrow night, so you must do it sometime after eight.' It was necessary to plan the exit carefully, as leaving a province was just as problematic as entering one if you didn't register on the security system.

The following evening, Hawsley arrived promptly at seven o'clock outside Janice's apartment block, and just as he pulled up, she came out of the main entrance door. She quickly made her way across to his car and got in.

'Hello, Mr Hawsley,' said Janice coyly, sounding awkward and unsure of herself. Almost any woman would probably feel much the same. Especially if they had made a secret rendezvous at night with the most powerful man in the land, someone they hardly knew, to travel to an unknown destination.

'Call me Aiden - that's absolutely fine - out of office,' he replied quietly. It sounded almost like a reprimand but with a pacifying smile, reassuringly softening the initially harsh inflection. He was unaccustomed to treading tentatively around anybody. Least of all, a woman - in his employ. But on this occasion, he was prepared to make an exception.

'We don't want strangers to know what we are doing, do we?' he whispered conspiratorially. He sensed she was feeling slightly hesitant, but the reassurance put her at ease. A smile flashed across her face, and she relaxed slightly as she settled into the passenger seat and put on her safety belt. She was suddenly aware of a frisson of excitement at the expectation of what might happen when they reached their destination.

461

'Thank you for doing this,' said Janice.

'It's the least I can do,' replied Aiden. Janice thought he sounded a little tense but put it down to the clandestine nature of their journey.

'How did you get away from your security people?'

'Oh, that's not too hard,' he replied. 'They're used to me not doing anything out of the ordinary. So, this is not something they would expect. They still think I'm at home with my feet up, watching the holavision and having a cup of hot cocoa. It's never really a problem getting away for an hour or two... if I really want to... if I need to.'

He added the last words almost as if he wanted Janice to know how easy it was to evade his protectors. He felt driven by an uncontrollable, self-destructive desire. The necessity to make a damming admission just to demonstrate how clever he was - to pierce his own pomposity. But that moment would have to wait; he knew that. He had to maintain control of his faculties for just a bit longer.

'Oh, I see,' said Janice, unaware of the gravity of that statement.

Aiden instructed the computer to go towards the security gate, which was nearly an hour away. He spoke little during the journey, appearing distracted. Janice presumed he was merely preoccupied with avoiding his security staff.

'I spoke to my friend Catherine today,' said Janice after a while, endeavouring to restart the conversation.

'About tonight?' replied Aiden a little abruptly.

'No, not about tonight. You said not to mention it to anybody, so I haven't. I just mentioned that I had some additional information about who the man who raped me might be, and I was checking it out. She is an old uni friend who has been very helpful. It was Catherine who suggested I spoke to you first before speaking to her husband.'

'Oh yes, I remember you telling me about her now. Didn't you say she was married to a police inspector?'

'Yes, that's right,' replied Janice, a little surprised that Hawsley had remembered that tiny detail. He was a last resort if I didn't get anywhere, but obviously, I don't need to speak to him now.' Aiden smiled but said nothing.

'You did it the right way round, Janice. We can sort this out without the police becoming involved.' Janice thought that was an odd thing to say.

'But they will become involved eventually, won't they?' she queried, slightly puzzled.

'If you want them to, of course, but you may change your mind once you've met him.'

'Oh, I see,' but she didn't. 'Does he know we're coming,' she asked?

'No, no, he doesn't. It will be a surprise.' Hawsley half smiled to himself, but Janice didn't notice.

They reached the security gate, and the eye scanner checked them both before releasing the barrier. Hawsley made a mental note to delete that security information from the system after he returned to Providence. They continued for another fifteen minutes before Hawsley took a slip road signposted for Winchester. The dazzling beams from the security searchlights that snaked out from the security towers were now just a faint afterglow in the night sky. The Atlas guidance system disengaged, giving the usual warnings, and Aiden took over manual control of the car. They continued towards Winchester on what Janice knew had to be an unmaintained road. As there was no street lighting, the only illumination came from the car's headlights.

Janice was a little surprised they had left the relative safety of the main highway, which was well-lit, to travel on this much rougher road. She presumed the person they were meeting must live off the beaten track.

'Does he live in the country?' she asked, indirectly querying the detour from the main road.

'I thought it best to stay off the main highway as it is closely monitored. It's a little longer this way but untrackable. The vehicle registration cameras might pick the car up. Before we knew it, one of my security teams would be flagging us down to escort us to wherever we were going, and we didn't want that to happen. Turning up anywhere with lots of flashing lights tends to alarm people. We don't want to warn him we are coming. We are in the Ghettazone now. It can be perilous at night out here,' said Aiden. 'And those guys can be a little overprotective at times.'

'I see what you mean,' said Janice, with some trepidation but reasonably mollified by the explanation.

'But you're okay. I will look after you,' reassured Aiden, glancing at her and smiling. 'We're quite safe as long as we don't attract attention.'

She smiled back. 'I know, thank you,' she replied.

Aiden drove on for another quarter of an hour before pulling over to the side of the road. 'I'm just going to stretch my legs for five minutes. It's a long journey.'

'I'll join you,' said Janice as she stepped out of the car. She preferred to stay with him rather than sit alone. Total darkness had descended now, and Aiden almost completely disappeared as he walked off ahead of her. Occasionally, the moon would come out from behind a cloud and cast a silver light on the deserted road as it twisted back into the darkness. Janice decided not to follow Aiden any further and stopped.

'It is a lovely night.' She had to raise her voice as she wasn't sure how far away he was. 'I miss being unable to go into this part of the country... as we used to... for picnics and things. During the day, of course.' She smiled to herself at her silly remark. She knew most people didn't have picnics in the dark, or did they.... She wasn't sure.

Her voice gently quivered with a tiny hint of tension, and she began rambling. This happened whenever she was a little scared. She hoped that Aiden would quickly return and they could resume their journey in the relative safety of the car. Then the clouds cleared from the moon, and she could see he had turned around and was making his way back.

'Where are you going?' he asked.

'Back to the car; it's too dark for me to see.'

'I understand,' he paused for a few moments. 'A lot of things have changed now, Janice,' said Hawsley. He was closer now, and she noticed a slight change in the pitch of his voice. He sounded sadder than before, as if he also missed those things. She could see him more clearly as he approached the car. That's when she noticed he was holding a gun.

'I didn't realise it was that dangerous out here,' she asked innocently.

'It is,' he said. Janice could just see his eyes in the moonlight, and they were looking straight at her. She became a little unnerved by his expression.

'What's the matter, Mr Hawsley?' She suddenly felt compelled to revert to a more formal title for some inexplicable reason.

'You can call me Aiden or Aid; either is okay,' said Hawsley.

'Aid,' she said cautiously, but he seemed slightly on edge. Maybe something was worrying him.

'I'm sorry about this, Janice,' said Hawsley. 'Really deeply sorry.'

'About what?' asked Janice, confused. 'Isn't he coming?'

'We're not going to meet anybody tonight. There is nobody here or anywhere come to that.'

'We're not...' she asked. 'But why not? Where is he? Why have we come this far if...? I don't understand why and....' The questions started piling up in her head, and for some reason, she couldn't get the right words together to finish a sentence. Everything was becoming a bit of a jumble.

'If there is no one here, what's the gun for?' But deep down in her stomach, she had a horrible feeling that she knew the answer.

'It's for you, Janice, for you,' he whispered while gazing down at her with a strange, bewildering expression.

'But why, what have I done?' She was baffled and confused, desperately trying to make sense of everything, but nothing made sense.

'You haven't done anything - that's the unfortunate thing. It's me. You're completely innocent of everything. You have done nothing, but I still have to kill you.'

'Kill me? Why?' Janice suddenly felt very cold. Nothing made any sense anymore. She could feel the sickening panic beginning to clutch at her stomach. She could feel a dampness between her legs and a cold shiver down her back; she was starting to shake.

'Because you know too much.'

'About what?' Exclaimed Janice, her voice now slightly raised as panic began to set in. She was desperate for some sort of explanation and was now visibly distressed. She could feel her legs tremble uncontrollably and suddenly felt very cold. 'What do I know too much about? I'm just a research assistant. I don't know anything.'

'Oh, but you do. The irony is that you just don't know what you know, but that doesn't change anything.'

'But I don't know anything!' exclaimed Janice. 'You're telling me I don't know what it is, I know, but I know something.' Janice suddenly realised how stupid the whole conversation sounded. It was turning into a bad comedy sketch full of riddles. She tried to laugh, but that wouldn't happen. She stopped talking, and her mind, spinning around in circles of sound and windmills of light, brought back flashing images of that night. She could suddenly hear something, something she had never remembered hearing before. Someone said something. What was it?

'Go on, Aid, give it to her.' It was as clear as day now. Why had she never remembered that until now? The long, dark memories buried so deep for so many years began to slowly surface, released from the darkness by the thought of imminent death.

'Go on, Aid, give it to her.' The words kept revolving in her brain in a montage of distorted memories, like the crazy mirrors at a funfair. Not again, she thought, not more suffering. I can't do that again…

She didn't have to. As the first shot punched into her chest, she collapsed, falling instantly to her knees. She felt no pain, just pressure and the inability to breathe correctly. She looked down and saw something seeping from her chest, forming a stain on her blouse. In the moonlight, it seemed to glisten like liquid silver. She put her hand on the stain, trying to stem the flow, but the blood continued seeping through her fingers. She felt weaker now and confused, unsure of what had just happened. Looking up at Hawsley, her eyes met his dark, soulless eyes looking down, devoid of emotion as he slowly levelled the revolver at her head.

She couldn't see him clearly as the moon was just behind his head, forming a strange halo-type effect. It gave him the bizarre appearance of a Russian religious icon - something she had once seen in a museum somewhere. But he wasn't religious, and he wasn't an icon either. He was just a rapist, and… *this can't be right, she thought - it can't be happening.* It wasn't fair, but life was seldom, if ever, fair.

'What did I do?' Pleaded Janice, every word now a muffled whisper as blood filled her lungs and began to gather in her throat. She started to choke as she tried to talk and breathe simultaneously.

'Nothing. I told you, it was me. I raped you, and this is my redemption. I am sorry.'

Janice didn't understand. 'You! But….' She tried to breathe again but couldn't. She still hadn't made the connection… then suddenly, it all clicked into place.

'Go on, Aid… Go on, Aid…' Aiden…Aiden Hawsley!

'I could have forgiven you… That is all I…' She gasped for air. 'All I wanted to do… all… Rose… daughter… Rose,' but the words would not come easily.

Hawsley looked at Janice on her knees, begging for her life, and realised what a pitiful person he had become. All this just to save himself. He felt utterly ashamed and slowly began to lower the gun.

'Please don't kill me... I want to live...' begged Janice. 'I want to grow old with my Rose... Our Rose... Our daughter. Please don't ki...

She never heard the second shot as the bullet smashed through her eye and shattered her brain instantly, blowing half her skull away. She died with her daughter's name on her lips.

Her body lurched back with the impact, and her expression of stunned bewilderment segued into one of serenity as death took control of her body. She slowly sank to the ground in a grotesque collage of body, blood, leaves, and silvery light and shadow. No longer did she need to concern herself with worldly trivia. The flames roared fiercely into the night as Hawsley drove away, and all the clocks in Janice's apartment stopped ticking.

The phone rang in Benny's office, and his secretary answered it, recognising the voice instantly.

'Lord Protector!' she exclaimed, listening carefully. 'He's right here,' she said after a few moments. She buzzed through to Maranno's office.

'It's the Lord Protector for you, Mr Maranno.' She passed the call through to Benny's office.

'Can you come up to see me? There's been a slight complication.'

'What?' asked Maranno.

'Not on the phone. Come to my office.'

'When?'

'Today would be good,' replied Hawsley. It wasn't a gracious suggestion. He kept the conversation short.

'I'll be there in half an hour,' said Maranno. He put the phone down, finished drinking his coffee, and mulled over what Hawsley could possibly be calling about. Reluctantly and not without some foreboding, he grabbed his coat, left the office, and drove hurriedly over to the CSP headquarters. He went straight up to the fourth floor but knocked before entering the room this time. He could see Hawsley sitting at his desk, talking on the telephone. Hawsley beckoned him over to sit down while he finished his conversation.

'How's the...?' Hawsley didn't finish the question but lifted an old paper file from his desk and waved it at Maranno.

'Going?'

'Gone,' replied Benny quietly. 'What about you?'

'She won't be coming back, so no need to worry.'

'Are you certain?' queried Benny.

'Quite certain,' replied Hawsley. 'What about Cleaver?'

'He's on gardening leave... permanently,' said Benny, grinning a little disturbingly while making a curious digging gesture. Strangely, there was no apparent evidence of his previous unwillingness to carry out his part of the plan. On the contrary, he now appeared imbued with calm confidence. Aiden's brotherly bonding gesture at their last meeting had transformed Benny's self-confidence beyond recognition. Hawsley almost admired him now and even managed half a smile.

'So, what's the problem?' asked Benny almost casually.

Hawsley's expression changed. 'There's somebody else we have to deal with,' Benny's expression changed.

'Oh, for fuck's sake, what now?' said Benny. His uncharacteristically cheerful disposition quickly segued into the resigned solemnity of his pre-hug period.

Aiden did not reply but put on his overcoat, scarf, and hat, walked over to the French doors, opened them, and gestured for Benny to come onto the balcony and join him.

Once Benny was outside, Aiden gently pushed the doors to, and they both stood gazing up the Mall as the snowflakes started to settle again. Benny began to shiver as a gust of freezing wind swept past the front of the palace, biting into everything it touched.

'I love this view,' said Hawsley. 'It inspires me. Do you know that?' Benny did not reply immediately; he was not in the mood for idle chit-chat. Hawsley looked at Benny for a response.

'It's magnificent,' replied Benny abruptly, but he wasn't interested. 'Why did you call me?' Benny felt a little edgy, impatient, and suddenly very cold.

'Janice spoke to a friend, Catherine Parish, and mentioned the DNA file. Apparently, they were going to do their own little freelance investigation if Janice's approach to me didn't work. This Catherine is married to a detective inspector. So, when she hears that Janice has disappeared, she may put two and two together and mention it to her husband, so we have to get rid of her quickly.'

'Christ, not another one. When will this stop?' exclaimed Benny.

Hawsley looked at Benny with expressionless disdain.

'It will stop just as soon as we have tidied up the last little problem,' replied Hawsley. He looked at Benny again, and Benny knew that he was expecting him to do something.

'Why me? This isn't my problem,' pleaded Benny.

'No, it is our problem, but I don't have the know-how to do anything.' He paused for just a moment before continuing. 'But you have.'

'Where does she live?' asked Maranno somewhat reluctantly. He knew he was in far too deep to walk away now.

'In Providence,' said Hawsley. 'I have her address.' He handed Benny a slip of paper; it was almost as if he was embarrassed by its content.

'Can you do something? can you help me?' Hawsley asked plaintively. It was at that moment that Benny noticed just how vulnerable Hawsley was. His voice had the uncharacteristic trace of weariness and bewilderment. It was almost a cry for empathy. This surprised Benny. He had never encountered the presence of compassion in Hawsley before today. He sounded drained and broken for the first time ever. It was like he had had enough and wanted it all to end.

Whether it was a clever emotional tactic by Hawsley or genuine remorse for all that had gone before, Benny couldn't tell. He would probably never know.

'Leave it with me. I'll sort it,' said Benny reluctantly. Hawsley was beginning to see his old friend in a different light.

Chapter 28

2026. The ping sounded, and Parish took the plastic dish out of the microwave, surveying, somewhat dispiritedly, the uninspiring lasagne al forno bubbling in front of him. He scooped it out of the container with a large green plastic spoon and placed it as best he could onto the plate, trying to maintain the original layered format, but he failed miserably. It collapsed into a pile of brownie-yellow goo. Parish sat at the small kitchen table and stared disconsolately at the plate and two empty chairs.

Suddenly, he did not feel hungry anymore. Parish picked up the glass of malt whisky he had carefully prepared with some ice cubes and just the right amount of water and took a swig. He leaned back in the chair and stared up at the ceiling as if looking for inspiration, and then his mobile rang. Had his prayer been answered? He looked at it briefly, deciding whether to ignore it. He didn't recognise the number. They would ring back later or leave a message if it were important. Seldom, if ever, did his mobile phone convey good news. But he answered anyway.... It was a habit.

'Parish?' asked the voice on the phone.

'Yes,' replied Parish, unable to place the voice immediately.

'It's Dinger, Dinger Grimes.' He spoke very quietly, not in the rumbustious tone that Parish had become accustomed to at their previous meetings.

'Professor, what can I do for you? Is everything all right? You sound...'

'My friend, I have to make an abject apology.' His manner had all the hallmarks of an act of earnest contrition.

'You do? Why?' asked Parish, indolently twirling a fork in the goo on his plate. He couldn't think of anything Dinger had to apologise for; he had been more than helpful.

'Well, I've discovered something which could mean everything I previously told you could be wrong; I may have completely misled you.'

Not good news, thought Parish. Should have known that was coming. For one fleeting second, he wondered whether Dinger had been got at but quickly discounted that possibility. He was a reasonable judge of character, and the professor never struck him as the kind of man who would readily succumb to threat or coercion. He inwardly scolded himself for even doubting his original opinion. It was becoming one of those cases where nothing and no one was quite what they seemed. That made him wary of relying too heavily on anything, whatever the provenance.

'Wrong?' enquired Parish gingerly. 'How do you mean wrong?'

'I'm sorry, but I don't think the DNA is from Drummond Cleaver after all.' There was silence for a few seconds as Parish absorbed what Dinger had just said.

'Not Drummond Cleaver... are you sure?'

'Yes.'

'Who was it then,' asked Parish, surprised and confused by the revelation? His mind began to race as the established facts and assumptions he had so carefully correlated and formulated into a reasonably workable theory slowly began to unravel, transitioning into an uncoordinated muddle of disjointed details and vague suppositions. The cohesive bond of rationality, the tenuous thread of commonality that ran through everything he knew and connected all the pieces, suddenly dissolved. Was he suddenly going to find himself back at the beginning, with just an unrelated assortment of lame what ifs and maybes?

'I'd rather not say on the phone, do you understand,' replied Dinger? Parish didn't, but there was a clear implication of caution in Dinger's tone, which did not require further explanation.

'So, what does that mean,' asked Parish? It was a rhetorical question, for he knew full well what it meant, and he realised afterwards that it was also pointless asking it.

'Can you come down to Deliverance again?' entreated Digby. 'I will explain everything.'

'Okay,' said Parish. He could sense Dinger's reluctance about going into further detail on the telephone. Parish had also noticed an uncharacteristic element of caution in his voice that was not evident at their last meeting. He couldn't remember the professor being anything other than gregariously extroverted and reassuringly confident. Whatever he had to tell Parish, he could not risk passing it over the network.

'I'll come tomorrow, around midday. Is that convenient,' asked Parish?

'That's good. I'll see you then. Thank you, goodbye.' Dinger hung up abruptly, and Parish touched the end call option on his mobile and placed it back on the table. He continued to play with the lasagne, wondering what could be so crucial for Dinger to summon him back to Deliverance. He messaged Heart, arranging to be picked up at nine o'clock the following day and advising him they were going back to see Professor Grimes.

After driving most of the morning, Parish and Heart arrived at the Data Centre building in Old Portsmouth, parking the car as before. They walked the last few yards to Professor Grimes's laboratory. Then they stood at the entrance for a moment, gazing up once more at the closing line on the sign over the door entrance:

> `But first, abandon hope.`
> `All ye who enter here.`
> `(just in case)`

Hopefully, that advice was not going to be too prophetic. Heart knocked on the laboratory door, and they heard the distinctive booming yet strangely comforting voice bellow again.

'Enter.' Heart felt sure the building shuddered.

Dinger met them just inside and warmly shook both their hands.

'Professor,' said Parish.

'Dinger, I still prefer that.' They smiled at each other. Digby didn't waste any time on pleasantries as they wandered back into the depths of the laboratory.

'Look, first, I have to apologise profusely for wasting your time with what I told you when you were last here and for dragging you all the way down here again, but... Well, let me try to explain.'

They followed him as he walked back to the middle of the laboratory, where the DNA air scanner was.

'You brought me two samples from two crime scenes, and they were the same person,' confirmed Dinger.

476

'Yes, Drummond Cleaver,' replied Parish.

'No!' replied Dinger slowly and deliberately. 'No, it's not.'

'It's not!' exclaimed Parish. 'So, there's been a mistake?

'Well, it's not exactly a mistake, but...' he paused momentarily while gathering his thoughts. 'There is no easy or quick explanation, so I will just explain the discrepancies and let you draw your own conclusions. It may make more sense to you,' Heart and Parish nodded.

'Any crime committed after the old criminal records computer was blown up was obviously not on the database I'm reconstructing.' He looked at Parish for an acknowledgement, and Parish nodded.

'So how did you come up with Drummond Cleaver,' asked Parish? Dinger indicated with his fingers, almost as if he were about to perform a magician's trick, that he needed to continue with the explanation.

'At the original rape enquiry, the police took DNA samples from everybody at the university and anybody who knew Janice. These were the obvious suspects.'

'Yes,' murmured Heart.

'Aiden Hawsley, Drummond Cleaver and Benny Maranno all gave samples because they had all worked with her in the BNP party headquarters on the night in question. But none matched the semen taken from Janice.'

'I'm with you so far,' said Parish, carefully absorbing every word.

'The sample you brought me last time from the semen sample found in Dhalia Vingali's virginal vault matched Drummond Cleaver's DNA from the sample taken at the Janice Watson rape.' He looked at Parish and Heart to ensure they were still with him.

'Yes,' said Parish. 'So, what's the problem?' Dinger smiled.

'There's no problem as such, but what the forensic people didn't do was cross-check the DNA samples to see if any of those matched.'

'Cross matched with whom?' asked Parish.

'With each other,' replied Dinger, now beaming with enthusiasm.

'Each other?' said Heart. 'Well, they wouldn't, would they? Why should they?'

'Why should they indeed?' repeated Dinger, nodding and acknowledging Heart's observation. 'But that's precisely what I did.'

'But why?' asked Heart.

'Just a hunch,' replied Dinger with a devilish air. 'Something just didn't seem quite right.'

'I still don't understand how you managed to locate the original DNA files. I thought they were supposed to be destroyed once a potential suspect is eliminated from an enquiry. That is the law,' said Parish.

Dinger's expression of naïve incredulity soon put Parish right on that misconception. Dinger's eyebrows arched like a McDonald's sign.

'What! You're telling me they aren't destroyed?' asked Parish, genuinely surprised by this revelation.

'Not as far as I am aware,' replied Dinger. 'They never were.'

'So, what did you find?' asked Parish.

'Two of them were identical.'

'But how? What were they, twin brothers?' asked Heart.

'No, they would still be different. Many similarities, but they are still easy to tell apart. No, it was the same sample,' clarified Dinger. 'Two people used the same blood sample.'

'Same sample?' asked Heart. 'So, what you are saying is....'

'Precisely,' replied Dinger. The penny dropped for Heart.

'So, which two of them was it?' asked Parish.

'Cleaver and...' Dinger paused for a second, realising the importance of what he was about to say... 'Hawsley.'

'Cleaver and Hawsley. So, was there a mix-up?' asked Parish.

'No, I don't think so. I believe that whichever one of them raped Janice persuaded the other to supply a sample under the pretence of being him. There was probably a lot of confusion at the time. Two men of similar age and build could be mistaken for each other if the person taking the samples didn't know them.'

'So, the police never had a chance?'

'Well, they were obviously close. But pulling a body switch was ingenious and very risky, but they, or should I say he, managed it somehow,' said Dinger.

'Wouldn't the nurse taking the DNA samples have asked for a passport or a driving licence – something to confirm identity,' asked Heart?

'Probably, but maybe he or she didn't look too closely at the photograph. They were probably taking hundreds of samples every day.

'So, we're still no better off. We can't find Cleaver, and we have no reason to ask Hawsley for a second DNA when we already have his air scan DNA sample, and that doesn't match.

'Well, yes, you are, actually,' replied Dinger.

'Why, what else have you got?' asked Parish, now intrigued.

'I've found another sample of the DNA, and it matches your suspect,' said Dinger, smiling with a calm assurance that belied his razor-edged insight. 'That should help you a bit,' he added as a casual afterthought. 'In fact, quite a bit.'

The joy of watching how one small, insignificant piece of information could make other people happy always gave him so much more pleasure than he would have ever derived personally from the discovery. He lived in a world where minor differences made interesting anomalies; they lived in a world where the same distinction could change people's lives.

'And?' said Parish, anxiously prompting Dinger to elaborate further.

'Well, there was a drunk driving offence in two thousand and five, and DNA was taken from the driver at the scene. He had his driving licence with him, so it's reasonable to assume it's the right DNA for that person.'

'So, his DNA had always been on the system. But if that is the case, why wasn't it cross-matched with the rape DNA. That was still an outstanding unsolved crime?'

'No idea on that one. It was just never processed, or it was simply missed.'

'So, the DNA from the drunken driving offence matches the Janice Watson rape DNA?'

'Yes,' replied Dinger.

'And it matches the semen DNA on Dhalia-Rose?' asked Parish.

'Yes.'

'And the baby that Rose was carrying?

'Yes.'

'So, the DNA is definitely from Rose's father?'

'Obviously.'

'So, who is it?' asked Heart, still unsure which one it was.

'Aiden Hawsley was the name on the driving offence report,' said Dinger, 'but if you run it through Artemis, it shows up as belonging to Drummond Cleaver.' Heart went quiet for a moment, not sure where that left them.

'So Hawsley must have switched his DNA on the computer systems more than once,' exclaimed Parish? Heart smiled to himself, suddenly realising what must have happened.

'So, it would appear,' said Dinger.

'So, we need to find Cleaver to prove what has happened,' said Parish.

'But he hasn't been seen or recorded anywhere for nearly three years.'

'Hawsley must have had him killed. Extremely dangerous to have him walking around,' said Heart mockingly, but Dinger and Parish didn't laugh. The realisation that, of course, Cleaver must be dead suddenly dawned on them all.

'So, all the DNA we have pointing to Cleaver actually belongs to Hawsley. Any samples we find will default back to Cleaver because the Artemis and Balingo system have the wrong DNA allocated to Hawsley. And that means that Hawsley can do what he likes and leave his DNA anywhere. And will always show up as belonging to Cleaver?'

'That's the way I see it,' said Dinger.

'And we can't change the data on Balingo to show the correct DNA ownership?' asked Parish.

'Can't be done. Nobody can change anything on the system. You can only add new information; you can't delete or alter anything existing. The option doesn't exist.

'But Hawsley did,' said Parish.

'Yes, he did, didn't he?' said Dinger, his eyes looking upwards through his bushy eyebrows. 'Probably the guy who wrote the program knows how to do it. They always leave a back door.'

'Who designed it?' asked Parish.

'Interesting question,' replied Dinger. 'A certain Mr Benny Maranno sanctioned the design team's budget.'

'Benny fucking Maranno,' mumbled Heart uncharacteristically. 'That's it. That's how he did it.'

'Maybe,' said Dinger, 'but proving that will be much harder.'

'Why can't we just get Hawsley to take another DNA test?' said Heart.

'Because even if you could prove that his DNA profile was the same as that on the victim's body, he would only argue that the computer has made a mistake. And somehow, had muddled up his profile with Cleavers. He will rely on Artemis as the ultimate arbiter of truth - and when it produces a report that states that Cleaver's DNA was on your victim, he's off the hook. You must remember that the Balingo system still indicates he was in the room according to the air scans, so he doesn't have to deny he was there. Their entire system had been corrupted to his advantage,' replied Dinger.

'So, he's virtually untouchable?' said Heart.

'Just about, unless you can get Maranno to say that he changed the records on Balingo. But if he does, then the integrity of the whole security system is thrown into jeopardy, and what chaos that would cause,' replied Dinger. 'He could still get away with it.'

'The only way I can see that we can crack this is to speak to Cleaver. That way, we can prove his DNA is not the DNA on our victim's body?' suggested Parish.

'So, how will you do that,' asked Dinger rhetorically.

'Unfortunately, the most likely way is through a medium,' mumbled Heart drolly.

Neither Parish nor Dinger said anything to contradict Heart's suggestion.

'We could appeal to Hawsley's sense of justice and integrity and ask him to confess?' suggested Heart after a few moments of strained silence. But the expression of stunned disbelief from Dinger and Parish quickly put that notion to the sword.

'We definitely need to find Cleaver,' replied Parish. But even he was beginning to doubt the probability of that happening.

'I'm sorry I got it all wrong the first time around,' said Dinger.

'No apology needed,' said Parish. 'You didn't have a chance, not with what he'd been doing. It wouldn't have made a lot of difference anyway. It would have taken a little longer, but I think we're on our way now, thanks to what you told us. At least we know which direction we're going.'

'I hope so,' said Dinger. 'I do hope so.' They all shook hands, and Heart and Parish left to start the long drive back to Providence. They arrived after midnight, and Heart dropped Parish off at home and drove off into the night. Parish fumbled around for his security tag and opened the front door. The blue skirting lights came on automatically. He shut the door and punched in the code to the alarm system, which beeped three times. He took his coat and hat off, dropped them on a chair in the hall, entered the lounge, and collapsed on the sofa. He stretched out his arms on both sides, took a deep breath, looked skywards, and prayed for inspiration.

Chapter 29
The last day

It was raining outside and still bitterly cold, but Parish hardly noticed it as he drove into the old palace. His mind struggled to arrange all his assumptions, suppositions, and conclusions into a cohesive narrative - a compelling argument that could effectively withstand a robust challenge. It was a gamble, showing all his cards simultaneously, but one he had to take as the disparate parts of his speculative theory were too flimsy on their own. He was lining all his ducks up at a shooting gallery to pick them off one at a time, in the correct order. But some of the ducks were missing, some were going the wrong way, and some weren't even ducks. And now he had one extra duck to play with, but he didn't know where it was… And more importantly, this duck had a smoking gun. If all else failed, he would just have to wing it and hope he got lucky. Parish smiled at the unintentional pun.

He had rung earlier and asked for an appointment with Hawsley alone, and somewhat surprisingly, his request had been granted. He arrived at Hawsley's office and gently knocked. Hawsley answered the door.

'Good morning, Inspector, come in, come in.' Hawsley waved his hand in a nonsensical flourish, welcoming Parish into his office.

'Good morning, Lord Protector,' replied Parish. 'Thank you for seeing me at such short notice.'

'Always ready to assist the police,' replied Hawsley, 'the eternal invigilators of law and order.'

Parish detected a slight hint of cynicism but nothing he could actually put his finger on. 'You weren't wired, so

I'm advised?' (*The security guards had been particularly rigorous when he arrived that morning. This was a little unusual as he had already handed over his weapon before being searched. Now he knew why*).

'No. Why should I be?' asked Parish, sounding surprised but to a carefully measured degree.

'No reason. I was just intrigued, Inspector. You said you were coming alone and specifically asked me not to bring my....' He paused for a moment and smiled at Parish. He was obviously amused by something that had just crossed his mind.

'Pet, so I just wondered what you were after.'

'I'm not after anything,' said Parish. 'May I?' He pointed at the chair in front of Hawsley's desk. Hawsley nodded, and Parish sat down. Hawsley walked round to the other side and sat in the chair opposite.

'I have actually come to give you something,' said Parish.

'Have you indeed?' said Hawsley. 'And what, pray tell me, is the nature of this gift you have brought me? I'm intrigued.'

'The opportunity to make a final act of contrition,' replied Parish. It was a high-risk strategy; if he got it wrong, his career would probably be over... or worse.

'I didn't know you were a priest,' said Hawsley with a derisory smirk.

'I'm not, well, not in the strictly secular sense of the word. It's more the... penitential dimension that I'm interested in,' replied Parish, 'the act of atonement....'

'I'm not sure that's something I need,' replied Hawsley wryly while lifting a bottle of scotch and two glasses from his desk drawer. He placed the glasses on the desk and unscrewed the whiskey bottle. He looked at Parish, smiled, and waggled the bottle at him. 'I have this for my moments of absolution.'

Parish nodded imperturbably; Hawsley poured more whiskey in both glasses and half-smiled. Every movement by them now deliberately measured, contained, and carefully controlled, neither wishing to expose any sign of weakness. The stealth and cunning of the lion as it stalks its prey before the kill. Which, in a way, it was, except neither of them was quite sure who was who?

'I'm not supposed to drink on duty,' said Parish.

'I'm running the country, and I have a drink when I'm "on duty", replied Hawsley, almost admonishing him for his probity, 'join me... please?'

Parish picked up the glass, and they clinked them together.

'Happy Days,' said Hawsley, swallowing the contents.

Parish smiled, took a tiny sip, but said nothing. He could feel his body becoming tense and his throat becoming dryer. He hesitated momentarily to pace himself, collect all his thoughts together - and take a deep breath.

'I think you killed Dhalia Vingali... and I've worked out how you did it.'

He had said it; it was now out in the open. All he had to do now was wait for a reaction and the inevitable fallout, but there wasn't any. Hawsley stayed remarkably calm and began pouring more whisky into the two tumblers, not looking at Parish but carefully concentrating on not spilling a drop.

'Have you?' replied Hawsley, smiling, not hesitating for a moment until both glasses were half full. He stopped, put the bottle on the table, and glanced at Parish.

'You look... apprehensive, Inspector. I think you had better have this.' He pushed the glass back towards Parish, then leaned back in his chair and took a sip from his. Parish lifted his glass took another large swig of the warm liquor, and the dryness in his throat almost immediately disappeared. He placed the glass back down on the desk.

Hawsley looked at the glass he was holding and swirled the golden liquid around before holding it up like an offering to heaven as if it were the elixir of life. 'Sixty years matured in an oak barrel. About the only thing the Scots are any good at. Fucking useless at football. I would have finished them off at Culloden if I'd had anything to do with it, but if we'd put them all to the sword, we wouldn't be drinking this now, so...' He took another sip. 'So, temperate mercy reaps temperate rewards, but not often....'

Parish wasn't sure what he was referring to. Hawsley put his glass down and looked up with an icy stare that unnervingly seemed to focus just behind Parish's head. He leaned forward on his desk, clasped his hands together under his chin, refocused his eyes on Parish and, with quiet deliberation, asked,

'Do you believe in God, Inspector?'

The question took Parish by surprise. 'A God... possibly, but I've never thought that much about it. Why?' It seemed irrelevant to what they were discussing and where they were going.

'You should think about it. It's an intrinsic part of making any decision,' said Hawsley. 'As you lie on your death bed, croaking out those last groans and grunts of life. As those last moments are slowing ebbing away, and you haven't the strength to breathe in the air you so desperately need to hang on for just a little longer, well, it's not an ideal time to be indecisive. You should already know the answers to all the important questions, or you will leave this world in mental turmoil... Do you believe in being merciful?'

'That's not up to me to say. That's for the Courts and God to decide,' replied Parish prosaically, subtly attempting to divert the conversation away from the philosophical and down a more pedestrian pathway.

'The Courts of Justice?' said Hawsley, smiling and sounding surprised. 'But you can't prove anything.' He leaned back and took another sip of whisky.

'I think I can,' replied Parish. Hawsley looked up at the ceiling but didn't answer immediately.

'I'm not a bad person,' he looked back at Parish reflectively. 'It's not easy doing all this, you know.' He waved his arms around the room in a sort of biblical gesture. Parish thought it pretentious but said nothing. 'What was it that Cromwell said? *"Uneasy lies the head that wears the crown." I know how he felt. I don't sleep well.*'

'Shakespeare, actually. *Henry IV*' corrected Parish. It was one of the few quotes where he knew the source. 'And I don't sleep much either, not for the last three years anyway, not since....' but he didn't finish.

'Shakespeare was it?' replied Hawsley, ignoring Parish's last comment. 'Oh well, whatever. So, what have you worked out, Inspector? Please enlighten me.' Hawsley smiled again, unnerving Parish a little.

'How you did it and why.'

'I'm all ears,' said Hawsley, lying back in his chair, looking remarkably calm. 'Please continue. I've always wanted to experience an epiphany. Maybe this is it.'

'Well, let me tell you what I think,' said Parish quietly. He spoke with a steely confidence that was growing stronger by the minute. He would leave the biblical rhetoric to Hawsley.

'Back in 2001, you and Cleaver and Maranno were at a party somewhere celebrating something. I don't know what precisely; maybe it has something to do with the old BNP. Anyway, one of your helpers was a young girl, only fourteen years old, who returned to your office. She had been conscientiously working for you, handing out pamphlets or making the tea all day, something like that. And because you found her attractive, you decided to take her out and get her drunk. During the evening, one of you, probably Cleaver, spiked her drink with a drug concoction, probably some variant of Rohypnol. He was training to become a chemist and knew about those things. That would be a real benefit to you years later. Anyway, it worked, and when she was entirely out of it, you took her somewhere, probably your hotel, where you brutally raped her. I did think it might have been all three of you at first.' Parish paused for a moment to take another sip of whisky.

'She didn't remember anything about what happened, and she obviously didn't remember you despite coming to work for you years later. So how am I doing so far?' asked Parish.

'You can't prove any of that. It's all supposition.' replied Hawsley, listening attentively to Parish while sipping his whisky.

'I think I could, but we will return to that later. Let me continue.' Hawsley gave Parish a half smile and waved his hand nonchalantly as if urging him to get on with it as he was in a hurry to be elsewhere.

Parish took no notice. 'After the rape, you took this fourteen-year-old girl out in your car and dumped her somewhere, and the next day, the police found her wandering around still drugged and took her to the hospital. There, they determined she had been raped, so they took some vaginal swabs and found semen and the DNA of the rapist. Then, the police conducted a mass DNA test on everybody who knew Janice. But you were cleverer than that; somehow, you managed to persuade somebody, who we now know was Drummond Cleaver, to give two samples, the second one pretending to be you. That's why they never traced the rape to you. Maranno's DNA never came up on the mass DNA test because he didn't join in for some reason. It was just you. Am I correct so far?' Hawsley chuckled, not indicating whether he agreed or disagreed and continued listening.

'Of course, when they checked your sample, it didn't match, so you were in the clear. You got away with it, for the time being, anyway. But this girl you raped had a child nine months later, a daughter. Did you know that?' Hawsley did not respond.

'Janice Watson was the name of the girl you raped, and she built a rapport with one of the constables on the rape enquiry. He kept her informed about how matters were progressing – or not, as the police got nowhere. The case was eventually filed as unsolved. After a few years had passed, Janice went back to see that police officer, and she asked him to do something for her. Do you know what that was?'

'No idea. Please enlighten me,' said Hawsley.

'Well, she asked this impressionable young constable if, as they had all but closed the case, he could obtain a copy of her assailant's DNA record on the premise that she could look into it herself sometime in the future. This constable wasn't very keen on this at first, but she persuaded him, and he managed to acquire the report and gave it to her. Unbeknown to that constable and Janice, that simple deed, foolish maybe, illegal definitely, and professionally irresponsible, would eventually cost the lives of six people, including hers.' Hawsley's expression began to change as parts of the puzzle that had so far evaded him began to fall into place

'By the way, Rose Watson, or Dhalia Vingali as you knew her, was pregnant. Did you know that?' Hawsley didn't respond, so Parish continued.

'The pathologist analysed the unborn baby's DNA, and do you know what he found?'

'No idea. Surprise me, Inspector,' replied Hawsley with a jaded expression.

'There was a familial link with whoever raped her mother, so you murdered your daughter and granddaughter as well...' Hawsley didn't respond. 'Incidentally, that constable who was so helpful was eventually promoted. He's now a Sergeant, Sergeant Heart, in fact. He probably remained a sergeant all these years because he cared about the victims and got too emotionally involved. You had the wrong man when you framed Chief Superintendent Marshall Hayden.'

Parish stood up, wandered over to the French doors and gazed up the Mall.

'So what else do you have to support this ridiculous story, Inspector?' asked Hawsley. 'I hate to slay a beautiful theory, but the simple ugly truth is, you have no evidence, which is a fact. It all sounds just a bit too far-fetched. Legally speaking, circumstantial and inadmissible in a court.'

'I do have a little more,' continued Parish. 'Everything went quiet after the rape, for thirteen years to be precise. But you still knew your DNA was in an unsolved rape file out there, somewhere, waiting to destroy you. The second you make a mistake, and your DNA is taken and checked against CRO records, up would pop a match with the unsolved rape DNA and bingo, career over. Which wouldn't have mattered much had it not been for your serendipitous good fortune in being elected leader of the BNP in 2009.

Then, would you believe it? In 2014, your party, now cleverly rebranded as the Christian Socialist Party, which in hindsight was probably a bit fanciful, won the general election. You are suddenly elevated to the highest position of power in your newly created hierarchy as Lord Protector of the United Republic of Great Britain? But now, that irritating little problem from the past is a much bigger problem for you. A nasty skeleton dangling quietly, precariously in the cupboard, was now beginning to rattle on the door. The one little detail that could finish your career.' Parish made a swishing gesture with his hand and smiled, his confidence returning. He walked back over to the desk and sat down.

'So, what do you do about this problem? Well, you promoted Benny to Head of Internal Security and Logistics. Then you concoct a plan to get him to switch your computer DNA record with somebody else, and who did you choose? Well, there was only ever one dispensable person, Drummond Cleaver. It worked for you the last time, didn't it, so why not again? That was it, you thought; problem solved. And if a problem did turn up, it would look like Cleaver. In the clear, you thought, but of course, the weakness was still Cleaver. With him walking about, he could easily ruin your clever little plan one day. Any day, in fact, just by making a simple mistake. You can't allow that to happen, so he must disappear, but you put it off. It's not urgent, not right now, anyway. So, you leave it for a while... for years.'

'Still sounds like a fairy tale,' sneered Hawsley. 'I can't see a lot of evidence, and it still looks like a happy ending for me.'

'No, I agree, and you have been fortunate,' replied Parish. 'Incredibly so.'

'Fortune favours the brave, Inspector,' said Hawsley with a leisurely air of arrogance.

'You have definitely been fortunate. I'll give you that. You had another bit of luck in 2014. That was when the protesters found out you intended to throw all convicted criminals, social welfare claimants, the unemployed and various other religious groups out of the new provinces after the walls were finished. They started rioting and blew up the Criminal Record Office computers to try and disrupt your plans, but you had already printed out the list of people who would be expelled. Your secret police already had their names, so that was a waste of time. But what a stroke of luck that the DNA record of the rape was gone. So you were doubly in the clear – except that you didn't know that Janice still had her paper copy of the investigation file with your DNA.

Then, in two thousand and fifteen, when the province walls had been completed, and you initiated the Balingo security system, your DNA had to go on the new system. But that wasn't a problem as this was all new, and there were no old records to refer to. And anyway, your DNA file on Artemis comes up as unknown because you've had the Cleaver file erased. So, whenever you leave your DNA somewhere, it flags up as unidentifiable. Cleaver is still a threat; he could ruin everything if his DNA turned up by accident, so you will have to do something about him, but still, there's no rush, so you do nothing.'

'That's all hypothetical, and it doesn't prove anything,' interrupted Hawsley. He finished his whiskey and carefully placed the glass on his desk. 'I think you're pissing in the wind, and it's blowing back in your face.'

'There is more,'

'Oh, well, do go on. I'm intrigued, if a little unimpressed. I was told you were clever!'

'Not clever, just stubborn. I don't like to fail.'

Hawsley smiled. 'Neither do I, Detective, neither do I.'

'Then things started to unravel when one of your employees, Janice Watson, came to see you one day in 2023 and told you her story. Then, she gave you a DNA record to check against the Artemis database. You got your people to check out the DNA, but they must have checked it against the Balingo system instead, and hey presto, your name popped up as a match. So, once you were over the shock of realising who she was and what she could do, you had to make some quick plans. So, you told her some story, took her out into the Ghettazone, shot her in the head, and then set fire to her body.

You betrayed her for the last time. Then, just to ensure you had covered your tracks, you or Benny killed Drummond Cleaver in case another copy of that DNA file was floating around. This would ensure his DNA never turned up anywhere. It would have appeared very odd if one sample perfectly matched two people. We already had your air scan evidence to prove you were there, so the Cleaver/Hawsley DNA would make it conclusive. How am I doing?' asked Parish.

'More Scotch?' asked Hawsley, glancing up at Parish. Parish nodded. 'I'm becoming quite excited. Haven't had someone read me a fairy story since my dear old mum died. All sounds very Grimm to me.' Parish half-smiled at the pun, more out of sympathy than anything else. Hawsley poured more whisky into Parish's glass.

'I hope it has a happy ending.' Hawsley actually appeared to be enjoying this exposition. Parish thought that a little strange but continued...

'Then, of course, there was the other problem. During your chat with Janice, she mentioned that she had talked about her rape and the DNA file to an old friend she went to university with. So that was someone else who knew too much and someone else you would have to get rid. So you asked Maranno to help. He was now in charge of the AMG system and security so he could orchestrate an accident in which the woman Janice spoke to would be killed. Unfortunately, the woman had her daughter in the car at the time arranged, so they were both killed.

Parish paused for a moment. He could feel something deeply unpleasant in the pit of his stomach. For a moment, he thought he would be sick, but it passed.

That didn't worry you too much – just a little unfortunate. But... finally, you thought you would be in the clear. You had tied up all the loose ends.' Hawsley became a little subdued and took another sip of his whiskey. He went to say something but then changed his mind.

'That woman, Catherine... who you somehow had killed in a car crash, was my wife, and the girl with her was my daughter Jade, and you had them crushed to death to protect yourself.' Parish appeared devoid of any emotion as he made the accusation. It was as if he were

496

talking about two people he didn't know... casual acquaintances.

'There wasn't enough on their bodies left to fill a shoebox, did you know that?'

Hawsley winced, shutting his eyes for a second.

'That was an accident,' said Hawsley quietly, but he knew it wasn't. His bravado was slowly being replaced by contemplative resignation as his hand slowly slipped into the top drawer of his desk. He drew out a revolver and laid it on the top. Parish didn't react quite how Hawsley expected. He just continued to talk, occasionally glancing at the gun but not really taking any notice. It posed no threat to him, for Parish had stared at his own gun many times before with envy. This was always the final exit route from the living hell he endured every single day, but the path from which Catherine always pulled him back. The gun held no fear for him, only release and deliverance. He almost wished Hawsley would have the guts to use it, for he had nothing to lose.

Parish continued. 'Then, three years later, would you believe it? You have been having sex with high-class prostitute Dhalia Vingali for some years. You and Benny that is, which I thought was very chummy. Then, one day, she lets slip that her mother used to work in your office and was murdered in two thousand and twenty-three. You can't believe it; you have been having sex with your own daughter. This thing just won't ever go away, and in a fit of carefully controlled, frenzied rage, you arrange to meet her at her house one night and feed her Benacane, your drug of choice by now. While she is drugged and unable to resist your demands, you get her to kneel naked in front of you. Of course, she agrees, and then you probably tell her what you were going to do, and she probably understands, but she can't do anything about it because of the drug's effect on her. Then, while she smiles helplessly up at you, her father, unable to fully comprehend what is about to happen, you beheaded her with the samurai sword.

'That's the bit I still didn't quite understand: the humiliation thing. But you even planned that very carefully. You knew your security people had installed the air scan system in Dhalia's bedroom to protect you. But of course, had it been working, it would have destroyed the air scan evidence you needed to be found after you murdered her. You knew you were in the clear anyway, so sometime before you killed her, you disconnected the system. That way, the techies' air scan equipment would throw up Drummond's DNA, which was, in fact, yours, and of course, that of all her other clients that night, including Maranno. Ironically, you needed that system to fail to protect you, and that's what confused me for a long time.'

Hawsley took another sip of his whisky and topped up his glass. He offered more to Parish, but he refused.

'Surely that must be the end, you think. What is there left? Well, there is something, and this is the good news. Dhalia gave you AIDS, and you will die horribly, hopefully in excruciating pain. Probably not in prison, but that won't make any difference. You see, Dhalia knew you did it, and she knew you would probably get away with it. That's why she's killing you by proxy first.'

'How did you...?' Hawsley didn't finish.

'Janice gave Dhalia a note before you took her to see the man who had supposedly raped her. All it said was that you were taking her to meet the man who raped her. We found the note.'

'Where?' asked Hawsley.

'Does it matter? We found it. That's all you have to worry about.'

'So Dhalia had worked it all out, but she didn't just want to kill you. No, that would have been far too easy and much too quick; she wanted much more. She wanted you to endure months of pain and agony and have plenty of time to reflect on what you had done. So, she went to her doctor friend and asked him what would be the most efficient way to pass on the AIDS virus to you and be certain you wouldn't recover. And he told her that anal sex was virtually guaranteed, as it invariably causes tiny fissures in the penis and the anus, facilitating the free transfer of body fluids. So, do you know what she did?'

'No, surprise me,' said Hawsley.

She persuaded her doctor friend to inject her with a highly virulent strain of a full-blown HIV virus, one that wouldn't respond to drugs. Probably paid him an enormous fee for that. That's what he was doing for her. Not trying to help her get rid of it but infecting her – and all for you. Then she had as much sex with you as she could stomach, and I bet she made you sodomise her. It probably became very demanding: lots of body fluids going back and forth, I would imagine, even some bleeding, which was absolutely essential, of course.'

The expression on Hawsley's face confirmed that Parish wasn't far from the truth. 'And then when she was sure she had infected you, and there was nothing you could do about it, Dhalia told you what she had done....'

'The fucking bitch actually laughed at me,' whispered Hawsley. 'She just laughed and told me I was going to die, and there was nothing I could do.'

'Well, of course she did,' said Parish. 'You raped and killed her mother. She was sure of that, and she was

carrying your baby. Well, there was no way she was taking
that full term, but she probably didn't think you would kill
her as well. There was no point, but she didn't care. She
was dying anyway. One way or another, she was taking
you with her on the road to oblivion. No wonder she was
laughing - she'd picked her battle well, and in the end,
she'd beaten you.

I do have a couple of questions, though, two things I
couldn't work out,' continued Parish.

'What?' said Hawsley, still surprisingly subdued.

'You were on the way to the airport, so how did you get
back to Dhalia's?'

'That's for you to figure out. You're the clever one,'
said Hawsley. He held his finger up and waggled it about.

'Okay,' said Parish. 'The samurai sword. Why that?'

'I'd always fancied beheading somebody I knew. I had
been practising for a long time for that,' said Hawsley
without any expression.

'So that's why it was so neat?' said Parish.

'It was, wasn't it? I was quite proud of that one."
Parish looked stunned as Hawsley's expression became
more demented.

'What did you practice on?' asked Parish out of
curiosity.

'Not what, Inspector, who?'

'Who, then?' said Parish, unsure what he was about to
hear.

'On those fucking Glundes. I've been popping out in
my car, giving them some "Bene", and chopping a few
heads off whenever I got bored. That's all they're good
for. They're just bloody vermin. The more I killed, the
better it would be, and the better I became at it.' Parish had

trouble absorbing this detail; he hadn't gotten quite that far.

'You're completely mad,' retorted Parish.

'Mad!' exclaimed Hawsley. 'What? For making The United Republic of Britain a safer place to live? That's not insanity - that's evolution.' The irony of his words was not lost on Parish, but it seemed to have entirely bypassed Hawsley.

'I still think you're insane.'

'Am I?' said Hawsley. 'Does it really matter? You still can't prove any of this.'

'I think I can - in fact, I have. But it doesn't matter, does it? You are going to die anyway. That's all that matters. We went to see Professor Grimes, who confirmed that the semen sample we gave him from Dhalia Vingali matched yours. You forgot one thing.

'Did I?' said Hawsley.

The drink-driving incident in 2005. The police took your DNA and logged it onto the old computer system. Digby found the file, proving that your DNA matched the one found in Dhalia. So, Janice Watson's rape when she was fourteen and her murder twenty-two years later, both apparently by Drummond Cleaver, was, in fact, carried out by you. I think you'd already killed Cleaver, probably two or three years ago. Having him around was a bit dangerous as you were using his DNA to cover your tracks, so it's unlikely he killed Dhalia. Your mistake was killing Cleaver too soon; with him gone, your DNA alibi for any future murders was gone.

'Very clever, Inspector. I can see I underestimated you a little, but as I said, it makes no difference. You will never prove any of this in court. You still haven't got my DNA, and the law doesn't allow you to arrest me without it. And you can't take it from me unless you arrest me, as you already have it on file, so it would be inadmissible in court.'

'But we will, eventually,' replied Parish. Soon, when you become ill, you'll need blood to prolong your miserable life. Then we'll have your actual DNA, which the hospital can take legally, and when we have that, you will be convicted and sent to live, or should I say die, out there.' Parish pointed upwards, but Hawsley knew what he meant.

'But I'll be nearly dead,' said Hawsley, smiling wryly.

'Well, not quite. Hopefully, you won't die too fast, and there will be pain, lots of pain, but no morphine for you. I guarantee you that much. You'll be in the Ghettazone you created, and they don't have many drugs out there. Not the sort you'll need, anyway. I don't think you'll be able to intimidate anybody out there by telling them who you were; they'd just kill you.' He looked straight into Hawsley's eyes. 'So, you're fucked any which way.' Parish smiled discreetly.

'This is all Cleaver and Maranno's fault. I had nothing to do with it!' exclaimed Hawsley. 'They can prove I had nothing to do with any of it.'

'Possibly they might have, but from what I can tell, you've already killed Cleaver, so that's one person who can't defend you.'

'Maranno will back me up,' said Hawsley after a moment's hesitation, virtually condemning himself as an accomplice in Cleaver's death.

'Well, no, actually. You see, Maranno shot himself this morning in his garden. But he left an exceedingly long note clearly explaining everything....' The air suddenly

502

went quiet, and Parish thought he saw a tear fall from Hawsley's right eye and slowly down his cheek.

'Benny dead,' said Hawsley

'Yes,' replied Parish.

'*Tant pis,*' Hawsley muttered, his face now saddened.

'Sorry,' said Parish?

'*Tant pis.* It's Latin.'

'Is it,' said Parish?

'Never mind. The situation is regrettable but now beyond change. That's a rough translation,' muttered Hawsley, adopting a resigned expression. The news of Maranno's suicide had affected Hawsley far more than Parish had expected. It had affected Aiden more than Aiden had expected.

'It was the best way out, in the end, to tell the truth,' said Parish.

'I suppose that's all that matters before you die,' said Hawsley.

'There are two things that matter before you die,' said Parish.

'And what are they?' asked Hawsley with haunting bewilderment and resignation.

'How you go and what you leave behind, and you have control over both.

'Do I?' said Hawsley.

Parish looked at the corner of the desk where Hawsley had laid his gun and then at Hawsley. 'I'll come back later with the warrant.'

'Yes, that would be good. I look forward to seeing you. Thank you,' said Hawsley.

It was just after midday. As Parish drove out through the palace gates, he heard a loud clap and caught sight of a body falling from a balcony. He slowed down briefly, thinking of Catherine and Jade, and then drove on.

Chapter 30
Lara

2023. Janice continued talking to Rose, retelling every minute detail of her conversations with her great-grandmother, Lara. At times, she spoke as if she were Lara – inhabiting her soul's space and spirit in a strangely ethereal manifestation.

'It was a dark Russian winter... and it was cold - icy cold. The hearth fire kept Lara and Mia warm... it gave them life. If the fire had gone out for just a few hours, they would have frozen to death, and you would not be here today. That is what the fire meant... Life!' Rose poured a little more wine into both their glasses.

'Your great-great-grandfather Vladin was a good man. He kept our family alive when we surely should have died.' Janice often repeated this haunting exhortation whenever she spoke about those days.'

'Lara and Mia only survived because Lara kept the fire going through the long winter nights with the wood Vladin had collected before the snow came. They would eat bread Lara made from the flour they had hidden away. The flour not stolen by the Germans. Lara would make a stew from the vegetables they kept frozen in the snow and whatever animals Vladin could kill in the woods. Sometimes, he would bring rabbits home. Sometimes, he would bring home rats as large as rabbits, for they had grown fat, feasting on the bodies that lay everywhere. Lara would keep this stew going all winter. 'Feasting on friends' was how she thought of it; this was the only way she could come to terms with a lamentable reality.'

The room grew a little colder as Janice continued her story. Rose wrapped herself up a little tighter in her jacket.

'It was 1940 when the German army began sweeping through Eastern Europe on their way to crush Moscow and Stalingrad. And the deepest winter by the time they arrived at Lara and Vladin's house.

Even now, I can still remember the emptiness in my great-grandmother's eyes as she cast her mind back all those years. A foreboding, strangely subservient tone in her voice. The sour odour of subjugation and depravity seeping out from every pore of her skin, infusing and stifling the air, creating a stale, pervasive stench of hopelessness.' Janice took a deep breath and continued.

'The officer knocked on the door. He was very polite at first. He asked if she had anything to eat and drink for himself and two of his men as their field rations had run out because they had been moving forward too fast. They had encountered far less resistance than expected.'

At first, the people of Lithuania were pleased to see the arrival of the German army. Saviours, they thought. From the oppression of Stalin, who particularly hated them and had made every effort to exterminate them. *'The vermin that existed in the sewers of the Russian empire.'* That's what he called us. We were not pure like the White Russians. We were the runt of the litter, and he wanted us gone from the face of the earth. He just couldn't kill us fast enough. Even Hitler could have learnt a thing or two from his methods for annihilation. The Germans were traditionally thought to be a fairer race, more clinical but even-handed, and more civilised than the Russians - but in the cold reality of war, that was proved to be terribly wrong. They were just the same when it came to creating new techniques for extinction in their own killing plan.

'Lara told the officer they had hardly enough food to feed themselves, but he took no notice. Without explanation or invitation, he brushed past her into her farmhouse and sat down near the fire, slamming one leg on the bare kitchen table. Then he leaned back with his malevolent Aryan arrogance, carefully balancing the chair on its two back legs. The two soldiers stayed by the door, smoked cigarettes, and watched but said nothing.'

'Have you nothing at all?' he asked. But Lara did not move; she couldn't move. He repeated his words in a menacingly suppressed tone, his real intention slowly becoming evident. He cast his eyes slowly around the room, searching for any place where food could be hidden.

'Have you nothing at all, woman,' he asked again?

Janice soulfully repeated the words as if she had been there and had witnessed it herself. So intense was the depth of immersive introspection conveyed by Lara when she retold the story to Janice that it was almost as if Janice was reading a fairy tale to a child. Not someone recalling the harrowing memories of someone else's darkest hours.

'He didn't bother raising his voice. It wasn't necessary. All the malice and fear he wanted to convey were so effortlessly conveyed through the subtlety of intonation alone.'

'A little bread, some stew and some water, that is all we have,' murmured Lara, her voice quivering with fear, her body trembling with cold. She kept her eyes rigidly fixed on the scrubbed floorboards, somehow believing that if she did not make eye contact, he would eat the food and leave her house. He would have no interest in a simple Lithuanian peasant girl and would do her no harm. But it would not have made any difference if she were ugly and wan or beautiful, for he didn't care. What he desired was

507

not a thing of beauty but merely an orifice for his transient carnal pleasure.'

'Bring it to me,' he ordered quietly and politely, but the underlying tone of his voice instilled terror. Lara hurried to the cupboard and took out the only thing left: half a loaf of stale bread. Then she ladled some stew, cooking in a cauldron hanging in the hearth, into a bowl and gave it to him. He looked at it and sneered before breaking the bread in two and throwing half to one of his men, who split it in two to share it with the other soldier.'

'He tried a mouthful of the stew but spat it out. 'What is this shit?' he exclaimed. Lara apologised. 'It's all we have.'

'It tastes like rat!' shouted the officer. Lara said nothing. It was a rat, but she dared not tell him.

'I'm sorry. I have nothing else.'

'Water!' he demanded, and Lara quickly fetched the water jug from under the sink and gave it to him with a cup. She knew that this day would not end well and prayed that Vladin, who fortunately was away in the hills looking for food, would not come back before they had gone, for if he did, they would have surely killed him. She kept her head bowed low, avoided eye contact, and tried to make herself look slighter than she really was by crouching her body as small as she could manage.'

'The officer with his nice, clean uniform and shiny buttons finished the bread and drank the water before beckoning his two men to drink from the jug. This they did before returning to their position by the door. He stood up and started moving around the room, carefully surveying everything but still closely watching Lara. A sparrowhawk circling a field waiting for that miniscule, tell-tale movement that its nervous prey far below would eventually

make. The prey, a tiny mouse, senses the predator is high above them somewhere but does not know if it has been seen. The predator hasn't seen the mouse, so it hovers, swoops, and turns to intimidate the prey, waiting for it to panic and run, which it does, thus exposing its position. The predator swoops and swiftly kills. His gaze jerked back to Lara, who was gazing at the shiny buttons on his coat.'

Janice remembered the shiny buttons so clearly because Lara had told her the story many times - in minute detail.

'I was beautiful then,' said Lara. 'Twenty-two years old, married four years to my lovely Vladin, and our precious daughter Mia was nearly three.'

'He stopped at the table and poured more water into the cup, drank it, then moved around until he was behind me.'

Janice turned away from Rose's gaze and stared into the roaring fire as she continued her story as Lara had told her.

'He grabbed the back of my dress and slowly dragged me upright. I knew what he was going to do, but I did not know precisely how it would begin. From behind, he slowly ripped my dress down the back. It fell to the floor, leaving me standing naked and shivering. I dared not move. I clasped my hands to my body to protect what modesty I had left. He kicked the chair away and pushed me down onto the table.

He was going to rape me, but I could do nothing. My whole body was paralysed with fear for me and concern for Mia, who I knew was watching. With his left hand, he pushed my head down onto the table, and for a few seconds, I shut my eyes. When I opened them again, I could only see his two men standing by the door, still smoking and watching what was happening. But they were utterly unconcerned by the brutality about to be inflicted upon my body. Any sense of humanity stripped away, lost forever on the long journey from Berlin to Moscow.'

'He ran a finger slowly up and down my backbone – a cold sensation that brought further panic to my trembling body. I could hear his breathing slightly faster now, and I could feel and smell his warm, stinking breath over my shoulder; that made the hairs on the back of my neck stand up. Then he started to hum Liszt's Les Préludes.' Many years later, I learned this was Hitler's chosen anthem for the Barbarossa campaign. He wanted different pieces of inspirational music for every campaign. Whenever I hear it now, I wet myself.'

'With his left foot, he kicked my left leg sideways to open me up. Then, after fumbling with the fly buttons on his trousers, he forced his penis into me and started thrusting violently - but I was dry, and the pain was excruciating. It must have hurt him, too. I think he tore his foreskin as he screamed out, but he carried on. He grabbed the water from the table and poured the remaining contents onto where we were joined to ease the dryness - and the pain eased a little for me. He took hold of my right breast and squeezed it so hard I cried out, but he carried on, forcing himself into me for three or four minutes before he screamed again and came into me. All the time, Mia was watching from her bedroom door, too afraid to cry out or move.'

'When at last he withdrew, I thought the ordeal was over. He stood me up and ordered me to get some water to wash his cock, which was bleeding. When I finished cleaning it, he carefully put it away and slapped me hard across the face with the back of his hand. I fell to the floor.

He gestured to his two men with his fingers to take me, and they both raped me in turn while the officer watched and smoked a cigarette.'

'Then, when they had finished, their attention switched to my precious Mia, who had come out from the bedroom to comfort me as I was curled up in the corner of the room crying. I looked up at the officer, but he just sneered and nodded at his men. One of them, the shorter one, lifted Mia onto the table to view her. She was shaking, crying, and holding herself tightly. I feared for what they were about to do to her, but the officer just stared at me and shouted, 'What do you think we are? Animals? You fucking Russian peasants.'

'I don't know why he stopped them, but he did. Then he snatched Mia from the table and ripped her dress off. She was only three, but he fucked her, and she screamed and screamed, and blood poured from her body, and when he was finished, he threw her back to me, and the two soldiers just laughed.

'Always remember,' he said, 'I gave you your life and kept you alive. Never forget that.'

'No! I thought Vladin kept us alive.'

'The officer and his two men eventually left the house, and we huddled together for nearly an hour before we could move. I tried to wake Mia, but she was cold and would not wake. Blood was all over the floor, and I knew she was dead. I cleaned everything up because I knew Vladin would be home that night. When he got home, I told him that Mia had started to bleed and died, and I could do nothing. Vladin believed me, comforted me, and asked no questions. What purpose would it have served?' Vladin carried her body into the woods. We kissed Mia and *buried her as deeply as possible so the foxes and rats couldn't dig her up.*

Janice took a small sip of wine, set the glass on the floor, took another deep breath and continued with the story.

Three years later, towards the end of 1943, the remnants of the defeated German army passed through our village once more. This time, it was the worst winter in twenty years, much worse than the last time they passed through. They were no longer the conquering heroes - now the vanquished foe, beaten not by Stalingrad's brave defenders but by mother nature, Russia's staunchest comrade in arms. The one who never betrayed her, deserted her, let her down, and always stood by her side.

She had crushed another invader in 1812, and Tchaikovsky later wrote music to commemorate that momentous occasion. This time, the music had already been composed, and the outcome was written once again in the snow with rivers of frozen blood. Hitler was listening to the wrong music this time. They did not stop this time. They just carried on walking; they wanted to go home to die in the warm. Now they would be happy to eat rat stew.'

'*Lara watched through a small gap in the curtains as the occasional solder ambled past the farmhouse. Now, they gazed permanently at the ground in confusion and desperation, hoping to return to a home that few would ever see again. When the knock came at the door, Lara sensed who it might be, and it was. He was alone, bedraggled, unshaven and much thinner this time. He stood and waited for her to allow him to enter, and for whatever reason, she did. Gone now the Germanic arrogance. This time, he was humble, and she almost* pitied his soul, for she knew his life too must soon be over.'

'He sat down at the table and took his cap off. The room was warm, and Lara could see that he had been cold for a long time as he pulled his chair closer to the fire. She asked him what he wanted, and he just said he needed somewhere to sleep for the night and would be gone by the morning, and she agreed without saying anything. He asked where Mia was, which alarmed Lara, but he explained in his much-improved Russian that he only asked about her as he noticed she was not there. Lara told him she was sleeping.' 'I have a daughter the same age,' he began to tell Lara. 'She will be five next month. I have not seen her for four years. I would love to see my daughter one more time.' He seemed to know he would soon be dead.

And did you and your friends kill and rape her and rape her mother? Lara thought.

'Anna, now nearly three years old, came into the kitchen half-asleep. The sound of talking had awoken her. She asked her mother for some water. The officer looked at her, then looked at Lara. 'Why is she so small? She must be nearly six now,' he asked, looking at her curiously.'

'Lara told him they had had little food for three years, so the village children grew very slowly. The officer seemed mollified with the answer but puzzled. Anna walked over to the man she did not know, said goodnight, kissed him on the cheek and then smiled, and he smiled back at her. Then she walked over to Lara and kissed her before returning to the bedroom.'

'She is so small,' remarked the officer once again. 'So very, very small, but so exceptionally beautiful. You are very fortunate.'

'After giving him some bread and water, she sat opposite him. Not afraid any longer, she looked directly at him and asked, 'Why did you rape me?' Her eyes never straying from his.'

'He didn't answer at first but momentarily looked down at the table, then back up at her. 'Do you know that throughout history, invading armies were ordered to rape the women of any country they invaded, and do you know why?'

Lara did not answer; she did not care.

'Because it would eventually create a generation of children of the conquerors with a biological allegiance to both their father's and their mother's country, bringing lasting peace between warring nations. For brother would not take up arms against brother and a son would not take up arms against his father.' 'He apparently believed what he had been told, however flawed the argument was.'

'Lara didn't reply straight away. I can't have babies anymore. You did so much damage to me three years ago. Do you know that?' she told him.'

'I am sorry,' he said and started to weep - but she could see no sadness in his eyes, no remorse, only the humiliation of defeat.'

'Lara got up and moved slowly around the table to stand behind his head and comfort him. While his head was bent down weeping, she whispered quietly, gently holding his head, 'Why did you rape my child?'

'I don't know. I'm so sorry. It was wrong. I know it was wrong... It's war... It makes you do things...' 'Lara took out the small razor-sharp kitchen knife she had been hiding in her dress pocket and calmly but firmly plunged it deep into his neck, almost immediately slicing through the carotid artery just under his left ear. She continued pulling

the knife slowly across his throat with all her strength. She half-decapitated him so gently that he didn't notice immediately as his body was still numb with the cold. He made no attempt to resist her. To Lara, it felt no different from killing a goat, and Lara had done that many times before. She moved round in front of him and knelt down, watching his face as the last few moments of life drained from his body, but she didn't smile - there was no pleasure and no victory.'

'He opened his mouth to say something, but nothing came out. Just a quiet gurgle of blood seeping into his oesophagus and from his torn throat onto his tattered tunic. As he looked down, he could see Lara begin to say something. Slowly, she whispered, 'Deine Tochter.' He didn't immediately understand what she was saying, and Lara could see confusion in his eyes. 'My daughter... she is your daughter, Deine Tochter.' He smiled back, but she gave him no absolution. This moment of retribution was hers to savour, and she took it for she owned it. Slowly, he crumpled to the floor, bleeding to death as Lara looked on.'

'Later, when it was dark, Lara pulled his body out of the house and buried it in the snow just outside. When the snow began to thaw in the spring, Vladin moved the body to the woods and never asked Lara about him.'

'In 1960, when Anna was nineteen, she moved to London and married a painter, and Tatiana was born. In 1987, when Tatiana was twenty-seven, she gave birth to me. The rest, you know.'

Janice smiled at Rose. They held each other for the last time in front of the fire, and Rose made a promise. She would pick her battle well, and she would win. And she did.

The End

A Brief Summary of the United Republic of Britain.

Aiden Hawsley declared in his pre-election manifesto that when his party was elected to power in the following year's general election, there would be a significant geographical reorganisation of Great Britain into four high-security gated provinces. Hawsley promised that, above all else, the safety and well-being of hardworking, honest UK residents would be protected at any cost and that any person convicted of a crime would lose his right to live within one of these communities. He had drawn a line in the sand, but it was deeper and broader than anybody could have anticipated.

It was a brave, ambitious, almost foolhardy policy. And it brought tears of derisive laughter from the other political parties when he announced it one wet Thursday afternoon in March 2013. Implementation of such a plan would be prohibitively expensive. It would almost certainly fall at the first hurdle if it appeared to breach European civil liberties and human rights law, which it undoubtedly would. However, Hawsley had captured the voters' mood, and his contempt towards the European parliament further endeared him to the British people.

The ruling Conservative Party thought he was mad to propose such a radical change. But although he did not realise it then, he had accidentally stumbled upon the holy political grail, and victory was suddenly within his grasp. Foolishly, the Conservatives condemned the 'nutty Nazi notion,' as they always referred to it, as the ridiculous jingoistic ranting of a madman. (another common theme) They suggested it smacked of puritanical elitism and fascist ideology. Ultimately, it would further polarise the antagonistic class structure and create widespread unrest, discontent, and even civil war. Hawsley had already carefully considered that possibility and had made contingency plans to deal with it.

The government also believed that not only were the technical problems of building such a mammoth construction insurmountable, but the crippling financial costs, fifty billion pounds - were unrecoverable. It was unlikely to attract sponsors or private investors when the very nature of the construction would severely reduce the number of people it would benefit.

However, they had grossly miscalculated the plan's socio-economic structure. Those entitled to live in a gated province would only be the affluent A-C groups controlling 85% of the country's wealth. Most of the social-eco groups D and E would be automatically excluded. A rumour circulated that the government had already considered the scheme in-camera but discarded it as political suicide.

Hawsley had researched his subject well and was convinced he had detected an undercurrent of exploitable malcontent. He was confident his reforms were precisely what the proletarian masses desired. His conviction was proved unerringly correct when they almost unanimously voted to put his party into power in 2014. The people had had enough of underpinning a morally bankrupt government. One that was too weak to make pivotal decisions on the issues of mass unemployment, rampant crime, the proliferation of illegal drugs, unrestrained immigration, loss of social decency and the continuing subsidisation of corrupt third-world regimes. Why should those who had worked hard to give themselves a decent life be taxed into poverty just to support those who had never worked, did not want to work, and never had any intention of working.

These people who depended on the government for permanent, all-inclusive social welfare wanted to spend their days indulging in illegal drugs and alcohol or tripping on counterfeit VRS (Virtual Reality Simulator) chips. The Conservative way wasn't working, and Aiden Hawsley promised change and that he would deliver.

The electoral mandate was simple, unambiguous, and effective. There was never any real doubt that there would be a significant swing to the CSP. Pre-election polls were indicating a landslide victory.

Although a little unclear on detail, all but the very naïve or profoundly stupid should have realised that many hard-line supporters would paradoxically be excluded from social registration. Fortunately, the mass hysteria that seemed to be affecting CSP followers blinded them to the frightening scenario for which they were signing up. Britain for the British, the rest can go to hell, the banners read. It had been a landslide.

Who or how you defined someone as British and how you could tell the difference was a trivial detail that did not concern them at the time. The CSP wanted to run the country's industries, and the state and Aiden Hawsley were their frontmen. He would be valuable and instrumental in attaining that goal. He was charming, articulate, amusing and captivating when addressing a crowd. However, he became a demonstrative, demonic megalomaniac when addressing his cohorts and inner cabinet. Hawsley once walked across the floor of the House and stood a few inches from the face of one of the few remaining Labour MPs. He had been arguing passionately and, annoyingly for Hawsley, somewhat eloquently on a relatively innocuous race issue. For some reason, Hawsley had taken a personal dislike to the man.

The MP appeared to be winning the debate up to that point, but he went noticeably quiet when Hawsley confronted him. Hawsley whispered something inaudible (to the chamber) into his ear. The MP smiled, turned around, picked up his papers, left the house and five minutes later jumped off one of the turrets into the Thames and drowned.

After Hawsley's election, the country was split into five new areas. Four gated Province communities, two residential and two industrial. Everything else became the Ghettazone. Each province would be surrounded by a twenty-foot-high security wall. Lord Protector Hawsley dropped the use of 'Prime Minister' after his election, preferring the more pious-sounding Cromwellian title. He personally allotted the designated areas for each new Bunyanesque-inspired ' Province.'

They were a Southern residential and farming area stretching from Plymouth to the Isle of Sheppey, which he named Deliverance. The area around London, encircled by the existing M25, which he named Providence, and two industrial and farming provinces, one in Wales called Progress and one incorporating Birmingham, Manchester, Nottingham, and Sheffield named Redemption.

In the beginning, there were vague references to how the entitlement of each inhabitant to live within a province would work. Early indications were that the qualification would primarily be based on an individual's criminal record and other unspecified social and economic factors. In reality, it soon became apparent that it would also be dependent upon academic qualifications, physical ability/disability, professional experience, and level of dependence on the National Health Service. In particular, a specific weight-to-height programme was to be initiated. Anybody exceeding the prescribed limits could be excluded. Employment status, a potential security risk to the state, and many other undisclosed minor physiognomies were also reasons for disqualification. Distinctly Orwellian elements quickly came into play, which mainly went unnoticed initially.

Those qualified to live inside a province were perfectly happy with the arrangement. But those excluded quickly became disenchanted with the utopian dream they had been sold – a beautiful illusion that promptly morphed into a dystopian nightmare. Sporadic civil riots began to break out in late 2014, just as the construction of the province walls began.

After the sudden and humiliating destruction of the Conservative majority and the almost total annihilation of Labour and the other minor parties at the 2014 general election, the so-called opposition occupied so few seats that it became necessary to adjust the seating arrangement in the House of Parliament to accommodate the CSP's majority. They now filled both the left and the right seating banks. The remaining minor parties languished in a tiny corner of the chamber. But even that was only temporary. The concept of sitting members of parliament was also being phased out and replaced by district High Sheriffs, selected personally by the Lord Protector. They administered the customary law, justice, and security issues for their designated areas from local justice offices.

With a 93% majority and control of the Commons and judiciary, the CSP could formulate, move to statute and enforce new laws with remarkable alacrity and impunity. The Conservative Party could do very little with only 5% of the votes, and their choice was stark but simple. Join the CSP as a passive coalition partner and be awarded some nominal position or be condemned forever to obscurity. They joined. Hawsley had subtly threatened another general election to consolidate his position if the Conservatives did not conform. So they deferred, choosing to become a humiliatingly small part of something - rather than a substantially more significant portion of nothing.

Discretion being the better part of valour, they quietly fell into line behind Hawsley. At least they had retained some dignity, but even that didn't last for long.

The Labour Party members were marked men and consigned to imminent extinction under the PRE1 (Political Rationalisation Edict No 1) that the CSP had quietly published before the election. It clearly defined the concept and practicality of a one-party system being in the electorate's best interest. Although the Conservatives had the right to object to any proposal in the early days of the new parliament, their 5% minority meant there was not the remotest possibility they could ever make any difference to the outcome.

Aiden Hawsley had previously collated a dossier on every Conservative party member with the judicious and systematic research of his SDSD Department. Each report contained sufficient data about unorthodox activities, sexual harassment, expense fraud, tax evasion, and other personal details to cancel the Identity Registration of 90% of the Conservative Party members still in office, if necessary. The dossier's very existence and the knowledge that Hawsley would have no compunction in releasing the information to the relevant authorities and the press was enough to guarantee a favourable decision on any contentious legislation. Once the High Sheriffs were elected, stragglers would eventually be phased out of the system anyway.

Civil liberties and human rights legislation no longer applied to anybody residing in the UK. Amnesty International and other quasi-political organisations were banned. Parliament and the Monarchy were finally dissolved in 2018.

By the end of 2026, the CSP had successfully controlled Britain for twelve traumatic years…

The Social and Criminal Reform Act of 2016.

Under this act, any person could have his social registration cancelled if a discrepancy was discovered in their social security records. All previous claimants for any disability benefit were rigorously interviewed and reassessed by specially trained medical examiners. The examiners were extraordinarily vigilant, for they were also threatened with losing their own residential registration permits if they diagnosed someone as disabled, and the claimant was subsequently found not to be. A one-year moratorium was introduced before they were requested to attend a disability reassessment review. Surprisingly, many people claiming benefits cancelled their claims before the review date.

All other social security benefits were cancelled. Anybody losing their job would be expelled after three months if they did not find alternative employment and could not support themselves financially. The retirement age was now seventy, and there was no state pension. If you had not saved sufficient funds for your retirement and could not prove you could support yourself indefinitely, you would also be expelled from the province.

Under the act, conviction of any crime could mean your registration could be cancelled (depending on the judge that day), and you could be expelled from the province. Expulsion was for life with no appeal. It was also within the judge's remit to sentence and evict any immediate family if he believed they may have contributed to the primary offence.

The Cost of Crime Act was passed on to the statute books in 2016. This legislation effectively charged all criminals and their families with the total cost of any prosecution. This would be reclaimed automatically by the court from the disposal of realisable assets. There was no requirement to prove contributory factors or influence as this was at the judge's sole discretion, and they exercised this power with a Stalinist efficiency. Without registration, you couldn't pass through the automatic Balingo DNA scanner security gates to enter a gated province. Within the Province, crime had dropped dramatically by the end of 2017. Each Province had an average population of ten million inhabitants with less than a thousand police officers. They spent most of their time watching security monitors. Street presence was rare except when a major incident occurred.

After the civil riots in two thousand and fifteen, all major supermarket chains were nationalised under the SCOMTEL banner. The national marketing strategy's dramatic and unsophisticated redirection was immediately introduced, driving everything towards a uniformly utilitarian advertising format. It no longer bore any resemblance to the amusingly benign advertising campaigns created during the genteel days of playful competition of the previous seventy years. Sales advertisements were always perceived as the driving force to attract customers to a particular store or product. But as a marketing format, it was now redundant, having been supplanted by far simpler messages efficiently delivered to the customer.

There was no necessity for sophistication anymore. The price was all that mattered. Since nationalisation, expensive and amusing marketing campaigns were no longer necessary. Most small high-street shops closed immediately after the SCOMTEL consolidation. The remaining independent, owner-operated chains disappeared within a few years, unable to compete commercially. They were continually frustrated by the lack of regular deliveries that seemed to be disproportionately affected by spot regulation and compliance issues, indecipherable legislation, and logistical delivery errors from manufacturers. The Hawley administration covertly militated against the independent retailer. The shops that did manage to stay open were looted continuously or burnt and eventually succumbed to the inevitable.

The government blamed the manufacturers for not producing enough goods. The retailers believed it was because SCOMTEL controlled the supply lines by imposing stringent rules on manufacturers in return for large orders. Manufacturers argued that the government had applied strict austerity measures to avoid wastage. They were only authorised to produce sufficient product quantities to satisfy immediate market demands. The market demand was calculated by the Government Statistics Department for every product. In fact, the GSD determined how much of anything was manufactured. And by default, how much would be available to each shop. The general idea was that this would reduce wastage, which in turn would benefit the environment. The only problem was nobody outside of a province was remotely interested in saving the environment anymore. There didn't seem to be any point.

Hawsley's government had, as a means of population control and, for other reasons, quietly encouraged the riots in what was a crude but remarkably effective political campaign. Two million people died in the Ghettazone riots, nearly fifty per cent of whom were minority faiths. 'It was a jolly good start at sorting the "problem" out.' As Hawsley had so succinctly put it when discussing the colossal loss of life a few years later in a holavision documentary. It was hosted by Christopher Pennington, one of the most venerated intellectuals of the day.

Pennington had then asked Hawsley if he realised that making a statement so contentious, crass, insensitive, and disrespectful was bound to inflame the extremists in the minority groups - those most affected in the riots. This would undoubtedly reignite the smouldering embers of discontent. Without any sense of remorse, regret, or obvious concern for the possible repercussions, Hawsley had unequivocally indicated that he had always anticipated a more significant loss of life and was disappointed that the final toll had not been higher. Hawsley had cleverly orchestrated the virtual annihilation of a substantial segment of the social-economic D and E groups. These were the unproductive elements he did not want in his new society.

This he had pledged to do in his manifesto in 2010. Although it had taken a little longer than expected, he had effectively fulfilled his promise by 2019.

SCOMTEL eventually became the only authorised retailer for all consumer goods. Advertising was just information about the availability of a SCOMTEL product. The choice was simple: you either wanted it or didn't. The old maxim about the paradox of choice was put to death. There was one type of everything, and that was it.

My acknowledgement to Edith Hamilton and her book on mythology. And to all the other writers not acknowledged in the book from whom I may have subconsciously and unintentionally borrowed interesting phrases, I plead Cryptomnesia. This is the disadvantage of reading books while simultaneously writing one. And finally, apologies for creating new words as yet undefined in the Oxford dictionary.

A Letter

This story is based on the events that befell my family between 1941 and today. Some names and places have been changed to obscure identities for reasons that will soon become obvious. I have also taken the liberty of extending the timeline to 2026 when I have assumed all parties will be dead. I have written a postscript to this story, which will be published after my death. This will reveal the true identity of the people involved and the places mentioned.

The nature of events has made it necessary for me to embellish, extemporise and create specific details to cloak or obfuscate the truth. I have taken the liberty of introducing various scientific developments, discoveries, and technical advances, some of which are currently under research and development, some of which may become available in the future. This has been necessary to obscure some of the actual facts.

Some of the conversations are hypothetical or conjectural. They are based on discussions, reminiscences and information supplied by witnesses, acquaintances, and friends. Therefore, the content can only be presumed to be correct. Some of the details were recorded contemporaneously.

I hope and pray that the people still living depicted in this story do not recognise themselves with the changes I have made. However, if I should suddenly disappear or mysteriously die in unusual circumstances after the publication of this book, then I have failed. But in this failure will come my final redemption.

Angel Vingali, 2014

Please leave a comment on Amazon if you enjoyed this book.
Contact the writer at **butchmoss111@gmail.com**

If you enjoyed this book, why not try the first in the Story Teller Pentalogy. Each tale explores a relationship and how it can change. Death of a Sparrow.

CHAPTER 1. DEATH OF A SPARROW
Marissa's story.

Many things happen that make sense, but so many more do not. I have tried to unscramble one from the other. But as time passed, a mist of uncertainty, confusion and doubt descended over what happened on that first day and all the days that followed. I could blame this on a declining memory, but that would be disingenuous - to you as the reader and to me as the writer. The proverb goes, *reason will prevail when tension is becalmed*, and I believe the tension was stilled for a few brief moments. And in those few moments, reason determined the destiny of the world. I have no desire to tell an untruth or to mislead, but I may. If I do, please forgive me, for it will not be by intent.

This is my story of what happened during the eight days of Hanukkah in 1943.

The Second Night of Hanukkah 1943.

Nica was clearly not happy. His glazed expression, a curious montage of disheartenment, confusion and, to a lesser degree, resigned acceptance. Each emotion pulled him in a different direction. Each vying for overall control, endeavouring to assert itself as the dominant force to be reckoned with. He was clearly in a bit of a muddle.

At times, he could also be infuriating and stupid and many other things, but I could trust him, and in a way, I loved him. He was honest, tolerable (most of the time), and amiable. I would probably marry him one day when we were old enough. If nobody more suitable came along and the Germans hadn't shot him in the meantime. But of course, he didn't know that - not back then, but neither did I... not really.

Those who did know him - knew him well, that is, would have understood him. They could read his face and, with a reasonable degree of certainty, determine where his mind was at, but not today. Considering the incalculable number of subtle variants of mannerisms, demeanour and emotion in play, it would have been virtually impossible.

He was struggling with one of the two suitcases he was carrying across the platform. That was obvious. I later discovered that he had no problem with his own case, just the one belonging to his sister, Tania.

For a brief moment, Nica wondered why he was carrying it at all. Tania's case was obviously much heavier than his, and this annoyed him intensely. But his father had asked him to carry it, and he had respectfully agreed. Nica seldom argued or disagreed with his father's requests; there was never any point. His father knew many things that he did not, and he understood that his own desire to learn was perfectly matched by his father's desire to teach him all he knew.

A delicate sense of equilibrium existed between them, which would remain for the foreseeable future. To this much, he was resigned. One day, however, he would become as knowledgeable as his father, possibly more so and then no longer would the equilibrium be maintained. He would then not just be a son but a man in his own right. He would then make his own decisions, but until that time....

Shuffling across the station platform in the howling wind and snow, dragging two suitcases was not exactly how Nica had imagined spending the first day of Hanukkah. But then much had happened over the last few days that would change how he might celebrate the festival of Light in the future - and how he would remember Hanukkah 1943. It would be indelibly transcribed into his brain for the rest of his life, however long or short.

For a moment, he wondered what Tania could have packed that made her case so much heavier than his. Standing at the steps to the carriage, he took a deep breath. Then he hoisted the two cases, one at a time, onto the small backplate platform before quickly clambering up behind them. His father had taught him to always take a deep breath before engaging in any activity requiring a sudden energy spurt.

Nica and Tania were only allowed one small suitcase each for the journey. Their parents, Dr Franz and Mary Schiller, had carefully packed them the night before with essential clothing, a few personal items, a little food, and in Tania's case, half a dozen house bricks, just in case... That was the best explanation Nica could come up with.

Standing on the tiny backplate, he hesitated momentarily and glanced back at the ocean of bewildered faces. The unmistakable haze of desolation and sadness rose from the crowd like the steam from a freshly cooked bread pudding. He could feel it, almost touch it, as it penetrated every pore of his body. Overwhelmed by this episodic wave of sorrow and anguish – he was drowning - he might never breathe again...

He half hoped, in desperation, to see at least one familiar face amongst the hundreds of confused faces waiting to board the train, but he did not. He saw uncertainty and puzzlement in each tiny pink moon, obediently shuffling forward. He knew this was to be expected, for he, too, felt the same. What he had not expected to see, suffused amidst these unsolicited sensations, was the tiny glimmer of hope, but this was, by far, the frailest sense.

The blizzard, which had been blowing relentlessly since early morning, now shrouded and transformed every huddled body into a blanket of undulating white velvet. It effectively obliterated any possibility of meaningful recognition. All the frenetic energy of the swirling snowflakes, each contemptuously gyrating in a tiny vortex of ecstasy. Each diametrically opposed to the almost motionless lines of children waiting patiently to board the train.

'Hurry up!' somebody half-heartedly shouted. 'I'm freezing my bollicks off out here,' but Nica did not reply, for he did not hear the plea. His mind was elsewhere as he shook the snow from his coat and entered the carriage. Tania, who was following just behind, still appeared to be half asleep - utterly unaware of what was happening around her or even where she was, for that matter.

This was not like Tania; she had always been the curious one. The one who asked too many questions. The one with such acute peripheral awareness that, at times, she seemed to know precisely what was happening behind her head and in front of it. Today, however, she was aware of nothing.   She was still confused by the sense of wretchedness that had totally overwhelmed her the previous night when her parents had explained what would happen the following day. The words bounced around the kitchen, desperately looking for somewhere to land before her brain conceded to the inevitable and allowed them to enter. Still, they made no sense.

––––––

Before passing through the station's final barrier, their parents kissed them both. They held them tightly - bidding them farewell and a "Happy Hanukkah." Happy Hanukkah! It sounded strange – meaningless and absurd – without purpose. Tania wondered how they could wish them happiness when they were being made to leave their home and everything they had ever known. They were going to a place they had never been before - to live with people they did not know – and they had no idea when, if ever, they would see their parents again.

Nica tried to open the door to the carriage but couldn't - the handle was frozen and very stiff. He wrenched it a second time, and it opened. He glanced at Tania and smiled.

Inside the carriage, he saw the other children scurrying around, lifting bags onto racks, and deciding whether to sit by the window or gangway. He started to edge his way through the chaos and confusion, closely followed by Tania, slowly making their way down the centre aisle. Eventually, he found a four-seater section near the interconnecting door at the end of the carriage. There were three spare spaces. One of his friends, Janez, was already sitting in the fourth space reading a book. Nica hoisted the two suitcases onto the overhead storage rack, struggling a little with Tania's, before eventually dropping down onto the wooden bench and sliding up to the window. Tania sat down beside him, facing Janez.

'What did you pack in your case?' asked Nica, turning briefly to Tania with a sarcastic smirk, 'half a ton of coal?'

'No, just some essentials, thank you,' muttered Tania with rueful indifference. This was oddly out of character - she was usually more forthright. Her reply, bordering on the edge of courteousness, was strangely unnerving for Nica.

Nica shrugged with a hint of curiosity. He was not entirely satisfied with Tania's answer - but felt disinclined to interrogate her further; it wasn't that important. He thought that was the best course of action in the circumstances.

Janez looked up at them, casually acknowledging their arrival with a quick smile. He glanced at the large ushanka hat that Nica was wearing but made no comment. 'Thought you two weren't coming?' He flashed them an inquisitorial expression.

'Wouldn't miss it for the world - I love a day out,' mused Tania.

'Well, we did think about not bothering, but the krauts insisted,' replied Nica, with a derisory air of defiant arrogance.

'Did you get breakfast before you left home?' asked Janez.

'Yes,' replied Nica, 'why?'

'I don't think they will be giving us anything, I did ask – out of curiosity, but the shitlicker just grunted.'

'The shit-lickers wouldn't give you the drippings from their arses,' added Nica with a sneer.

Hungarian soldiers were called many things by Slovenians after the German invasion. But shit-lickers was by far their favourite term of abuse. The Slavic attitude towards their former neighbours changed dramatically after the extreme north-eastern zone of Slovenia, Prekmurje, was transferred to Hungary in April 1941. This was by way of an axis power arrangement when Germany dismembered Slovenia. The rest of the country was divided between Austria and Italy. The northeastern zone was controlled by Hungarian soldiers but with German officers. The Germans didn't trust their new allies that much.

'Aaaah,' squelched Tania, screwing her face up in disgust and sticking her tongue out as if she were about to vomit. 'I wish you wouldn't use that word,' glaring at her brother with half-closed eyes. He knew she hated it when he cursed publicly, but he did it anyway. She thought it demeaning and common and hated being associated with him when he was like this. He would never have used the word in front of his parents.

'What word?' replied Nica, feigning puzzlement.

'You know what word. That word... it's disgusting. Father would chastise you if he heard you, and the soldiers will shoot you dead in a heartbeat if they hear it.'

'Father's not here, so he can't say anything - and the shit-lickers are stupid and deaf,' snapped Nica. His expression didn't change this time, but a noticeable hint of resentment and contempt hovered in his tone. It was as if he held his father responsible for him being where he was today.

'No, but I am here, and I did, so I must act in loco parentis, so to speak, and monitor your language,' replied Tania in a moralizing tone. Nica shrugged disagreeably at Tania's presumptive assertion.

'Must you, really?' he replied impertinently, curtly shaking his head.

'Yes!' replied Tania, adopting a strange matriarchal glaze.

Nica gave in, as he always did with Tania. He thought he would have a stab at sarcasm instead. 'I guess it beats sitting around a cosy roaring fire, eating hot chestnuts, drinking mulled wine, and singing happy Hanukkah songs. Yes, I definitely prefer to be starving on a train while freezing off my testicalia.'

'Aaaaaah,' murmured Tania, even louder than before. She also hated hearing any words related to male genitalia. Unfortunately, Nica had an encyclopaedic knowledge of the subject, having read the relevant section in every one of his father's reference books, and there were many. Tania mumbled, 'I don't feel well,' then she shut her eyes and pretended to sleep.

'What's loco parentis?' asked Janez, a little puzzled.

With a curious expression, Tania half opened her eyes. With a hint of a smirk, she explained, 'It means I am acting as Nica's parents while our real parents aren't here.' She smirked at Nica.

'So you are in charge of Nica?' inquired Janez, obviously baiting their conversation.

'Yes, because I am the sensible one.'

'In your dreams,' interrupted Nica, grinning at Tania.

'I have to be in charge to ensure you keep your mouth clean,' replied Tania with a scowling expression. 'It's like a toilet sometimes.'

Nica didn't reply, and Tania shut her eyes again. Momentarily, she reopened them.

'Is that even a word?'

'What word?' replied Nica, Goading Tania to utter another word she found repulsive.

'You know what word,' replied Tania, realizing she had backed herself into a corner again.

'The horrible word you just said.'

'TES-TI-CAL-I-A, you mean?' He pronounced it very slowly, over-emphasising the five syllables.

'Yes.'

'Well, it is a proper word. I found it in a book,' replied Nica proudly.

'Did you,' replied Tania condescendingly. She fervently believed that he only read books simply to discover unpleasant words to taunt her with.

'Yes.'

'Right.' Tania shut her eyes again and stuck her fingers in her ears.

Janez grinned at Nica's spat with Tania. It amused him. 'Where's Marissa?' he asked.

'Don't know, haven't seen her,' replied Nica. 'I glanced around the platform before boarding, but it was pandemonium. I couldn't see anybody clearly. Thought she might already be here with you.'

Janez shook his head. 'I kept a place for her,' he nodded to the empty space where he had left his suitcase, 'but I haven't seen her.'

It went quiet for a while as they gazed out of the carriage window, looking at the other children on the platform, still waiting to board the train.

'Do I look stupid in this?' asked Nica, gingerly peeking out from under the curiously large brown Ushanka hat he was wearing. It had large, dangly flaps hanging down on both sides to cover his ears, obviously to stop them from freezing. But it also gave him the appearance of a dangerously oversized demented hare.

'Do you really want me to answer that?' chipped in Tania, opening one eye - desperately trying not to laugh.

The hat was far too big for him; it almost covered his eyes, but it kept his head warm – and that was all that really mattered. It had been his father's till today, but Franz had placed it on Nica's head at the railway station just before he and his sister passed through the final barrier. Now, it was his.

'Not at all,' replied Janez, smiling at Tania's reply. He enjoyed watching them bicker. 'I did wonder about the size, though.'

Nica glared at Tania. 'Ah, you're back with us again; I was getting worried about you, and I asked Janez for his opinion, not yours.'

'Were you?' asked Tania, smirking.

'Yes.'

'Well, I thought I would stick my nose in any way.'

'I thought you weren't well?' asked Nica.

'It's only some of the words you use that make me sick, but I'm feeling a little better now, thank you,' said Tania with another squinty smirk.

'I can tell,' mumbled Nica.

'But I'm still a bit sad,' said Tania.

'We're all sad, but we must put up with it for now and put on a brave face.'

'Yes, I know,' said Tania, 'but...'

'It's a lovely ushanka, interrupted Janez without any hint of sarcasm. 'Is your head hot?'

Tania glanced at Janez in disbelief - stunned by the banality of the question.

'It's actually just right... It was my dad's. That's why it's too big,' replied Nica.

'I sort of guessed it wasn't yours,' replied Janez with a tiny smirk before returning to his book.

'Don't lose the ushanka!' His father, Franz, had plaintively shouted just as Nica and Tania stepped into the carriage. But his plea had been drowned out by the howling winds whipping through the station and the heavy muttering of parental uncertainty filling the air. Nica never considered that those few innocuous words might be the last he would ever hear from his father.

Three slender threads of commonality connected Dr. Franz Schiller and his wife, Mary, with the other parents left standing on the platform. The first was a small yellow cloth badge in the shape of the Star of David, preeminent on every coat breast embroidered with the word žid.

The second was a visceral sense of confusion and trepidation, suffocating the air like a heavy mist of warm

treacle. Conversely, the more prosaic ice-cold driving winds and snow cut through the atmosphere like a warm knife slicing through butter. The third was that only children were boarding the train, their
children. In a trance-like state, Mary watched as each child stepped regimentally into their chosen carriage in a strangely mechanical manner. It reminded her of clockwork soldiers she had once seen in a toyshop window in Lendava before the war. The shop wasn't there anymore. There was no longer a demand or the money for frivolous expenditure on children's toys - especially those with military connotations.

For no particular reason, the children had, without prior instruction, formed themselves into four orderly queues and were waiting to board their selected carriage. Slowly, they were devoured as tiny morsels of nourishment for this metal monster. But the monster's appetite would never be satisfied until it had consumed every last vestige of innocence.

Herded like cattle behind the ominously tall, rusty grey metal barriers, the corralled parents painted an inglorious picture of enforced incarceration. The Hungarian guards erected the barricades to prevent last-minute fraternisation or emotional outbursts between parent and child. Anything that could cause a delay in the loading process was to be avoided at any cost. At this, the final moment of parting, denial of compassion, the last remnant of humanity - the unconscionable act of a thief in the night stealing time - inflicting heartache.

But it mattered not, for the parents and the children had already said their goodbyes.

Frail and withered by years of war, Mary had to endure the final attrition - losing her children, probably forever.

She knew she would not see another summer, only the glorious apricity of one more winter before her days were done. Her spindly blue fingers, skin like gossamer, tightly grasped the wire barrier. She hoped for one last glimpse of Tania and Nica before they boarded the train, but they were lost in the crowd. Mary wept quietly, unobtrusively. That was her way, not for her the vacuous piety of grief; there was no reverence that could be shared; it was hers and hers alone. Franz kept his feelings in check, as he always did. Of course, he loved his children as much as Mary and would miss them just as much after they were gone, but he did not show it – he would not show it, not yet. There would be time enough later for sorrow and remorse, but not now; that was his way. He was powerless to change anything, and hopefully, Mary would understand.

The night before was the first night of Hanukkah, and they had recited the three Maariv prayers together. Nica had lit the Shammash and the first candle, a custom he looked forward to each year since his Bar mitzvah.

He would not be lighting any more candles at home this year. After prayers, they sat in the kitchen to eat fried potato pancakes. Franz explained to Nica and Tania that they would be going on a long journey the following day. They even managed to laugh a little. Hanukkah was always a joyful time. But in their minds, they all wondered when and if they would ever celebrate as a family again. And what the circumstances might be....

Tomorrow, they would travel on a train with hundreds of other children to their new home. But Franz and Mary would not be going with them. They had never been separated before.

'So tell me, Father,' said Nica, 'Where are we going?'

'You are being evacuated to Switzerland for your own safety.'

'But why Switzerland?' asked Tania curiously.

'Because that is where they are taking you.' Tania wondered who the "they" were but said nothing. She knew her parents would not send them anywhere if it was not necessary. Let alone on a journey to a different country where they were uncertain of the destination and who would be there to meet them.

'Switzerland is a good place,' replied Franz reassuringly. 'It is a neutral country not involved in the war, so you will be better off there than here. So tonight, after supper, you must prepare for the journey. It should take about two to three days to get there, but once you arrive at your new home, you will be safe until you return to us after the war is over.

Tania and Nica couldn't see any sense in being separated from their parents. But their concerns had been partially alleviated by their parent's reassurances that they would soon be reunited....

If you enjoyed this book, why not try the second in the Story Teller Pentalogy. Each tale explores a relationship and how it can change. The Tusitala.

Chapter 1. The Tusitala
1984

This story starts long before it begins and finishes long after it ends. In fact, the end is the beginning, in a manner of speaking. You must decide where and when it reaches its conclusion and from where it could have begun. This is only one small episode of a much larger story…

Blake Thornton sat in his study. Leaning back in his tattered, green leather captain's chair, gazing at the photograph of his wife Catherine and their two children, Max and Claudia. The antique silver picture frame had been a present from Catherine on his thirty-fourth birthday back in 1981, along with the portrait she had commissioned from a professional photographer. Receiving that gift was one of the happiest moments in his life, although he didn't realise that at the time.

'Something to inspire your wearisome days,' she had whispered as she gave him the present. 'Something to look at daily, to remind you that no matter what happens, we will always love you.' Then she gently kissed him. It was a declaration of love, unlike anything he had experienced before. Thornton was enraptured by its intensity. But he had failed to notice the tiny hint of dark foreboding deeply couched within the words.

Catherine then took hold of his hands and eased him slowly out of the chair. 'Dance with me, Thornton,' she whispered forcefully. 'Show me how much you love me.' She wrapped her arms around his body, and he slipped his arms around her tiny waist. Thornton smiled demurely, for he could not resist her – he never could.

He was not a particularly good dancer and had always been self-conscious about his awkwardness, but it felt different with Catherine. It was as if nothing else in the world mattered - it was just the two of them. 'Dance as though no one can see you' – that was what Catherine always told him. She touched the play button on the stereo system, Billy Joel started to play, and they began...

'By the way,' whispered Catherine, looking up at Blake. 'I have another birthday present for you.'

'What?' asked Blake.

'I'm pregnant.' Blake smiled and kissed her again before they slowly fell back onto the sofa, kissing and caressing each other, eventually sliding to the floor, where they made love. The children were fast asleep in bed...

Catherine's plaintive words had comforted Blake. He had never really felt the need before. But for some reason, he found the solace strangely reassuring on that occasion. But little did he appreciate the prophetic irony of what she had said.

He cherished the photograph and the sentiment; it reminded him of how uncomplicated things had been before the manuscript of Prospect Road had arrived at his office. It also marked one other significant moment in his life. The year, he had officially taken over from Reggie Clanford as the owner of Clanford and Fox publishers and literary agents. A few months later, Catherine lost the unborn baby. Thinking back, Blake wondered if maybe that was when things had begun to change.

He gazed up at the ceiling, and his mind wandered back even further to 1968, when he had first joined Clanford and Fox as a new manuscript reader and copy editor. He was twenty-one and fresh out of university, gaining a double first in English Literature and History. He was unsure what he wanted to do with his life. He had considered going into television or the newspaper business. Then, one day, while drinking in a Chelsea wine bar with Sean, an old friend from university, he mentioned this vacancy.

'Why don't you apply for this job?' Sean asked. He showed Blake the advert. 'It's a publishing company. I've already accepted another offer, so I'm not bothering with the interview. There's no reason you shouldn't apply. You are better qualified than I am, so it could be right up your street.'

Blake thought it sounded interesting; he was broke, so he telephoned the company and arranged an interview. He was offered the job on the spot and accepted it, little realising how much that decision would affect the rest of his life.

Blake got on well with Reggie Clanford right from the start. Reggie took him under his wing, and within a couple of years, he was treating him like the son he never had.

One day, Blake was in Reggie's office. They were discussing something completely innocuous when, quite unexpectedly, Reggie came out and said it. 'Blake, I want you to take over the business when I'm gone.'

'Me? But I've only been here for a couple of years. In all honesty, I don't really know anything about it. Everybody else understands the business far better than I do.'

Blake was insistent about his lack of professional experience, but it brooked no sympathy from Reggie. His continued self-disqualification on the grounds of inexperience only further cemented Reggie's decision. He was the perfect man for the job.

'Yes, you do,' replied Reggie, smiling phlegmatically at Blake's modesty. 'It's not just about what you know. You... you have a natural flair for the business. You get on well with the authors and understand their silly quirks, idiosyncrasies, eccentricities, whims, fancies, and occasional strange ways. That is what's important. This is a people business; we don't make anything here. We find dreams, fantasies, and illusions and put them on paper for people to read. Reggie gestured to a chair.

'Sit down for a moment, Blake, and let me give you some fatherly advice. Authors – and I use that word sparingly.' He made a wry expression – 'will happily inhabit their existence with the ease of a tortoise permanently ensconced in its shell. Their most highly valued asset is the independence and freedom they have won by creating stories. Stories which other people want to read. Stories that allow their readers to temporarily escape their own humdrum existence. That freedom is most important to them. They work to be free of the world. And you must defend this status quo – to the death if necessary.' He added the last few words in a Churchillian tone - more for the dramatic effect than any literal sense. Blake smiled.

Reggie took another sip of coffee, leaned back in his old captain's chair, and gazed up at the ceiling.

'Over the years, I have concluded that writers live in their own microcosmic world. They are totally detached from the reality of a normal existence. This is essential if they are to continue creating interesting characters and engaging stories. They must be protected from the real world; reality and creativity are never good bedfellows. You must nurture their ideas and ambitions and listen to their problems, but never ingratiate yourself or give in to obsequiousness. That would demean and eventually destroy the delicate balance and dynamic of your relationship. Do you understand what I am saying?'

Blake nodded, but Reggie was still staring at the ceiling.

Reggie looked back at Blake, and, in a hushed, conspiratorial tone, he continued.

'Hopefully, they will repay this empathetic indulgence by remaining loyal to our company once they become successful. Some of our current authors could have sold more books by switching to larger publishers. But writers generally write for something more incorporeal than mere financial gain. This much I know you understand.' He took another sip of coffee, 'this is the most important thing to remember above everything else.' He paused for a moment, gathering his thoughts. He chose not to mention one more critical detail; he would talk about that another time.

'Did you know that Clanford and Fox have been agents and book publishers for over seventy years?'

'No, I didn't,' replied Blake, listening carefully. Visions of more extraordinary things were beginning to form in his mind.

'It was started by Joshua Clanford and Obadiah Fox in the early 1900s. They majored in writers of the ilk of Dickens and Conan Doyle, storytellers with a hint of darkness about them. Unfortunately, none of our authors has achieved quite the same recognition and popularity as Dickens or Doyle. But we have still had commercial success with the ones we have published, so we cannot complain. We have stayed in business to the present day, which is no mean accomplishment in these challenging times for the publishing industry. I am sure it will continue for another seventy years.' He smiled at Blake.

They had been salient words from the heart and had made a deep impression on Blake. Now, the business was his. Reginald Clanford had retired, and one year later, just before he died, he handed over the last remnants of control and all his shares in the company.

There was one other thing that Reggie had mentioned at the time, which suddenly came back to mind. It was about Freddy Fox, Obadiah's son and Reggie's junior partner until he died in 1966 - a couple of years before Blake started working for the firm.

Freddie killed himself, leaving a puzzling note that nobody could understand. It merely said, 'For the sins that must be atoned.' It was all curiously enigmatic and made no sense to Reggie or Freddie's wife, Amelia. The other oddity was that Freddy had left his entire shareholding in Clanford and Fox to Reggie, and, for some inexplicable reason, he had left none to his wife.

So, Reggie Clanford owned all the shares in the company. Oddly, the legacy had been added as a codicil only weeks before Freddie died. Neither Reggie nor Amelia could understand why he had written this clause into his will, and neither would ever know.

'Not every suicide comes with an explanation,' said Reggie quietly, staring into the distance, 'but there is usually some rationale. In Freddy's case, however, there was nothing apart from the cryptic note. He was happy at work and home, and the business was doing well.'

Reggie had never gone into further detail except to say they had been best friends for many years, never having a cross word. Suddenly, one day, Freddy's demeanour changed, and three months later, he committed suicide.

Blake's mind shot forward to 1982, just over two years ago. He had been sitting in the same office talking to his assistant Jamie about the schedule of manuscripts they had to read over the long May bank holiday weekend. Fortunately, or maybe not, he could work at home whenever it pleased him, doing what he enjoyed most: reading stories.

Manuscripts that had successfully passed through the first reading process in the outer office were then passed to Blake. This happened with Prospect Road, an autobiographical novel by Anthony Theodore Clackle when it arrived at the office that March. Jamie had read the whole manuscript, which he thought was promising. He then passed it to Blake with his editorial comments, ready for a final decision on whether they should publish it.

THE TUSITALA.
PROSPECT ROAD: CHAPTER ONE
Written by
Anthony Theodore Clackle
Thomas Drayton's Story

My name is Thomas Edward Drayton, and I was born in July 1947. It was a sweltering summer following one of the coldest winters on record. I do not remember being born; neither do I have any recollection of that long, hot summer. I was only informed of these details after I had reached an age when I could understand their relevance.

My first full-colour memory of my existence on Earth was Coronation Day, 2nd June 1953, a national holiday. I was nearly six years old. Undoubtedly, all the preceding days had been blessed with colour, but this one was the most memorable for me. It was so utterly different from all the other days of my life up to that point. It was a little overcast to start – it had rained overnight and left things a little damp. But the temperature warmed up as the hours slowly passed.

It eventually became an unforgettable day, and I had a wonderful time.

Looking back, I remember it as a day full of promise - many promises, in fact, during a period of great excitement and overflowing enthusiasm. The lust for life had vanquished the cloud of despair that had hovered over us for so long.

There was a smile and encouraging words from everyone I met. 'Alright, lad' or 'Are you having a lovely day, my boy?'

We had been delivered from the carnage of a world war eight years previously. I was not actually around then, merely a by-product of the continuing celebrations after six years of bitter conflict.

Food rationing was still in place, but we had enough to keep our bellies happy. In the air, a hint of exhilaration and a sense of expectancy. The feeling that things would change was inescapable. No one seemed to know how things would change, just that they would, and it would "all be for the better," as everybody kept saying...

It was as if we were at the beginning of something beautiful, a journey into the unknown. It felt like those last few days of eager anticipation and excitement just before starting out on holiday. We had not arrived yet, but we knew that when we did, it would be fun, and we would enjoy every minute of it. The country had suffered from all kinds of shortages for years. But now things were going to be different - better. Fortunately, I did not suffer from these shortages, as I had never been aware of them in the first place. My mother used to say what you never had, you never missed.

Apparently, me and everybody else had a ubiquitous relative whom we all referred to as "Uncle Jim." No matter what the familial relationship was. I called him Uncle Jim, my mother called him Uncle Jim, and all the people in the shops, even the "old bill," called him Uncle Jim. It was all a little odd and very confusing at times.

I found out later that being called Uncle was a local tradition. This was an epithet decorously granted to anybody who could always be relied upon to find whatever anybody wanted (within reason). Be it sugar, butter, nylons, coffee, bananas or even petrol, and of course, chocolate. He had been successfully plying his trade throughout the war and some years after.

He appeared to be utterly unaffected by the vagaries of Mr. Hitler's attempts to prevent us from enjoying such luxuries and utterly oblivious to the government's rationing legislation (whatever that was). Parsimony and frugality were alien concepts to Uncle Jim. A complete contradiction to his liberal theories on free trade, which he would articulately defend on any night of the week in the Sailor's Return Public House on the corner of Prospect Road.

Once again, as with so many of my earlier recollections, they almost entirely depend on third-hand information passed on to me much later in my life. But so vividly were they retold that I now feel confident that I must have heard them first-hand after all, however inconceivable that may sound.

Uncle Jim was a fascinating character. The like of which undoubtedly turned up all over the country during this period, tinker traders who kept everybody adequately supplied with the essentials and a few simple luxuries. He carried on his lucrative business right up until 1954, when rationing eventually came to an end. After that, food, clothes, and luxury items became more generally available in the shops if you had the money to buy them.

Just after that, like a wisp of smoke in a gentle breeze, he was suddenly gone, and I never saw him again. I often wondered what became of Uncle Jim.

I later learnt that he was of Romany extraction, a fact that was, a little oddly, always greeted with a hushed mysticism and mild disdain whenever mentioned in general conversation. I never managed to figure out precisely why this should make any difference to his innate ability to procure these little luxuries. Or why he was apparently exempt from conscription.

'Where do you come from, Uncle Jim?' I dared to ask him on one of his visits to our house.

He looked down at me and scratched his belly. 'You're a cheeky little sod, aren't you?' I smiled, and he gave me a piece of chocolate but did not answer my question. I later learnt that this was because he was *enigmatic,* whatever that meant.

Uncle Jim had been living with my grandmother during the war, apparently as a lodger. My grandfather (Grandad Bob) had been away in North Africa at the time. He was a bit unlucky, forty-three years old at the outbreak of hostilities and therefore still subject to the call-up.

During the war and for some time after it had ended, Uncle Jim brazenly drove around Portsmouth in his enormous pink Cadillac motor car, selling black-market goods from its vast boot. I can vaguely remember the Cadillac making flying visits to various houses on Prospect Road around the time of the Coronation. I only remember this because the lurid colour stood out so vividly in a predominantly dour landscape. The warships moored at the end of the road, and the pavements were grey. Rusty corrugated iron, which was everywhere, was brown. Everything else that could be painted seemed to be painted black, and everything else not painted black was painted dark green. Bright colours were a rarity in those days.

Many years later, I pondered how Uncle Jim managed to avoid the long arm of the law for so long when he drove around conducting his business in Portsmouth's most outrageously ostentatious car. I concluded that they, too, must also have been grateful recipients of his generosity and trading activities. All this was, of course, apocryphal. Undoubtedly colourfully embellished over time. I was unaware of what Uncle Jim did until I was about five or six; by then, his luxury goods empire had begun to crumble.

Now was the time to rebuild our damaged country and mend our broken lives. We were encouraged to plan for the future, and most of us did, one way or another. My mother, Mary Florence Drayton, known by everybody as Flo, was always making plans for something or other. On Coronation Day, she dressed me up in some Satin supplied by the infamous Uncle Jim to look like Sabu the Elephant Boy. I believe he was a Kipling character immortalised in a popular film of the same name from the late 1930s.

My mother covered my body with a peculiar-smelling brown liquid, which she had concocted from potassium permanganate and mud as far as I could make out. She only told me this when I was much older and could process the information philosophically. As I later learned, my life would be peppered with many strange experiences relating to potions, mixtures, concoctions, and customs. Macbeth's weird sisters had nothing on my mother.

I remember trying to remove the stain between my toes weeks after the party had finished. Eventually, I had to resort to having a bath… ahhh.

Twenty years later, I distinctly remember using this same concoction to soak my feet (without the mud this time.)

Apparently, it prevented them from smelling so cheesy, a severe problem when trying to attract members of the opposite sex (this was another suggestion from my mother).

Like most mothers, Flo played a large part in forming my views on life and what I could expect. "The world was my oyster," she would say. I did not know what an oyster was. "You just have to pick out the shiny little pearls." I didn't know what they were, either. But I smiled and made a mental note.

Fortunately, I also inherited her innate ability to think for herself. This would stand me in good stead for the rest of my life. It would not make me wealthy, but it would make me happy – very happy for a while. Fortunately, I did not inherit my mother's idiosyncratic tendencies, one of which was a peculiar ritual she enacted every Halloween. For some reason I could never fathom, she always used the occasion to play questionable games with the devil and the occult. This concerned me much, and I have often wondered whether she was sowing bad seed for the future.

On the night in question, several of my precious lead soldiers, Christmas presents, I hasten to add, would mysteriously disappear, never to return. Coincidentally, during the latter part of the evening, my mother would start to heat up a saucepan, which, unbeknown to me, had my lead soldiers in it. Once they had melted, she would have my sister Lizzie and me stand around a large basin of cold water. Then she would put her hand on one of our heads, utter a strange incantation, then drop some boiling lead into the water. This would instantly form a very odd shape, which she would retrieve from the water and carefully view before telling us what our futures held. As you can imagine, we were both in awe of this quasi-demonic ceremony, which she regularly conducted on the same night every year. That was until my army of lead soldiers was all gone. Little of what she predicted came true.

Flo made a turban out of green satin, which she carefully wrapped around my head. She completed the ensemble with a sort of Indian shirt and baggy trousers, which she had made from red satin material. She was a dab hand on the Singer sewing machine; most mothers were just after the war. I must have looked a picture wandering up and down Prospect Road, giving the impression of a refugee with serious sartorial issues. Or possibly a miniature trainee pimp from a Bombay harem (I did not know what a pimp was then).

My sister Elizabeth was dressed up as Nell Gwynne. Surprisingly, as Uncle Jim could not source real oranges, Lizzie had to make do with green apples painted orange. They may have been dipped in the same concoction I had been coated with. And so, we spent that fantastic day wandering up and down Prospect Road, in and out of everybody's house, eating and drinking whatever treats we were given.

The centre of the road was taken up with tables covered in Union Jack paper, and bunting was strung between the houses. Where there were houses still standing, that is. Directly opposite Number four, where we lived, the houses numbered one through to seven had been hit by a bomb and were no more. My Uncle Keith and Auntie Jenny lived at Number Nine. Families lived together in little communes in those days, much like today in some more deprived areas. But the family ties and community commitment were beginning to be eroded by radical social engineering. Back then, the terraced houses were small and basic, but the people were friendly. It was adequate for our needs. The new tower block developments were entirely different, deconstructing social interaction and divisively alienating communities.

I have never again experienced that same feeling of family togetherness, unity, and community as I did during those early years. Something was satisfying and comforting about living within walking distance of your relations. A sensation that I believe is primitive in its concept. Although tempered by the absence of privacy, I still found it profoundly friendly, welcoming, and heartening. There was a sense of well-being and wholesomeness. I suppose even a nod to Puritanism in its most secular form. Utilitarian religion was also significantly important in those days.

We looked forward to baptisms, confirmations, and weddings, the affirmations of life and commitment. These were extraordinary days; Lizzie and I always went to church on Sundays. I did not know what it was all about, but I suppose it served as a moral compass, giving us direction. That simple life lifted my spirits and roused my soul every single day. Something, sadly, that I do not believe happens quite so much these days. Now, there is intensity, tension, and anxiety in almost everything we do. I am not that naïve to think that rape, murder, or robbery are any more prevalent today than they were back then. I just didn't notice it when I was a child.

On this unforgettable day, the tables were covered in plates of sausage rolls, lemonade, Cherryade, Tizer, crumpets, sandwiches, cakes, blancmange, sweets and even some chocolate. In the latter part of the afternoon, I remember hearing the distant sound of a plaintive trumpet, sounding like the United States cavalry announcing its arrival just in time to save the day. I regularly saw this heart-wrenching yet exhilarating spectacle on Saturday mornings when I visited the local fleapit, the Forum cinema. Then, I began to feel the distinctive thud of the bass drum, relentlessly pounding out the infectious rhythm of life, becoming louder with every heartbeat.

Then suddenly, we were confronted with the awe-inspiring sight of the Salvation Army brass band swinging around the corner, marching majestically down Prospect Road. They were playing their hearts out as they made their way towards us with all the pomp and circumstance befitting this magisterial occasion. The buttons on their uniforms sparkled like diamonds in the afternoon sun. Their brass instruments, highly polished and gleaming, deflected streaks of sunlight in every direction.

All the older men –probably not that old, they just seemed that way to me – who had been drinking in the Sailor's Return on the corner came out of the pub with pints of beer raised in the air and cheered the band as it passed. It was an enormously rousing and uplifting occasion, and I felt oddly euphoric about the whole thing. It was something I had not experienced before and seldom since...

They continued down to the dockside at the end of the road, and for one terrible moment, I thought they were going to march straight down the slipway and into Portsmouth Harbour. My immediate concern was the appalling effect the mud would have on their shiny boots, but they did not. Slowly, with sweeping majestical elongation and precision, they turned through ninety degrees into the road. Then, they carefully turned again and began marching back up the other side. Once again, they passed all the bedecked tables, and once again, they received a roaring ovation. Eventually, having made their way to the top of the road, they turned the corner. Then, they slowly disappeared into the sunset, continuing their journey to unknown destinations and destinies.

The celebrations went on into the night. I remember Lizzie and me looking out of the bedroom window down at the street below, completely mesmerised by the evening spectacle slowly unfolding before us. We watched as the tables were moved to one side, and the adults began dancing the night away to the sounds of Mantovani and the Joe Loss band on a record player. The street lights cast an ethereal glow on the proceedings. The sounds of laughter carried on long after we had eventually fallen asleep. I will remember that day for the rest of my life.

The Tusitala.
Prospect Road: Chapter Two
Written by
Anthony Theodore Clackle

The following day was also a holiday, so we, Barry Lee, Carol Mansbridge and I – went down to the slipway at the end of Prospect Road to play in the mud for a while.

The sailors on the destroyers and cruisers moored to the quayside would throw pennies over the side for us to find in the sludge. They always threw more money if Carol was there. She had already mastered the art of smiling coquettishly, and her beguiling expression of heartfelt appreciation for the small gifts raining down seemed to work wonders. I was still relatively naïve in such matters and didn't completely understand the hidden agenda. But precocious Carol had already fully realised how best to exploit her femininity.

Barry lived at number fifteen, and Carol lived on the next road but always came to play with us. When I was about six or seven, I thought I would like to marry Carol because she made such splendid mud castles. When I went to her house for tea, her mum always gave me a packet of Smith's crisps. Mind you, the Smith's factory was not that far away, and everybody seemed to have a big square tin of Smith's crisps hidden under the stairs.

I remember how the big blue lorries used to park overnight at the end of the road on another bomb site. Some days, we would walk around the other bombsite and try to guess how many packets of crisps were inside the lorries. Some days, you could smell the boiling fat from the factory where they were made. In summer, you could taste the cooked potato in the air. They only had one flavour, potato, with or without salt, which came wrapped up in a little blue twirl of waxed paper.

I remember one very terrifying experience with Carol. Well, not exactly with Carol; it had more to do with her mum and my mum. It was when we were about seven and pretending to be married. One day, we went back to my house to play a game of mummies and daddies in my bedroom and decided to get into bed as husbands and wives do. We were cuddled up and happily chatting away, completely oblivious to the sexual connotations of the situation. We had shared a bed many times before when we were much younger. Typically, when my mum was going out for the evening, I stayed overnight at Carol's mum's house. It all seemed perfectly innocent to us.

Suddenly, my mum burst in, looking horrified. She began shouting, screaming, and leaping up and down, which frightened us both. I thought she had gone mad. We jumped out of bed, and then, for no reason that I was aware of, my mother started to beat me on my legs with a cane while continuing to shout at me. I did not have the slightest idea of what was going on. Then Carol started crying profusely, totally confused by what was happening. My mother did not let up on the raging and ranting and beating. Then, out of nowhere, Carol's mum suddenly appeared at the bedroom door.

There was more shouting, screaming, jumping up and down, and then whacking with another cane. It was absolute bedlam. Carol's mum started beating Carol's legs until they were covered in wheals and welts. We collapsed on the floor, crying our eyes out, without a clue as to why we were being punished. Eventually, it all stopped, and her mother marched Carol home. I stayed in my room for days, except when it was time for food, or I wanted to go to the toilet.

Ten years later, I began understanding what had gone through our mothers' minds. It was a classic example of childhood innocence being cruelly destroyed in an instant. Lost forever because of a simple misunderstanding and our parents' seriously flawed and hypocritical morality. They had judged us by their corrupt standards – a valuable lesson I would remember for the rest of my life.

Anyway, the tide was coming in, so we started to make our way back up the slipway to the road and went to play on to the bombsite where numbers 1, 3, 5 and 7 Prospect Road once stood. All the bricks had now been taken away, leaving lots of pieces of wood, complete doors, corrugated iron sheets, odd bits of metal (probably bits of a bomb with my luck) and deep trenches everywhere. Some had been used for dumping a variety of unspeakable things over the years. This, in turn, created a mysterious, musty pong, which I will never completely forget. The smell was always much worse in winter when the earth was wet.

Years later, I would think back to those trenches and wonder how they compared to the First World War trenches in France. As I grew older, I occasionally caught a whiff of something similar, invariably in an entirely unrelated environment. I would instantly be transported back to my childhood - the bomb site and our underground kingdom. It is so strange how an aroma, pleasant or nasty, can do that. Those moments happened less and less as I grew older.

We would cover the top of the trench with sheets of corrugated iron or old wooden doors. And as we were roughly the same height as the trenches, we could wander around our malodorous subterranean village, undisturbed by the rest of the world. I do not remember much about what we did there, but we would spend hours running around pretending to do something. We were possibly preparing our defence of Prospect Road against an invasion from outer space or even red Indians.

Whenever it was lunchtime or teatime, my mum stood outside Number 4 and bellowed out my name. I would pop up from our subterranean world with my head just visible above ground level and wave to her so she knew I had heard her. She always smiled when she saw me. I still remember that. Everybody in the road (possibly the next road, too) probably heard her. She had a loud voice – just how loud it could be, I found out during the bedroom incident with Carol. I thought then that my ears were going to bleed. Still, I think she loved me quite a lot.

During the daytime, my mum always wore one of those flowered housecoats and a scarf. I remember she would go through a routine of polishing the front doorstep with Cardinal red polish at least once a week. I think it was on a Friday because we used to have fish and chips for tea. I have no idea why she did this on Friday other than everybody else did it on the same day. Some Fridays, we would be *on duty* in our trench gazing across the road - watching the curious sight of our mothers polishing.

It would entertain us for ages. All on their knees - head covered in cotton scarves, happily polishing their steps in perfect synchronisation while simultaneously conducting various unconnected conversations. This made no sense at all to me. I could only describe it as an incredibly surreal setting for a West End-stage musical song routine. Once again, this memory has been partially enhanced by the passing of time. Something which has undoubtedly lent it some enchantment. I would not have known what a musical was at that time.

Some house windows were still boarded up eight years after the war. Occasionally, washing lines would be hung out across the road, with carpets hanging on them, making it look like a Moroccan marketplace. I did not know what to make of it then, and I still don't nearly thirty years later. The road had been blown to bits in places; a quarter of the houses were gone. And yet, amid all this carnage and destruction, my mum was polishing some bricks. It seemed an ironic juxtaposition. Maybe a bright, shining front doorstep was a beacon of defiance. Perhaps it was a bylaw that you had to keep your doorstep polished at all times?

I also remember a character known as Bertie Coggins, the local rag, bone, and scrap metal merchant. All the stuff he collected was stacked inside and outside his junkyard at the end of the road. He stood out in my memory because everybody thought he was no more than a beggar. Then, one day, he turned up in a brand new, dark-blue Humber Super Snipe motor car, the best car I had ever seen. This proves the old Northern saying, 'Where there's muck, there's brass.' Everybody spoke highly of Bert, or Bertram, as he preferred to be known after buying the Humber (though we all continued to call him Bert, much to his displeasure).

When I had no money, I would walk around the houses, gather newspapers, and take them to Bert. He would give me a penny a pound in weight. I also collected empty beer bottles and returned them to the pub for the deposit refund. I think it was about a halfpenny a bottle. All the money I made invariably went over the counter in 'Auntie' Maureen's sweet shop, just around the corner on Commercial Road. It also sold Woodbine cigarettes and matches. Next door to Auntie Maureen's was, and I am not making this up, 'Auntie' Doreen's.

Doreen Cover and her husband, Jack, sold fruit and vegetables. Maureen and Doreen (which always made me giggle for some inexplicably puerile reason) were good friends with Mum. They would come to all her parties - my mum loved to have a party - and they were always kind to me. Auntie Maureen – she was not a real Auntie – would bring me sweets when she came to babysit, so I was always pleased when Mum told me she was coming around.

Next door to Auntie Doreen was Eric Dimblebee, Barber and Hairdresser. What had always fascinated me about Mr Dimblebee was that as well as cutting hair, he also sold Durex 'Johnnies'. They were invariably stored tantalisingly high up in a glass cabinet in front as you sat in the chair.

I knew what they were, more or less, or to be more accurate, I knew there was a tenuous link with sex, but I had no idea what that specific purpose was until much later in life. But the mysterious connection between barber and condom stuck in my mind for many years. Up to the age of thirteen, I genuinely believed you could not have sex until you had your hair cut. I eagerly looked forward to having my monthly snip. I half expected something wonderful and miraculous would happen to me one day, as it appeared to happen to the other men who entered Eric's shop.

'Something for the weekend, sir?' That immutable phrase was muttered surreptitiously into the customer's ear. I waited patiently for the day when it would be uttered clandestinely into mine, but it never was. Oh, those wistful days spent in expectation of wondrous things that would happen to me in the future. But they never did, not for a long time. Not until I was nearly nineteen, despite having many haircuts, some of which weren't strictly necessary.

The following two shops were not there, just a large hole, then it was Wilson's the Butcher and finally, The Royal Oak

Public House on the corner. As I remember, there seemed to be a Brickwood's pub on the corner of every street in Portsmouth. All Brickwood's pubs were ornately tiled inside and out, usually in shiny dark reds, greens, and browns. Very depressing, really. Looking back, they were not dissimilar in design to public toilets and didn't smell any better either.

Further along the road was a cemetery with tall iron railings parallel to the main road. In the middle was a large ornate arched cast-iron entrance with two imposing gates. I half expected St Peter to be hanging around somewhere. The gates would open when the procession arrived with its latest arrival... I suppose departed might have been more technically accurate. Barry and I would often lean on the railings, watching the proceedings - discussing the merits of being dead - in some depth. The list was endless: no school, no requirement to tidy our bedrooms, not having to be in bed early, not having to eat our greens, and not having to wash. On balance, though, we unanimously decided to stay as we were for now, as being dead looked a little bit boring.

I only sort of half-understood what was really happening. A few years later, I passed the cemetery and noticed all the headstones had been lifted and stacked against the back wall. I did wonder if there was a time limit on how long you could stay in the ground and whether that limit had now expired. But then, that did not make any sense. Some of the plots had only been filled a year or two earlier.

It turned out the church had sold the graveyard to a petrol company, and they would build a filling station on it. The next we knew, all the stones had gone, and a new petrol station with four pumps, a large canopy, and a shop had been built on the site. I often wondered what happened to the souls of the departed bodies that had not had enough time to make the final transition. One day in the future, I might find out.

Anyway, back to Prospect Road. Quite often, there were piles of horseshit left in the road from the tradesman's carthorses. Initially, canny Bert never bothered to pick up his horse's dung. He very kindly left it for budding entrepreneurs like me to handle that end of the market. I suppose if I had made a success of it, he might have considered taking me on as an apprentice shit shoveller. But I didn't fancy it as a career.

During the summer, especially during the holidays, Lizzie and I would collect the horseshit and then knock on doors to see if anybody wanted to buy it to put on their vegetables. Mum used to shout at me if I called it horseshit. She told me to call it garden manure or dung. I would wait patiently for the coalman or the milkman to pay the street a visit, and then I would be off.

'We're just going out to collect some horse shit, Mum,' I would shout endearingly up the stairs as we hurriedly left with bucket and coal shovel in hand. I especially used the shit word. I could be very irritating when I was young, having become aware of my mother's and her friends' delicate sensibilities. I loved hearing her shout despairingly, 'It's dung, darling, manure, or pooh, but not that word.' She always sounded so disdainful, which only made it worse as we found her oddly pretentious inflection even more amusing.

'Yes, Mummy,' we would reply and then wander off up the road saying to each other, 'It's not horseshit, darling, it's pooh.' To which Lizzie would reply, 'We are off to collect some poo... not shit... poo.'

'Manure sounds nicer,' I would say, and Elizabeth would reply, 'What! Nicer than poo or nicer than horseshit?' 'Oh

566

yes, definitely nicer than horseshit.' This would be the general tone of the conversation as we wandered door to door. Until we got bored or found a new customer.

But of course, Mum knew best, as we would eventually come to learn. I did not realise then that she had plans for much better things for all of us.

'Would you like to buy some horse manure, penny a bucket,' we would politely ask when knocking on doors.

'Yes, please, they would say. Could you take it around the back alley?'

Lizzie and I would fall about in fits of laughter when a customer told us he would put it on his rhubarb... you know the rest.

A year or two later - the milkman, the coalman and the dustman stopped using horses and switched to electric floats and lorries with petrol engines. Hence, our supply of merchandise began to literally dry up. Bert, the rag and bone man, was the only trader left who still used a horse. I am sure he only did this to prop up the image of humble impecuniosity he had created. However, his new car had done to death any such illusion he may have thought we were labouring under.

As our last local produce supplier - stock was becoming increasingly harder to find. On top of that, Bert had become more astute and even sharper, which I did not believe was possible. He had obviously taken careful note of my profitable side-line. Bert was now collecting his horse's dung and selling it on his travels through the highways and byways of Portsmouth as "freshly made quality fertiliser." So that enterprise was coming to an end, as we couldn't afford a production facility. We still collected newspapers and sold them to Bert right up to the day we moved away.

The French onion man, who came on a bike, was always a slightly questionable character. I knew France was far away and could not figure out why he would come from France to England to sell a few rings of onions he'd hung around his neck. It just didn't seem financially viable even to my naïve business brain. I could understand the horseshit trade. On this, I was virtually an expert, knowing it inside out - back to front in a manner of speaking, and that made perfect financial sense, but his did not.

I stayed awake for hours at night, worrying about how he made a living with all the costs of going backwards and forwards to France daily. A few years later, I discovered that Onion Johnny had been living with Auntie Doreen's sister Doris all along. Her husband was permanently stationed in Hong Kong. Onion Johnny had done a deal with Jack (Doreen's husband) to store his onions in Jack's warehouse and store himself in Doris's bed.

So, he went to the warehouse daily and picked up more onions to sling around his neck. He would put on his silly beret and striped jumper, and then off, he would peddle for the day. Apparently, he had not been back to France since the end of the war. I later learnt that the onions came from a farm in Petersfield. I was learning something new every day. For some reason, everybody thought that Onion Johnny's onions tasted better than English onions. How little did they know?

The crumpet man came on a bicycle pushing a tiny trailer in front. That was not much use to me or my horticultural growth enhancement business.

I do not have many recollections of my dad from those days. He was nearly always away during the week in Andover, Bournemouth, Guildford or one of the many other faraway places where he worked. But I would see him on most weekends. He worked as a window dresser for Hepworth's.

Many years later, in my early twenties, I reflected on this strange quasi-nomadic occupation he had chosen, forever travelling from town to town. Only then, after lengthy interrogative conversations with my mother, did I come to understand something significant. He had been rampantly homosexual for most of his life. His occupation facilitated his predilection towards younger trainee window dressers of similar persuasion. They were available in every town.

Occasionally, he would bring one of the trainees home to stay with us for a few days. Heaven knows what the sleeping arrangements were. Fortunately, all this was unknown to me then. The invention of sex and promiscuity ushered in with the sexual revolution of the 1960s, along with the decriminalisation of homosexuality in 1967, was still to come. So, I remained ignorant of such things.

Many years later, after learning the ways of the world, I would eventually understand the true nature of my father's inclinations and my mother's tacit acceptance of this peculiar ménage à trois. Despite this strange arrangement, my parents appeared devoted to each other and remained so until my father's death.

Much as before, my weekdays were taken up with school. But it had now become a little more serious. We had to learn many subjects to prepare for an important exam we would take when we reached the age of eleven. The outcome would determine where we would continue our education. Either at a grammar school wearing a nice uniform or at a secondary modern, where we could wear whatever we liked because we weren't so bright – so I was told.

Evenings were still spent playing marbles and games in the street or messing around in the mud (usually only at weekends). I visited the underground kingdom less and less now. I had grown too tall and had to bend over to walk underneath the corrugated iron. If I behaved, I had been promised a bicycle for Christmas, so I was doing my best.

In 1955, somebody new arrived in our life: Uncle Bruce, my mum's brother. He was in the Navy and had been in Singapore since the war. But now, he had been posted home and started to live with us for a while. As Dad was still away most weekdays, I tended to treat Uncle Bruce more as a father than an uncle. We made battleships out of Player's cigarette packets with guns made from silver paper and matchsticks. Bruce was not married (at least I had never seen his wife), though as far as I know, he was not homosexual like Dad. Of course, I am writing this with the benefit of hindsight, which makes me sound far more aware of my surroundings than I was at the time.

Uncle Bruce smoked (RN naval issue cigarettes) and drank Old Navy Rum. Strangely, he never fell over, which could not be said for some of the men who frequented the Sailor's Return public house on the corner. I remember Bruce brought us some presents from Singapore when he came home. One was a 3D viewer scope, which looked like a pair of binoculars into which you placed photographic 3D slides. This allowed you to see the fantastic sights of the world in unique three-dimensional colours. It almost felt as if you were there. Bruce died suddenly in November 1956 after falling down a hatchway on his ship while still in the harbour.

The coroner's report said he was heavily intoxicated at the time. It was an ignominious end for someone who had courageously battled through six years of war and had been sunk twice without a scratch. My mother harboured severe misgivings about the verdict until her dying day, based on the simple premise that she had never seen him incapably drunk. She swore blind he was pushed, but it did not seem likely, as he was such a likeable person. There is a lesson to be learnt in there, somewhere, but I have no idea what it is.

Somewhat ironically, only a few months earlier, Bruce had a win on the pools, a sort of weekly lottery based on which football teams scored a draw each Saturday. If you managed to pick eight score drawers, that gave you 24 points - the jackpot! Bruce did not score 24 points, just 23, but that was enough to win him a prize of over £2,000. This was a lot of money in 1956. He gave half to my Mum, who said she would now buy a house in the posher part of Portsmouth. The house on Prospect Road was rented, but we did not move immediately for some reason and stayed for another six months. Something to do with the lease, I think.

My mum later inherited the balance of the pool's prize from Bruce. He had not spent a penny of it, so the future looked very rosy for all of us – except, of course, for Bruce…

Dad apparently did not earn much money, so Mum started taking in a lodger. She had the money from Uncle Bruce's Littlewoods Pools win, but that was 'sacrosanct', whatever that meant. She would say this whenever anybody mentioned using it if we were a bit broke. That did not happen very often, as Uncle Bruce used to bring us home many things when he was not away at sea, but of course, that had all come to a sudden end.

We usually only had one lodger who would stay Monday to Friday, so Lizzie and I would move into Mum's bedroom, and our room would be rented out. I remember we met some lovely people during that period. One, in particular, was Christine, whom we called Auntie Christine. We called all the women Auntie, but oddly, all the men were misters until we knew them better.

Auntie Christine would remain a family friend for many years. What I learned many years later changed my understanding of many events during this period. Christine was a beautiful woman. She was about twenty and worked on the next road in the corset and brassiere factory. I remember Christine came home very tearful one day, something I do not remember adults doing very often. She had a long talk with Mum in the front room (we were not allowed in). Christine was ill and stayed in bed for a few days but was as right as rain afterwards. Anyway, it turned out she had been pregnant and, with some help from my mum, she became un-pregnant.

She eventually married a footballer who played for Ipswich Town. My mum had many other friends, so life was always hectic but mostly enjoyable. When she gave us our pocket money on Saturday morning (if we had behaved all week), we would trot off to Woollies and spend it. So, come Sunday, I was broke again. Lizzie somehow used to save some of hers every week. I never understood how she managed that.

Sadly, in 1958, my adorable sister Lizzie was killed in a freak car accident. That left a big hole in my world. I missed her terribly, not least because she had been an integral part of the crop fertiliser business. She was the senior partner in charge of stock control. (I looked after sales and marketing).

I grew closer to my father after Lizzie died. But I always knew that he and my mother never really overcame her early death. I don't suppose any parent would. Sometimes, I would come in to find them sitting together in the lounge, holding each other tightly and gently weeping over a photograph they'd had specially made. It was a sort of monochrome with some parts of it hand coloured. They kept it on the sideboard. These were the precious moments I always remembered long after I had forgotten many other things about them. Most fathers tend to be closer to their daughters, which was true of mine. I felt that something left him that fateful day and never came back. We still got on okay, although I tended to be closer to my mother as she was always around.

She staunchly defended him until her death just a few years after his. Vehemently condemning anybody who dared say anything untoward about his 'funny way' (as she put it.) I often wondered if she really knew what they got up to, such was her trusting and empathetic understanding of his inclination.

Whatever memories they had together, only they shared, and they were something I would never fully understand. Every relationship that lasts a lifetime does so for reasons far beyond rational comprehension. My one regret is that I never really got to know my father until the very end, and I think he also had regrets about the time he had not spent with me when I was younger... It was a father-son relationship that never quite blossomed due to circumstances beyond his and my control.

This probably happens more often than it should in the busy, complicated lives that we all now lead. I feel sad when I think back to what might have been. Occasionally, I grieve for the lost opportunity to get to know the man my father was and the chance to understand what makes somebody what they become. We all start out as one kind of person. Slowly, through circumstances, destiny, and serendipitous luck, sometimes good - sometimes not so good, we change into a different type of person. I sometimes wonder what really controls this strange chronological metamorphosis.

The Tusitala.

Please leave a comment on Amazon if you enjoyed this book.
Contact the writer at **butchmoss111@gmail.com**

☐